LOST SOULS

LOST SOULS

KATIE JAROS

Text copyright © 2015 by Katie Jaros

ISBN: 978-0-9968176-1-5

Second Edition

This book saved my life.

There are many dark places in the world... some that are not so easy to crawl out of. Sometimes you need to build your own ladder... a lifeboat... and that is what Lost Souls was for me at one of my hardest moments. It has changed me in ways I am still discovering.

I want to dedicate this story to my Estabon... my love, my life... the guy holding the lantern steadfast over me while I hammered in the dark. I love you.

PROLOGUE

TEENAGE BOYS HAVE their own special smell. It's made of pheromones—a reminder from simpler times that there is a perfect match for us all. The boys that I'm riding with right now, though, just smell like cigarettes and beer.

"Riley! Pull in here!" Tom calls out from the passenger seat.

Riley takes a sharp right into a 7-Eleven parking lot. I lurch across the backseat, my open can of Pabst sloshing on the cloth interior. Whatever—this car is older than I am. Tom looks back at me from the front, his eyes quickly scanning down to my bag.

"Make sure you bring that in with you. I'm having a mad Doritos craving... Gotta get me some!" he ululates, his head twitching from side to side.

I reach over and smack him on the arm. "Ssshhh!" I laugh, my eyes darting to the store window. "They can probably hear you already. You are the worst criminal mastermind in the history of ever!" Tom blows a raspberry and puts his tongue out for a kiss.

"OhmygodChristalloveyousomuch..." he pants, his eyes rolled back in his head. I squeal and bat his face away.

"Gross!" I snort. "Such a jerk!"

Riley glares at Tom and puts his arm up between us. "Quit slobbering all over my ride!" he yells. "And to be crystal, if anyone is the mastermind here, it's me." I arch an eyebrow at that, but

Riley slurs, "Come on, girls." He opens his door, adding, "And I swear to God, Tom: if you jack this up, you are walking your own ass home!" He slaps Tom hard on the chest as we get out of the car and make our way into the shop.

Behind the counter sits a middle-aged Korean man and his very pregnant wife. They both eye us suspiciously as we walk past the aisles of auto supplies, mac and cheese, and baby diapers, until we finally reach the back where they stock the stoner food. Riley reaches into a cooler and grabs a six-pack of Heineken, an impish grin stretched across his face.

"Distraction time. You two get busy," he mutters. He saunters up to the front and slams the beer on the counter.

"Service, please! I demand to be serviced!" he bellows.

"You got ID?" the shopkeeper replies, his eyes narrowed.

Riley pats down his Sacred Heart jersey and pants. "Yeah, I know it's here somewhere…"

The man sighs as Riley slowly turns out all his pockets. Tom covers me as I shove candy bars and bags of chips into my purse. He snorts and stumbles into a rack of Little Debbie snack cakes, sending cupcakes skating across the floor. He starts to laugh uncontrollably as I scramble to straighten the display.

"What the…" I glance towards the checkout counter; the owner is still occupied with Riley. I shush Tom violently and smack him on the arm.

"Tom, shut up!" I mouth. "Help me…" He nods drunkenly and quickly pushes a couple more bags of chips into my purse. When it's full, we walk back toward the front door. Riley is still stalling, looking for his license.

"Maybe I left it in my car… Hang on a sec," Riley mumbles as he follows us out. When he bumps into my purse, a bag of Fritos falls out.

The shopkeeper's eyes widen. "Hey! Come back here! Thief! Thief! Stop!" he cries.

"Run, Christa! Go, go!" Riley laughs, shoving me through the door. We dart back to the car, but when I rush over to the passenger side and grab the handle, it's locked.

"Riley, the keys! Hurry up!" I squeal. Riley reaches into his pocket and fumbles, finally getting the keys into the door and turning the lock. I wrench it open and jump inside. Tom falls into the back as Riley stuffs his large linebacker frame into the driver's seat and jams the key into the ignition. The Asian man is standing in front of his store, waving his arms and screaming at us. Riley speeds out of the parking lot and bursts into laughter.

"Oh my God, did you see that guy's face? That was AWESOME!" he yells. "I swear, one of these days, we're gonna get arrested. What was the haul?" He checks his blind spot over his shoulder.

I unload my bag onto the armrest. "Three bags of Doritos, a Ruffles, two Twix, couple Kit Kats, and some of those generic lemon drops I know you love." I grin, tossing the bag into his lap.

Riley leans over and kisses me sloppily on the lips. "Aww... You shouldn't have, babe. I knew there was a reason we kept you around."

Tom pretends to gag in the back and then lets out a yowl as his hand finds the spot where my beer hit the seat earlier.

"What gives, Christa? Did you piss yourself back here?" he shouts.

I chuck a bag of Doritos at his head. "You're one to talk, Tom."

Riley sits back, his head grazing the roof of the car as we get onto the 10. "Children, if you don't stop bickering, I'll turn this car right around and take you both back to school," he sniggers.

As we all laugh, I ease into my seat, taking in the view out the window—miles and miles of endless road coursing through a sprawling suburbia. L.A. flashes before me like a series of photographs... Pink's Hotdogs, the Santa Monica pier, rows of palm trees lining crowded thoroughfares. It's a city that offers so much promise to the many transplants that make their way here each year, but, more often, turns out to be a Venus fly trap where dreams come to die. I've lived here my whole life and, with the exception of the occasional celebrity sighting at The Griddle, I may as well live on Mars. We cruise along happily, snacking away.

Riley merges onto PCH, the ocean only several hundred feet from us, its waves steadily lapping at the shore. I spot a couple of huddled masses around a garbage can fire, members of L.A.'s infamous homeless population getting ready for another long, cold night. Between the stars and the water, this doesn't seem like such a bad place to be down on your luck.

Darkness comes on early, though, a sign that winter will be here soon. The heat in the car isn't working; I'm glad I had the foresight to take a jacket when I left the apartment this morning. I catch a glimpse of myself in the side mirror. Tired gray eyes stare back at me. I sweep my long brown hair up into a knot on the top of my head and try to pinch a little color into my cheeks. I don't want to look like the walking dead when we make it to the club.

Riley parks a few blocks away, down on Sunset. The line to get into Trinity is already around the corner. We join the collection of club kids, hipsters, and junkies waiting for the bouncer to give them their chance to rub elbows with the rich and famous. I fiddle with the zipper on the top of my boot, making sure my key and phone that I tucked away are still in there. We finally make our way to the front of the line, where the bouncer, wearing an earpiece, holds his hand up to us while he confers with someone inside. IDs aren't necessary at Trinity—if you have the right look, you're in. He takes in my plaid skirt, fishnets, and tight black sweater.

"Okay, sweetheart, you can go in—but your friends have to wait out here for a while." He motions me with his hand. Tom and Riley start to protest and push forward, but Earpiece holds them at bay.

"I can send your asses to the back of the line if you're gonna trick off," he barks in a deep voice. Tom and Riley shrink back against the barricade. I give the boys a sympathetic smile as the bouncer stamps my hand.

"See you inside," I sing-song.

Tom shakes his head. "So typical, Christa. I can shake my ass too, you know!" he yells, his hand placed jauntily on his hip. "Get me a drink, okay?"

I roll my eyes and enter through the red double doors. Trinity is a renovated Catholic church—although the only things worshiped here are sex, drugs, and Usher. The walls are plastered with crosses and mirrors, reflecting dancing couples pressed hotly against each other. I chew at my lip and maneuver through a sea of people over to the LED light-covered bar in the back of the club. I catch the bartender's eye and order a whiskey and Coke. I'm still pretty buzzed from the car, but I need a little more liquid courage before I'm ready to hit the dance floor. I sip my drink slowly and feel the bass resonate in my stomach, my hips starting to sway as I take in the orgy-like mass of bodies pulsating before me. Beats from the wall-to-wall speakers bounce off of the exposed ceiling pipes as the crowd gathers in tighter and tighter around the bar. I have my eyes closed, rocking back on my heels, when some spaz in an orange Day-Glo tank top shoves me into someone sitting on one of the bar stools, my drink pouring all over my sweater. I wince as the icy liquid hits my skin. Day-Glo glances at me and dramatically feigns surprise.

"Oh my God! I am *so* sorry!" he chortles as a skanky girl rubs up behind him, running her hand under his mesh shirt. I look away, disgusted.

"It's fine. Whatever," I grimace, looking around for a napkin. Day-Glo and his gross girlfriend snicker and dance off. I give them both a withering glare before turning to the guy on the barstool.

"Sorry about that. Did I get you too?" I mutter.

He looks up at me with piercing blue eyes, the club lights glimmering in his coal black hair. I catch myself mid-gasp as I take in his aquiline nose and perfect mouth. His eyes go wide for a minute, before he picks up a napkin from the bar and coolly dabs at his jacket. He then hands it to me.

"Nothing I can't handle. Looks like you got the worst of it," he answers in a thick Irish brogue. I smile sheepishly as I attempt to pat my sweater dry.

"I like your accent. Where are you from?" I yell over the music, tucking the napkin into my skirt pocket.

"West Hollywood," he jokes, then adds, "No, I'm originally from Limerick." As he obviously checks me out, I tuck my tongue into my cheek.

"Limerick, like those cheesy five-line poems you have to practice writing in English class?" I ask. "You know, there was an old man from Nantucket... something about peeing in a bucket..." I give a little flourish with my hand. He smiles politely and nods, glancing down at the floor. I feel my face redden.

"Sorry, that was really lame. That probably wasn't the first time you've heard that line before." I cringe. He looks up and pats my arm kindly.

"No, I was actually trying to remember the one about the lady from Dublin." He chuckles. I sigh, grateful, and move in a little closer.

"So, what's your name?" I ask.

"Maybe I should ask you the same question," he replies, arching his eyebrows. "Or your age, with all this talk of English class." His accent chews his consonants.

I bite my lip. "It's Hollywood. The younger the better, right?" I glance up at him coyly. He can't be more than 21, himself.

He chuckles and stands, offering me the stool. I take it, and he puts his hand on my knee, leaning in. My skin flushes where he touches me.

"Can you see me?" he purrs.

I shake my head, confused. "I mean, it's a little dim in here, with the lights… but, yeah, I see you." I laugh.

He grins and puts his lips to my ear. "And I can certainly see you." Despite the noisy club, his voice is crystal clear. "Alden. My name is Alden."

"I'm Christa." I shiver, staring into his eyes.

"Can I buy you a drink, Christa?" he asks, the corners of his mouth twitching. "Your other one didn't last so long,"

I blush. "Um, yeah. I'll have a whiskey and Coke."

Alden gestures to the bartender, who instantly brings over a new cocktail. He leans against the bar as I sip it, ice cubes clinking on my teeth. He eyes me hungrily and brushes his finger across the side of my cheek. I down the rest of my drink and spin the stool towards him, wrapping my legs around him. He looks down at me and raises his eyebrows. I can tell that we're both surprised by my boldness. I tuck a loose strand of hair behind my ear.

"D-do you want to dance?" I stutter. He takes my hands in his, lifting me off the seat.

"Always," he murmurs.

He leads me through the surging throng of dancers, over to an elevated private alcove made up of three-way mirrors. From this angle, I can see every beat that vibrates through us, watch every caress he makes down my arm, touching my hands and waist, pulling my hips into his. I can feel the alcohol kicking in, and my head dizzies and falls back as he presses into me, his lips grazing my neck. His scent fills my nose—burnt paper. We spin around and face our reflections. The girl who I see looking back at me is one I barely recognize, her eyes huge and cat-like. Heat courses through my veins as Alden pushes up behind me, his hand on my navel. For a moment, I completely surrender and melt into him and the music, forgetting everyone else in the club. He turns me around and pulls my hair out of its bun, coiling it in his hand like a rope and gently winching my head back. My eyes flutter shut and I arch my lips up to his. Just as we're about to kiss, someone comes up behind us and wrenches me out of Alden's grasp. I open my eyes abruptly and see Riley, his mouth pressed into a thin line.

"What are you doing? Who is this guy?" he demands.

I shake my head. "We were just dancing. It was nothing..." I turn back to Alden, whose eyes have narrowed. He crosses over and shoves Riley into the mirror. I stagger back, my buzz gone.

"Hey—don't... It's fine—" I stammer, putting my hand on Alden's shoulder. Heat radiates off of his back as he pushes Riley harder.

"You've got guts, getting in between me and her," he growls. Riley's eyes widen as Alden pins him against the wall, clenching the collar of his football jersey. Even being almost half a foot taller, I can tell that Riley is stuck. He huffs and struggles to even move his shoulders.

"Things don't go well for those who get between me and what I want," Alden sneers.

"Seriously—stop!" I cry, looking nervously out at the club for help. Alden glances back at me, his blue eyes searing. He takes a breath and steps away, a menacing grin spreading across his face. Riley straightens up and shakes his head.

"This is messed up! I don't know what's going on here, but she's *my* girlfriend, asshole!" Riley glares in my direction. "Maybe she forgot to mention that, but I've got no problem breaking it down for you." He gives Alden a small shove and adds, "Back off, dickwad, before we have to take this to the next level."

Alden stares back at him, unflinching, before bursting into a round of applause. My eyes dart between them, confused.

"Hey, no worries, man. I didn't know she was yours." He laughs, putting his hands up in mock surrender. "I wouldn't want to mess with a big boy like you," he adds smugly. Riley nods and then steps out of the alcove.

"Are you coming?" he asks, looking back at me.

I nod. "Just give me a second."

Riley shakes his head. "I'll be at the bar," he calls as he stalks off. I turn back to Alden, my face red.

"That was a little much," I say, looking down at the floor.

He sighs. "Sorry, I'm not big on interruptions. Especially when it involves a pretty girl like you." He lifts my chin with his thumb. I blush. "I hope I didn't upset you." The corners of his eyes crinkle.

I let out a nervous laugh. "Yeah, well, I'm not a big fan when *anyone* decides to go all Hulk Smash." I look at him quizzically. "How did you do that, anyway? Riley's got, like, sixty pounds on you." I look down at his arms. I can tell he's built underneath his jacket, but he's no football player.

Alden grins. "Adrenaline, I guess. Gives me superhuman strength." He leans over me. "But usually, I like to use my powers for more… savory activities." He runs his fingers down my side. My head dizzies again and I smile stupidly.

"Dancing with you… It was… nice," I manage.

"Understatement. You were shining so bright I couldn't take my eyes off of you," he breathes, resting his hand on the small of my back. My whole body starts to quiver.

"I really have to go," I murmur, my eyes closed.

"No, you don't." He smirks, taking my hand. "Forget him. Stay." He stares at me, his eyes cool. I bite my lip and pull my hand away slowly, not really wanting to let go.

He nods. "Wouldn't want to keep your boyfriend waiting." He puts his hands in his pockets. "No worries, I can take a hint." He gives me a tight smile and turns to walk away. I startle.

"No, wait—Alden!" I call. He spins halfway on his heels, glancing back at me slyly. "Don't you want my number or something?" I shrug.

He chuckles. "You'll find me," he teases, "when you're ready."

He arches his eyebrows playfully and disappears into the crowd. I grab onto the wall, everything below my waist begging me to follow him. I take a breath before looking disparagingly toward the bar. I can just make out the top of Riley's head above the other club-goers. I sigh and drag myself away from the alcove.

"What the hell was that all about, Christa?" Riley barks when I arrive.

"Riley, chill. We were just dancing…" I plop down onto a stool.

"Looked like more than that," he scoffs. "Whatever. You wanna slut it up all over town, that's your business."

"Hey!" I scowl, purposefully staring down at a stack of singles, a pretty meager tip for the bartender. I debate pocketing it and calling a cab. Riley paces behind me.

"Seriously, Christa! What do you have to say for yourself?!" he yells. I purse my lips and spin around to face him.

"I don't need to say anything, Riley! Why are you being such a dick?" I shout.

He shakes his head and points in my face. "No, you don't get to be mad!" he snaps. "I'm the one that walked in on you about to hook up with some random dude at a club! I'm the one who gets to freak here, not you!"

I jump as he slams his hand against the bar. "Back off!" I give him a warning punch on the arm. He straightens up and steps away. I sigh and run my fingers through my hair.

"Riley… what you saw back there—"

"Meant nothing. Yeah, yeah. Save it, Christa. You can say whatever you want to cover your ass, but we both know what was going on back there." He waves a hand and turns toward the dancers. "You looked… possessed or something! Obviously, that guy has some major game, and I'm not even gonna try to compete with that." He lets out a huff. "I just feel like a douche for thinking that you and I had something." He shakes his head and arches an eyebrow. "Most girls I know would have felt more of a connection after all the stuff we did."

I bite the inside of my cheek. "Well, I guess I'm not like most girls."

He snorts. "Got that right. Yeah, maybe this is my fault." He scratches the back of his head. "When I first met you, I thought, 'Well, she doesn't have a lot going on up front, but she's got a nice ass, so... what the hell.'" He shrugs.

I roll my eyes. "Wow, thanks."

"And I knew you had attachment issues, but I just thought that kind of crazy would make you a freaky lay," he continues. "I never thought it would come back and get me like this, not in a million years." He shakes his head and stares out at the club.

I wince. "Riley, I'm sorry. Really, we were just dancing. I don't even know him—he's just some guy I met at the bar."

He wrinkles his nose. "That's supposed to make me feel better? The way you were looking at him in the mirror, the way *he* was looking at *you*—" He flushes. "The whole thing was just embarrassing! Seriously, Christa, I thought you had a little more dignity." He picks up his drink from the bar and puts the rest of it back.

I laugh. "Huh... That's kind of amazing, *you* shaming *me*." I hop off of the stool. "This from the biggest man-whore at Sacred Heart. Nice double standard." I turn back to the crowd.

Riley's eyes bug out. "*That* is totally different, and you know it! I've never hooked up with some other chick right in front of you... What you did was completely disrespectful!" He smacks the back of the stool with his palm. I roll my eyes.

"God, I didn't know you took this all so seriously. I thought we were just having fun," I grumble, picking at my fingernails.

Riley shakes his head. "Yeah. Sure. Really fun watching you mack on a total stranger."

"Oh please, get over yourself! I wasn't going to have sex with him, Riley!" I grit through my teeth. "Either you trust me or you don't—"

"Well, I guess I don't, then," he interrupts. "We're done now."

I look down at the floor as he turns back toward the bar, trying to get the waiter's attention. I sigh and turn away, watching Tom trying to twerk with two tall blonde women out on the dance floor. They take one look at him and burst out laughing, yelling something in what sounds like Russian before moving further into the club. He glances away, dejected, before seeing me. He bounds over like a puppy all out of breath.

"Looks like you're having a rough night, too," I lament, patting Tom's back. He waves his hand and smiles.

"Aww, they'll be all over me by the end of the night. These mail-order girls can't get enough of *this*." He smooths his t-shirt. "Besides, I didn't want to leave you two wallflowers hanging by your lonesome. What are we drinking?" He pushes back his sweaty bleach-blond hair as he cozies up to the bar.

Riley clears his throat and taps the bartender on the shoulder. "Three Snakebites." He gestures with his fingers. I sigh: there is order to the universe. Riley never lets a fight get in the way of getting totally hammered. The bartender nods and lines the shot glasses up in a row. He pours, and we all raise a glass.

"To friendship and self-respect," Riley toasts, glaring in my direction. I clench my jaw as I slam my drink back, the alcohol burning my throat.

"And hot Russian ass," Tom adds, his drink spilling over the side of the shooter.

*

"This place is dead. I'm ready to call it," Riley mumbles after a couple of hours. He leans over and nudges Tom with his shoulder. Tom turns and motions with his hand before spinning back around to a drunken girl who is talking to her friend on his right.

"I gotta bounce, Oxana. It's been real." He gives her a light slap on the butt. The girl rolls her eyes and goes back to talking with her friend. I sigh and pull on my jacket.

This evening has been one huge disappointment. After unsuccessfully trying to find Alden again, I spent the rest of the night listening to Riley and Tom try to out *Simpsons*-quote each other while they got more and more trashed. I should have taken the sexy Irish guy up on his offer when I had the chance.

We stumble to the car, where I lay down in the backseat, hoping to avoid an angry, drunken lecture from Riley. We pull away from Trinity as Tom starts replaying the night's events.

"… And I think I would have totally hooked up with that chick from Ukraine if her stupid friend hadn't been hanging around the whole time," he says with a shake of his head.

"That was never gonna happen, Tom. Sorry," Riley chortles from the driver's seat. "Maybe you should ask Christa for some tips on how to win over the international circle. She's an expert at drawing in Eurotrash."

I scowl and sit up, rubbing tiredly at my face. My brain is foggy with too much booze and not enough sleep. I trace small circles around my knees, picking at my stockings where Alden's fingers touched my skin. I exhale slowly.

Get a grip, Christa, I tell myself. *He was just some guy at a club, a one-time thing.* I snuggle back into the seat, gazing out my window, a gentle rain beating against the glass and the city lights keeping me company. I sigh and close my eyes…

I'm already fast asleep when the car swerves and we crash headfirst into a concrete wall.

CHAPTER 1

I HEAR HIS VOICE before I ever see his face. "Hey, Nurse? Can I get an update?"

"Sure, hon. Her tox screens just came back. No drugs, but her blood alcohol was .10. She's not as bad as the driver—I heard he blew a .12 at the scene. She should be coming out of it soon." She clears her throat. "Are you a friend or family?"

The voice pauses. "Uh, friend, I guess. I saw the accident happen."

My eyes flutter open and I swallow, painfully. I take in the room with its popcorn ceiling and complicated-looking computer monitors. I'm in a hospital, full of sterile, bright lights and noisy medical machinery. I turn my head and see two female nurses standing together, talking casually just outside of my door.

"Well, is she going to leave him?" the one with dark hair whispers. The older woman shakes her head.

"I don't know," she mutters. "She keeps telling me she wants to, but she's got a baby with him, doesn't want to break up the family over something small... If it were me, I would have been out of there *years* ago." She raises her eyebrows knowingly as she reaches up and takes a file off the wall. "I'll be right back. I need to get this to Turner."

She nods and shuffles away in her purple scrubs. The other woman walks back to the nurses' station and sits behind the desk.

I take a deep breath and stare down at my bed. I'm still wearing my own clothes, but I notice an IV drip snaking out of my right hand. I take stock of all my parts: ten fingers, ten toes, two arms, two legs, one pounding headache. My hand trembles up to my temple, skimming a thick bandage that's wrapped around my forehead like a horrible '80s headband. Great—just what I needed.

I hear footsteps coming down the hall and try to prop myself up on my elbows to see who it is. My body has other plans, though, and, after a crippling dizzy spell, I slump back into the pillows. I sigh and try to breathe evenly.

Expecting to see a nurse or a doctor, I snap to attention when a tall boy in a red knit cap carrying two cups of water walks into my room. His eyes widen when he sees that I'm up, and he hastily puts the cups down on the side table.

"You're awake! Hang on…" He crosses over to me and presses a button on the side support rail, lifting the top of my bed slightly. Blearily, I can make out his faded brown leather jacket and blue jeans. He reaches down and brushes my arm.

"How are you doing? Do you want some water?" he asks softly.

I nod as he holds one of the cups up to my lips, cooling my scratchy throat. I cough and he puts the water aside so that he can wipe my mouth with a tissue. I blink.

"Where am I?" I rasp.

"Westside Hospital. You were in a car accident earlier… Hit your head pretty bad." He leans in closer, looking at me intently with warm brown eyes. His curly blond hair pokes out from underneath his hat, and he's wearing an old Rolling Stones t-shirt. He looks to be about my age, maybe 19 or 20. He sees me staring and smiles.

"You have very straight teeth," I coo.

He laughs. "I'll make sure to send your compliments on to my orthodontist." He picks up the water again. "Do you want more?"

I nod and take the cup. "Thanks." I look at him and squint, trying to focus through my headache. "Are you a volunteer or something?" I ask, sipping the water.

"Uh…" He straightens up and rubs the back of his neck. "In a matter of speaking, yes."

I stare at him curiously, gripping the cup with my fingers. He gives me a tight smile and looks around to the door. "I think I hear your nurse. Hold on."

His sneakers squeak on the tile as he rushes out of the room. I inch up the bed until I'm in a sitting position, the room spinning for a moment before leveling out. I sit very still, waiting for the vertigo to pass, then take another drink.

Mystery Date returns with the older nurse from earlier. She grins widely before stepping over to the computer and beginning to type. The boy sits on a stool right next to my bed. I glance over at his beat-up blue jeans and see smears of what looks like blood on them. Yeah, he's definitely not a candy striper. I quickly look away.

"Do you know your name, hon?" the nurse asks as she looks up from her keyboard.

"Christa Nichols."

"How old are you?"

"17… No, 18," I correct myself quickly. "I, um, just turned 18."

"Birthdate?" She punches a few of the keys.

"November 1st." I look over at Mystery Date, wondering why he's still here. He nods pleasantly.

The nurse bats my hand. "Ooh, just last week! Me, too—well, the 3rd… Although, I've lost count of how many at this point!" She laughs, pointing up at her gray hair. "Can you tell me who the president is right now?"

These questions are getting weird. I blink a few times. "Why are you asking me that?"

She sighs. "Well, Christa, you were in a nasty car wreck earlier tonight. You hit your head pretty bad. Do you remember any of that?"

I comb my fingers through the ends of my hair, trying to recall the car ride home. I had fallen asleep, but I remember hearing Riley and Tom talking, and then Tom yelling to watch it, or maybe to slow down... I start to feel dizzy again and let out a groan. The boy takes my hand and tries to read my face. I look at him, surprised that he's touching me, and pull my hand away. I turn my attention back to the nurse. I can read her name tag: *Shirley*. She glances down at me, her fingers still typing away.

"I *really* need you to answer these questions before I can discharge you. Do you know where you are?" she asks firmly.

"L.A.... Los Angeles." I reply, attempting to sound coherent.

"Great." Shirley smiles. "One more: were you wearing a seatbelt at the time of the accident?"

I let out a little chuckle. Seatbelts? Yeah, right. We'd nicknamed Riley's car *Deathtrap*.

"No." I lick my chapped lips. "Are my friends okay? Riley Anderson and Tom Wyndam?" I sit up, trying to get a look at the computer screen.

She furrows her brow at the monitor and clicks the mouse a couple of times.

"Riley Anderson was admitted with superficial injuries and was released to police custody for questioning about an hour ago," she reads verbatim. "And it looks like... Tom Wyndam... is still in surgery." She blinks.

I close my eyes and take a deep breath. I can feel tears starting to prickle behind my eyelids. I put my palm over my face.

"Is Tom going to be okay?" I whimper.

Shirley shakes her head. "I don't know, hon. He's not on my service."

I take my hand away from my eyes and stare up at the ceiling, wondering if this night can get any worse.

"Okay," Shirley sighs, trying to shift gears. "You had a blood alcohol level of .10 when you came in. Standard protocol when you're unconscious and over the legal limit is to pump your stomach. Your throat might be a little sore for the next couple days." She looks at me as I massage my neck self-consciously.

"Dr. Turner did get a chance to review the results from your CT scan. Looks like no serious damage was done. There's a little bit of bruising, but no signs of concussion. You're going to want to keep the ice and bandage on for another half hour or so." She lightly touches the icepack strapped to my head. "As you are under-age and have been drinking, you will have to attend the hospital's Sober Students Together program. It's a sixteen-week course that meets weekly." She pauses and taps the mouse. "The next session starts this Saturday. It *is* mandatory, if you want to avoid jail time."

I grimace. Perfect.

Shirley looks at me. "Is there someone we should call to come and get you? Mom? Dad?"

Yeah, that's not going to happen anytime this century. I shake my head.

She frowns. "Okay," she says softly. "We'll want you back here in a week for a follow-up. Do you have a way to get back then?" she asks, her eyes round.

I shift in the bed, less dizzy this time. "I'll figure it out."

"I'll make sure she's here," Mystery Date interjects from his perch. I break into a fit of coughing.

"I'm sorry," I say to Shirley. "Who is this guy?" I shake my head.

Shirley lets out a giggle. "Cute. Little head trauma humor, there." She smiles as she pulls a pen and pad out of her a pocket in her scrubs and scribbles down a note. "You have a few cuts and bruises from the window shattering. Report to the pharmacy on Level 2 before you leave and pick up your pain meds and antiseptic cream at the counter." She glances down at her hip, her pager vibrating, then quickly unhooks my IV and starts to move out of the room.

"That's all I've got. The doctor has already cleared you. Take your time—your friend can help you when you're ready."

"Wait, I *really* don't know him—" I call, waving my hand listlessly at the boy. The nurse, however, has already zipped out into the hallway. We sit and stare at each other for a moment before he raise an eyebrow.

"Huh." He puts his hands in his jacket pockets and stands. "Well, I guess we should get your coat."

My eyes bug out of my head. "Okay, time out!" I manage to sputter. "This whole thing has gone far enough." I clench my jaw and start to swing my legs off the bed, my knees shaking like jelly.

"Um—she said to take your time…" he cautions, coming up behind me. I slap his arm away.

"Thanks, I got it." I glare. "So… I know I'm missing some key details from tonight, but—who are you?"

"Like I told the nurses, I found you at the scene—at the underpass…" he mumbles, staring down at his muddy sneakers.

I shake my head. "Yeah, that doesn't answer my question. Why are you here? And why was that nurse okay leaving me with you?" I wince and grab my head as I sit up.

He sighs. "You *asked* me to come. You seemed pretty adamant about it at the time."

I grab onto the bed rail for support as he moves to my side and tries to take my hand again. I swat him away.

"*Don't* touch me! And I'm not going anywhere with you!" I yell. My head starts to throb and I let out a moan, slumping back onto the bed. He sits down on the stool again.

"That's fair." He nods. "You've been through a lot tonight." He wheels a little closer to the bed. "We'll just take it a step at a time… Everything is going to be fine, just—"

I look at him and start to laugh hysterically.

"You have got to be kidding me!" I interrupt. "Everything is *not* fine! This thing on my head—" I point at the bandage, "—is the least of my problems! Did you not hear what the nurse just said?" I shut my eyes and rub tiredly at the bridge of my nose. "I've got one friend in surgery and the other in jail. There's a pending underage drinking charge against me unless I go to some wacky support group, and I probably look like I've been mauled by a mountain lion." I bite my lip. "The last thing I need is some deranged homeless guy following me around trying to turn me into a project."

I feel bad the minute the last part comes out of my mouth. "Sorry if that's an inaccurate description," I mutter, glancing at him out of the corner of my eye.

He exhales, his hands on his knees, and pushes back from the bed, the wheels of his stool screeching against the linoleum. "It's fine. I've been called worse." He stands and starts to chuckle.

"I just assumed—from the dirty clothes…" I trail off. He smiles.

"Yeah, laundry day's Sunday. I wait 'til people go off to church and then sneak into their basements and run a load." He coughs, looking down at his shirt. "Sorry if the blood is a turn off, but I thought you might be willing to overlook it since, I don't know, I saved your life and all."

"Okay, seriously…" I roll my eyes. "You don't have to get surly."

He snorts. "Well, how would you like me to be, Christa? All sweet and syrupy, kiss your boo-boos and tell you that what happened to you is no big deal?" He shakes his head. "Poor Christa… She didn't know what she was doing when she got mad wasted, or should I say, 'It's not her fault that she got into that car with a drunk driver; she's not known for her great life choices.'" He pouts.

I balk at him, aghast. "You can't talk to me that way!"

He raises his voice. "Someone has to!"

"Don't yell at me! You don't know anything about me or my life…" I take a deep breath, turning away.

He rolls his eyes. "Please—don't flatter yourself. I could write that book in my sleep. It would be titled *Wrong Turn: The Christa Nichols Story.*" He laughs.

I feel my face contort. "This is… unbelievable. You just need to get away from me—whoever you are. If this is some creepy ploy to get into my pants, you're barking up the wrong tree!"

When he does nothing but roll his eyes, I start to stand up and growl, "Like that didn't cross your mind. I don't know what happened tonight—"

"You almost died," he interjects, folding his arms.

I feel the wind get knocked out of me and lean back against the side of the bed. "You're kidding, right?" I whisper.

He looks down at his hands, fidgeting with the button on his jacket. "Wish I was. If it hadn't been for me, you'd be extra crispy, just like your friend in surgery."

I feel my face redden. "That is… disgusting." My voice cracks. "You can't say things like that."

He moves over to the wall. "It's true. I'm sorry, Christa… You were both in serious trouble tonight." He looks at me, his expression grave. "Can you remember anything from earlier?"

I shake my head. "No," I mumble. "I remember leaving the club and getting in the car… and that's about it." I shrug.

He sighs and slowly steps over to me. "I was at the underpass, talking with my friend. It was raining pretty hard and we were both trying to stay dry."

When I grimace apologetically, he grins and adds, "It's okay, really! You don't need to feel bad for me! Anyway," he continues, "we see your car come barreling around the corner; it's pretty obvious that whoever is driving is trashed. We had about three seconds to jump out of the way before you guys crashed headfirst into the side wall."

He leans next to me and looks down at the floor. "The car burst into flames. I helped Riley out first; he was still awake. I could hear your friend Tom screaming, but I couldn't get him. His door was wedged against the wall…"

I feel my throat tighten. He purses his lips. "But I could get to you—through your window. You were just coming to. I got you out and waited 'til the ambulance arrived." He sighs. "I rode over with you, and… here we are." He spreads his arms and shrugs.

I nod, touching the side of my head and feeling the scratchy bandage. "I guess that sounds about right." I clench my jaw and mutter, "I'm sure it will all come rushing back at some point like a bad made-for-TV movie."

He nods, looking at the floor. "I stayed because you asked me to," he says quietly. "The last thing I want to do is weird you out."

"Thank you," I sigh after a moment. "You didn't have to help me, and you did. That's… something that not a lot of people would do."

Without even thinking about it, I put my hand on top of his, our fingers lacing together familiarly. We both stare at our hands before he clears his throat and pulls away.

"You're welcome," he murmurs, getting up. "We should get you home. It's getting late—or early, depending on how you look at it." He arches an eyebrow, looking out the window.

I nod, coming out of my daze. "Yeah, you're right. I want to get out of here." I stand shakily and reach for my coat. He gets up to help me into it, and I let him.

I pull my hair from my collar and turn to him. "This night is so weird. It started out with ditching school and ends with a massive head injury." I snort. "Should probably come up with a better plan next time I want to miss a Calc exam." The corners of my mouth twitch.

He nods. "Yeah. Complaining about an upset stomach will usually do the trick." He smiles, and I notice a small white scar just above his top lip, the kind of imperfection that makes me want to take a second look. I exhale and look up at him.

"I don't even know your name." I say.

He takes a breath. "It's Daniel," he answers. I nod, waiting for more.

"Just Daniel?" I smile. "Daniel...?"

He cocks his head to the side. "Just Daniel. Like Cher or... Oprah." He laughs.

I roll my eyes. "Okay, fine... Be all cryptic," I start to walk towards the door. "But if you burst into a sudden rendition of 'If I Could Turn Back Time,' I am so outta here."

*

"Thanks for the coffee," I murmur, blowing steam off the top of the cup. I take a sip and hand it back to Daniel.

"Sure. Sorry I didn't have enough for two." He blushes, looking down at the sidewalk. The rain has stopped since we arrived a few hours ago, now limited to the occasional drip from the tall palm trees above us. But we're still huddling under the rain shelter with a few other people, waiting for the Number 7 bus into the Valley.

"It's fine—I don't mind sharing." I smooth the back of my head with my hand, now bandage-free. "I shouldn't have let you pay at all. *I'm* the one who should be buying you a lifetime's supply of... coffee, shower gel, dog food, whatever you want." I smile.

He laughs. "Your gratitude was plenty. Seriously, I'm not looking for a curtain call." He crosses his arms and leans against the shelter wall. "But if you've got a pair of tickets to the next Stones reunion tour, I wouldn't say no." He winks. I look down at his shirt, where the big, red Rolling Stones tongue and lips are splattered in my blood.

"You some kind of super fan?" I ask.

"More like a love affair that's lasted a lifetime!" he exclaims, offering me the coffee. "I've um, followed them for… a while." He grins sheepishly.

"I got that." I snicker, taking a drink. The heat feels good on my sore throat, but my head is still pounding. I wince and touch my forehead where a giant goose egg is forming.

Daniel looks at me, concerned. "The pharmacist said you could take one of those green pills now if you're in pain." He glances down at my bag.

I nod. "Yeah, I know. I'm just trying to hold off a little longer." I draw in a big breath of cool morning air. "It hurts… but this is the first time all night that I've felt like myself." I shrug.

He rests his head against the wall. "I get that. Just don't try to be a hero," he says airily.

"Yeah, I don't know if this bus stop could handle that. Only room for one Superman," I tease, slapping him playfully on the arm. He sniggers and steps out onto the curb, looking down the road for the bus. I turn and check out the other people waiting: a couple of nurses coming off of their shift change, an older man sitting on the bench trying to read a book in the dim street light, and, next to him, an Indian woman cradling a young boy in pajamas—I'm guessing a late-night flu situation. I catch a glimpse of my reflection in the shelter glass and startle as I take in the full damage from the accident. My face is covered in small, deep cuts from the shattered window, and I have a particularly nasty bruise on my right cheekbone—all excellent compliments to the giant bulge on top of my head.

"I'm surprised I haven't sent everyone screaming into the hills," I mutter, wincing as I gently graze one of the cuts with my finger. Daniel turns and walks back over to me.

"Ach, it's just a flesh wound!" he says, doing his best Arnold Schwarzenegger impersonation.

When I giggle and shake my head, he juts out his chin. "You're a tough girl. In a couple days, you'll be back to taking names and breaking hearts."

"Oh my God, who talks like that?" I laugh, looking down at the sidewalk. "You're like something straight out of an old movie."

"I will take that and say thank you." He smiles, looking back at the street. "Do you have a watch? I feel like this thing should be here by now." He clucks his tongue.

"Yeah, I've got my phone... Hang on a sec," I rifle through my purse and pull out my iPhone. "It's 5:46. Does that mean anything?" I ask.

"It comes on the 10s, usually," one of the nurses answers.

Daniel and I both nod. "Thanks," I reply, scanning through my contacts list. I push Riley's number and put my phone to my ear. Daniel furrows his brow. "Hang on a sec," I mumble, turning away.

The call goes straight to voicemail. "Hey, it's me," I sigh into the receiver. "Just wondering how you're doing... The nurse said you were in police custody. Hope you're okay." I pause, biting my lip. "I know things are really messed up between us, but call me when you can." I hang up, about to put my phone back in my bag, then look at Daniel and grin. "Let me take your picture."

Daniel grimaces. "Now? Like this?" He flashes his messed up shirt.

I nod. "Yeah, now!" I laugh.

He shakes his head. "Aw, no... I'm not camera-ready." He arches a brow, saying, "Let me take *your* picture," and gesturing for the phone.

I hold it away slyly. "Ha ha... I am *definitely* not camera-ready." I motion to my face dramatically. "Come on, give me something to remember tonight with. The good part anyway." I cock my head and look at him sweetly.

He makes a face and nods. "Well, when you put it that way…" He sighs. "Okay—fine. What do you want me to do?" He poses awkwardly.

I smile. "Just zip up your jacket and lean against that post." I wave at the shelter wall, taking a step back. He rolls his eyes, but does as instructed.

I hold up my phone and focus. "Take your hat off! Be a person!" I yell.

He puts his hands on his hips. "Seriously?" he gripes.

I grin. "Just do it!"

Daniel sighs and pulls the cap off, stuffing it in his coat. He runs a hand through his blond mane, his rock-star curls sweeping his shoulders. I smirk coyly and snap the photo. "Very James Dean," I croon. "Thank you for obliging this poor invalid girl." I save the picture and put my phone away.

"Yeah, yeah." He stares into the distance, his hands in his pockets. I sidle up next to him and rest against the bus stop wall.

"All I want right now is a long soak in a tub and then to sleep for a million years," I yawn, closing my eyes. Daniel pats me on the shoulder.

"Soon. We'll get you home," he murmurs. I shift uncomfortably against the hard metal of the rain shelter; trying in vain to find a good position. For a second, I consider leaning on Daniel.

"*CATALYST!* I see you! I found you!"

My eyes are jarred open by someone screaming and grabbing my arm.

"Whoa! Cool it, man! Get your hands off her!" Daniel shouts, pulling me behind him.

Teetering in front of us is a light-set man, his face worn and gaunt with dark circles under his eyes. He's wearing dirty gray sweatpants and a thin red t-shirt. He's shivering, but I don't know if it's from the cold or something else.

"No... I saw it! I saw it from across the street!" he barks, tugging in frustration at his matted brown hair. "It's mine! MINE!"

I shrink behind Daniel, trying to make myself as small as possible. I look over at the young mother, who is now clutching her child. Both sets of eyes are wide as they watch the man waver and slobber all over the sidewalk.

Daniel shakes his head and steps toward the crazy guy. "Listen, we've got nothing for you." He puts up his hands calmly and points back to me. "She's had a really rough night, so why don't you go find another bus stop to terrorize, okay?"

The man swings haphazardly with his hand, missing Daniel's face by a couple of inches. Daniel steps back and protects me with his arm. "I'm only going to say this one more time, man," he warns. "Just walk away, all right? Turn around, go find somewhere else to sleep it off and leave us alone. You're freaking everybody out!" He gestures to the others, who have all quietly moved out of the rain shelter.

The man bares his teeth and claws at his own arms. "I'm not afraid of you, *Guardian!*" he spits. Daniel sighs and rubs his forehead as the man continues. "I see you, too; don't for a second think you're fooling anyone! I see *everything*!" His voice cracks and he falls to the ground, smashing his fists into his eyes.

I zip up my jacket and take Daniel's arm. "Daniel, I want to go... Let's just start walking. We'll find another stop." I keep my gaze down.

Daniel opens his mouth to answer, but gets cut off. "I will follow you, Catalyst! Until the end of the world, 'til the end of days—you can't run from me!" the man bellows, lunging forward. Daniel catches him and pitches him against the shelter, the back of the man's head bouncing off the wall.

I gasp as he slumps down, crumpling like a rag doll. I clutch at Daniel. "Oh my God! Is he...?" I cry, but I get my answer when he bolts back up like *Night of the Living Dead* and starts running toward us again.

The other people scatter into the parking lot. "What the hell is he on?" I shriek, grabbing Daniel's waist.

"Christa—get back!" Daniel orders. I let out a little scream and scramble to the other side of the glass shelter wall. Zompocalypse shoves Daniel aside and throws himself at the window like a dog crashing into a screen door.

His face and hands press grotesquely against it in front of me, but the wall holds. I can see every popped blood vessel and sweat stain. His mouth works quietly against the glass. "I see you... see you..." he rasps.

My jaw falls open as Daniel rushes over and takes my hand. "Come on—the bus is here!" he yells, almost wrenching my arm out of its socket. We dash over to the street as the Number 7 takes its time turning the corner into the hospital lot. The man is still peeling himself from the glass as the bus doors swing open and we bolt up the stairs. We fall into the seat behind the driver.

"Don't let that guy on!" Daniel shouts, pointing at Zompocalypse. "He's completely insane!"

The bus driver slowly looks back at us. "Well, who do you think rides the bus?" he drawls.

Daniel and I jerk to the window; the man is now shambling toward us. "Oh my God, Daniel!" I scream.

Daniel beats the back of the driver's chair with his palm. "Shut the door! Shut the door!" he howls. The driver lets out a grunt and eases into his seat, calmly reaching over and pulling the door handle closed. We hear a bang against the side of the bus as we pull away from the hospital.

I finally exhale as we get on the freeway, Daniel thumping his head against the seat rest. "What *was* that?" I pant, trying to catch my breath. Daniel shakes his head.

"I don't know..." he heaves, breaking into a sudden coughing fit. I lean forward and pat his back.

"You okay?" I ask, a small grin creeping across my face.

He nods, holding his hand up to his mouth. The coughing subsides. "Yeah, just... a little high action back there." He chuckles, sitting back.

I laugh. "No kidding! Jeez, he just showed up out of nowhere." I clutch my bag in my lap. "And all that crazy stuff he was spouting..."

"Well, nothing like a day ending in Y to bring out the crazies in L.A.," Daniel scoffs, glancing out the window. "But I've never had one come at me like that."

I stare at him and scrunch my brow. "Hey, you've got a little something right there." I point to a smudge at the corner of his mouth. He reaches up with his finger to touch it. "Here, I think I have a tissue or something." I check my coat pockets before reaching into my skirt. I pull out the napkin from Trinity and hand it to him.

"Thanks." Daniel quickly wipes his lips and gives it back to me. Images of Alden and I dancing flash in my mind; that feels like a lifetime ago, after tonight. I smile and look out at the highway, the sun just starting to peek over the horizon. I sigh and snuggle into the seat, resting my head on Daniel's shoulder.

"Is this okay?" I mumble, closing my eyes. "I need to get off at the Van Nuys Sepulveda stop." I yawn, then add, "I just want to sit here for a minute." I press my face into his arm, closing my eyes. The scent of the leather from his jacket mingles with warm kitchen spices: cinnamon and ginger. He smells like home.

I hear him smile as he hunches down into the seat for me. "Sure. I'll wake you when we're there."

*

"Hey." Daniel gently nudges me awake. "I think this is it."

I rub my eyes and sit up, looking out the window. Across the street, the Coffee Bean and Tea Leaf is just opening for business, the lights at Nasty Jim's Tattoos and Piercing next door still off. I nod and get up, stretching.

"Yeah, thanks," I mumble as Daniel stands and lets me out into the aisle.

"Hey, I'll walk you to your door." He puts his hat back on. "If that's okay," he adds hesitantly. I smile and shrug.

"Sure. I'd like that." I swing my bag over my shoulder. "It's not far, just a couple blocks."

We thank the driver and step off the bus, the pavement still damp from last night's rain. A homeless man sleeps in an abandoned doorway, a piece of wet cardboard draped over his head. I look at Daniel and cringe as we start to walk. "Not exactly Beverly Hills," I mutter.

Daniel shrugs and puts his hands in his jacket. "You don't need to make excuses to me. I've been there." He glances down at his dirty clothes. "Still there, I guess." He laughs.

I cross my arms over my chest, studying my boots as we move. "So... where will you go? I mean, after this," I ask slowly.

He scrunches his brow. "I was thinking the Denny's down on Sherman. There's a waitress there that's pretty generous with the leftover home fries." He looks at me and grins.

I sigh. "You know what I mean. Do you have somewhere to... stay?"

"You offering?" He chuckles. "Little couch surfing at the Nichols' residence?"

I blush. "Yeah, I guess I am." I stop and look at him. "I don't like the idea of the guy who saved my life *twice* sleeping under a bridge... or worse." I shake my head. "I know we don't know each other... like at all..." I trail off.

Daniel's face softens and he stares down at his sneakers. "You shouldn't go inviting strangers to stay at your house. It's not a very good survival strategy." He shakes his head.

I shrug. "Well, given that I currently look like I just took a bunch of power tools to my face, survival strategies are not at the top of my list." I sigh. "I don't know… You don't feel… *strange.*" I bite my lip.

He looks at me. "Stranger than you know," he murmurs. "That is really a very kind invitation, Christa, but I'm good—I promise. The last person you need to worry about is me." He breaks into a large grin as we begin walking again. "But, if you're in the market for a roommate, I think that guy from the bus stop is looking for a place to crash. Seemed pretty eager to get to know you." He laughs.

I roll my eyes. "Zompocalypse? Yeah, that's never going to happen." I snicker.

Daniel stops in his tracks. "I'm sorry—what did you call him?" His eyes crinkle. "*Zompocalypse?*"

I turn and arch a brow. "I like nicknames. It's just something I do." I shrug. He nods appreciatively.

"That's a good one. Pretty fitting." He smiles. "Got any for me?"

I smile slightly, saying, "Maybe a couple." I clear my throat and gesture to the building that we've stopped in front of. "This is me."

I reach down and pull my key out of my boot before turning and look at him. "Thank you for everything," I sigh, rubbing my jaw with my hand. "God, I feel like that doesn't even begin to cover it."

Daniel nods and pats me on the arm. "Don't mention it. All in a day's work." He rocks back on his heels.

"Off to go rescue a bunch of kids from a burning building; maybe help an old lady cross the street?" I joke.

"No… I thought I heard a cat crying in a tree a few blocks back; I'll probably start there." His eyes flash as he leans against the wall.

I shake my head. "So cheesy," I mutter, trying to keep myself from smiling.

"Yeah, but you're laughing, so it's worth it," he replies.

"Only because you look so ridiculous standing there like that, like you're the Fonz or something." I smirk, batting his stomach.

He fake winces and pops off the wall, moving over to the entrance. "I'll take what I can get. I like that you make me work for it." He looks at the door and tilts his head. "You should get inside."

I nod. "Ugh, time to face the music," I grumble, staring at him. "So... is this it?"

He looks away. "Yeah, guess so," he sighs. "Got you back, safe and sound." He smiles wistfully.

I scuff my boot against the sidewalk. "Can I call you? Do you have a phone or... anything?"

He shakes his head.

"Am I ever going to see you again?" I ask quietly.

Daniel lets out a laugh. "Probably sooner than you'd like!" He gestures down the street. "I saw a great alleyway back there, thought I'd take up residence," he teases, tapping my elbow.

When I scoff, he adds, "Nah," and points up to my building. "I know where you live, now. I'll try to stop by sometime." He keeps his tone casual.

I sigh. "So that means *never*." I nod, stepping onto the threshold. "I got it."

He puts out his arm, stopping me. "No, that means *surprise*; good surprise, I hope." He turns his head. "I don't have the most... predictable lifestyle." He scrunches his nose. "Wish I had a better idea of what tomorrow was gonna look like, but consistency is kind of a luxury, you know?" He stares at me intently. "I *will* come back, I promise." He reaches out and brushes my hand.

I turn away from him and smile secretively. "Okay," I murmur, "Mystery Date." I push against the door.

"I like it." Daniel grins, walking backwards. "Maybe next time we could, I don't know, get some coffee, but skip the ambulance ride. What do you say?" He holds out his hands, weighing the two options.

"I say 'okay,'" I chuckle.

He winks back at me, tugging his hat over his ears. "Then I'll see you when I see you."

He salutes. I wave and close the door.

CHAPTER 2

THE APARTMENT IS still dark when I enter. I can make out a pile of blankets on the couch that is slowly rising and falling, the occasional snore rattling against the cushions. I quietly shut the door behind me and tiptoe into the kitchen.

Everything is in its usual disaster state, the counter covered in a mosaic of dirty dishes and half-empty liquor bottles, a weird green film growing along the edge of the sink. I check my phone to see if Riley called, but there are no new messages. I slam my purse onto the stovetop and sweep a few bottles into the trash; the glass clatters noisily as it falls. Clearly, Mom had a date with Jim Bean last night.

"Such a dump," I breathe as I forage through the cabinets for something to eat, my appetite having finally returned with a roar. I find a cup of insta-soup, but settle on an open box of cereal instead. One quick look in the sink tells me there are no clean bowls, so I opt for a more direct approach: digging out handful after handful of Cap'n Crunch and dejectedly shoving it into my mouth. The cereal is stale, giving me an instant case of cotton mouth. I toss the box aside and run my lips under the sink faucet.

"Home, sweet home," I mutter, wiping my mouth with my sleeve. This place is definitely not our old house in Brentwood, with its clean Spanish tile and sprawling backyard. I still miss that place, along with actual breakfast. I glare at the half-empty box of puffed sugar. I can't exactly remember when we became a cereal family, but I hate it. Mom used to get up every morning super early before work and put together a full spread, with pancakes, eggs, fruit, juice... I glance over at her old tote bag hanging off the backdoor handle, where the words *We Love You, Mrs. Nichols!*, scrawled in multicolored puffy paint, are now flaking away. Her first class of second graders made her that, after she switched from teaching kindergarten. Maybe that's when the homemade breakfasts stopped—right around the time she lost her job.

I hear rustling coming from the living room, so I take a look at myself in the microwave door and hastily comb my hair over my face. Mom shambles into the kitchen and grabs a mug from the cabinet. She's still wearing the same blue t-shirt and jeans that I saw her put on two days ago, her long auburn hair matted to the side of her head. Her grey eyes stare vacantly at the counter, red-rimmed and unfocused.

"Do we have any tea?" she asks blearily.

I shake my head and look away, trying to avoid eye contact. "I dunno. Check underneath."

"Mmm... okay." She stumbles past me and starts rummaging through spices and expired baking supplies in the Lazy Susan. She finds an old box of English Breakfast and turns on the pilot light under the teakettle, then stretches and scratches her dirty hair, a total hot mess.

I sigh as I reach up for a drinking glass. "You look terrible," I mutter, unable to stop myself as I fill my glass at the tap.

Mom slumps, holding onto the oven door and nodding slowly. "Thanks, Christa. You're always such a ray of sunshine." I see her squint in my direction as I sip my water. Quick as a flash, she's standing in front of me, pawing at my face.

I flinch, batting her hand away. "Hey! Quit it!"

"What is this?" she slurs, grabbing my wrists with her hands, prying them aside to get a better look at me.

I stare at the floor. "Nothing."

She shakes her head, letting me go. "Bull, Christa! This is *not* nothing!" She touches the swollen bump on my head. I wince and pull away, trying to busy myself around the kitchen, but Mom stands back and stares at me, her eyes wide. "You look like you just survived World War III! What the hell happened?" She crosses her arms over her chest.

"I'm fine," I mumble as I pretend to scrub with a sponge at a pot in the sink. "It's honestly no big deal. I was just out with Tom and Riley last night…"

"TOM AND RILEY!" she bellows, slapping her thighs. "I told you those boys were trouble! Did they do this to you?" She motions to my face. "Did they do anything *else*?" Her eyes scan down to my knees.

I balk, knowing exactly what she's implying. "God, Mom, no! They're my friends! If you would just stop yelling and listen—"

"We need to call the police! And take you to a doctor…" she interrupts, frantically looking around the kitchen. "Where's my purse? I need to find Dr. Coliani's number… Doctor Collini—Colera…" she mumbles, searching under the counter.

I roll my eyes and throw my sponge into the water. "Save it. I've already been to the hospital." I grab my purse off the stove and shake it violently, my prescription rattling around inside. "Got meds and everything. I'll make sure to hide them where you can't find them so you don't feel tempted." I stomp out of the kitchen, heading back to my bedroom.

"Watch your tone, young lady!" she shouts, following me down the hall. "You have no right to speak to me that way!"

When I don't respond, she sighs and leans against the doorframe, watching me rifle through the pile of clothes by the closet. I find a clean plaid skirt and peel off my boots and stockings. "What are you doing?" She shakes her head.

"What does it look like? Getting ready for school," I grumble, stripping off my black sweater. I hear her gasp as I turn to look for a new blouse. I roll my head back petulantly. "Don't sound so surprised—it's Friday. Have to at least make an appearance for Tater Tot Day." I grimace.

"Jesus, Christa..." she breathes. I glance down to see what she's staring at.

A constellation of purpling bruises runs across the right side of my ribcage, down past my hip. I touch one and wince before grabbing a clean shirt from one of the lone hangers on the top rack. Something the ER nurse forgot to mention, I guess. I scramble into the shirt and hastily start on the buttons.

"It's fine," I mumble, watching Mom shift in the doorway.

"Christa, talk to me, please!" she cries, wringing her hands. "What happened?"

I let out an exasperated sigh. "I was in a car accident, okay?!" I yell. "Riley was drunk, and he crashed the car into an underpass wall."

She starts to tear up. "I spent the night at the hospital," I continue. "They ran a bunch of tests, and I'm totally fine—it's just a couple bumps and scratches. It really *is* no big deal." I tuck my shirt into my waistband and step over to where my makeup bag sits on top of the desk.

I can hear Mom gnashing her teeth. "No big deal? How can you say that?" she exclaims. I purse my lips and look for my eyeliner. "You spent the night in the hospital and you didn't call me?!" she continues. "Unbelievable."

"I didn't think you'd come." I turn to the mirror and pull down my lower eyelid. I quickly smudge a little black around my eye and move onto concealer; I'm going to need the whole bottle today. I can see my mother's reflection behind me, her face pinched.

"Of course I would have come! When stuff like this happens, I am your first phone call!" She slams her hand against the door.

"Okay, Mom," I grumble, shaking my head.

She crosses over to my bed and slowly sits down, smoothing my purple leopard print comforter with her palm. "And what were you thinking, getting into a car with a drunk driver? I know you know better than that," she scolds, putting her head in her hands.

I roll my eyes. "Oh, please," I snigger. "I get in the car with *you* every day, and I'm still standing."

She leans back on her elbows and glares at me. "The way you talk to me—if I had even tried half the crap *you* pull with Nana…" She shakes her head.

"Nana was a sweet old lady who played Mahjong every Thursday and dressed her dogs up in homemade pom-pom sweaters," I tsk. "You are definitely not Nana." I painfully pat powder over my cuts.

Mom sits up. "What's that supposed to mean?"

I glance at her scornfully, then turn back to the mirror. "You know what it means." I put a touch of glitter at the corners of my eyes and step back and take myself in. No amount of sparkle and lip gloss is going to hide the fact that I still look like I went ten rounds with a lawnmower. I sigh and give up, tossing my makeup back into the bag.

Mom gets up, her jaw clenched. "Well, all I have to say is that you can kiss your social life goodbye. You are grounded, Christa— no friends, no driving, no raves or clubs or wherever the hell you go when you're out with those losers. Just school and then home," she spits, moving towards the door. "I mean it— for, like, a month."

I shrug and look at the floor. "Fine, whatever," I mumble. She'll forget all about grounding me by Happy Hour.

She stares at me and sighs. "You know I don't want to be the bad guy, Christa, but you are seriously out of control!" She looks at me pleadingly. "If you would just talk to me, tell me what's going on with you… maybe I could help."

I furrow my brow and turn back to the desk. "I don't need your help. I don't need anything."

She looks down and scratches the back of her neck. "You used to tell me everything. About school, your friends, the boys that you liked…" She presses her lips together. "But ever since Daddy—"

I feel my shoulders tighten. "You don't get to talk to me about him," I hiss. She shuts her mouth. I bite my tongue and grab the side of the desk.

"Sorry," she whispers.

I inhale and clear my throat. "I need to finish getting ready for school. Can you please leave now?" I tuck my hair behind my ears.

Mom bows her head and shuffles onto the threshold. "You don't have to go to school if you don't want to," she mumbles. "You know, if you just want to take a sick day and stay home."

I close my eyes and sigh.

"Like I said, I'm fine. I have a big test in Bio today. I don't want to miss it," I lie. She nods and shuts the door behind her. I huff through my nose and grab my boots from the floor, knocking my green rabbit's foot off the desk. I stop and pick it up; I got it when I was 7 after putting a quarter into one of those vending machines at the mall. I scored that day and got two for the price of one, two baubles popping out at the same time with the exact same prize. I gave Dad the matching foot. *Lucky us, Sweet Girl. Unlucky rabbit…* he used to joke. Lucky or not, he made sure he traveled with it for every business trip from there on out. *Sweet Girl…* He'd probably been the only person in the history of ever to think that about me. I sigh and give my rabbit's foot a little rub before setting it carefully back on the shelf, then grab my backpack off the desk chair.

"On second thought…" I reach back and retrieve the rabbit's foot, tucking it into my backpack. "I could use a little luck right now."

*

"Late, Ms. Nichols."

"Sorry, Mr. Trundi. I couldn't get a bus out of the Valley this morning." I grimace, hastily crossing the front of the class. Everyone spins around in their chairs to watch me shuffle to my lab table in the back. Mr. Trundi glances up from his PowerPoint presentation and frowns, taking in my injuries. A low grumble emits around the room as I slouch in my seat.

"Oh my God, Christa! Your face!" Marcus Brady gasps from across the aisle, his brown eyes wide. I glare at him irritably as I open my backpack and take out my textbook.

"All right, everyone, eyes forward," Mr. Trundi sighs, rubbing his jaw. He points to Dexter Whitman in the second row.

"Okay, Dexter, give me the definition of an invader species, then list three examples we've covered so far this semester."

Dexter looks down nervously at his notes and starts to ramble off an answer. Mr. Trundi shifts his large frame on his stool, nodding slowly and occasionally shooting a concerned look in my direction, his bushy mustache twitching. I hunch down behind my book, willing myself to become invisible. Dexter finishes, and Mr. Trundi stands.

"Great, Dexter. Did everyone get that down?" He turns his head. "If you haven't figured it out already," he speaks in a stage whisper, "these are probably going to show up again on the final." The class laughs as he raises his eyebrows dramatically and returns to his slides.

I peek over the top of my book; everyone has pretty much gone back to ignoring me, except the pair of horn-rimmed glasses to my right. I see Jodie staring at me, her jaw clenched and her dark, straight hair hanging like a curtain over her shoulder. When I clear my throat, she quickly looks down, scrawling something in her notebook before tearing the paper away and folding it into a football. When Mr. Trundi isn't looking, she tosses it in front of me.

I sigh and open the message. *Are you okay???* it asks with three question marks. I tuck my hair behind my ear and shrug. Jodie rolls her eyes and mimes writing with her finger.

I purse my lips and pick up my pen. *What do you care?* I scribble and send back across the aisle when Trundi's back is turned. I watch Jodie read it, a pained expression clouding her face. I feel my stomach clench guiltily, but quickly push the feeling aside and pretend to focus on the lecture. Jodie writes frantically for a while, her nose pressed close to the paper. I shake my head as she passes it back, waiting a minute before opening it.

Of course I care, Christa. The fact that you think I wouldn't really hurts. When I heard about what happened, I tried to call you during 1st and 2nd, but your phone said it was disconnected. Did you get a new number? I'm worried about you... Please don't shut me out.

I look up at her, my brow furrowing. How does she know what happened?

The bell rings and everyone gets up, grabbing their stuff.

"Okay, guys. From here 'til exams, I'm going to have after-school study hours if you want to come in and use the lab, review my slides, or ask questions. I should be here 'til about 5 every day, except for this afternoon... Science Club has a presentation."

Mr. Trundi watches the class stuffing notes and books into backpacks. "Please take advantage of this time, people! This test is 40% of your semester grade! I know that a lot of you seniors already have your college plans set for next year, but don't check out yet! These first-term grades are just as important as your last three years!" He shuts off his computer and steps over to his desk. "And if passing your exam isn't enough of a reason to show up, there will be snacks."

The room clears out, and I turn to Jodie. She gives me a weak smile, her large backpack balanced on the lab table, heavy with books. She still has the *Vampires Suck!* pin stuck to the front pocket that I gave her when we were 14, from when Dad took me to a live TV taping. I let out a sigh.

"Hey," I murmur, looking down at the floor.

She readjusts the zippers on her bag. "Hi." The couple of feet between us feel like a mile. We haven't spoken in almost a year. I've known Jodie since the 2nd grade, back when her family moved into the house next to ours in Brentwood. We became instant best friends while hunting for bugs in my mother's garden, picking little green caterpillars off the tomato plants. We attended the same small private elementary school, and she's the reason I decided to go to Sacred Heart. At the time, we dreaded the thought of going to different high schools and cheered each other on as our acceptance letters arrived in the mail. That seems like a thousand years ago now. I watch her fidget with the safety pin at her waistband, the skirt no doubt an oversized hand-me-down from her sister, Francine.

I clear my throat. "So…"

She looks up at me expectantly.

"Christa? Can I get a quick word?" Mr. Trundi interrupts from across the room. I stare at Jodie, my mouth agape. Jodie hesitates, her hand on her bag.

"Ms. Phan," he states calmly, "you'll see her in a minute." Jodie nods and hurries out of the room. I exhale and slouch over to Mr. Trundi's desk.

He looks up at me from his office chair and scratches his temple. "You wanna tell me what's going on?" he grunts, spinning to face me. I tug at my backpack straps.

"I, um… I was in a car accident last night. With Riley and Tom," I mutter.

He frowns. "Anderson and Wyndam?"

"Yeah," I murmur, trying to avoid eye contact.

Mr. Trundi shakes his head and blows out his cheeks. "Well, are you okay? Should you even be here today?" He runs a hand through his thinning hair, his eyes soft.

I smile and shrug. "I'm fine, Mr. Trundi, really." I glance down at my boots. "I'm sorry I was late. My mom meant to write a note, but things got... busy. It won't happen again."

He rolls his eyes. "Yeah, I won't hold my breath on that one." He picks up a pink Koosh ball from his desk and tosses it back and forth. "Listen, we really need to talk about your classroom performance this term." He sets down the Koosh and flips open his gradebook. I cringe as he runs his finger down the page.

"This isn't looking good, Christa... and I don't get it." He shakes his head. "You used to be one of my top students. You aced every unit, freshman and sophomore year. You told me your big dream was to attend Stanford's bio-chem program... Is that something you still want?" He looks at me hopefully.

Yeah, like we could ever afford that now. I shrug and stare down at the desk. "I dunno..." I mumble.

Mr. Trundi rests his chin on his palm. "Well, with grades like this, there's no way they'll even consider you. I need to see a severe turnaround in the next couple of weeks, or you can kiss that one goodbye." He sits back in his chair and folds his hands over his big belly. "I know that things have been tough since your dad... That's to be expected. But I know that he wouldn't want you to throw your life away." When I cross my arms over my chest, he sighs. "I'm sorry. I know it's hard for you to talk about."

I smile tightly. "It's fine."

I glance over at the framed photos on his desk, pictures of him and his family on vacation somewhere tropical, one of his young sons holding a giant coconut drink with a tiki umbrella poking out. Mr. Trundi's nose is sunburned, and he has a huge grin on his face, his arm wrapped affectionately around his plump, cheerful wife. They all look really happy.

"You coming to Science Club tonight?" Mr. Trundi asks, his eyes following mine to the photo.

I shake my head. "Why would I? I don't have anything prepared... I haven't been there all year."

Mr. Trundi nods. "You could just sit in and listen to the presentations. I know we all miss you—some more than others." He shifts his gaze out into the hallway, where Jodie is slowly pacing by a bay of lockers.

I sigh. "I don't think so… Not today." I shrug.

He sits forward. "You were never one of my typical Club kids, Christa." He folds his hands. "You look more like one of Coach's, and you always stuck out like a sore thumb. But you were good at it, and I could tell you loved every minute, from the research all the way to competition."

He glances up at me and sighs. "I know Science Club isn't what the 'cool kids' are doing." He flashes his fingers in air quotes while I shift back and forth awkwardly. "I *know* it's not what Anderson and Wyndam are doing, but I also know that Anderson and Wyndam don't dream about Stanford." He rolls his eyes. "I don't really want to know *what* those two dream about. I can only imagine." He grimaces and holds his hands up in mock terror.

I let out a small chuckle.

"Just think about it, okay?" Mr. Trundi smiles, hoisting himself out of his chair.

I nod. "I will, promise."

"All right, get outta here before you're late for your next class, too." He shoos me out with his hand.

I start to amble towards the door. "And Christa?" he calls behind me. "I really need you to hit the ground running on Monday. It would be in your best interest to be at every extra study session next week. Seriously." He looks at me gravely.

I bite my lip. "Okay… Thanks, Mr. Trundi."

I step out into the busy hallway, now a crowded sea of green and blue plaid. I walk up to Jodie, who is half-heartedly trying to figure out the combination of a random locker. She turns and arches her eyebrows when she sees me. "Everything okay?" She jerks her head towards the classroom.

I nod as we start to walk. "Yeah… Trundi was just on my ass to come back to Science Club. Guess my beautiful mind is sorely missed." I snicker, leaving out the part about my failing bio grade.

Jodie nods. "You *should* come back. Everyone still talks about the project you did where you compared biodiversity to punk bands. Remember? The one with the mushrooms?" She smiles warmly.

"I remember." I grin. "It took me like… five tries to get those things to grow inside." We navigate around a pocket of junior girls, their eyes bugging out of their heads when they get a look at my face. I sigh and turn towards Jodie.

"Plus, Ethan Liu is completely out of control," she continues. "If you thought he was a know-it-all last year, think again." She shakes her head. "Without you there to keep him in check, it's like Fukushima on steroids."

She stops and steps into an empty classroom doorway. I follow her out of the passing period traffic. Jodie reaches over timidly and pats my elbow. "How did your mom take it?"

I snort and look away. "In typical Julie Nichols fashion— explode first, ask questions later. I'm sure she's downing half a liquor store right now. You know, coping." I shrug.

Jodie gives me a tight smile. "We both know she's dealing with more than last night."

"Aren't we all," I reply sarcastically.

She takes a deep breath. "How are *you*, really?" she sighs.

I laugh. "Oh, hanging in there. We have a big ski trip planned for Thanksgiving, and I just don't know if I can show my face in Aspen looking like this." I smirk, then add, "But I'm surviving. Thanks so much for your concern."

Jodie crosses her arms. "Don't be like that. I was really worried when I heard about the accident. I didn't know how bad you had been hurt, if you were even still at the hospital." She surveys my cuts and bruises. "I wish you had called me."

I rub the back of my neck. "I didn't think you'd recognize the number," I admit. "Besides, I know your parents don't approve of you talking to losers, or whatever weird Vietnamese word they called me."

Jodie looks down sadly. "I've been wanting to talk to you about last Christmas for a while. I wanted to say I'm sorry." She shakes her head. "They had no right to talk about you that way... and I wouldn't have let them if I knew it would have meant I was going to lose my best friend," she whispers.

I shrug. "It's fine. I wouldn't want my daughter hanging around with someone like me either." I exhale. "Besides, I didn't think the first time we talked should be me saying, 'Hey—what's going on? I almost died in a fiery car crash last night... Can you pick me up from the ER?'" I roll my eyes as she stares at me, her lips pursed. "Also, how do you know about what happened?" I wrinkle my forehead. "I just got here like—twenty minutes ago."

Jodie looks at me quizzically. "Everyone knows. Riley—"

"OH MY GOD—CHRISTA!" Marcus Brady barrels over to us through the crowd. "You look like hell! Did you need to have surgery? How's Tom? Is he going to die?!" He gawks at me, his eyes wild.

I stumble backwards, my shoulders pressed up against the wall. "Wow, Marcus—take a breath!" I bark. "I'm fine, thanks for asking," My eyes dart between them. "How does everyone know what happened?"

Jodie opens her mouth to answer, but Marcus cuts her off. "Riley—duh! It was all he could talk about in Poli Sci this morning. And why wouldn't he?" Marcus simpers. "It's, like, the biggest news in the history of ever. God, this school is so boring."

I shake my head. "I'm sorry, what? Riley is *here*? At school... today?"

They both nod. "He was a little late for first period English, but yeah, he's here," Jodie murmurs.

I run my hands through my hair, accidentally winging the

bump on my forehead. I wince and bite the inside of my cheek to keep from crying out. "Well... why didn't he call me?!" I shout, making a group of passing freshmen boys jump.

Jodie shakes her head. "I don't know... I'm sure he's worried about you, Christa." Her tone is conciliatory.

"Or it's his way of showing you the door." Marcus grins, casually inspecting his fingernails.

Jodie clucks her tongue and smacks him on the arm. "What? I'm only saying what we're all thinking." He shrugs, brushing his floppy brown hair out of his eyes. "It's common knowledge that you two have a pretty... *passionate*... relationship." Marcus crinkles his nose as he searches for the right word. "One minute you're tearing each other's heads off in the hall, the next you're tearing each other's clothes off in the hall closet." He rolls his eyes. "It was always going to end badly—one might say in a burning blaze of glory?"

I narrow my eyes and take a step forward. Marcus puts up his hands defensively. "Sorry! Sorry! Too soon, I guess."

"Don't you have somewhere to be?" Jodie growls. "Like... anywhere but here?" Marcus chuckles and swings his bag onto his shoulder. "Wow, church mouse has got a little bite in her! I'm so scared..." he taunts.

Jodie crosses her arms waspishly. I lean back and sigh. "I just can't believe he hasn't tried to find me... to at least see if I'm okay," I mutter.

Marcus rolls his eyes. "Doesn't Riley have gym next period with all the rest of the football players? Why don't you just go talk to him like a normal person and find out what's going on?" He waves a hand patronizingly.

I straighten up and nod. "Yeah, I think I will." I stomp into the hallway, Jodie and Marcus hot on my heels.

"Christa, I don't think that's such a good idea..." Jodie calls.

I shake my head. "Not now, Jodie. This is just something I have to do." I stalk forward, determined.

"But... you'll miss Calc!" she cries. Marcus lets out a snort.

"Mouse, you should know by now: if given the choice between math and sex, Ms. Nichols always chooses the latter." He snaps his fingers. "Get it, girl!"

"Christa!" Jodie yells behind me. I spin around to face her. "Call me, okay?" she says, exasperated. I nod and turn the corner, leaving them in my wake.

I zip through the busy hallway, making a beeline for the girls' locker room, the fastest way to get into the gym. I shove open the door and walk past the never-used showers and rows of tiny lockers. I stop when I hear laughing.

"Did you see her face? It's totally messed up... crazy cuts and this ginormous bruise right over her eye. So gross," one girl jeers. I hear others giggle.

"Looks like someone isn't going to get a date to Winter Formal," another chimes in.

I peek around the wall and see the same group of junior girls I passed in the hall a few minutes ago, changing for gym.

"I heard she was hitting on some random guy, and that's what sent Riley over the edge. She was practically having sex in the club," the first girl mutters, sweeping her long blonde hair into a ponytail. I recognize her: Brit Cornell. She's in gymnastics with Jodie. I grit my teeth.

"That girl is such a slut. She slept with the entire basketball team last year... like, gangbang style," a short one with dark hair murmurs as she scrunches into her sports bra. Brit looks at her and raises her eyebrows.

"What?" the shrimpy girl scoffs, grabbing her deodorant. "It's supposed to be on YouTube."

"What is a varsity quarterback doing with someone like her?" another girl asks.

"Probably getting blow jobs during passing periods! I mean... I get it, she *is* really pretty." Brit shrugs, adjusting her gym shirt.

"Not anymore!" Shrimpy snickers. They all laugh. Brit sighs.

"I just don't think Riley knew what he was getting into. When you play in the trash, you're gonna get dirty." She crosses over to the mirror and rolls the waistband of her shorts, the back hem just grazing her tan ass.

Shrimpy grins mischievously. "So, it sounds like Riley's a free agent now. You thinking of making a play, Brit?" The other girls gather in tighter, waiting for her answer.

Brit pouts into the mirror, checking her lip gloss. "I imagine he might need a shoulder to cry on right now... I mean, his best friend *is* still in the hospital." She winks at herself. "I can be a really nurturing person—you know, when I want to be."

Shrimpy nods in agreement. I roll my eyes and step out from behind the wall. "That's really nice of you, Brit. You're practically Mother Teresa, always putting others first. Riley's lucky to have you." I tuck my hand into my jacket.

The other girls gasp when they see me. "What are you doing here?" Brit snaps. "You're not in this class!"

I lean against the wall coolly. "My ears were burning... Thought I might stop by and catch up on the latest." I smile down at Shrimpy. "Also, it was only *half* the basketball team. Get your facts straight."

"Oh my God..." She blushes and slithers to the door. The other girls follow awkwardly, leaving Brit solo by the mirror.

She glares at me, her lips pursed, before breaking into a huge, fake smile. "How are you, Christa? I heard about last night! So glad your injuries were only... superficial." She simpers, crossing her arms.

I nod and chuckle. "Thanks, Brit. I wouldn't expect any less from such a kind, *nurturing* person." I raise my eyebrows and saunter toward the gym. "If you need any ideas on how best to comfort Riley, I've got some pro-tips." I smile and grab the door handle.

She clenches her jaw and looks down at the floor. "Whore," she mutters.

I sigh, turning back around. "You wanna repeat that?" I reply, taking a step closer.

She stares at me with cold blue eyes. "You heard me." She arches a well-manicured eyebrow.

I scoff and shake my head. "Whatever, Brit… Takes one to know one, I guess." I start to leave again.

"It's not just me who thinks that, Christa. The whole school knows about you—what a freak you are, how you'll screw anything with a pulse." Her mouth twists unattractively. "We've all been waiting for you to do something stupid like get pregnant or jump out a window stoned, thinking you can fly." She tucks a loose hair behind her ear. "Last night was just a preview of the rest of your life, loser." She grins, resting against the mirror.

I feel my face go red and my fists tighten. Brit looks down at my hands and laughs. "You gonna hit me? Go for it. I'll get you thrown out of here so fast your head will spin." She stops and leans into my ear. "And there's no daddy around to bail you out with his money anymore."

I glare at her as she strolls by and opens the gym door. "Now, if you'll excuse me, there is a certain football player who needs my love and support." She scrunches her nose and leaves.

I pause, listening to the empty locker room sounds, before breaking into a feral snarl and kicking the wooden bench in front of me.

"Damn it!" I howl, grabbing my throbbing toe. I take a deep breath and close my eyes, counting backwards from ten before walking out of the room.

I step out into the hall and poke my head into the gym, seeing a bunch of juniors and seniors, including Brit, lining up for class. I scan the group; Riley's not there. I sigh and walk back into the hall, pacing in front of the boys' locker room. A couple of guys come out, take one look at me, and quickly shuffle past. The warning bell rings, and still no Riley. My patience running thin, I shove open the locker room door and march inside.

"Whoa—what the fuck!?" Caleb Jones curses, grabbing his shorts to cover himself. I shake my head and whisk past several other football players, all in various states of undress.

"You can't be in here, Nichols! This is... this is sexual harassment!" Adam Cotswald stutters, slamming his locker. I ignore him and stomp into the bathroom stalls, ramming them open with the heel of my hand. Empty. I turn back to the guys.

"Where's Riley? Is he here?" I bark. They look down sheepishly. "Riley B. Anderson... Anybody gonna tell me where he is?"

"Hey, baby," Andy Monroe coos next to me. I glare at him as he wets his lips and flexes his pecks. "I don't know about Riley, but *I* dig crazy bitches who are DTF... You know what I'm saying?" He cocks his head back toward the stalls. "You wanna...?"

I roll my eyes. "Oh my God—seriously, Andy!" I stare at the other boys. "Where the hell is he?"

Tito Gonzales points to the showers. "He's back there, with Johnny P. You should leave it alone, Christa!" he calls as I tramp down the corridor.

I smell weed the minute I turn the corner; Riley and Johnny stand under an open window, passing a joint back and forth.

Johnny glances up, his mouth full of smoke, and sees me. "Yo, homes, isn't that your girl?" he coughs, handing Riley the joint.

Riley turns, his eyes wide. "Holy shit." He accidentally drops the joint down the shower drain, getting ash on his jersey. "Fuck... Christa! What are you doing here?"

I bite my nails dramatically. "Oh, crap! Must have made a wrong turn at the gym... How the hell did I end up in here?" I shake my head in disgust. "I wanted to thank you personally for all the concerned phone calls, the flowers, the sweet Get Well Soon wishes." I cross my arms. "Oh wait, none of that ever happened!"

Riley stares down silently at the floor.

Johnny looks at us both and clears his throat. "Looks like you two have some shit to sort out," he murmurs, patting Riley on the back. "Catch you later, bro." He shakes his head and quickly scoots past me.

Riley sighs and rubs his eyes. "Well?" I snap, crossing my arms. "What happened? Last time I saw you was from the backseat of Deathtrap, thinking you were driving me home." I put my hands on my hips. "Next thing I know, I'm waking up in a hospital bed to some homeless kid holding my hand! Why didn't you wait for me?"

Riley exhales as he punches the shower wall with the side of his fist. "You know why! The cops had a fuck-ton of questions about the crash. I was down at the station 'til like 6 a.m. this morning!" he yells.

I nod angrily. "So you *did* get my message!" I shout. "Would it have killed you to send a text letting me know you were okay, and, I don't know… *not* in jail?!"

Riley clenches his jaw and runs a hand raggedly through his hair. I give him a quick onceover: aside from a scratch across his right cheek, he's come out totally unscathed. I shake my head and scuff my boot on the faded beige tile.

"You have got to be… the most selfish person on earth," I mutter, looking up at the ceiling.

Riley lets out a mean laugh. "Wow, *you* saying that to *me*…" He chuckles darkly. "That is like, the most epic thing that's ever happened." He gazes out the window.

I grimace. "What are you talking about?" I yip.

"You're the reason we crashed!" he shouts. "You know I

wouldn't have drank so much if I hadn't caught you with that English guy's hand up your skirt."

"Irish!" I correct. He rolls his eyes. "And are you kidding me!?" I continue. "Are you really going to blame *me* for you drinking yourself under the table and then driving your car into a concrete wall?" I hold up my hands. "And I thought I was the one with the brain injury." I lean against the shower stall.

His eyes trace up to the bump on my forehead.

"Are you... okay?" he asks sullenly after a minute.

I sniff. "*Now* he asks." I scowl. "Yes, Riley... I'm going to be fine. It looks worse than it is." I put my fists in my pockets.

He steps a little closer. "I'm sorry," he mutters, looking away. "Just... for everything." He scratches the back of his head.

I nod. "Okay." I sigh, staring up at him. "How's Tom? Do you know anything?"

He rubs his neck. "Last I heard, he was still in critical condition." He frowns. "My mom is supposed to call if things... change." He crosses his arms. "This is all so fucked up."

I bite my cheek. "I know. He's going to be okay, Riley." I glance down at the drain.

He shakes his head. "You don't know that. Whatever... Guess we'll just have to wait and see." He gives a weak smile.

I reach out and touch his wrist. "Are we going to talk about the... other stuff from last night?" I whisper.

He looks at me and raises his eyebrows. "I don't know what there's left to say." He smirks. "You made it pretty clear you want to see other people."

I cluck my tongue. "I honestly didn't know that what we had was an exclusive thing. We never established any labels." I tuck my hair behind my ears.

Riley sighs. "I figured, after all the crap we'd pulled together, it was pretty clear how I felt about you." He purses his lips as I look away shyly. "Since the first time we hooked up, I have been nothing but loyal to you."

I roll my eyes. "It's true!" he declares. "I know my history, but you're the only girl I've been with this whole time..." He looks out into the locker room. "And I know *your* history, too. I hang out with several of your past exploits on a pretty regular basis," he tuts. "But I thought we had both moved beyond that. So, seeing you with that jerk last night... it really fuckin' hurt, Christa." His voice cracks a little. I keep my eyes trained on the floor.

"And I know I'm not as smart as you, but I've realized something now," he continues. "None of this shit has anything to do with me. It has everything to do with you hating yourself." He steps back and feigns an explosion with his fists. "Boom."

I stand for a second, nodding at the tile. "Gee, thanks, Doc," I finally say with a glower. "I must have been out cold when you got your MD in psycho-babble bullshit." The corners of my mouth twitch as I start to pace again.

Riley grabs my arm. "Hey—calm down..."

I shrug out of his grip. "Don't touch me! You don't know a damn thing about me!" I yell.

His eyes dart down the hall. "I know you get really loud when you're pissed... Just chill out," he mumbles.

I laugh. "You don't get to tell me to do anything after what you did to me! God, Riley! You have the nerve to try to analyze me after you almost got me killed?! You are unbelievable!" I get in his face and shove his chest.

He holds steady. "You asked me about last night! We both know this is over, and I already said I was sorry! What more do you want from me?!" he shouts back.

"For you to fucking care!" I cry.

We both grab our ears as a shrill whistle blast echoes around the locker room. "HEY! Anderson! Nichols! What the hell is going on in here?" a gravelly voice growls.

We both spin around to see Coach Cryer, a soccer ball perched in the crook of his elbow, his face flushed and ruddy. I look out the window as he shifts in his inappropriate, ill-fitting shorts, making Brit Cornell look downright matronly. Riley hangs his head and quickly steps away from me.

"Nichols!" Coach yells. "What the hell are you doing in the men's locker room?! Do you know how many rules you're breaking right now?"

I cower against the wall. Coach opens his mouth, but quickly shuts it and inhales through his nose. "And… is that…" He sniffs the air. "Is that… grass?" His eyes narrow. "Are you two smoking marijuana?" His nostrils flare like a dragon's as he waits for an answer.

"Uh…" I shake my head, dumbfounded, while Riley puffs out his cheeks and says, "Busted."

Coach Cryer jerks his thumb. "Both of you—Schaffer's office. NOW!"

I cringe. "Wait! I can explain…"

Coach shakes his head. "Save it, Nichols." He points to the door.

I sigh and body-check Riley indignantly as we stumble out of the shower stall. "You could have at least told him I wasn't smoking! Way to take me down with you," I grit through my teeth.

Riley grins. "Until the bloody, gory end, baby."

*

"Cutting class, smoking an illegal substance on school property, harassing other students, blatant disregard for the sanctity of single-sex locker rooms… have I missed anything?" Principal Schaffer leans back in her chair.

"No, ma'am," Riley answers sweetly. I roll my eyes at his attempt to be polite. "But you have to understand something: I was just minding my own business, getting ready for class, when Christa barged in, completely out of her head, screaming about a bunch of stuff, and I had no idea what she was talking about." He sits back and shrugs, raising his palms in surrender. "*She* wanted to talk to *me*... Her coming into the locker room, it was all her." He waves his hands dismissively.

I shake my head. "That is such a load of crap, and you know it! I was there because you left me hanging in the ER!" I yell, slapping him on the arm.

Principal Schaffer pounds her fist on the desk like a gavel. "Hands to yourself, Ms. Nichols!" she orders, her mouth set. I slump in my seat, pressing my knuckles between my thighs.

"Now," she tucks her short, freshly dyed black hair behind her ears. "Who brought the pot?" Her eyes dart back and forth between us. I press my lips into a tight line; Riley sits next to me in stony silence. As angry as I am, I'm no snitch.

"Fine," Schaffer sighs. "I don't know if I'm going to get a straight story from either of you. The two of you are both repeat offenders, and if I had my way, I would just expel you and be done with it." She smooths her blue pantsuit and clears her throat.

"But there are other circumstances to consider, here." She looks at Riley, her brows arched. "Mr. Anderson is our star quarterback." Riley grins and sits up a little straighter. "As I think we all know, there is a very big game coming up this weekend against Holy Name. There's no way Sacred Heart can win without you playing... which won't make our alumni very happy." She crosses her arms and glares at him over the top of her glasses.

"Do you think if I let this one slide, Mr. Anderson, you can keep your head down and stay out of trouble until at least the end of semester?" she asks, her tone severe.

Riley sits forward and nods vigorously. "Of course, ma'am. I never wanted any trouble anyway." He grins.

Principal Schaffer clenches her jaw. "Of course not." She sighs, turning to me. "Now, Ms. Nichols... What are we going to do with you?" She narrows her eyes and picks up her pen, scrawling down a note on a yellow legal pad.

"Um... maybe you could let it slide for me, too?" I mumble hopefully. She doesn't look up from her pen. "I've uh..." I clear my throat and gesture to my face. "I've had a really hard couple days here..."

She nods. "Hmm, you certainly have." She drops her pen and tears away the paper from the pad. "Which is why I am recommending a five-day suspension, starting now." She folds the note and hands it to me. "I think some time apart for the two of you is just what the doctor ordered. Present this to all of your teachers before you leave to pick up any work that you'll be missing." She places the cap back on her pen with conviction.

I stare at her, my mouth hanging open. Riley tucks his chin into his chest, trying to keep from laughing.

"I'm sorry—what?!" I finally cry. "Suspension?" I look back and forth between the two of them frantically. "He gets to stay and be the hometown hero, and I get kicked to the curb?!" Riley shrugs, his lips hiding a smile. "But that's so unfair!" I shriek at Schaffer.

Her head shoots up. "I think, given the offenses, it's very fair, Ms. Nichols! I'm sorry. If the roles had been reversed and it was a *boy* bolting into the *girls'* locker room, I would have the local news waiting on my front lawn!" She shakes her head. "No, I won't abide that double standard. Consider yourself lucky and excused."

I open my mouth to protest, but nothing comes out. She nods and spins around in her office chair. "That's all. Back to class, Mr. Anderson. Ms. Nichols, we'll see you next week."

I sigh and sling my backpack onto my shoulder, not looking at either of them as I leave the office.

"Christa—" I hear Riley call behind me once we're both out in the hall.

"Thanks for sticking up for me in there," I hiss over my shoulder. "Such a fucking prince."

*

When I get home, the living room is empty. I turn on a light and toss my stuff onto the easy chair, kicking my boots off at the door.

"Mom?" I call out, receiving no reply. Her disarrayed nest of pillows and blankets on the couch is exactly the way she left it this morning. I didn't see her car downstairs, so she must have gone out. I let out a heavy sigh, relieved to not have to explain my little Staycation until tomorrow.

I walk back to my bedroom, strip off my uniform, and wad it into a ball before hopping into the shower. I stay in for a long time, letting the hot water course over my tender spots, washing away last night. I get out and twist my wet, clean hair into a knot on the top of my head before applying some of the antibiotic cream the pharmacy gave me to my open cuts and bruises. I try not to spend too much time looking at my messed up face in the mirror and quickly shrug into my favorite gray sweatpants and Dad's old Vanderbilt shirt. It's several sizes too big and almost see-through from twenty-five years of wash and dry cycles, but I love it.

Feeling cozy, I head into the kitchen and make the cup of insta-soup I saw earlier, scalding my fingers as I carry it back into my room and snuggle into bed. As I wait for my dinner to cool, I pull out my phone and text Jodie.

So this is me... new 213 area code. Probably the only way you can reach me the next couple days, as I have become recently suspended.:/ You were right, as usual.

I slurp my soup and start thumbing through old photos: Dad and I carving a Halloween pumpkin together, me and Jodie at Lucky Strike, and one of Mom smiling at the beach. When I get to the most recent, I stop and giggle. I recognize the leather jacket and the sandy blond hair instantly—Daniel. It's the picture I took at the bus stop, him leaning sexily against the rain shelter, the hospital parking lot in the background. I bite my lip as I reflect on how hot he is, with his big grin and charming brown eyes. I think about what it would be like to kiss him… and more. I stop myself guiltily, remembering everything Riley said today.

"Screw it," I mumble, tracing my finger over his face. "It's not like I'm ever going to see you again." I squint and look a little closer at the photo.

It's not horribly noticeable, but there's a faint aura around him, like a burning golden light. I shrug. My flash must have done something weird to compensate for the early morning dimness. I turn off my bedside lamp and cuddle up with my phone, smiling as Daniel's image gleams up at me like a nightlight. I peacefully drift off, his face imprinted behind my eyelids. For the first time in almost two days, I sleep soundly with no dreams.

CHAPTER 3

I WAKE ABRUPTLY TO the sound of someone pounding on the apartment door. I fumble for my phone and check the time—9:30 a.m.

"Practically in hibernation mode," I mumble, clearing my throat. The knocking grows louder.

I groan. "MOM! Can you get the door?!" I wait for an answer and get nothing, then drowsily rub my face and haul myself out of bed, feet first. The banging turns into a full-on assault.

"Holy cow, calm down! I'm coming!" I yell, glancing over at the couch as I stumble into the living room. No Mom… It doesn't even look like she came home last night, as her warren of blankets and pillows is undisturbed.

I shake my head. She's probably the one losing her mind in the hallway. I roll my eyes and turn the deadbolt.

"God, relax! Next time you forget your key, just call my phone. You don't have to go all Blitzkrieg on me," I mutter, wrenching open the front door.

I startle when I see Daniel waiting on our welcome mat, wearing a clean t-shirt and two cups of coffee in hand. He grins and does a little tap dance as he gives me one of the cups. I take it and lean against the door.

"Morning, sunshine! Thought you might need some caffeine

for your big day," he says. "I took a guess on the milk and sugar, just did the same as the other night." He scratches the back of his neck.

"No, that's how I like it." I bashfully reach up with my free hand and pat the rat's nest on the side of my head. I realize I have no idea what I actually look like right now—probably like something akin to Bigfoot or the Abominable Snowman.

"This is a surprise," I murmur, glancing at my coffee.

He bites his lip. "Good surprise, I hope?" He looks up at me expectantly. I smile, remembering how I fell asleep to his picture last night. I catch myself blushing and try to shake it off.

"Yes, good surprise." I hold open the door and gesture with my cup. "Thank you, and... come in." I stare down at my sweats, hastily repositioning my coffee in front of me.

"Okay." He puts his hands in his jacket pockets and steps inside. I close the door and motion to the living room.

"You can sit down, if you want... Oh." I scurry in front of him over to the couch and push the blankets out of the way. I turn back, flustered. Daniel chuckles.

"Sorry... My mom left her stuff out. It's not usually this bad." I grimace. "I... uh, just haven't had a chance to clean up..." I attempt to straighten the coffee table, stacking old tabloids and shoving them under the couch. I get up and tuck a loose strand of hair behind my ear.

"Anyway, this is it." I perch myself on the edge of the easy chair as he moves over to the couch.

He nods and looks out of the big picture window. "It's nice. Not a bad view you've got here." He motions to it as he sits.

I laugh. "Yeah, the 405 really sings at this time of day," I joke, slowly sipping my coffee. "I , um, didn't think I was going to get to see you again." I lean back and smile, spinning the easy chair with the ball of my foot.

Daniel looks at me. "I said I'd stop by." He glances around

nervously. "Did… did you not want me to come? I can go…" He starts to stand up.

I shake my head. "No, no!" I laugh. "I'm really glad you're here. Just… when most guys say they'll stop by, or call, or… whatever…" I shrug. "That usually means they won't."

He snorts and sits back. "Well, that's really dumb. If I didn't want to see you, I'd just tell you I didn't want to see you." He shakes his head and holds his cup up to his mouth.

I nod. "That kind of attitude is not something you see around here very often; it's… refreshing." I watch him drink his coffee, his light hair curling behind his ears. He's not wearing his hat today. I clear my throat.

"So… what brings you to my little corner of the universe?" I murmur, picking at a loose thread on the chair arm.

He stares at me disbelievingly. "Don't you remember? You need to be back at the hospital, in like…" He looks around the room, grabbing my old SpongeBob clock off the end table. "Two hours!" He puckers his lips. "I know that sounds like a lot of time, but you've got to figure for traffic." He looks me over matter-of-factly, stopping at my feet. "You ready to go? You need shoes." He furrows his brow.

I shake my head. "I'm sorry… What are you talking about?" I snicker, tucking my feet under me before taking another draw off my cup.

Daniel sighs and sets his coffee down on the table. "Big meeting: Sober Students Together!" He claps. "You don't want to be late for your first day!"

I let out a moan. "Oh my God! You have got to be kidding me… That's seriously today?" I put my face in my hand. "Can't I call in sick?"

He shakes his head and grins. "Not unless you're willing to take your chances in court. Come on, it won't be so bad." He reaches over and lightly taps my leg. "Have you eaten yet?"

I shake my head. "No... I'll be fine, just let me go throw on some clothes," I mutter.

He stands up and clucks his tongue. "This thing goes all afternoon! And after what you've been through, no, you need your strength." He points, walking out of the living room. "Kitchen is this way, I'm assuming?" He turns back and grins.

I cringe and jump out of my chair, spilling hot coffee on myself as I do so. "Ouch! Yes, that's the kitchen..." I wince and suck my burnt thumb, joining him in the doorway. "But it's..."

I watch him survey the damage, stepping into the galley. "We, um... don't cook much." I mumble as he gingerly picks up a frying pan from the sink that's covered in some sort of biological warfare.

"I can see that," he murmurs, nodding appreciatively.

I blush. "Seriously, I can just grab something on the way... or nothing! Really, I'm not that hungry," I ramble. "I don't think we have anything to make, anyway..."

He takes off his jacket and tosses it over one of the stools, then turns and opens the fridge, holding up a hand. "Hey, I got this." He looks back to where I lean against the doorframe, wrinkling my nose. "You go get dressed, and I'll take care of the food, okay?" he says with a smile.

I shake my head and raise a brow. "Um... okay. I don't know if there is much to 'take care' of..." I scoff. "Maybe a couple of moldy strawberries and some expired creamer."

He gives me a look from behind the refrigerator door and waves me away. I put my hands up and walk toward my room.

"Okay, fine! Good luck, Godspeed... but don't say I didn't warn you!" I chuckle as he pulls a few unrecognizable items out and puts them on the counter. I patter down the hall and close my door behind me.

Once inside, I rush over to the pile by my closet and frantically throw clothes all over, looking for something cute and hopefully clean to wear. I settle on my skinny jeans and a tight red thermal top. I grab my sexiest bra and matching black thong before detangling the elastic tie out of my hair and going over to the mirror, cringing when I see myself. Most of my cuts have scabbed over, and my bruises are starting to green. While I know that these are all signs of recovery, I still look completely putrid.

"I don't know if you're going to be enough," I whine to the push-up bra in my right hand. I sigh and shimmy into my clothes, hoping that Estee Lauder can work miracles.

"Wow…" Daniel breathes as he looks me over, leaning back from the sink. I smile as I step into the kitchen, my hair bouncy and full, only a slight shadow of bruising around the big bump on my forehead. I spin on one of the breakfast bar stools and place my elbows on the countertop, resting my chin demurely on my hands. Daniel smiles from the other side of the counter and tosses a dish towel over his shoulder, setting my coffee down in front of me.

"Man, if I knew I'd be cooking for a movie star today, I would have sprung for the good stuff, not this swill!" He laughs, gesturing at the cup. I grin and sit back, taking in the kitchen. It's the cleanest I've ever seen, the sink empty, the tile sparkling, and a delicious smell coming from the stovetop. My eyes go wide.

"You are a magician! How did you…?" I look around, awestruck.

He grins and quirks his eyebrows. "Let's see if you still feel that way after you try breakfast. How do you like your eggs?"

"Not crunchy," I reply, watching him work over the stove. He snickers and shuffles a spatula around the pan.

"I don't know if they teach that one at culinary school. Here." He grins, turning around with a plate of food. I almost fall off my stool; he's made fried egg, chorizo, toast and jam, and a pair of thin apple slices carved into delicate hearts. I hold one up and shake my head in wonder. The seeds are still intact, the red of the peel just trimming the edges.

"This is beautiful... and more advanced than your standard weekend breakfast fare," I murmur.

Daniel smiles. "Well, I didn't bring flowers." He runs a hand shyly through his hair.

I blush, setting the apple next to the toast. He nods at my plate. "Dig in."

I sit back and pick up my fork. The fragrance is so overwhelmingly appealing, my hands shake as I cut into the egg. When I take a bite, my eyes close, and I let out a little moan as the egg melts in my mouth.

"Oh my God," I purr in between bites. "This is... out of control." I let my silverware clink against the plate as I open my eyes and stare at him skeptically.

"Where did all of this come from? Did you like... skip out to the store while I was getting ready?" I ask as I shovel more egg onto my toast.

Daniel shakes his head as he dries the frying pan with his towel. "All of this stuff was here." He points to my plate. "The eggs and milk were purchased in the last couple of days. Someone in this house keeps the fridge well-stocked."

I narrow my eyes as I clean the back of my teeth with my tongue. "Guess Mom must have run to the store yesterday. Shocking," I mutter, staring down at my food.

Daniel puts the pan aside and starts wiping down the counter. "That's unusual?" he asks offhandedly.

I shrug. "Yeah, sort of. She hasn't really been your typical mom since..." I stop myself and push my toast around my plate. He looks up. "Well, for a while," I finish. "To tell you the truth, I don't really know what's going on with her. We don't talk all that much anymore." I spear one of the apple hearts with my fork.

"Who's choice was that?" He sweeps a little pile of debris into the trash can.

I give him a tight smile and shift on my stool. "I feel bad that you're cleaning, and you cooked for me… I should be cooking for you." I place my hand on top of his to get him to stop. Daniel pauses and looks at our hands, then pulls away with a grin and walks over to the refrigerator.

"So, while you were getting ready, I found something while I was cleaning…" He reaches up to the top of the fridge.

"You mean, other than a sink full of hazardous waste?" I snicker, finishing up my breakfast.

He rolls his eyes and pulls down a dusty old trophy. I blush and cover my face with my hands. "Oh my God," I mumble, dropping my knife noisily.

"2nd place at the Los Angeles County Science Fair. Looks like… three years ago?" Daniel smiles, placing it in front of me.

I snatch the trophy and look up at him peevishly, hiding it under the counter. "What's that all about?" he crows, coming around and sitting next to me. "That's something to be proud of! 2nd place at the county science fair is no joke, seriously!" He gently takes it out of my hands and sets it between us, shining it a little with his dishcloth.

I sigh. "We should have gotten first, but there were these kids from Glendale… total ringers." I purse my lips. "I think they actually went to UCLA and were just bored, or something."

Daniel rests his chin on his palm. "So you're pretty smart, then, right? Running around, doing experiments, chattering off the numbers from pi like it's no big deal…" He grins.

I roll my eyes. "Not that smart, apparently," I grumble, glancing down at my lap. "I found out yesterday that I'm failing my favorite class." I look up at him earnestly. "You can probably guess how I'm doing in my not-so-favorite ones." I nod and bite my lip. "Not like it's a big surprise… Helps if you show up every once in a while to, I don't know, do the work."

Daniel scratches his chin and shrugs. "So fix it. Show up."

I smile weakly. "Yeah… there's kind of a kink in that plan, too. I um… got suspended yesterday." I wince.

Daniel crosses his arms and leans back on his stool, smirking. "Go on—I'm intrigued."

I tuck my hair behind my ears. "Long story short… I ran into the boys' locker room, accosted my ex-boyfriend, and got framed for smoking pot." I sigh. "Not my finest hour."

Daniel laughs. "Pretty good, pretty good," he murmurs, standing up. "But I don't think you should let all that sway you from doing what you love." He gestures to the trophy. "You didn't have to do that for class, right? You just did it cuz you wanted to?" When I nod, he says, "Well, there you go. That's pretty special." He puts the trophy back on top of the refrigerator. "I never won anything like that. Where I come from, that's a big deal."

I hop off my stool and walk over to him. "And where's that?" I ask with a smile.

He puts his hands in his jean pockets and looks away. "You should get your coat. We gotta get rolling,"

I click my teeth irritably. He arches a brow. "Two can play at that game, Christa." He grins, grabbing his jacket. "Come on, get your stuff. You don't want to be late."

I take a breath, about to ask him again where he's from, when I hear a key turn in the door. My head jerks toward the living room.

"Shit," I mutter, rubbing my face. "Talk about perfect timing."

Daniel peeks through the doorframe. "Who is it?" he asks.

I roll my eyes. "My mom. Just ignore whatever she says." I sigh, slinging my bag over my shoulder.

Daniel wrinkles his nose. "That doesn't sound like very good advice!" he chuckles. "Come on, introduce me… Moms love me." He puts on his most winning smile.

I shake my head and quickly zip up my jacket, grimacing as the front door opens. "Doesn't look like I'm going to get much of a choice," I grit out. I stomp into the living room, Daniel following close behind.

Mom stands on the threshold, trying to juggle her purse and a couple of unmarked grocery bags, her big, bug-eye sunglasses covering half of her face. I sigh; at least she looks like she showered sometime within the last 24 hours, since she's now wearing clean clothes and her hair is swept into a side braid.

She turns and sees me, kneeing the door shut before dropping the bags onto the floor. "You're up early for a Saturday," she says, pushing her glasses up on her head, her eyes studying the two of us.

I cross my arms. "I could say the same for you, if you'd bothered to come home last night," I reply, my voice monotone.

She sighs and licks her lips. "Things went late with some of my old coworkers from Kingsley. I figured you'd be okay on your own for a couple of hours."

"I was." I arch a brow.

She clenches her jaw and is about to say something, but stops and sniffs the air. "Did you... did you cook?" She gawks at me.

Daniel smiles and gives a little wave. "I did! Hope that's okay." He steps over. "There's still a little left in the pan if you're hungry—some eggs and sausage." He hops on the balls of his feet. "You picked a beautiful pig."

Both Mom and I do a double take. "She did!" Daniel turns to me. "That was some top-shelf chorizo!"

Mom raises her eyebrows and looks at me. "Who's this?" she asks, nodding to Daniel.

"Just someone I know..." I grumble.

Daniel reaches over and offers his hand. "I'm Daniel, Mrs. Nichols, Christa's friend." He grins as she cautiously takes his hand. "It's really nice to meet you."

"Um, yeah," she grimaces. She takes her hand away and clears her throat. "I'm sorry, but I've never heard Christa mention you."

She scratches the back of her neck. "How do you guys know each other?"

Daniel opens his mouth, but I cut him off. "He's from school. We're working on a project for history together." I jut out my chin. Daniel furrows his brow.

"At 9 a.m. on a weekend?" Mom murmurs, her lips pursed.

Daniel lets out a nervous laugh. "I just thought she might want some coffee…" He shrugs, putting a hand on his hip.

I roll my eyes and step forward. "It's fine, Daniel," I snap.

Mom hones in on my bag and boots. "Are you going out?" she asks, blocking the doorway. "Because last I checked, you were still grounded."

"Obviously, I'm going out," I sneer. "Can you move?"

She flushes. "I'm sorry—what did you just say?" Her voice rises.

I shake my head as Daniel steps between us. "It's just that Christa needs to go back to the hospital, Mrs. Nichols," he interjects warmly. "With all of the commotion from the accident, she probably forgot to tell you that her Sober Students Together meeting is today, and she can't miss it." He nods for emphasis.

Mom leans back against the door and glares at me. "Sober Students Together? What is he talking about, Christa?" she barks.

I put my hands in my pockets. "It's just this thing I have to go to if I want to avoid… jail time," I mutter.

Her eyes widen. "*Jail?* Why would you need to worry about jail? I thought it was Riley who caused the accident!" she yells, tossing her purse on the floor by the wall.

I sigh and glance at Daniel. "Yeah, it's because I'd been drinking," I reply slowly. "You know… at a club."

She crosses her arms and stares at the floor. "Right," she scoffs. "That makes perfect sense." She steps aside and opens the door. "Well, by all means… please, go." She shakes her head at me. "Hopefully you'll learn something and turn your life around before it's too late." She rubs the bridge of her nose. "God knows nothing else has gotten through your thick skull."

I nod angrily and march out the door. "Thanks for the pep talk, Mom," I hiss.

Daniel hustles behind me. "Again, really nice to meet you, Mrs. Nichols." He smiles.

I see Mom look up, bewildered, as he closes the door.

We move down the stairs, my teeth about to crack from clenching my jaw so hard.

"I'm really glad I got to meet her!" Daniel exclaims sincerely. "I could absolutely see the family resemblance when you two were standing next to each other… The apple doesn't fall far from the tree, right?" He quickens his pace to keep up with me.

I punch open the security door, bright sunlight pouring into the main foyer. "Shut up. Just please, don't say anything else," I growl.

He clears his throat, a smile dancing behind his lips. I look at him and sigh. He scrunches his nose.

"Go ahead, before you burst," I spit.

"Like… you have the same eyes! It was almost creepy." He laughs as we walk toward the bus stop. "The way they bug out when you both get mad—" He shakes his head. "Like mother, like daughter."

"Yeah, in more ways than one, apparently," I mutter. "This day sucks."

*

We arrive at the hospital with a few minutes to spare. Daniel leads me down a corridor to a bank of elevators. I watch him curiously as he punches the down button.

He looks over at me. "It's in the basement: Conference Room B."

I poke my tongue in my cheek. "You seem to know a lot

about this thing today—where they meet, what time it starts…" I raise an eyebrow. "What's the deal? Are you like, a support group junkie?"

Daniel laughs. "They *do* usually have pretty good munchies—but sadly, no." The elevator doors open, and we get inside. "Nah, this place is like a second home for me. I spend a lot of time here." The doors close, and I feel a pull in my gut as we slowly descend into the basement. I shake my head.

"Here? At Westside?" I chortle.

He nods enthusiastically. "They make an amazing Reuben down in the cafeteria. You should try it." He grins.

I slap his arm. "Seriously, Daniel! How do you know so much?"

He points to a bright orange flyer taped to the inside of the elevator. I quickly read it. "*Sober Students Together: Fighting Underage Drinking and Drug Use with Positivity—Meets Every Saturday, Noon start time. Conference Room B, Westside Basement. Changing the Future, One Path at a Time!* Huh."

"They're plastered all over the hospital; I saw it when we walked in," he whispers in my ear.

I nod and roll my eyes. "Of course you did."

The elevator reopens, and we step out into a fluorescent-lit hallway. Conference Room B is directly in front of us. I turn to Daniel and let out a nervous breath.

"Okay, well… I guess this is my stop," I sigh. "Thanks again for breakfast." I cross my arms and stare sullenly at the floor.

He nudges my shoulder. "Try not to look like your favorite cat just got squashed by a bus," he chuckles. When I bite my lip, he adds, "It's going to be fine. It'll be over before you know it." He squeezes my arm before moving down the hall.

I jerk my head to follow him. "Where are you going?" I ask.

He points to a sign overhead—*Cafeteria*. "I wasn't lying about that Reuben," he says with a wink.

I smile and wrinkle my nose. "You'll wait?"

He reaches into his back pocket and pulls out an old paperback. "Came prepared."

I cover my mouth with the back of my hand to hide my giant grin. "Okay." I blush, stepping into the threshold. "I guess I'll see you later, then."

He nods. "Yep, count on it. Have fun." He waves and turns the corner.

I close my eyes and sigh, butterflies beating madly in my chest, before walking inside.

A gangly, dark-haired boy with a bad case of acne ambushes me at the door, pulling me into a klutzy hug. "Hello! We are so glad you could join us today!"

My eyes go wide in surprise. "Um... hi." I smile awkwardly.

He pulls away and pats me on the back. "Sorry if the hug seems a bit much." He shrugs, handing me a pamphlet. "We just want to impress upon each and every one of you that this is a safe space." He motions around the room. I turn and see a circle of brightly colored floor pillows.

The boy puts his hand on his heart. "I'm Seth, and I'll be assisting Mary Carmen on your journey while you're with us." He grins, his left bicuspid missing, and holds up a clipboard. "Can I get your name?"

I purse my lips and look at his list. "It's Christa Nichols... right there." I point to my name.

He nods and checks me off with a yellow highlighter. "Great to have you, Christa." He gestures to the pillows. "Please, find a seat with your fellow travelers in the circle. We have coffee, juice, and pastries in the back if you require any refreshments." He bounces on the balls of his feet and smiles. "Make yourself at home, and I'll be right here if you have questions."

"Thanks," I mutter, looking down at the pamphlet; it reads, *Sober Students Together: Lessons in Sobriety.* There's a picture of a bunch of happy teenagers from 1992 holding hands on a bright green lawn.

This is going to be totally painful.

Seth pats my shoulder and moves on to greet the next person who just arrived, a girl with short blonde hair. I sigh, relieved to be left alone, and head over to size up the snack table. I check out the muffins and danishes, but decide stick with coffee: I'm still full from Daniel's breakfast. I take a deep breath and glance over at the circle.

"Okay, fellow travelers," I grumble to myself. "Who do we have here?"

There's a girl who can't be more than 14 decked out in head-to-toe Goth gear, a tough-looking black kid in baggy sweats checking his phone, and some guy dressed like the Unabomber, complete with dark sunglasses and his sweatshirt hood up. He's staring right at me, his mouth agape.

"Always the unhinged ones." I roll my eyes and walk over to a blue and gold floor pillow on the opposite side of the circle, sitting cross-legged and blowing on my coffee to help it cool.

The girl who came in after me sits down on the pink pillow next to me and gives me a small smile. I nod in acknowledgement, looking down at her lap. She's also hit up the snack table and has a stack of cookies in front of her. She tucks her short blonde hair behind her ears and chuckles at the pamphlet before shoving a cookie into her mouth.

"This is just how I wanted to spend my Saturday." She chews.

I smile. "Yeah, really." She seems normal.

"At least the food is pretty good. Reason to show up," she says, wiping her lips with her sleeve. She has a familiar twang to her voice. I furrow my brow as she puts her hand out. "I'm Livie," she says, swallowing the rest of her cookie.

"Christa," I reply, taking her hand.

She bites her lip and nods up at my forehead. "Pretty nasty shiner you got there, Christa. Mind if I ask what happened?"

I grin. "Sure… Underage drinking followed by grisly car wreck." I shrug. "It looks worse than it is." I jut out my chin at her. "What about you?"

Livie rolls her eyes and holds up her wrists, which I now notice are covered in bright white bandages. "Mandatory 5150 after I got really messed up on my mother's Xanax prescription and pretended to try to kill myself." She cocks her head to the side. "Obviously, I was a little too convincing." She sighs. "I've been up on 10 all week. Supposedly, they're going to let me out tonight if everything goes okay today."

I look at her, my face pinched. "What's *10*?" I ask.

She purses her lips. "Psych floor, where they put all the looney toons." She shivers a little, then laughs heartily. "Nice to come down here and get a break!"

I nod and glance down at my pillow. "I'm sorry. I hope they let you go home." I can't imagine why someone as friendly as this girl would want to hurt herself, even if she was just faking it.

"Yeah, me too." She smiles and looks around the circle, stopping when she gets to Unabomber, who is watching us over his knees.

Livie blinks. "Well, there's an… intense… one." She nods. "What do you think he's in here for?"

"My guess is: getting wasted in Griffith Park Woods and sacrificing neighborhood pets while attempting to summon a demon," I stage-whisper. Livie snorts, quickly covering her nose.

"That," I continue, "or huffing Whip-Its during his shift at Dairy Queen." I watch her laugh and clear my throat. "You wouldn't happen to be from Tennessee, would you? Maybe Kentucky?" I ask, my eyes crinkling.

She breaks into a huge grin. "Oh my God, yes! Gatlinburg! We just moved a few months ago. Good ear… Everyone here thinks

I'm from Louisiana or Mississippi." She shakes her head as I give her a tight smile and asks, "How'd you know?"

"My dad," I murmur. "My dad's from Memphis." I look down at my boots.

She nods knowingly. "Nothing like getting a talkin' to by a southern daddy." She rolls her eyes. "Bet he just *loves* that you're here. Can't get away with anything."

I nod at the floor. "No, you can't."

At a quarter past noon, a beautiful Hispanic woman breezes into the room. Her long, dark hair is pulled into a bun on the top of her head, and she wears a dark purple sweater dress. She glides over to the circle and sinks down on an unoccupied pillow. She shakes out her hands as she gets comfortable, a row of silver bangles jangling down one arm. She looks up and smiles warmly at the group.

"Hello, I'm Mary Carmen. Thank you so much for coming today." Her heavily accented voice lilts. Seth scurries over to her side with a clipboard, gawking as he hands it to her.

"Oh, thank you, Seth." She counts the names on the list and then does a quick scan of the circle. I see her eyes flicker when she gets to me, taking a few extra seconds before moving on to Livie. She clears her throat and gives the clipboard back to Seth.

"Great… Okay, it looks like we're all here." She grins, clapping her hands. "I really appreciate everyone's dedication to punctuality."

She looks over to her left. "Ah! I see we have some repeat travelers. It's wonderful to see you again, Bryan." She glows and pats Unabomber on the knee. He fiddles with his sunglasses and nods down at the floor.

Mary Carmen casually gathers her bracelets into a bunch and takes them off, placing them on the floor next to her. "For those of you who haven't been here before, this is a safe space for us to talk about your life experiences and work on changing our own paths in a positive way." Her eyebrows quirk. Everyone except Unabomber looks down at the floor.

"To begin, we are all going to introduce ourselves and say one thing that you like about yourself. All I ask is that you be as genuine as possible." She pauses for a minute to take her hair clip out, her dark hair cascading down her back. She shakes out her mane and looks at the clipboard before turning to the Goth girl.

"Are you Michela?" Mary Carmen asks. Wednesday Addams nods. "How about you get us started?"

Michela shrinks back, trying to disappear into the floor completely. "Um, there really isn't anything interesting about me," she mutters, picking at her black nail polish.

"I don't believe that for a minute," Mary Carmen says with a smile. She points to the logo on Michela's t-shirt. "What about this? Ray-zer-Bee-me?" She wrinkles her forehead as she sounds out the word scrawled across the front.

Michela sighs. "It's pronounced 'Razor Beam,'" she corrects irritably. Mary Carmen nods, her eyes focused. "It's my boyfriend's band, and his name is Ray, so that's why they spelled it that way. They're going to be huge... They play all the clubs here around town." Michela looks out at the rest of us. "Well, the good clubs, anyway." The black kid rolls his eyes, his phone in hand, while Michela shifts her gaze to the floor. "Sometimes I sing with them, and that's pretty cool."

"I think that's really cool!" Mary Carmen exclaims. Michela looks up at her sullenly. "Really, Michela, that's not something everyone can do—get up in front of a big group of people and perform." Mary Carmen nods at us. "I still sometimes get nervous just talking in a small group! So... that's pretty big." She smiles, Seth nodding passionately along with her from the back of the room.

Michela shrugs. "Okay... So I guess, then, I'm Michela and I like to sing... That's my interesting thing." She blushes. "Somebody else go."

"Yes, fine!" Mary Carmen beams and glances down at her list. "How about… Jackson?"

The black kid looks up from his phone and exhales. "Okay, hi—I'm Jackson." He clears his throat and scratches the tattoo on the side of his neck. "What I like best about myself is my eyes. They change color depending on what I'm wearing, and I think that's cool." He pops his gum and goes back to his phone.

"Eyes *are* the windows to the soul," Mary Carmen says encouragingly, "but what do you think yours say about you, Jackson?" She pulls her legs to her chest and rests her chin on her knees.

Jackson looks at her, confused. "What do you mean?"

Mary Carmen cocks her head to the side. "Are you approachable or intimidating? Do you shut people out, or do you let them in?" She motions with her hands. "Are you available to the people in your life? These are all things that the eyes can show. What do yours show?"

Jackson sits back and puts down his phone. "I guess…" He crosses his arms and sets his jaw, lost in thought. "I guess a lot of people know I'm hard, livin' the life." He pauses. "But once you get to know me, you'd see that I'm sensitive. I get choked up at those stupid coffee commercials with the grandma and the baby, and I love my moms and shit."

Mary Carmen's eyes warm. Jackson nods at her before clearing his throat and glaring back at the rest of us. "But I don't talk like that with my boys, because… that'd be gay," he spits.

Mary Carmen winces at his slur. "Thank you for sharing, Jackson," she murmurs, "but let's remember that this is a safe space, and we want to try to use positive language when expressing our emotions. We don't call things 'gay' in here."

Jackson nods. "Oh, yeah—sorry." His eyes dart back to Seth, who is straightening up the snack table. "I meant… that'd be… retarded." He nods.

Mary Carmen smiles weakly. "Okay." She looks down at her list. "Livie, why don't you tell us something about yourself?"

Livie sits up straight. "Hey y'all, I'm Livie," she says with a little wave. "And… I guess the thing I like best about myself is my love for animals. Dogs, cats, birds, spiders—I don't care. I think they're all pretty neat."

She rests back on her knees. "When I was still back home, there was this sweet little black bear who would hang around, going through our garbage, looking for food." Livie smiles. "He would show up every morning early and get into the trash box… You're supposed to lock up your trash in the mountains to keep the bears out, but he was really smart—got the lock off and everything!" She laughs.

Jackson and Michela look at her like she's totally nuts; Unabomber sits enthralled. "Anyway," she continues, "I named him Joey and started leaving him little snacks: apples, peanuts, an open can of tuna one time—he loved that!" She sighs. "He started to become pretty familiar. I could sit out on the front porch and watch him eat his food, and then he'd stay a while, find a tree to scratch up against and then go back into the woods. I left him a big thing of raspberries before I left… I still wonder if he came back after we moved. I miss him." Her voice turns sad. "Haven't seen any bears out here. There's not much wildlife in Thousand Oaks, where I live now." She shrugs.

"Thank God," Michela sneers, rolling her eyes. Mary Carmen clears her throat.

"You can see mountain lions and coyotes if you go up to Topanga," Unabomber whispers. We all stare at him. "You have to wait for them." He snuggles down into his sweatshirt, looking mouthless.

Everyone slowly looks back at Livie.

"Anyway, that's my special thing! Hope that's okay." Livie grins, relieved to be done.

Mary Carmen nods in approval. "Yes, thank you, Livie! That kindness *is* very special; you should aim to cultivate that in everything you do." She glances around at the group. "We all have something special to offer one another—a talent, intuitiveness, kindness." She looks at Michela, Jackson, Livie, and then stops at me. "As we go along today, I want you to each take some time to really think about what you can contribute to your families, your community, and ultimately, the world." She grins. "Thank you, Livie. Let's continue."

It's just me and Unabomber now. Mary Carmen turns to her left. "How about you, Bryan?" She bows her head and peers up at him. "Would you mind taking off your sunglasses so we can all see you?"

Unabomber shakes his head, but complies and takes off his glasses, revealing a pair of closely set blue eyes. He looks up at the group, speaking barely above a whisper. "I'm Bryan and I'm really good at Jenga." He pulls his hood over his face.

Nobody says anything. Mary Carmen nods warmly, patting him on the knee. "That is one of my favorite games, too. Thank you, Bryan."

She pauses for a moment and then looks me straight in the eye. "You must be Christa. Please, share with us," she murmurs, her gaze intense.

I squirm uncomfortably on my pillow and take a deep breath. "Okay, um… Hi, I'm Christa." I clear my throat and tuck my hair behind my ears. My mind races as I try to think of something to say.

"All right, something I like about myself." I sigh. I can't focus; my mind keeps going back to Daniel in the hall and the smell of his jacket. "Okay, yeah—I'm pretty good at science." I picture him holding my stupid trophy and shake my head. "I uh, used to be in my school's science club and did a bunch of experiments, research." I catch myself worrying my hands and quickly cross my arms. "You know, it was just something I did, and I guess that's interesting."

That was so lame. I glance at Mary Carmen to see if she bought it. She's slowly nodding her head.

"So… you're like, a nerd?" Michela snickers from across the circle. Jackson and Livie giggle.

"Positive language please, Michela," Mary Carmen interjects.

"I didn't mean it as an insult." Michela shakes her dark pigtails indignantly. "She just doesn't look… smart." She glares at me.

"I don't think that's true," Livie tuts. She nudges me with her knee. I shrug.

"I think she looks hot," Jackson mumbles, checking his phone.

Michela rolls her eyes. "That's my point," she exhales. "I have a hard time picturing Cheerleader Barbie modeling lab goggles and standing over a microscope… 'Ooh! Look at me! I'm a *scientist*!'" She starts to pout. "She'd probably be too worried about her hair getting messed up."

I let out a laugh. "This coming from someone who probably spends a couple of hours every morning in front of a mirror making sure her Harley Quinn makeup is on just right," I chuckle. Michela frowns. "Whatever, dude." I purse my lips. "Think what you want. It doesn't make a difference to me." I lean back on my pillow next to Livie.

Mary Carmen clears her throat. "I'm hearing a lot of talk about external appearances right now," she states, sitting up straight. "While I think it would be beneficial for us to explore why we think that's important, I want our focus today to be on our internal perceptions." She rests her palm on her chest and adds, "What's in here."

She gets Seth's attention, and he comes running over with a stack of clipboards. Mary Carmen takes them and hands them around the circle. Each one has a pen, a blank sheet of paper, and an envelope clipped to it. Mary Carmen claps her hands.

"Our first exercise together is one that I want you to work on individually," she instructs, standing up. "You are all going to write letters to your future selves, the people you will be after you complete this course in a few months." She starts to stroll around the circle. "I want you to think about how you are feeling right now: your hopes, dreams, and fears." Her hips sway as she walks. "Do you have any goals for yourself? Are you the person you want to be right now? Dig deep. Be honest with yourselves. You are going to be the only ones to see your letter. I will return them to you as you leave our last workshop." She smiles and waves her arms. "All right, get to it!"

I watch as everyone bows their heads over their clipboards and starts to write. Livie hunches over her paper, her tongue pressed between her lips, her tight, cramped handwriting starting to fill the page. Jackson sits back on his pillow with a surprised expression on his face, while Michela attacks her letter with intense stoicism. I glance over at Unabomber, who is still staring at me. I jut out my chin aggressively in his direction, and he shakes his head before wildly scribbling away. I sigh and look down at my own blank page, not knowing where to begin. Everyone else seems to have a lot to say to themselves, but, really, I'm the last person that I would want to hear from. *Am I the person who I want to be right now?* I wonder. Um... that would be a big, fat no. I shift on my pillow and see Mary Carmen hovering in the back of the room with Seth, engaged in quiet conversation. They're probably discussing whatever mundane method of torture they're going to inflict on us next. Livie flips her page over and starts writing on the back. I sigh and tap my pen on my knee. My mind wanders out into the hall and wonders what Daniel is doing right now, what book is he reading, if he got something to eat, if he's even still waiting for me. He said he would, and he hasn't seemed like someone that would go back on his word so far...

God, this is so dumb! I grit my teeth and take the cap off

my pen, doodling a small spiral in the upper right hand corner. I pause and then write:

Dear Christa,

I nod to myself. Good start.

Mary Carmen steps over, glancing up at the wall clock. "Maybe another five minutes. Okay, everyone?" She smiles and puts her hair back up in a sloppy bun, sexy tendrils framing her face.

Crap. I stare at my letter (or lack of letter). Hopes, dreams, fears, goals… the five-minute version. Okay.

Dear Christa,

Here are several goals that I, your former self, think would be great things to strive for in an effort to un-jack your life:

Stop getting into cars with stupid boys. It's probably best to just stick with public transportation for the time being. Case in point: bump on head.

Stop hooking up with stupid boys. Try to only hook up with un-stupid boys. I bite my lip, my eyes scanning between the clock and the door.

3. When given the chance, find the nearest exit and run. Always sound advice.

Take it or leave it—

Love, the Ghost of Christmas Past

"Great. That's time, everyone!" Mary Carmen moves back over to the circle. "If you could seal your letters into your envelopes and pass them to me—thank you." I turn to pass mine to Livie, who has tears in her eyes.

"You okay?" I ask cautiously.

She nods and smiles. "Oh my gosh, yeah! Never better!" She shakes her head, wiping her tears away. "I guess I didn't realize how much I needed that." She looks at me. "How did it go for you?"

I blow out my cheeks. "You know... the same." I cringe, scratching the back of my head. "It was hard, but, um... really good to clear the air."

Livie nods knowingly.

"All right, we are going to take a ten minute break right now," Mary Carmen calls out. "If you go out into the corridor, the bathrooms will be on your left, just around the corner." Everyone stands up; I take time to stretch out my sore joints. "We'll continue with our group work after that. See you in a bit." Mary Carmen smiles and steps into the hallway.

I quirk my eyebrows at Livie. "I'm going to go check out the cafeteria. Do you want anything?" I ask.

She shakes her head and slings her purse across her chest. "Oh, I'm good, thanks! Well," she pauses and clucks her tongue, "maybe, if you see a pack of M&Ms or something? I could really use some chocolate. I'll pay you back!" she adds quickly.

I snicker. "I think I can spring for the 89 cents or whatever it costs. Don't worry about it." I pat her warmly on the arm. "I'll be back in a few."

We walk out. Livie goes left as I go right down the hall.

The cafeteria is busy, doctors and nurses grouped together at small tables according to scrub color, creating a patchwork of purple, blue, and surgical green. I head over to the candy racks and grab a pack of M&Ms, scanning the crowd for Daniel as I wait by the register. I start to get antsy as I pay the attendant and can't find a mop of golden-brown hair anywhere. I do a quick walk-thru just to be sure, grunting as I accidentally run into a pair of doctors in white lab coats.

"Oh, sorry," I mumble, my eyes darting around the hall. They nod kindly and move on with their trays. I bite my lip.

He's not here.

My heart sinks into my stomach as I slowly make my way back to the front of the cafeteria. I look around once more before walking back to the classroom.

Of course he wouldn't stay. Why would he? I'm such an idiot. I shuffle down the hall, my arms wrapped around myself as I stare at the floor.

"… *Creo que uno de mis otros niños pueden verla. No deje a su lado… aun permitirla ir a casa ayer por la noche fue una mala idea. Ella es un objetivo en movimiento*," I hear someone say in very quick Spanish.

"*¿No crees que lo sé? Pasé toda la noche en el alley… uh… callejón… por su apartamento. No quiero que… que… asustarla*," a guy's voice answers. I look up and see Daniel and Mary Carmen, leaning together against the wall outside of Conference Room B. My pulse skips a beat as I hustle over to them.

"Your Spanish is getting rusty," Mary Carmen murmurs, patting him on the arm.

He shakes his head and looks up, his face brightening as he sees me. "Hey!" he calls out. I grin and catch myself trotting the last couple feet over to him. "I was wondering when you'd show up." He chucks me affectionately on the shoulder. Mary Carmen clears her throat and stands up straight.

"I was in the cafeteria, looking for you," I answer, slightly out of breath. I glance between the two of them. "You guys know each other?"

Mary Carmen smiles and steps toward the classroom door. Daniel chuckles. "Sure… I told you I came here a lot!" He gives the wall a little kick with his sneaker. "Mary Carmen and I go way back. She's, like… a national landmark around here." He cocks his head toward her. She blushes.

My jaw tightens, all of this suddenly feeling very weird. "And… you speak Spanish?" I ask.

"*Un poco.*" He holds up his hand and rubs his fingers together. "*Hablas español?*"

I shake my head. Mary Carmen sighs and raps the door with her knuckles. "I'll see you inside, Christa." She nods at both of us before going back in. Daniel waves, then turns back to me.

"So," I state, trying to keep my tone even, "I thought you were going to wait for me down the hall. I couldn't find you."

His brow crinkles. "I *was* waiting. Got half way through my book." He grins and holds up his paperback. I roll my eyes as he adds, "But I went upstairs to see if I could find Tom. I thought you might want to go visit after you were done here."

My gaze softens. "You saw Tom?" I whisper.

Daniel nods. "Yeah, he's still in the ICU, but the nurse said that family and friends were allowed. Your name's on the list and everything," he replies.

I clear my throat, trying to keep the tears at bay. "I *would* like to go see him, thanks." I look down at the floor. Daniel leans against the door. "Did they… did they say if he was going to be okay or not?"

He shakes his head. "They wouldn't tell me anything, Christa. I'm sorry." He winces. "But he's alive right now, and that's something."

I nod. "Yeah, it is." I glance into the conference room. "I should get back in there." I look into his eyes. "Seriously, thank you for waiting. For… being here today. It means a lot."

Daniel steps towards me. "I wouldn't want to be anywhere else," he whispers.

Heat creeps up over my collar as I sense his closeness. I take a deep breath and rub my neck. "Okay, so… I'll see you in a little bit." I tuck my hair behind my ears and step inside.

He nods and takes a seat on the tile floor right outside the door. "Okay—you got it." He opens his book and smiles. "I promise not to wander off again."

I have to be the color of a stop sign as I shut the door behind me.

Back inside, everyone is sitting in their spots. I plop down next to Livie, tossing her the M&Ms.

"What's going on?" I glance back to Mary Carmen, who is standing by the snack table, organizing what looks like several balls of brightly colored yarn.

"I dunno." Livie shrugs. "Some kind of group thing." She grins as she tears open the bag of candy, popping a couple into her mouth. "Thanks for these."

"Sure." I nod, watching Mary Carmen as she places the yarn in a basket. She smiles and walks over to the circle.

"I hope you feel reenergized now after a little break. We are going to have one more exercise before you all have to head out back into the world." She moves around the circle and hands everyone their own ball of yarn. "All right—everyone stand up; Seth, you join us too."

Seth dashes over in between Michaela and Livie. Mary Carmen hands me a red ball of yarn; Livie takes blue.

"So, this game is going to work a lot like the drinking game, 'I've Never.' I am sure some of you have played it with your friends." Her eyes dart mischievously around the circle.

Michela sighs. "Ironic much?"

Mary Carmen chuckles. "In this version of the game, instead of trying to see what dirty deeds your friends have gotten up to, you are all going to state a truth about yourselves in the negative." She takes her spot in the circle. "So someone who has been to Hawaii on vacation could say, 'I've never been to Hawaii,' and then they would take a drink. Everyone else who has visited Hawaii would also take a drink. We are going to replace the drink with yarn." She holds up a yellow ball of yarn.

"Please tie your yarn around your finger now." Everyone does as they're told. "We are all going to state a truth about ourselves using the statement 'I've never.' If you have also had this truth happen to you, throw your ball to the speaker. The speaker will hook your yarn around his or her finger and then throw your ball back to you so that you can participate on the next turn. Does this make sense?"

Everyone nods. "Okay, Seth, please get us started." Mary Carmen turns to him and smiles. Seth gives her a goofy grin and begins.

"Okay, I've never… eaten spaghetti." Everyone giggles, and we all pitch our yarn to Seth. He bumbles as he picks them all up, hooking each color around his finger and throwing the balls back to their respective owners. We all twist our yarn around our own fingers, and the next round begins. Mary Carmen nods at Jackson.

"Um… I've never stayed up all night." Again, we all laugh, and everyone tosses their yarn to him. We go around the circle once with fairly bland confessions, until it's Seth's turn again. He takes a deep breath.

"I've never been so wasted I forgot where I was," he says, the corners of his mouth twitching. We all stand in silence, before Michela chucks her yarn at him, followed by Jackson and Livie. I sigh and throw mine, too. Livie reaches over and gives my hand a squeeze.

"Party at Clingmans Dome with my ex-boyfriend," she whispers.

"Hollywood Bowl, last summer," I reply. Seth tosses back the yarn. It's Michela's turn now.

"Well, if that's how it's gonna be…" She sighs. "I've never…

had sex with a stranger." I hold onto my yarn this time, but, surprisingly, Mary Carmen throws hers. All of us look at her.

"Life can be long and varied." She arches an eyebrow. I quickly wipe the shocked expression off my face. "Thank you, Michela," she adds before nodding at Unabomber. "You're up, Bryan."

He wavers, grasping his yarn. "I've never tried to kill myself before," he mumbles, barely audible. Both Michela and Jackson flinch a little as Livie throws her ball to Unabomber.

"Well, duh." She shrugs, holding up her wrists.

Unabomber leers at her. "Did you mean it?" he asks simply.

Livie gasps and shakes her head. "I don't... know..." She fidgets, looking down at the floor.

Unabomber blinks. "That's not part of this game, Bryan. Only 'I've Nevers,'" Mary Carmen interjects, her demeanor calm.

Unabomber sinks back into his sweatshirt. "Sorry," he mutters.

Mary Carmen clears her throat. "I've never..." She pauses and looks straight at me. "Lost somebody important."

Jackson tosses his yarn to her. "My auntie; cancer." He coughs, his eyes focused on the wall.

Mary Carmen stares at me, like she's waiting—like she knows. I shift uncomfortably. Everyone is glancing between themselves, starting to notice that this round is taking longer. Mary Carmen keeps her gaze trained on me. I can feel my face redden as I get madder and madder. How dare she make an example of me in this cheap imitation of *The Breakfast Club*. Mary Carmen looks on placidly. In a huff, I hurl my yarn at her. She gently rocks back onto her heels at the impact, glancing down at the floor.

Michela turns towards me, her kohl-smudged eyes wide. "Wow. Nerd Barbie, what's that all about?" she huffs.

Livie looks at me, her eyes sad. "I'm sorry," she whispers.

I shake my head and bite my tongue. "It's fine," I grit. "I'm fine—don't make it a thing."

Livie shrinks back. "Okay..."

. Mary Carmen takes a deep breath and stares out at the group. "All right, I think this is good. Let's take a minute to appreciate the amazing art that your honesty has created." We all look toward the center of our circles, a stunning rainbow web tremoring as each of us shift in our places. Even through my anger, I can recognize how cool it is. We stand, reveling in the web's beauty.

"Please, let's all sit back down… carefully," Mary Carmen instructs after a minute. We slowly sink to our pillows again.

"Next time, when you feel alone, or scared, or out of control, I want you to think about this web and the connections you have built here today with one another," she breathes. Everyone eyes each other.

"You are not alone in this world," Mary Carmen continues with a smile. "There are others who share your experiences and can help you. I hope you leave today full of life and possibility. This web is just a piece of the beauty that lives inside each of you." She pulls her hand from her strings and then comes around with a pair of scissors, cutting the ties that bind us to the center and leaving us each a piece of our original yarn to keep. As she comes around to me, she squeezes my shoulder.

I bite my lip. We all get up to leave.

"Thank you so much for coming today," Mary Carmen exclaims as we gather our things. "I will treasure your truths and think of you often over the next few days. See you next week!" She smiles as she and Seth start to clean up. Livie gives me a little wave as she leaves.

I grimace and shove the piece of yarn into my coat pocket before grabbing my bag. "Christa?" I hear Mary Carmen call.

I roll my eyes and turn to her. "Yeah?"

She saunters over to me. "Are you okay?" She reaches for my elbow.

I pull back, avoiding her touch. "Yeah. Like I said, I'm fine,"

I bark. "Why does everyone keep asking me that?" Am I really that obvious?

She gathers her long hair and pulls it over her shoulder. "It feels like that last activity was a little hard on you, especially at the end." She furrows her brow. "I wanted to see if there was anything you wanted to talk about in private." She tilts her head to the side.

I cross my arms over my chest. "No… I just don't like being singled out." I clench my jaw. "It was like you were… baiting me, or something." I look down at the floor.

Mary Carmen sighs. "I certainly wasn't trying to do that. Everyone comes in here with a clean slate; I value whatever you decide to share with me." She watches me intently.

I put my jacket on in a hurry. "Fine, whatever," I glower. "Can I go now?" I glance toward the door.

"Of course." She nods and steps aside. "See you next week."

"Okay, bye," I mutter, jetting for the exit. I stalk into the hallway, almost tripping over Daniel on the other side of the doorway.

He hastily gets to his feet. "All done?" he asks, tucking his book back into his jeans. "Ready to go up?"

I march across the hallway and punch the elevator button. "Yeah," I say as the doors open. "I'm just so sick of everyone thinking they know my life story—especially a know-it-all, self-help wannabe." I shake my head and step inside.

Daniel reaches over and taps Level 8. "Sorry," he says, his voice calm. "I'm sure she was only trying to help."

I snort. "Yeah, I'm so sure. She probably needs to meet a quota by the end of the month… Like, 'Ooh, look at me! Savior to the masses with my huge boobs and phony accent!'" I wave my hands. Daniel lets out a small laugh. I turn to him, my eyes narrowed.

"What *were* you and Mary Carmen talking about earlier, anyway?" I ask suspiciously.

Daniel gazes up at the ceiling. "Oh, just catching up," he replies with a little cough. "It's been a while since I got a chance to practice my Spanish." He wipes his mouth with the back of his hand. I shake my head and look down at the floor.

"I hope so… cuz it's not like I would have any idea what you guys were talking about, what with the whole lost in translation thing." I scowl. "I hope it goes without saying that what you and I talked about earlier was private." I motion between us. "You know, the stuff with my mom."

Daniel nods. "I promise you, I didn't repeat anything from breakfast." He stares at me. "What happened in there?"

I sigh. "Nothing—just a bunch of sob stories and self-congrat- ulatory B.S. You would have loved it," I add with a sneer.

The doors open on Level 8. Daniel points to the right. "He's this way." He looks at me hesitantly. "You sure you're ready for this?"

I nod. "As ready as anyone can be to watch one of their best friends stare death in the face." I exhale and close my eyes. "God, I really hate this place."

Daniel nods and walks me out of the elevator.

Tom's room is dimly lit by the stack of life-support monitors next to the wall, the shades drawn. The table under the window is cov- ered with flower arrangements and Get Well Soon cards. Tom lies non-responsive in the bed, his eyes shut and his mouth vomiting out a bouquet of tubes and plastic. He wheezes quietly as his chest rises and falls.

I stop in the doorway, a lump caught in my throat. "I don't know if I can do this," I rasp.

Daniel places his hand on my shoulder. "Yes, you can," he murmurs in my ear. "You'll be happy you came; it's good for him too." He pats me reassuringly. "Just go say hi."

I nod and take a few wobbly steps over to the side of the

bed, wrapping my fingers around the bedrail. Daniel hovers in the doorway.

"Hey, jerk," I breathe, caressing the top of Tom's head. I can see his eyes shifting under his taped lids. I bend down and gently kiss his forehead, careful to avoid the freshly burned skin on the right side of his face, shiny with some sort of medical goo.

"Some mess we've gotten ourselves into now, huh?" I mutter, crouching next to the bed. "Really screwed up."

Hot tears leak down my cheeks. I notice a machine on the other side of the bed, a balloon compressing like an accordion in time with Tom's chest and creating a tragic symphony with the chorus of other buzzes and beeps around the room. I sit back on my heels and fold my hands over his on the sheet.

"I guess there is a silver lining, though." I clear my throat. "This new look you've got going…" I point to his face. "… It's an instant chick magnet. Stacy Asher and Monica Harris should be showing up anytime now, wearing skin-tight 'Get Well Soon, Tom!' shirts." I chuckle, jerking my chin toward the table of gifts.

"And I'm sure there's got to be at least one card over there from Principal Schaffer telling you not to worry about school… You'll probably ace all of your classes for, like, the first time ever." I sniffle, watching the corners of his mouth sag around the ventilator. "So, you've just got to get better so you can come back and enjoy the free ride. You're… you're really good at that."

My face crumples, and I quickly cover my eyes with my palms, sobs wracking my shoulders. I rest my forehead against the bed, rocking in time with his breathing.

"What the fuck, Tom?" My voice quivers as I wipe my tears away. "Two days ago, we were sitting in the back of Brit Lit making fart jokes, and now you're, like… comatose?" I grab a tissue from the nightstand and blow my nose. "No—just, no." I shake my head and stand up. "I—I forbid you to die, Tom. Sorry." I nod. "You better deal with it and turn all this around."

Daniel spins and stares at me as I motion at the bed. "You're not allowed to die. This was never part of our plan!" I bark fiercely. "You're supposed to become a famous comedian and buy me a new house, a Ducati, designer clothes, a pack of purebred Akitas to guard my mansion…" My jaw tightens. "And every time you come hang out, you step in dog shit, remember?" I take a breath. "So just wake up already, all right?!" I stop and look at his face, waiting for that magic movie moment.

Nothing.

I sink down by the bedside again. "Please, Tom," I sigh, placing my hand back over his limp ones. "Please, don't make me do this again." I squeeze his fingers, almost succeeding in convincing myself that he squeezed back—but I know that the only real movement is coming from the machine that's breathing for him.

"Okay." I nod, giving Tom a final, watery smile. "Feel better, and… I'll see you soon." I get up and walk over to Daniel. "I'm ready to leave now," I tell him, suddenly feeling completely drained.

Daniel nods. "You got it. We can get out this way." He takes my hand and leads me past rows of partitioned-off exam rooms. The corridor is busy, overflow patients waiting on stretchers in the hall.

"Are you hungry? I know a spot nearby where we can get a burger." He looks over at me.

I nod. "Yeah, something quick might be good… I haven't really eaten since breakfast." I groan and rub my face. "Oh my God, I'm probably a total mess right now." I picture long, dark lines of mascara streaking down my cheeks.

Daniel smiles and gives my hand a squeeze.

"Don't worry: you're gorgeous." He bumps me with his shoulder as we walk. "Even though you look a little like Frankenstein with these lights." He points up to the fluorescents and grins.

I shove into him playfully. "Shut up!" I smile, staying close to him. "At least I don't have Thousand Island on my shirt." I point to a splotch near his neckline.

He looks down and grabs his collar. "Are you serious?! Man, that sandwich was all over the place today!" He licks it. "Mmm... Still good."

"Gross!" I laugh, accidentally walking into an occupied stretcher against the wall. I turn and put out my hand. "Oh jeez, I'm so sorry!" I exclaim. "Are you okay?" I crane my neck to see the person's face at the other end of the bed.

"*Catalyssssst...*" he hisses, slowly pulling himself into an upright position.

My eyes go wide, and I stumble back against Daniel. "Oh my God, *is that...?*" I cry. Zompocalypse, the crazy guy from the parking lot the other night? Daniel pulls me behind him. "What the hell is he doing here?" I yell, gripping onto his leather jacket.

"I don't know—but don't get too close." Daniel shields me with his back. Zompocalypse wavers before falling back onto the stretcher, his eyes half-lidded. He's shirtless, every rib visible as he gasps for air.

"What's wrong with him?" I whisper, peeking over Daniel's shoulder to get a better look. "He looks even more messed up than the last time we saw him, which I would have never thought possible." I shake my head. It's true: his face is covered in a million little cuts, and his skin carries a grayish, mottled tone. His eyes roll in his head as he tries to focus on us.

Daniel moves in slowly. "Hey, man," he murmurs, reaching out and carefully placing a hand on Zompocalypse's shoulder. The man flinches, but doesn't pull away. "What happened to you?"

Zompocalypse opens and closes his mouth like a fish, nothing but spit bubbles coming out. Daniel cranes his ear down to his lips. I take a tentative step forward.

"Please... please... I need some more..." he pants, his hand fluttering as he reaches up and grabs Daniel's wrist, putting his nose to his skin like a dog looking for treats. Daniel frowns and gently pulls his hand away.

"I'm afraid I can't help you with that," he sighs. "Even if I could, you and I both know that's not what you need." Daniel pats him on the head. Zompocalypse points at me, his fingernails caked in dried blood. I make the connection between his hands and the cuts on his face: he's been trying to claw out his own eyes.

"If I bring her back, they'll give me some more. They told me they would!" he shouts, his mouth foaming. I shrink behind Daniel. "I told them all about how I saw the Catalyst, and they said I could have as much as I want whenever I want it if I take it to them!"

"What is he talking about?" I snipe. "That's the second time he's called me that: *Catalyst.*" I stare at Daniel.

Daniel opens his mouth to answer, but his focus shifts as Zompocalypse swings his legs off of the stretcher and tries to get up. "You have to come with me—NOW!" he slurs, his whole body shaking.

Daniel holds his arms up defensively. "Hey! Sit back down!" he yells. "Don't do this!"

We both stand back as Zompocalypse takes about two steps before collapsing to the floor, his chest heaving as he erupts into a fit of coughing. Daniel picks him up under the arms and hauls him back onto the stretcher.

Zompocalypse's teeth are tinged red. His arms and legs start to seize.

"Oh my God." I look around frantically. "Isn't this a fucking hospital?" I cry, panicked. "We need a doctor!" I step across the hall and wrench open one of the exam room curtains. "Hello! We need help!" I shout to an empty room. I rush back over to Daniel, who is holding Zompocalypse's head steady.

"Daniel, what's happening? Is he OD-ing?" I glare at him.

Daniel winces. "In a matter of speaking. There's not a whole lot they can do for him here." He looks down at Zompocalypse and smooths back his hair. "You've got to calm down, guy. Shhh, it's okay." He pets the man's head again, his tone steady.

Zompocalypse sputters, more blood spraying onto his chin. "*W-w-why?*" he gurgles, looking up at Daniel. Daniel stares back into his eyes intently. Zompocalypse reaches up and grabs onto his collar, pulling him close.

"Why what?" Daniel murmurs.

Zompocalypse whimpers, tears streaking down his cheeks. "Why couldn't you have found me first?" He cringes and releases Daniel, reaching back to a medical supply tray next to the stretcher and picking up a scalpel.

"DANIEL!" I shriek. Daniel turns to me, his face confused, as Zompocalypse pushes him aside and lunges off the stretcher, coming right for me. I scream as he smashes into my side, his rancid breath on my face, wielding the scalpel dangerously close to my eye.

"Get off her!" Daniel shouts, tearing him away.

I hold out my hands as they grapple. "Daniel—the knife!" I cry. But it's too late: Zompocalypse wrenches Daniel's shirt down and stabs him over and over again in the chest.

CHAPTER 4

"OH MY GOD— NO!!" I scream as Daniel reels back, the bloody scalpel clattering to the floor. "Somebody, help—HELP!"

I rush over to him, my breath catching in my chest.Behind me, Zompocalypse lets out a moan and flops back onto the bed, his whole body convulsing. I kneel next to Daniel, who is curled up against the wall, a bloody hand over his heart. I grab his shoulders and gingerly peel back his jacket, the inner lining covered in red.

"Christa—" he rasps. "Don't…"

"Oh my God! Don't talk—don't move!" I screech, twisting my neck around. "We need a doctor—NOW!!"

A team of white coats comes running from one of the rooms down the hall; I recognize them as the two from the cafeteria. Daniel's eyes go wide, and he staggers up, his mouth twisted in pain. He pulls me into a hug, pressing me tightly against him to hide his bloody t-shirt. The doctors bolt right past us to Zompocalypse, who's gone into a full-body spasm.

"Get the crash cart!" one of them yells, starting compressions on Zompocalypse's chest.

I look up and stare at Daniel. "What are you doing?" I yell. "You need help!" I turn to the doctor, who is now jumping onto the stretcher to straddle Zompocalypse. "Hey! We need help over *here*!" I scream.

Daniel jerks me by the shoulders. "Christa—stop! I'm fine!" he grits out, clenching my jacket. I bare my teeth and stare at him wildly.

"You're not fine, you idiot! You just got stabbed!" I yank down his shirt and reveal several deep, life-threatening gashes. I watch them gush blood and get woozy. "Oh my God…" I mumble, the hallway starting to spin. I place a hand haphazardly over the cuts in an attempt to staunch the bleeding and turn back to the doctors. "Please…" I whimper, my fingers slick.

Daniel grimaces and grabs my hand. "Stop." He tries to push me away, but I stand firm.

"No—we're supposed to apply pressure!" I cry, a flickering memory from 9th grade first aid coming to the forefront of my mind. I bunch up his t-shirt in my fist. "Here, hold this on top…" I pull my hand away, and my jaw drops.

Like watching a time-lapse video of a flower opening and closing, the incisions seal themselves up. In about ten seconds, the only reminder of the incident is a thin film of wet blood over tan skin, smooth and unblemished. I stare at Daniel, who is watching me in stony silence.

"What—" I gasp, taking a step back. I look at his chest and then at the mess on my hand. "But… but you're bleeding…"

Daniel shakes his head and zips up his jacket. "Be quiet, Christa," he whispers harshly.

I feel my legs turn to jelly and hold the wall for support. "H-how—???" I stammer. I stare at him, my mouth agape, extreme relief washing over me with shock and confusion quick on its heels.

Daniel grabs me by the waist and pulls me close, searching my eyes. "No, no, no…" he mutters, glancing away. "Not here, not now…" He takes a deep breath through his nose and looks down the hall. "Okay, we have to go." He nods affirmatively. "This way."

He starts to pull me down the corridor. I shake my head and dig my boots into the floor. "Wait—no!" I wrench my wrist away from him. "Daniel, I don't know what's going on! I just need a second..." I put my hand to my forehead, trying to keep from hyperventilating.

Daniel rubs his jaw. "Please, Christa! I promise I'll explain everything once we're outside." He glances over at the doctors. "We have to get out of here." His voice cracks.

I turn back around and stare at the stretcher. The other, older doctor has returned with the crash cart, and the one working on Zompocalypse points to us and murmurs something. The other doctor nods and dashes over.

"Crap," Daniel mutters, staring at the floor. "Don't say *anything.*"

I gawk at him, wide-eyed. "What would I even say?" My lower lip starts quivering. I must be losing my mind.

The doctor stops in front of us, out of breath. "You kids okay?" he asks, looking us over. I cross my arms and lean against the wall. Daniel nods and gives his best Cheshire cat grin.

"Oh yeah," he scoffs, tilting his head toward the stretcher. "Little exciting, but nothing we couldn't handle." He clears his throat.

The doctor frowns and looks at me. "Are you okay, Miss?" he asks.

I stare dully at the floor.

"She's fine, really," Daniel interjects, patting my shoulder. "My girlfriend's just not used to seeing crazy people in action." He shakes his head.

The doctor nods and folds his arms. "Sorry about that." He looks back at Zompocalypse. "We're still trying to figure out what that guy is on... Never seen anything like it."

I shudder as we all turn and watch the first doctor charging up a pair of cardiac paddles. "You sure you two are all right?" our doctor asks again, now zeroing in on Daniel.

Daniel smiles and wraps his arm around my waist. "Never better! But we really have to be going... We're meeting her mom for dinner." He coughs, starting to lead me away.

The doctor's eyes narrow. "Wait—I'm sorry... Is... is that blood?" He points to the little bit of t-shirt visible behind Daniel's jacket.

Daniel glances down and sighs. "Ketchup from lunch. Can't take me anywhere!"

I turn my head toward him as he bursts into a deep, chest-heaving cough. The doctor reaches out and puts his hand on Daniel's shoulder. "Son, I think we should take a look..." He tries to guide Daniel into one of the exam rooms.

Daniel bucks his hand off. "If you want to be helpful, you should really be more careful about where you leave your dangerous medical instruments!" he crows, his eyes wild. The doctor takes a step back. "Especially when there are mentally unstable people around. It's a lawsuit waiting to happen!" He glares angrily.

The doctor shakes his head and looks away. "That's what I thought!" Daniel barks, gripping my hips. "Come on, baby... Your mom's holding the table across the street." He coughs again, walking us briskly down the hall. I twist my neck to see the doctor staring at the floor before moving over to assist with Zompocalypse.

"Don't look back. Come on." Daniel winces, tugging at my waist. I face forward and see a bay of elevators a few feet away, then start to feel weak again as Daniel helps me inside.

"I just don't get it," I mutter. "I saw him cut you... I'm not crazy!"

Daniel wheezes and hits the door close button fervently. "Hang with me, Christa. Just for a little bit longer."

I put my face in my hands as we begin our descent.

It's dark outside when we leave the hospital. Daniel practically drags me into a nearby alleyway, where we stop and I catch my breath.

"Okay, you really need to start talking, or I am going to lose it!" I snap, grabbing my stomach, feeling like I'm going to upchuck all over the concrete.

Daniel nods, staring down at the ground. "I know... You deserve to know everything," he mumbles, scratching his neck.

I toss my head back and glare at him. "What the hell happened up there? How are you still..." I sputter into silence, shaking my head. "How are you not wearing a fucking toe tag in the morgue right now?"

Daniel smirks and crosses his arms, glancing out at the road. "Been there, done that, got the t-shirt..." he chuckles grimly. "Is that where I should be? I guess that would make things easier."

I clench my jaw. "Of course not! Of course I'm happy you're not..." I bite my lip. "None of this makes any sense, Daniel! What happened just isn't... normal!"

"You're right," he sighs, still focused on the street.

"Hey!" I roar, shoving him with my fists. "I know what I saw— don't try to tell me it didn't happen!" I rake my hands through my hair.

"I know." He swallows, staring down at his shoes. "You need answers, and I'm going to give them to you, but not here." He exhales, looking at the street again. "We need to keep moving." He reaches out to take my arm.

"NO!" I bat his hand away. "I'm not going anywhere with you until you explain to me..." I sigh. "Explain how I saw you... *heal?*" I look up at him questioningly. "Is that what happened?" My voice cracks.

He closes his eyes. "Yes," he whispers. "That's exactly what you saw."

I step back, gulping for air. "Oh my God." I crouch down

and put my head between my knees. "This isn't real... I must be hallucinating." I lie my hands flat against the cold pavement. "Or dreaming, or maybe it's my head..." My fingers flutter as I place them on top of the bump on my forehead. "I think I'm having an episode or something."

Daniel bends down next to me and cautiously places a hand on my back. "Christa... Take a breath, and we'll talk about this." He uses the same tone he used with Zompocalypse a few minutes ago.

I shake my head. "Oh my God... No, no, NO!" I shout, shooting up like a rocket, Daniel falling backwards. "Don't touch me—stay away!" I cry, pacing around the alleyway.

He gets to his feet and raises his palms. "Christa, calm down... Everything is okay. There is a lot I need to tell you, and I need to know you're not going to flip out." He smooths the air with his hands.

I laugh hysterically. "Flip out! FLIP OUT!" I yell. "Who are you—*what* are you?!"

Daniel sighs and looks up. "I'm an Angel... sort of." He shrugs.

I stop pacing and stare at him, my mouth hanging open. He puts his hands in his pockets, trying to read my face.

"Angels aren't real," I reply matter-of-factly after a moment. "And what do you mean, 'sort of'?"

He gives me a weak smile. "Well, technically, I'm a Guardian, having done the whole mortal thing before." He winces. "It's um, complicated." He turns and takes a few steps away.

"Are... are you kidding me?" I shake my head. "I want answers, Daniel, *real* answers!"

He exhales. "I promise you, Christa, this will all make sense soon." He turns and looks at the street again. "But we really, *really* should get moving."

"Why do you keep saying that?" I shout. He crosses his arms and sets his jaw. "Seriously?" I bark, stomping over to him.

"Because you're not safe here!" he finally yells, tearing at his hair as he cranes his neck around the corner.

I catch my breath. "Or I'm not safe with *you*," I snap. "I'm so outta here." I sling my bag over my shoulder and start to stalk out of the alleyway.

"No—Christa, don't!" He grabs my arm and swings me up against the wall.

My eyes go wide. "OW! Get your hands off of me!" I shove him away from me, hard.

He puts his face in his hands. "You may not understand this yet, but there are two Demons waiting for you a block up from here," he grits out. "We passed them on our way out of the hospital." He shakes his head. "You can't go out that way, not while you're Haloing... They'll see—they'll see *everything*." He looks down at the sidewalk.

"Oh, fuck my life!" I exclaim. He startles, so I add, "Guardians, Demons, Haloing? You are seriously deranged!" I march away from him down the other side of the alley toward the street.

"Christa, please!" he begs, following me. "You are super vulnerable right now—you don't even know!"

I huff and keep walking.

"Something happened to you when you saw me heal... Stop!" he shouts as I make it to the street. "You're the Catalyst!"

I turn to him, my eyes narrowed.

"You are. Just, please stop... stop," he pants, holding his chest.

I look down at the ground. "You know what that means, what Zompocalypse called me?" I ask.

He hangs his head. I glare at him. "You've known this whole time. Figures." I shake my head. "You two were probably working me together from day one."

"That's not true! Christa, come on!" He steps toward me.

"This is insane," I mutter, clearing my throat. "So, what does it mean, Daniel?" I arch an eyebrow. "Catalyst? Ooh, spooky, spooky…" I waggle my fingers menacingly.

He stares at me and shakes his head. "Come on, tell me," I tease and punch him lightly on the arm.

He focuses on the ground. "I don't know," he mumbles. "No one does. We just know that you're important." He leans against the wall.

I laugh. "If you don't know anything, how do you know it's even me?" I call, motioning with my hands.

Daniel chuckles and glances at the sky. "Oh, it's pretty obvious." He chews his lip sullenly. "None of this is going the way it was supposed to."

I jut out my chin. "And how was that, Daniel? Hm?" I jeer. "Little candlelight, some soft music… then you'd whip up some more amazing food and feed me a pack of lies? Is this your twisted way of picking up girls?"

He looks at the ground. "I'm not lying," he whispers.

I roll my eyes. "Of course you are! You can't even look at me—"

"I'm trying to be respectful!" he shouts, staring straight at me. "You have no idea what's happened and you're too bullheaded to just stop and listen—"

"Oh, I have heard enough!" I yell.

He turns and kicks the wall, placing his hands on his hips.

"The real crazy here isn't what I saw back at the hospital or if you're a conman, or a criminal, or whatever," I spit. "It's that I think you actually believe the shit you're spouting! God, Daniel!" I wince and tug at my hair. "I trusted you!"

He stares at me, crestfallen. I clench my jaw. "I trusted you, and I thought you were…" I pause, searching for the right words. "… someone I could count on. I am so stupid." I shake my head and step toward the road.

"Christa!" Daniel calls after me. "WAIT!"

I keep walking. "Screw you!" I yell over my shoulder. I look around for a bus stop, a car, anything. I see a line of cabs waiting outside a fancy restaurant a few blocks away. I break into a trot and head in that direction.

I hear Daniel following, his steps long and fast. "Christa, please! Listen to me..." He catches up, out of breath.

I scowl. "I told you to leave me alone."

He sighs. "I'm sorry, but I can't." He frowns, grabbing his chest.

I shake my head and readjust my bag as I stomp towards the cabs. "God, you're worse than I thought! If I had known what a psycho stalker you were, I would have never let you into my house!" I cross my arms. "Take a hint! I don't want anything to do with you or your crazy. Forget where I live. Forget you know me... Just stay away!" I'm about a hundred feet from the restaurant. I speed up.

"Like I said—I'm sorry!" he shouts, breaking into a run. "That's not how any of this works... There's so much you need to know—can you slow down?!"

When, he reaches for my sleeve, I see red. "I said don't touch me!" I snarl, pulling my arm back and cracking him against the chin. He spins cartoonishly on the sidewalk.

"OW!" Daniel stops and grabs his face, readjusting his jaw. "You've got a wicked right hook!"

I wince and shake out my fist, having finally reached the line of cabs. I jump into one.

"That's good!" Daniel calls as I slam the door shut behind me. "Do that to anyone who tries to come at you, makes you feel weird, looks at you funny..." He taps the window with his finger.

I turn and shoot daggers with my eyes, but he's still talking. "Please, Christa," he says, his voice muffled by the glass. "I know you're mad right now, but just go home, okay? Promise me!" He winces and pounds his fist on the window. "Go straight home!"

I roll my eyes and don't answer.

"You ready to go?" the driver asks from the front seat.

"Oh yeah," I huff, "so ready."

As the cab pulls away, I turn to look back through the rearview window. Daniel stands forlornly in front of the restaurant, watching me go. We turn a corner, and he's gone. I spin back around in my seat and sigh.

"Where to?" the cabbie murmurs.

"Um… Van Nuys—" I start to say, then catch myself. Screw Daniel for thinking he can tell me what to do.

"Actually, can you take me to Trinity on Sunset?"

*

The line in front of the club is double what it was a few nights ago, stretching around the corner and halfway up the next block. I sigh and pull out my phone.

"You want me to drop you here?" the driver asks. I check my messages and smile at a pic from Jodie. She's decked out in her cupcake print pajamas, holding a pint of ice cream with an episode of *Vampires Suck!* on in the background. The text reads *Marathon!!! Feel like grabbing a spoon with me?*

"More than you know," I mumble.

The cabbie clears his throat. "Hey? Is this okay?" he says a little louder. I glance out the window, startled.

"Oh yeah—this is fine, thanks." I chuck a wad of cash at the front seat and step out onto the sidewalk, taking in the line.

"Great… This is going to steal, like, twenty years of my life," I mutter. Everyone who is waiting seems restless, eager to get inside and start the night.

"Hey, Princess—come here! We've got mollies!" some asshat in line cat-calls to me. His stupid friends laugh and pat him on the back. I roll my eyes and turn back to the cab, strongly considering jumping back in and going to Brentwood. I freeze, though, when a familiar brogue catches my ear.

"No, no, no, not red!"

I spin around and see Alden pacing on my side of the rope, his phone up to his ear. He looks like a European model, wearing another perfectly tailored shirt with charcoal gray pants and his dark hair tousled just right. He's sexy, aloof, put together, and not Daniel. He's exactly what I need right now.

I check my lip gloss with my finger before sauntering over to him, hoping I did a good enough job in the cab on my makeup.

"I don't care if you have to drive all the way to New Jersey," he hisses into the phone, his back turned to me. "Pink! Get it right, or it's your head." His aggressiveness is a little daunting, but not necessarily a turn off. I clear my throat and 'accidentally' fall into his shoulder. He spins to see who bumped him, annoyed at first, but his eyes widen in delight when he recognizes me.

"I have to go." He hangs up and quickly shoves his phone into his pants pocket.

"Well, well, well… aren't you a sight," he purrs, seeming somehow wolf-like as he looks me over.

I coolly survey the line of people behind the velvet rope as they shift right and left to try to get the bouncer's attention. "Hi, Alden," I say, giving him a half-smile.

Alden grins as his eyes follow my gaze. "Christa, right? Where's the high school football star? No boyfriend tonight?" he asks casually.

I laugh. "Riley is *not* my boyfriend. No, I'm flying solo, looking for a little… fun." I arch my eyebrows meaningfully.

"I bet you are." He smiles and coils his arm around my hips. I grow flushed from his closeness. "I like fun," he whispers in my ear. "You wanna have a little fun with me?"

I bat my eyelashes coquettishly. "I would love to, but I just got here, and that's a *very* long line…" I cock my head.

Alden scoffs and walks me over to the red double doors. "I don't do lines—and tonight, neither do you." When he gives old Earpiece a wink, the bouncer nods and lets us through. I snicker to myself as I hear a chorus of groans from everyone still waiting.

It's Saturday night at Trinity, and the place is packed wall-to-wall. The music is blasting, beautiful people writhing across the dance floor and making out with each other like their lives depend on it. I turn toward the bar and see a row of on-the-house shooters, filled to the brim with rainbow-colored alcohol. I grab two and offer one to Alden. He shakes his head and tugs me gently by the arm.

"Let's go somewhere quieter," he yells over the noise. I look at him quizzically. He smiles. "Come on, it's just this way."

I shrug, throw both of the shots back in succession, and leave the empty glasses on a tray as he leads me past the bar to a curtained-off hallway. This is a section of Trinity that I've never been to before. We can still hear the music from the main room, but the bass isn't quite as heavy anymore. Small, private rooms line the walls; we pass a couple of young guys laughing as they undress a pretty Asian woman. In another, a Trent Reznor look-alike shoots up some girl with what looks like black tar heroin. Her head lolls back onto a crushed red velvet chaise lounge, arm extended, eyelids fluttering like she's asleep.

I look at Alden and blush. "That's pretty... intense," I mutter.

He shrugs. "If they pay for the room and everyone's consenting, who are we to judge?" He grins rakishly as he guides me to an ominous black door all the way in the back.

"What's this?" I ask, glancing over my shoulder at the other rooms down the hall.

Alden chuckles. "Someplace quieter where we can chat, get to know each other better." I gasp as he runs a finger across my jaw. "Nothing... twitchy, if that's what you're worried about." He glances back toward the private rooms. "Scout's honor."

I bite my lip. "This looks like there should be an 'employees only' sticker on it." I crane my neck to see if anyone is coming. "We can't just barge in like we own the place."

Alden wrinkles his nose and twists the knob. "Sure we can." He quirks his eyebrows and gestures inside. "Please, come into my office."

I exhale as I take his hand. "Why, thank you," I murmur.

The room is not at all what I expected. Instead of red walls and long, low couches like in the rest of the club, there is an expensive-looking leather chair behind a huge wooden desk lit by a Tiffany lamp. The room is painted a mellow sky blue, and behind the desk is a wall-sized fish tank, putting the city aquarium to shame. Tiny white pebbles and beautiful coral line the bottom, with every kind of tropical fish imaginable flitting merrily amongst the bubbles.

"Wow..." I breathe, walking over and pressing my face up against the glass. I feel like a child, staring at sweet little clownfish and tetras as they pop in and out of the anemone. I turn and gape at Alden.

"I had no idea this was back here. It's amazing." I shake my head as a beautiful black and white angelfish flutters past.

He smiles puckishly. "I know." He leans against the desk, playing with the Newton's cradle that sits next to the phone, the metal balls clanging brightly against one another. "I much prefer it to the main room. I can hear myself think back here." He sits back, watching me admire the fish tank.

I smile and look around the rest of the room. "So, this really *is* your office?" I ask.

He nods. "I share it with the owner. I'm the lead promoter, so I actually spend most of my days back here on the phone, managing the club and our other properties around the world." He arches an eyebrow and smooths the wood with his hand. I look down and fidget with the zipper on my jacket, suddenly feeling intimidated not only by his looks, but also his overwhelming success.

"I can't believe you work here," I mumble. "You're... older than I thought."

He snickers. "You have no idea." He cocks his head to the side. "Is that a problem?"

I shake my head quickly. "No, no. It's just kind of weird that someone like you would want to hang out with..." I sigh and cross my arms. "... someone like me."

He laughs and steps next to me, both of us washed in glowing blue light from the aquarium. "I'm very happy to see you again, Christa," he says, reaching out and petting my arm. My knees knock together at his touch.

"I didn't know when we'd get to meet again," he continues, "especially after the way things ended the other night." He smiles tightly and puts his hands in his pockets.

"I'm sorry about that," I reply. "I tried to find you later, but things with Riley got really out of control." I look down at the floor and clench my jaw. "I should have never left with him."

Alden leans against the glass. "No matter; you're here now," he whispers, lifting my chin with his thumb, our eyes meeting. "And you are *very* pretty, standing there in the light like that."

I tremble as he brushes my hair out of my face. I stare deeply into his eyes, noting that our irises are almost the exact same shade of steely-blue.

I snap to attention as a quick rap sounds on the door. A gorgeous girl with pink hair enters, dressed in a black cocktail dress and carrying a tray of drinks. She gives Alden a thousand-megawatt smile and places two glasses of some sort of purple liquid on the desk. "Bruno told me you were back here. Thought you two might be thirsty," she sing-songs through her teeth.

Alden nods and breaks away from me, tapping her elbow familiarly. "Thank you, Cameron. That will be all."

She raises an eyebrow and tucks her tray under her arm. "Of course." She leaves, closing the door behind her.

Alden picks up the glasses and comes back over. "I'm not going to get in trouble with your mother if I offer you a drink, am I?" A wry smile teases his lips as he hands one to me.

I laugh, tossing my bag on the floor behind the desk. "Only if you didn't pour one for her first," I smirk, clinking our glasses together. "Cheers."

He holds his drink thoughtfully against his jaw as I put mine back. The icy liquid burns down my throat. "Strong!" I cough, setting my glass on the desk. "What is that?" I ask, my eyes tearing.

Alden chuckles. "It's called 'Purple Haze.' One of our bartenders invented it." He places his off to the side. "You're supposed to drink it quickly so that it doesn't hurt as much on the way down. Here, try again." He hands me back my glass. I look at him warily before taking a deep breath and shooting the rest of my drink. I clear my throat and nod.

"Better," I rasp.

Alden smiles and sits down on the leather chair, unbuttoning and rolling his cuffs. "Good. Now, why don't you tell me all about how you got that nasty bump on your head." He points, his forehead wrinkling.

"It's nothing. Really, I'm fine," I mutter, flustered that he even noticed.

Alden shakes his head. "It doesn't look like 'nothing,' Christa… Hmm." He spins and glances around the room. "I have to apologize for the lack of seating options around here." He bites his lower lip. "Where are we going to put you? Ah…"

I gasp as he reaches over and swiftly reels me in by the hips, setting me down on the desk in front of him. "That will do nicely," he murmurs, my legs straddled on either side of his. "I can get a good look at it in the light." He stands and angles the lamp closer, his face inches from mine. I catch myself holding my breath as he traces a finger over my forehead.

"Does that hurt?" he asks softly.

My eyelids flutter. "No," I breathe, my thighs pressed around his waist.

He nods and gently tilts my jaw toward the light. "Rough little shiner there," he tuts, offering me his drink. "You look like you need this more than I do."

I purse my lips and take the glass. "I'm never one to say no to free shit." I pitch the whole cocktail back in one swallow, my eyes pinching shut. "Fuck! Still burns…" I start to cough, handing the glass back.

He carefully sets the glass on the desk. "Have you been to a doctor?" he asks. I nod. "Good." He clears his throat and sits. "How did it happen?"

I sigh and lean back on the desk, disappointed that he's no longer touching me. "It happened the night we first met, actually." When his eyebrows raise in surprise, I add, "It's a pretty short story. Riley was pissed about us dancing, so he got really drunk and then got behind the wheel, and my friend and I were in the car." I look down at the desk. "We crashed into a concrete wall, and… that's it." I puff out my cheeks and grimace.

Alden stares at me, his gaze sympathetic. "I'm sorry," he murmurs, taking my hand.

I nod and squeeze back. "It's fine. I'm fine." I shrug. "We really don't need to talk about this right now."

I reach up with my other hand and slowly unzip my jacket, revealing my tight red thermal shirt underneath. I peel off my coat and Alden's lips pucker, his eyes darting between my chest and our fingers clasped together.

"Hm." He lets out a low chuckle. "And this?" he asks coyly, holding up my hand. I squint and then pull it away, noticing that there is still a little blood left on it from earlier.

"Oh shit, sorry… I thought I got all of that in the cab." I try to rub it off with the hem of my shirt. Alden shakes his head, taking my hand back and bringing it to his lips. He slowly kisses and licks the backside, then turns it and draws my fingers into his mouth. I pretty much pass out when he softly nips the fleshy space between my thumb and index finger.

"Oh my God," I pant, my breath ragged. Every part of me feels like it's on fire.

He rests my fingertips between his teeth, considering. "This isn't your blood," he states, his cool blue eyes watching me.

I shake my head feverishly. "What? No, it's not," I slur, suddenly feeling dizzy. I take my hand away. "It's, um… this guy I know…" I lick my lips and look down at the two empty glasses, now spinning, on the desk. "He got hurt earlier… I was… helping him—after he helped me…" I clear my throat and try to focus.

"That was very kind of you," Alden whispers, sitting back in his chair. "I'm sure he was ever so grateful." His mouth twists and he steeples his fingers.

I snort. "Actually, he turned out to be a total whack job… saying all this crazy paranoid crap about angels and demons…" I laugh and grab my forehead. "God, what was in that drink? I'm not usually such a lightweight." I close my eyes and take a deep breath, trying to count the number of drinks I've had since I got here. "Seriously—I feel like I just got hit by a train."

Alden slowly stands again and wraps his arms around me. I slouch against him, thinking how embarrassing it would be to throw up all over his nice shirt. "You're doing just fine," he mutters, holding me upright. "Now, Christa. I need you to think very carefully." I moan as he pushes my hair back. "Did that guy you know… did he give you anything?" he asks, his tone light.

"Nothing but a major headache!" I grunt, pressing my nose into his collar, his burnt paper smell overwhelming me. "I'm sorry, but I think I need to lie down…"

"It would have been small, like a pen or some other knick-knack," Alden continues, keeping me steady. "Think, Christa. This is important."

"What are you talking about?!" I bellow, trying to wave my arms around wildly. Alden startles and leans back. "I thought I came here to have a good time, and all you wanna do is talk about... boring... stuff." I leer up at him, my head pounding. "God, I feel like ass! Was there Wild Turkey in that thing you gave me?"

At that moment, the door bursts open. Alden bolts upright, and I lurch around to see what's going on. Two huge guys in dark suits enter the office, dragging a young black woman between them. She struggles and tries to pull away.

"Get off me! I swear, I am two seconds away from going full-on supernova!" she cries, her whole body shaking. She wrenches her arms free and drops to the floor. The men step back, glancing nervously at the door. She gets up, dusting off her dirty khakis before looking over at us, her hair wild and unkempt.

"What—no!" She gasps, her eyes going wide as she stares at me. I scrunch my nose and teeter on the edge of the desk. "What are you doing here?" she barks. "You can't be here!"

I glare at her belligerently as a figure steps into the doorway. The woman turns, taking an attack stance.

"No one is going anywhere without my say so," replies a gravelly voice. "Least of all you."

We all watch in silence as an old man enters the room. "Hello, Emily," he adds with a grin, stepping toward the woman.

I stare down at the desk and try to get a look at him out of the corner of my eye. He's maybe in his late sixties, but it's hard to tell from his thin, ravaged face. He wears an expensive black suit, his collar buttoned stiffly. I shudder when I see his eyes, which are such a light gray that they're almost invisible.

"Did... did you want us to restrain her, sir?" one of the guys mumbles. Emily hisses and bares her teeth.

"No. As long as we can keep her back here, we should be fine," the old man answers lazily, cracking his knuckles. "Watch the door, Vinny."

The guy on his right leaves, closing the door behind him.

"So glad you could join us," the old man says, reaching out to the captive woman tenderly.

Emily leans back on her haunches, ready to pounce. "You stay away from me, you son of a bitch! Don't come any closer!" She holds her fists up.

The man chuckles and leans against the desk, his back toward Alden and me. "Is that any way to talk to an old friend, Emily? Come on, put your dukes away, and let's talk about it," he drawls, putting his hands in his pockets.

She shakes her head. "We were never friends! Don't even play," she grits out through clenched teeth. "I know it was you! I saw what you did to them!"

The man nods. "Yes, Annie and Samir were very accommodating. So sweet, letting us join in on their Saturday morning. Wasn't that good coffee, Tony?" He turns to his thug.

"Love that French press, sir." Tony replies.

I shift apprehensively on the desk, glancing at the door. "Alden," I rasp. "I want to go…" Alden's eyes, however, narrow as he shakes his head ever so slightly, placing a hand on my shoulder. I look back at Emily, who is now perched on the balls of her feet.

"They mentioned that they met you on their honeymoon… Puerto Vallarta, I think?" the old man continues. "Said you helped them out of a tough spot—something about an attempted robbery?"

The woman sighs and stares down at the floor. "Such courage!" the old man exclaims. "You must have made quite the impact. They said you still stop by for Game Night every Thursday." He grins. "How adorable." He stands up and starts pacing around the room.

"Don't…" Emily snaps, her bottom lip trembling.

The old man clears his throat. "It seems like they're settling into married life nicely." He stops and straightens a picture by the door. "Although, I don't think they'll be getting in the family way anytime soon." The corner of his mouth twitches. "Given Annie's current condition."

Emily bites her lip. "Motherfucker," she curses under her breath.

"The guy cracked pretty quick after that," Tony interjects casually.

The old man nods. "Sure did. Good husband." He moves over to Emily. "But bad news for you."

"You bastard, you'll pay for this—every single one of you!" she snarls, her eyes darting around the room.

The old man arches a brow. "Come now, my dear; you know how this works," he replies smugly. "In this life, there are winners and losers." He flashes his teeth at her. "And, unfortunately, you picked the side that is always running to catch up." He turns and motions dismissively with his hand. Tony nods and takes a step toward Emily.

"NO!" she screams, taking a running leap at the old man. She knocks him to the ground and starts clawing at his face. Tony rushes in and wraps his arms around her waist, tearing her off.

"Don't touch me!" she screeches, flailing at Tony. "You can't do this... Let me go, let me go!"

The old man gets up, several thin lines of blood trickling down his cheek. He sighs and taps Emily's forehead with his pointer finger. In an instant, her whole body freezes, and she falls noiselessly to the ground. I cover my mouth to keep from screaming.

"I thought you had better manners than that, Emily," the old man mutters. He pulls a handkerchief from his breast pocket, wiping the blood from his face. "Guess I forgot who I was dealing with." He nudges her limp body with his toe before turning to Alden, who stands at attention like a solider.

"Working overtime, Mr. Murphy?" He smiles, his teeth weathered and cracked.

Alden nods. "No rest for the wicked, sir," he replies shortly.

The old man scoffs. "Got that right." His light eyes train onto me. "And what do we have here?" he whispers. I try to sit up, but I can't even get my hands underneath me, I'm so dizzy. "Aren't you a rare little thing… We've been waiting a long time for you." He steps over and pets my hair with the palm of his hand. I cringe, scrambling behind Alden.

The man laughs. "What did you do to her, Murphy? She can barely stand up!"

Alden sighs and wraps his arm around my waist. I cling to his protection. "Whatever!" the man continues. "Good work. Take her by the Warehouse later, once you're through with her." He grins maliciously, turning back to his guard. "Everyone'll be real excited."

"Yes, Vesper," Alden murmurs. The man waves toward the door.

"You two clear out. We need the room." He points to the woman on the floor. Tony steps forward and pulls her up, setting her in the office chair. Alden nods and quickly guides me to the door. I spin back around to see Emily's head lolling like a rag doll's, Tony taking a pair of zip ties out of his suit pocket and placing them on her wrists. He looks expectantly at the old man, who gives him a curt nod. I watch in horror as Tony reaches up and backhands her across the jaw, knocking her hard into the leather chair. A tiny wail escapes my lips as the door closes behind us.

"Oh my God… Alden!" I cry, my hands shaking as I hold onto his arm. He steers me past Vinny, who is lounging on the wall outside of the office. He straightens up and nods as we pass.

"Just relax, Christa," Alden mumbles, making a quick turn down another hallway, heading toward what looks like a fire exit. "Let's get you some fresh air."

"What the hell happened in there?" I slur, the old man's pale eyes flashing in my mind. "And who *was* that?"

"Vesper. He's the owner, my boss," he replies calmly, looking straight ahead. He pushes the door open, and a burst of cool night air beckons us into the abandoned back alleyway, the bass from the main room throbbing against the wall. A flight of concrete stairs leads down to the dark alley below, the only light coming from a bulb above the club door. I fill my lungs gratefully and grab onto the railing.

"Seriously, Alden, I'm really messed up," I mutter, holding my head as I watch the ground tilt beneath me.

He snickers and moves in close. "You just need a little fresh air. Give it a minute." He pushes me back against the wall and leans in to kiss my neck, his breath hot on my throat.

I cluck my tongue and give him a small shove. "Stop... I mean, no." I glare up at him. "What happened back there with that girl?"

He laughs. "Don't worry about it." He goes back to my neck, grazing his hand along the waistband of my jeans. His fingers make my skin tingle, but I'm still really freaked about what just happened in the office.

"Hey!" I push him off again.

Alden lets out an exasperated sigh and stares into my eyes. "Yes?" he snaps.

I jut out my chin stubbornly. "Why would they hurt her like that—Emily?" I shake my head. "And what was all that stuff about those other people, Annie and Samir?"

Alden rolls his eyes and steps back. "Probably just an unpaid bar tab!" he exclaims. I cross my arms over my chest. "Happens all the time," he continues. "Bums come in off the street, mooch a bunch of free drinks, and then the staff has to rough 'em up a bit so they stop coming 'round. I promise you, the same thing happens at every club down the street." He sniffs and puts his hands on his hips.

I look down at the sidewalk and tuck my hair behind my ears. "*That* wasn't an unpaid bar tab," I grumble.

Alden sighs. "We're going to have to do this the hard way, aren't we, Christa?" I gawk as he presses himself against me again. "Or maybe I should have said *Sweet Girl...*" he drawls into my ear.

The earth spins beneath me as he whispers the nickname that I haven't heard in almost two years. "Don't call me that!" I grit out, slamming my palms into his chest. "Okay, party's over..." I try to wriggle away, but he has me pinned against the wall. "Let go of me, Alden!" I snap.

He leers at me, his eyebrows raised comically. "I'm sorry, did that hit a nerve?" He laughs, shoving me lightly into the wall. "You were Haloing so bright, I just had to..." He nibbles at my earlobe as bile rises in my throat, remembering that Daniel used the same word outside of the hospital.

"What the hell is this? How do you know about that?" I shout, glued to the wall.

Alden glances up at me. "How do you not? Didn't Danny fill you in on all this? Come on, let's have a look." He grabs my chin and stares into my eyes, his pupils flicking back and forth. "Ahh, I see." He nods and purses his lips. "You never let him get that far—poor sod."

I try to tear my face away. "Don't touch me! And how do you know Daniel?"

Alden rolls his eyes and holds my head in place. "Let's save questions for the end of class, shall we?" He sighs as he pushes his knee between my legs. "And stop squirming around so much, I need to concentrate." He wrinkles his forehead.

"You're crazy!" I sputter, my eyes wild. "All of this—it's a joke, or some city-wide prank." I lurch my shoulders and try to wrestle out of his grasp. "You're all just a bunch of loser fucktards who got bored jacking off, so you decided to go out and mess with defenseless girls. You're disgusting."

Alden chuckles. "I can assure you, Danny and I haven't worked together in years! But *you* would think this is all a joke, the natural-born skeptic that you are." He leans in, tightening his grip at my temples, our noses touching. "I've got it all here on instant replay." He snickers. "Angels aren't real, you're such a liar, you've been working me since day one... *I'm not safe with you...*" He scrunches his nose. "Ouch! Bet that one hit him like a bag of bricks!" He shakes his head, keeping eye contact. "But he did tell you that you were the Catalyst, so that's something."

My knees go weak. "How do you know all this?" I breathe.

He sighs, loosening his hold on my face slightly. "Fine. If it's the role of teacher I must play, it's a task I take on begrudgingly." He clears his throat. "If you had managed to let old Danny finish a sentence, he would have told you that right now... your soul is showing!" He gasps dramatically and wiggles his fingers, stepping back.

I rub my cheekbones tenderly. "What?" I exhale.

He points to my eyes. "The old saying is true: 'windows to the soul'... Currently, yours are putting on quite the show. An unfortunate side effect caused by observing a spontaneous miracle!" His voice twangs like a roadside preacher's. I think back to the hospital and watching Daniel heal, cold dread welling in my stomach.

"That's right, Sweet Girl," Alden twitters, eyeing me intently. "That's the moment! God, front row seats." He laughs, staring into my eyes. I shrink back against the wall, suddenly feeling horribly exposed.

"Anywho... An individual with a certain skillset," he grins ghoulishly and gestures to himself, "and an aptitude for reading souls can really move in and take advantage of a rather... delicate situation." He looms over me. "I can see every dream, desire, fear, memory..." He strokes my cleavage with his forefinger. I bat his hand away. "It's quite intimate," he purrs, undaunted. "You really picked the worst possible place to come tonight."

He steps back and leans next to me on the wall, his arms crossed in front of him.

I glance down the alleyway, debating running for it even though I don't know if my legs can actually run right now, but something holds me in place. I wet my lips and close my eyes. "Are you an Angel, too?" I ask meekly.

Alden puts his head back and roars, peals of laughter echoing off the sides of the dark buildings above us. "Oh, my poor, naive girl!" he simpers after catching his breath. "If you think *I'm* an Angel, then you don't know how much trouble you're really in."

I take a shaky breath. "Then... are—are you a Demon?" I stammer.

Alden rolls his eyes and picks at a cuticle. "What does it matter?" He gazes at me. "You yourself said that none of this is real, just a load of rubbish." He raises an eyebrow.

I bow my head. "I just don't understand how any of this is possible." I rub the bridge of my nose, feeling the start of a splitting migraine coming on. "It goes against everything I ever believed in or knew to be... true, I guess," I whisper.

Alden sighs and pops off the wall. "Yes, yes, we're working against all of the basic laws of nature, cross your heart and close your eyes before taking a leap of faith... I know this is hard for you to make sense of." He paces impatiently. "It would have really been better for all of us if you'd stuck with Danny and had your end-of-innocence moment with him. He has a softer touch." He sniggers, crossing back over to me and placing his fists on either side of my head.

I stare up at him weakly.

"I know you're still coming back from having your mind totally blown," he says, checking his watch, "but there are other pressing matters that I must attend to before getting you over to the Warehouse." He turns my face by the ear.

I shake my head, coming out of my daze. "Wait… no! I'm not going anywhere with you!" I cry, trying to jerk away.

Alden clenches his jaw and rams his knuckles into my hair, my temples caught in a vice-like grip. "I wasn't *asking*," he growls. "Now, stop moving." He sandwiches me against the wall.

I watch him start scanning me again, and I quickly squeeze my eyes shut. "Ah… smart!" he exclaims. "Nice to see you're getting with the program, but I don't have time to play games." He slaps me lightly on the cheeks. I scrunch my nose, keeping my eyes closed.

He takes a step back. "Don't turn into a petulant child on me now, Christa!" he hisses. "Open your eyes like a good girl and let me get a look!" He grabs my chin again, giving it a hard knock. "Show me what I need to know!"

My eyes pop open, and I spit in his face. Alden winces and wipes it away with the back of his hand, then grabs me by the shoulders, slamming the back of my head into the brick. I slump listlessly as little stars erupt in the corners of my vision.

"Lovely," he grimaces, pulling me up. "Jesus, you're tall!" He wheezes as he pushes me back against the wall. "What are you—5'9", 5'10"?" My head bobs from side to side. "You're giving *me* a run for my money… but I bet he likes that, though—someone to dance cheek to cheek with."

He keeps holding me up by the jaw. "Now, if you could just stand still, I can be quick about it! I promise you, I'm *really* good at this." I whimper as the fight goes out of me. He stares deeply into my eyes.

"That's it… Where is it?" he mumbles to himself. His eyes widen. "Well, *that's* fascinating, but not what I want." He rattles my shoulders. "Come on, tell me!"

"She's not a Magic 8 Ball, you know." I hear footsteps coming down the alleyway. I slouch in front of the door as Alden spins around, his eyes searching the darkness.

"At any rate, I think *All signs point to No* right now, so how about you get off her and we'll call it a day?"

Daniel steps out of the shadows, his hands wedged into his jacket pockets. Alden breaks into a maniacal grin and hops down the stairs to the pavement.

"Danny Boy! I was starting to wonder when you'd turn up! Long time, no see!" he shouts, sauntering over to him.

Daniel glances at me anxiously. "You okay, Christa?" he calls.

I nod, rubbing the back of my head. "I'm fine. Just a little fuzzy," I reply, getting to my feet.

Alden chuckles. "You missed out on all the fun, Danny! We had a few drinks, a few laughs... You practically sent her to me gift-wrapped. Thanks for that." He reaches Daniel and pats him playfully on the arm. Daniel's jaw tightens. "I have to say, your new girl here is quite the firecracker... She's game for anything." He leans into Daniel's ear, raising a brow lasciviously, and adds, "I can see why you like her—really high charge. I could barely keep her off of me in the office a while ago, she wanted it so bad."

He winks, smoothing the collar on Daniel's jacket. "Don't worry, I got her all warmed up for you. With a girl like that, it doesn't take much." Alden wrinkles his nose.

Daniel's back has gone rigid. "If you touch her again, I will end you," he whispers. His eyes burn as he stares Alden down.

Alden laughs. "That would be something, wouldn't it? I would really love to see you follow through on that. Hm." He smiles charmingly.

"Come on, Christa. We're going." Daniel keeps his focus on Alden as I start to stagger down the stairs.

"That might prove to be more of a challenge than you think, Danny..." Alden clears his throat and tilts his head toward me as I grasp the railing. I lose my balance and tumble down the stairs, my left elbow crashing into the cement.

"Hey!" Daniel's eyes widen as he dashes over and gently helps me up. "Are you all right?"

I look up at him and smile. "You came back," I murmur, slumping against his side.

He nods and hoists me up, favoring my injured arm. "I should've been here sooner. I'm sorry," he breathes into my hair.

I press my nose against his t-shirt. "You smell *so* good!" I proclaim, relief washing over me as I inhale his familiar warm, spicy scent.

Daniel glares at Alden. "Sorry, she's had *a lot* to drink…" Alden sniggers. "Seriously, put a glass in front of that girl, and it's gone in a flash." He snaps his fingers. "Haven't seen skills like that since before I came ashore…"

Daniel's eyes narrow. "Every time I see you, you become less and less of a human being." He shakes his head, tucking me under his arm.

Alden smiles weakly. "Well, that's not surprising, given your condition. It's a wonder you recognize me at all… Everyday miracles, I suppose."

"What's wrong with you, man?" Daniel suddenly shouts. "You couldn't leave her alone for five minutes? Give her a chance to figure everything out first?" He tightens his grip around me as I start to sway.

"She found me!" Alden bellows in turn, waving his arms. "And she's lucky she did! It could have been a lot worse for her if one of the others had got to her first."

"Oh yeah," Daniel sneers. "Real lotto day. Let's not pretend you're doing me any favors, 'kay, pal?" He turns to me as I nuzzle into his jacket. "Do you think you can walk?" he asks quietly.

I shake my head. "I dunno… I feel so wonky." I close my eyes and rest my head on his shoulder. Daniel runs a hand through his hair.

Alden sighs. "She's going to need to sleep. We could lay her out on one of the couches in the back." He takes a few steps toward us.

Daniel raises a fist. "I swear to God, if you come any closer, I will knock you into next week!" he barks. "You've done enough!" He continues to watch me nervously.

"Come on, Danny! The *Catalyst* shows up all glowy and open for business, and you expect me to ignore that?" Alden snorts and rolls his eyes. "Do you honestly think it was coincidence that she just happened to waltz into the largest Demon club in L.A. while Haloing? Don't you think that says something?"

"It was a mistake!" Daniel yells.

"Or destiny," Alden huffs. "You know this thing can go one of two ways just as well as I do." He leans against the wall, his eyes bright.

"You don't know anything," Daniel mutters. "And roughing her up and pumping her full of booze isn't gonna help your case any." He squeezes me protectively.

"You have your methods, I have mine," Alden says with a simper. "We can't all rely on rock 'n' roll and boyish charm." He stands and puts his hands in his pockets.

I groan and sink down onto one of the stairs. "I just need to sit for a second," I mumble, feeling seasick as the alley rocks back and forth. I wrap my arms around myself and shiver. "God, it's freezing."

Daniel kneels down next to me and takes off his jacket. "Come on, let's get outta here." He snugs me inside his coat, the arms hanging off like a cape. I look up at him and nod.

Alden clears his throat and steps into the center of the road. "Sorry to be the bearer of bad news, but Christa and I have other plans." He looks back at the club door. "They're expecting us over at the Warehouse. Wouldn't want to disappoint."

I turn to Daniel, frantic, and watch as he slowly stands up, careful not to disturb my perch. "Well, you're just going to have to send her regards—because there is no way on this Earth that she is going *anywhere* with you," he seethes, stepping face to face with the other man.

Alden chuckles and crosses his arms. "Tough guy now, huh?" He smiles, pushing back his sleeves. "Is this how it's going to be, Danny Boy? You and I tearing it up like old times? 'Keep 'er light on yer feet, Danny!'" He hops on his toes and tosses a soft punch at Daniel's shoulder.

Daniel stares at him coldly. "Whatever it takes," he rasps.

Alden nods and scratches his ear. "Well…" He grins, pacing back and forth. "I love a good stroll down memory lane as much as the next bloke—" He leans against the alley wall. "—but we both know it would be a bloodbath, and I don't want to embarrass you in front of your girl." He gestures at me.

"You would lose," Daniel growls, his fists tightening at his sides.

Alden laughs. "Really? Hm… There is only one scenario where I can picture that actually happening—and you wouldn't do *that* in front of Christa right now, would you? Put her at risk like that?" He pouts, shaking his head.

Daniel sighs, his eyes darting back to me. "I would never do anything to hurt her." He straightens his shoulders. "But she's not leaving with you." He turns and gives me a small smile.

Alden's eyes narrow. "Interesting," he mumbles, his brows twitching. "Now, when you say 'she,' do you mean 'she, the Catalyst'?" He looks at me. "Or 'she… Christa'?" He raises his eyebrows.

Daniel shakes his head. "What are you getting at?" he grits out. "What does that even mean?"

Alden holds out his hands placatingly. "I'm just curious how much of this is professional interest, versus… personal." Daniel looks away, and Alden shrugs and chuckles. "It makes no difference to me, but I'm sure there are others out there who are determined to have their assets protected only by someone with the… *purest* of intentions."

"Stop," Daniel snaps.

"It's a compliment, really!" Alden protests. "I'm just noting your dedication to this particular case. I can tell that you're really putting *all* of yourself into your work, this time around."

Daniel stares down at the ground, his eyes dark. "Leave, *now*," he hisses.

Alden rolls his eyes and nods. "Fine." He walks toward me. Daniel's head shoots up, a snarl rising in his throat. Alden takes a step back.

"Relax, Danny! I'm just saying goodnight." He leans down and puts his mouth to my ear. "It's been fun, Christa, but I think we should quit while we're ahead." He nuzzles my hair with the tip of his nose. "But don't worry, I'll see you soon. Promise."

I close my eyes and shudder.

"Don't count on it." Daniel moves over to my side.

Alden snickers as he straightens up. "I never make a promise I don't intend to keep." He smiles and gives a small wave. "Until then."

He turns and heads into the dark, his shoes clacking against the pavement.

Once he's gone, I let out a gasp and fling my arms around Daniel's neck. "I'm so sorry!" I bawl, grasping him tightly. "I'm such an idiot! I should have never…" I cough and sputter as snot pours out of my nose.

Daniel leans back and wipes my face with his palms. "Hey! What are you talking about? You don't need to be sorry about anything!" he says sweetly.

I shake my head, tears dripping onto my shirt. "No, I was so mean to you at the hospital! You've been nothing but nice to me, and you helped me, and I should have listened…" I look down at my lap sheepishly. "I owed you that, and instead I messed everything up. I just totally freaked out." My face crumples as a fresh round of sobs comes over me.

Daniel holds me close. "You didn't mess anything up! Come on." He pulls me into his lap and rocks softly. "Anybody who knows about this stuff loses it the first time they hear about it... There'd be something wrong with you if you didn't." He tilts my chin up and grins. "I'm glad you told me to screw off—it means you've got guts!" He holds me a little tighter. "We're gonna need those guts."

I nod and nestle against his chest, reveling in his warmth. "I can't believe any of this is happening," I whisper. "I keep waiting to wake up and learn that it was all a dream, or that I'm stuck in a trick ending to some cheesy sitcom." I look down at my hands.

He sighs and pets my hair. "Me too," he murmurs. "Come on, let me take you home."

I shake my head. "I don't want to go home. I don't want to be alone... not after tonight." I sniffle.

Daniel nods. "Okay, well, unless we want to start paying rent in this alley, we should get outta here." He stands and helps me up, my knees trembling. "I've got a place. It's not far. Do you think you can make it?"

"Yeah, just... we have to go slow," I mumble, taking a few shaky steps.

Daniel smiles and holds my arm. "Take your time. It's not like I've got anywhere else to be—one of the perks of being a dead guy," he jokes.

I roll my eyes. "Okay, that was your one," I tease. "Any more cornball comments like that and I'm calling the whole thing off."

We step out of the alley and back onto the busy main road. He arches a brow and squeezes my arm. "You got it, Christa. You're the boss."

CHAPTER 5

WE HEAD AWAY from Sunset towards downtown, trading the clubs and glitz for old industrial buildings and abandoned sidewalks. If I were alone, I'd be completely terrified by the quiet and emptiness, waiting for something horrible to jump out at me—but right now, I've never felt safer. I weave my fingers through Daniel's as we walk.

"So, how did you find me?" I ask after a bit. "You know, after I left?"

He looks down at me and smiles. "I'm an Angel. We can smell trouble!"

I roll my eyes, and he laughs, nudging me with his shoulder. "No. In all seriousness, I've been able to sense you since the accident." He watches me hesitantly, waiting for my reaction.

"Like... you know what I'm doing all the time?" I blush, trying to recount my every action of the last three days.

Daniel shakes his head. "No, nothing like that!" he exclaims. "I have a general idea of where you are at any given moment, but I don't know what you're doing or how you're feeling, don't worry!" He grips my hand. "It's just one of those things that happens after we help someone; we become... linked, I guess. Just for as long as you need me." He stares down at the sidewalk, adding, "I'm sorry if that makes you uncomfortable. I know it's weird."

I smile and bite my lip. "No, it doesn't," I murmur. "I'm… grateful. It's what saved me tonight." I look up at him and notice that it's now his turn to blush. I clear my throat. "So, are you, like… linked with a bunch of other people right now?" I try to keep my tone casual.

He scratches his neck. "No, just you. I'm yours." He shakes his head, flustered. "Uhh… your Guardian, I mean."

"Of course." I grin.

We're now passing the L.A. Mission; I can hear men's voices cursing and banging on the doors, trying to get in. I look at Daniel and grip his fingers a little tighter. "That's not where we're going, is it?" I ask.

He squeezes my hand reassuringly. "Not tonight! I like the view from the east side of the street much better." He arches a brow as we cross the road, heading down an overgrown sidewalk. A light rain starts to patter around us, soothing on my forehead.

"It's just up ahead." Daniel points to a giant, decrepit factory straight out of *Ghost Hunters*, complete with shattered windows and crumbling brick. I take a deep breath. If I were with anyone else, this would never happen.

"This way," Daniel murmurs, leading me to the back of the building. He crouches down and pries open a broken double-hung window. He hops in and turns to take my hand. "Watch your head," he calls, pulling me in behind him. We're in the basement of the building.

Everything is covered in a thick blanket of dust except for a shoeprint trail that I can make out on the floor, going from the window down a dark hallway. Daniel turns and grimaces. "I'm sorry it's not nicer. All the lights and plumbing were pulled for scrap at some point, but we'll be out of the rain, and it's warm." He looks at his feet.

I take his hand and smile. "It's perfect. After what I've been through tonight, it's like the Ritz-Carlton." We follow the trail of footprints to the back.

"I've never seen anybody else in here. I've checked out upstairs—the flooring is pretty unstable, so it's not exactly a safe spot to crash. Pretty unattractive to most squatters." He shrugs. "This place used to be an old textile factory. There are a bunch of funny clothes from the '50s up there, if you feel like dressing up like *I Love Lucy*." He glances at me and grins boyishly. "I do a pretty mean Desi."

"I'm sure you do!" I laugh. "Maybe later. I'm pretty tired right now." I hold tight to his arm as we shuffle down the hall. I keep listening for the voices of dead factory girls or the whir of an ancient sewing machine. I shiver and pull his jacket tighter around my shoulders.

Daniel glances at me and stops in front of a doorway. "This is it. Hold on—I have a couple candles," he mumbles, slipping inside.

I place my hand on the doorframe as he picks something up off the floor, followed by the click of a lighter. The room fills with a rosy glow as he lights several jar candles that look like they were borrowed from a Mexican restaurant. There is a small window on one of the walls with a view of a streetlamp outside, glittering softly through the rain. In the candlelight, I make out a small chest of drawers with a couple of boxes on top and a twin mattress on the floor; next to it is a formidable stack of paperback books. It's surprisingly cozy, considering that this place was probably condemned fifty years ago. I move into the room and look at Daniel.

"Is this where you live?" I ask.

Daniel nods, stepping over to the dresser. "It's somewhere to hang my hat." He pulls his red knit cap out of the top drawer.

I smile and take it from him. "I was wondering where this was today! You don't look like you without it." I place it on top of his head.

"Ah!" he exclaims as he tugs it down around his ears. "That explains why you freaked out earlier: stranger danger." He raises an eyebrow at me.

I scrunch my nose and pick up one of the candles, walking over to the boxes on the dresser. I take the top off the first box and grin. "Are these records?" I ask, taking a couple out of the box. Led Zeppelin, the Ramones, and, not surprisingly, the Rolling Stones. I lift up the box and take it over to the bed, flopping down unceremoniously.

"I'm shocked you recognize them, being that they don't light up, call outer space, or show you where to find the best tomato soup in town," he jokes.

I roll my eyes and look back around the room. "Do you have a player? Can we listen to one?"

"Ask and you shall receive." He crosses over and rummages through the box, finally picking an album and taking it back to the second box on the dresser. It's a very old record player, the case cracked and covered in dirt.

I glance at him warily. "That thing still works?" I smirk.

He snorts. "Totally! I got a really good deal on this at an estate sale in Encino!" He shakes his head, laying the record on the turntable. "They were practically giving it away, and one man's trash…" He trails off and lifts the needle, the room filling with sweet, jazzy music. He grins smugly. "There we go!"

He hands the cover back and sits down next to me. It's *Astral Weeks* by Van Morrison. I recline back onto the mattress, my head on his pillow. Daniel smiles and pulls a red blanket from the floor, laying it over me and snugging it around my waist. He then leans back against the wall and closes his eyes, listening to the song.

"Do you know this?" he asks quietly.

I shake my head. "No… but I like it." I breathe evenly, letting the music wash over me.

He smiles and nods. "I thought we could use something a

little chill, after tonight." He looks down at his shirt and grunts, noticing that it's still covered in blood from the hospital. He sighs and gets up, going over to the dresser.

"I'm burning through these like a pack of matches! Who knew hanging out with you would be such messy business?" He chuckles, pulling off his dirty shirt and tossing it in the corner.

"Sorry," I snicker. "I'll get you a new one?"

"It's vintage," he sighs. "Irreplaceable." He digs through the drawer.

I smile and prop myself up on an elbow, watching him change. This is the first time I've seen him shirtless, and I catch myself holding my breath. His hair is long and shaggy, brushing his tan shoulders like the hair of one of the rock stars on the backs of his records, and his arms are more built then I'd realized, toned and muscular. The most startling thing about his appearance is the large tattoo scrawled across his entire back. I squint my eyes, trying to focus; it looks like a pair of folded wings. Not fairy wings or bird wings with feathers, but more geometrical—like you could break them down into a series of triangles, polygons, and rectangles. They remind me of a chrysalis or a honeycomb, something an insect would create. It's stunning.

"I like your tattoo," I murmur from the bed.

Daniel turns toward me, a long-sleeved gray thermal shirt in his hands. He blushes and smiles and starts to pull the shirt on over his head. "I can't take too much credit for it; if it had been my pick, I probably would have ended up with, like, a burning skull or a werewolf howling at the moon. Something more hardcore, you know? Something cool..." he mumbles through the fabric.

"Yeah, nothing screams 'cool' like werewolves." I giggle and study his chest, chiseled and smooth, as he pulls the sweater down. I wet my lips as his tight abs flex in the candlelight, my pulse quickening. Before he can tug the shirt over his stomach, I notice three small white scars glowing on his skin a few inches from his navel. I furrow my brow.

"What happened?" I ask, pointing.

"Hm?" He looks down at his new shirt, slightly fitted around the arms and chest and showing off his muscles. He finds a hole at the bottom of the shirt and pokes his finger through it, waggling it at me. He looks up with a grin.

"I know it's not Armani, Christa, but beggars can't be choosers. I actually thought this was a pretty good find…"

He starts to move back toward the bed. I grab his hem and lift it up, exposing the scars on his abdomen. I gently graze them with my fingers. "No, here." Each scar is about an inch long.

He quickly pulls his shirt back down and turns toward the dresser. "*That* is a long story for another time. And we have a lot of other stuff to get to tonight. But first—" He spins back around, holding a jar of peanut butter, a tube of saltine crackers, and a bottle of water. "A good host is always prepared."

My eyes widen with delight, and my stomach rumbles in agreement. I realize I haven't eaten anything since snack time at the hospital, and I'm suddenly ravenous. "Yes, please!" I beckon, and he tosses the crackers to me. I catch them as he opens the peanut butter and sits down again next to me on the bed. I dip a saltine in the jar and shove it into my mouth, licking my fingers as I do so. I can barely contain myself as I devour cracker after cracker, Daniel looking on, bemused. Before I know it, I've eaten almost the entire pack by myself. I glance at Daniel apologetically and offer him the last two crackers.

He laughs and pushes them toward me. "I'm okay right now. Go for it, you need your strength." He twists the cap off the water bottle and hands it to me. I take it and guzzle it back, washing the rest of the peanut butter down. I hadn't realized how worn out I really was, a little food making a big difference.

I cuddle up in the blanket, sated, my mind starting to swim

with questions. I take a deep breath and rub my face with the palm of my hand.

"So… I feel kind of crazy even mentioning it, but I know we have to talk about what happened earlier today," I mutter.

He sighs. "Yeah."

"What you said about being a… being…" I have a hard time saying the word, now that we're sitting here quietly.

"An Angel," he fills in, taking a sip of water.

"Yeah—that." I give an awkward laugh.

"Yes, I remember that moment pretty clearly. I also recall you spazzing out and running away like your hair was on fire." He arches an eyebrow.

I playfully smack his arm. "Um… okay. I had just watched you get stabbed by a crazed lunatic and then shake it off like it was a mosquito bite," I scoff. "I think, all things considered, I handled it pretty well. I'm here now, aren't I?" I twiddle a loose thread on the blanket.

"Yes, you are," he agrees, patting my leg.

I sigh. "So… you're an Angel. Like— pearly gates, playing harps, high fives with Jesus kind of stuff?"

He laughs. "It's a little more complex than that. Technically, I'm a Guardian."

I look at him quizzically. "Yeah, you've said that a few times. What's the difference?"

His eyes shift down to his sneakers, and he starts to fidget with the laces. He takes a breath. "There are three types of Angels," he begins. "The first are the True Angels that God created when He built the Universe." He glances at me. "These are your Archangels, and they pretty much run the show, going around walking on water and setting bushes on fire." He rolls his eyes. "They're arrogant and showy and love their pomp and circumstance—big lights, big sounds… It's sort of like going to a KISS concert any time they appear." He looks at me and smiles. I nod, still not believing this is an actual conversation.

"The second type are the people that led good lives on Earth. When they died, they went straight upstairs and are now happy little worker bees running errands around Heaven," he continues. "They're called the Seraphim, and they generally don't mingle with the mortals." He wrinkles his nose.

"Cuz that would be totally slumming it," I tease.

Daniel chuckles and draws his knees to his chest, clearing his throat. "And the third kind of Angel is a Guardian," he says, tucking his hair behind his ears.

"You mean the best kind." I grin, chucking him on the shoulder.

He nods slowly. "Well... not exactly." He stares down at his lap. "Guardians are people who wasted their lives on Earth. Junkies, prostitutes, petty criminals... a pretty miserable crew." His jaw tightens as he looks up at me hesitantly. "When they die, they don't go to Heaven, but instead are given a chance to redeem themselves by serving in the mortal world, saving people. Physically saving lives, but also helping people navigate the murky waters of... moral ambiguity, I guess." He grimaces. "So, that's what I'm doing, what I've been doing." He sits back and crosses his arms, watching me out of the corner of his eye.

I purse my lips. "Does that mean you were a bad person when you were alive?" I ask after a moment, looking at my hands.

Daniel sighs. "I, um... could have been better," he answers. "But I'm not that person anymore, Christa! You have to believe me on that." He reaches over and takes my hand.

I nod and smile at him. "I know... or, at least, I think I know." I exhale and pull my hand away. He looks at me expectantly. "This is all just a lot to take in."

Daniel nods. "I know. You're doing really well." He squeezes my foot through the blanket.

I frown. "So, how does this work? Will you ever get to go to Heaven? Or are you just… stuck here?"

"Yes!" he grins. "Once a Guardian proves themselves worthy, they Ascend into Heaven. Until then, we wander the human world looking for people to help." He smooths his jeans. "We try to blend in as best as possible. The more invisible you are, the better. Think janitors, car valets, the homeless." He gestures to himself.

I frown. "Homeless like that guy from the hospital, Zompocalypse? He knew what you were. He called you 'Guardian' the first time we saw him." I look at Daniel inquisitively. "Is he… *was* he a Guardian, too?"

Daniel takes a deep breath. "No. He's not. He's Smudged." He rubs his jaw. "He's a human who's addicted to Demon blood— really nasty stuff. Makes them slaves to their Demon masters, or Pets."

I shiver. "He… *drinks* Demon blood? That is so disgusting."

Daniel shrugs and sighs. "He's just as much a victim as the other people we're trying to save. We try, but we can't get to them all in time." He stares at the wall for a minute before going on. "Anyway, it's easier to go unnoticed when people are consciously trying *not* to look at you. It makes slipping into a drug den or pulling someone from the Pacific a lot easier."

"Or saving someone from a burning car wreck." I sigh, leaning back into the pillow. "So, it's kind of like Angel Rehab," I add thoughtfully.

He laughs. "Yeah, I guess." He leans against the wall. "I never really thought about it that way, but—sure." He smiles at me.

I bite my lip. "I mean, really, you couldn't have been *that* bad. Because… there is worse, right?" I look up at him, my face pinched.

Daniel's jaw tightens. "Yes, there is," he whispers.

I take a breath. "Alden. He's a Demon." I look at him gravely.

Daniel nods. "Yes." He keeps his eyes trained on the floor.

I scooch up, crossing my arms. "Well, how did that happen? Was he alive before, too? Or was he always a Demon?"

Daniel shakes his head. "Demons were all human, once." He sits on the edge of the bed. "They are the broken, the hopeless... the irredeemable." His eyes crinkle. I hold my knees. "When they die, they go straight to Hell, and only the smartest and most manipulative are allowed to work on Earth." He gives a little huff. "And Alden... is one of their best." He grabs the cracker wrapper from the bed and starts folding it into little squares.

I inch next to him. "It seemed like you two know each other," I murmur. "Tonight wasn't the first time you've met."

He shakes his head. "Yeah, we go way back." He rolls up the wrapper and tosses it at the wall. "We knew each other... before." He looks down, his face pinched.

"When you were alive?" I whisper. He nods. I reach over and rest my hand lightly on his shoulder.

Daniel exhales. "But like I said, *I* was different, he was different... Everything's changed. Since we've both crossed over, it's been one messed up game of cat and mouse after another." He snorts. "And now that he's sure you're the Catalyst and he knows we're together, it's only gonna get worse... Blood in the water." He looks at me.

I shake my head. "Yeah—about that. How is everyone so sure *I'm* the Catalyst?" I shrug. "And what does that even mean?"

Daniel laughs. "Well, for starters, you're *glowing*." He grins. "Kind of hard to miss."

He rolls his eyes and lies down next to me as I gasp and check my skin. I'm the same pasty shade I've been since mid-October. "No, I'm not!" I exclaim, holding up my arm. "Looks pretty normal to me!"

Daniel shakes his head and gently pushes my arm back. "Like the Vegas strip," he says with a smile. "*You* can't see it. You can't see any of us Angels and Demons... Your sight is still untouched."

I narrow my eyes. "Wait—you look different, too?"

He nods. "Yeah." He scratches the side of his head. "I'm still trying to figure out why you can't see any of us. Must be important…" He purses his lips.

I sigh and run my hands through my hair. "So what? I'm some weird shiny girl now who hangs out with the undead? This is so screwed up." I shrug irritably.

Daniel smiles and snuggles down on the pillow next to me. "I prefer 'mortally challenged.'" His mouth twitches.

I roll my eyes. "Seriously, Daniel! What does any of this mean? It seems pretty clear what you do… and what Alden does." I grimace. "But what am I? What does the Catalyst do?"

Daniel stares at me, sighs, and props himself up with the heel of his hand. "I don't know. I'm sorry," he murmurs. "I don't know anything except that you're incredibly special and need to be protected." He looks down at the blanket. "But I knew that from the first moment I saw you, Catalyst or not."

I blush. "Alden seemed to know more, back in the alley," I whisper. "Something about this thing going one of two ways… What did he mean by that?"

Daniel huffs and lays back on the bed. "He's all talk! He doesn't know anything that the rest of us don't." He shakes his head. "Demons are really good at puffing themselves up and making everybody else look like a bunch of amateurs, but everything they do is completely self-serving. At best, they speak in half-truths, twisting words around to get what they want." He looks at me severely. "It's their greatest weapon, Christa; never forget that, okay?"

"Okay," I mutter. He nods and crosses his arms, settling back into bed, his eyes closed.

"I just wish I knew more," I breathe, leaning back on my elbows. A lightbulb goes off in my head. "Hey." I pat Daniel on the chest. "Am I still Haloing?"

He sighs and opens his eyes. "Yes," he answers slowly. "You've probably got another couple hours left. It should fade by morning."

I shift toward him, the blanket cinching around my waist. "Well, maybe you could, I dunno, take a look?" I ask.

He frowns. "That's how it works, right?" I continue. "Maybe there is something in there that could tell us more about what I am, what I'm supposed to be doing." I raise my eyebrows.

Daniel turns to face me. "You don't really want me to do that." He clenches his jaw. "That's private."

I fidget with the blanket. "Alden seemed to learn a bunch of stuff pretty fast," I whisper, shuddering at how he turned my dad's nickname for me into a dirty word. "It just seems like, I don't know, he has an advantage over us now."

Daniel sighs and sits up. "Maybe. But just because he might know something we don't doesn't mean we should stoop to his level." He shakes his head. "I'm not going to... *violate* you like that, Christa! I can't." He shrugs and looks away.

I sit up and touch his arm. "It wouldn't be like it was with Alden," I murmur. "I... I want you to."

His face softens as he stares down at his knees. "You don't know what you're asking for, Christa," he sighs. "Every dream, every secret, it's on full display—your entire past and pieces of your future." I rock back onto the pillow, and he turns to me, voice rising. "Do you really want all of that out there?"

I look down at the blanket. "It's already out there," I grumble. "There's a deranged Irishman walking around right now who's already seen all my insides—except I didn't *ask* him to do it. He just went in and did what he wanted." I squeeze my shins. "So, maybe now I want to be the one who gets to decide who looks and who doesn't, and, in the end, *I'm* the one who gets to play Sherlock Holmes... Is that so much to ask for?" I glare at Daniel.

He sighs and sits back up, resting his head against the wall. "No," he whispers, "it's not."

I nod. "And it's not something I can do by myself, right? Can't just look in a magic mirror?" When he shakes his head, I add, "Okay, so I need you." I reach out and take his hand. "I know you won't hurt me."

He closes his eyes, taking a breath. "All right, fine," he mutters.

I grin and clutch his fingers. "Ahhh, awesome!" I squeal, my mind suddenly ablaze with possibilities.

As Daniel nods begrudgingly, I sit up on my knees and straighten my shoulders. "Okay, so... is this good?" I jut out my chin and shake out my arms. "Or do I need to be standing?" I start to get off the bed.

Daniel sighs and rubs the bridge of his nose. "Just relax for a second, okay? You don't need to go jumping around like a kid on a pogo stick."

I freeze and stare at him intently. He scratches the side of his neck and points, muttering, "Where you are is fine. Just don't move around too much."

I sit back on my haunches and try to breathe evenly through my nose. Daniel grunts and sits next to me on the edge of the bed. I smile as he gently places his hands on either side of my face. "I hope you like this as much as you think you're going to," he smirks.

I slap his thigh. "Come on, this is cool!" I warble. When he rolls his eyes, I add, "You could at least pretend to be excited! I *am* letting you into my innermost thoughts."

He sighs. "Anything in particular you want me to look for?"

I stop and think. "Well, anything about being the Catalyst, of course," I reply. "That's the most important thing. And maybe... if I'm ever going to be rich and famous?" I gasp. "You can do that, right? Tell my future? Am I going to have five kids? Who am I going to marry? Oh my God, it better not be Riley... or Ethan Liu. He is so gross!" I wrinkle my nose. "Will I honeymoon *on* the moon?" My eyes go wide. "How old will I be when I die?"

"Stop!" Daniel winces. "It doesn't really work that way." He speaks softly, cradling my chin.

I roll my eyes. "Well, come on! You gotta give me something! I thought you said you could see pieces of people's destinies…"

"You can—but that stuff's not as clear as things that have already happened or are happening." He smiles weakly, then sits up and straightens my head. "Okay, are you ready?" When I nod, he sighs and says, "Let's take a peek."

I quiet down and settle into his hands as he stares deeply into me. I watch his eyes flicker back and forth, his brown irises shining. I return his focused gaze, trying my best not to fidget. His pupils dart faster and faster, like they're devouring the entire *Harry Potter* series all at once. His breathing grows ragged, and I can feel heat rolling off of his skin as he leans in closer until our noses are touching. The rest of the room falls away, and I feel naked, never having stared anyone in the eyes for this long in my life. Part of me wants to look away out of modesty, but I force myself to stay still. Little droplets of perspiration break out on his forehead, his eyes still locked onto mine.

"Daniel?" I whisper after a while when my back starts to get sore. He doesn't answer, just grips my jaw a little tighter. I reach up and grab his wrists. "Can you hear me?"

His eyes keep scanning.

"Okay, I think that's enough…" I try to pry his hands away, but his fingers are rigid and unmoving.

"Daniel!" I cry, my tone panicked. "That's enough!" I push him hard in the chest, and he falls backwards, his head cracking against the wall. He lays there stunned, his chest heaving up and down.

"Oh my God, Daniel?" I scramble over to him. His limbs are splayed across the bed like a starfish as he stares glassy-eyed at the ceiling. "Daniel, talk to me!" I shout, lightly slapping his cheek.

When he startles and springs up, I fall back against the blanket, my heart racing. "How long was I gone?" he gasps, looking frantically around the room.

I shake my head. "What? Daniel, it's been like… ten minutes. What are you talking about?" I reach out and touch his arm. He flinches and bares his teeth, his face feral.

"Hey!" I lean back. "Calm down! Everything is cool!" I hold my hands up placatingly. "What the hell happened in there?"

He puts his face in his hands and runs them back through his hair, the nape of his neck damp with sweat. "Christa," he whispers, his head bowed.

I inch over to him and carefully take his hand. "Yeah, it's me." I cringe. "For a second there, it seemed like you forgot that." Oh my God, I broke my Angel. I squeeze his fingers, adding, "Are you okay?"

He stares down at the floor, his shoulders trembling. "Yeah," he mutters after a minute. "I'm fine." He pulls his hand away and tucks it between his knees.

I close my eyes and sigh. "You don't seem fine, Daniel," I murmur. I look around the room. It's quiet, the record now finished and spinning silently around the turntable, the needle catching every couple of rotations. I get up and switch off the player.

"Are you going to tell me what you saw?" I ask, turning to face him.

Daniel gazes up at me, his face pale. "Nothing. I saw nothing." He coughs.

I run my hands through my hair, frustrated. "How is that possible?" I bark, slapping my leg. He looks away. "No… Come on, Daniel! *That* was not nothing," I snap. "Something obviously happened in there, or you wouldn't be so messed up."

He exhales and claws at his legs. "Okay, yeah, I saw some stuff," he spits, "but nothing like what you were looking for." He clenches his jaw. "There wasn't anything about you being the Catalyst or what you're supposed to do next, no yellow brick road…"

My shoulders sag as he flops down and punches the pillow into place under his head. "But… there should be something," I whisper, leaning against the dresser. "If I'm really the Catalyst, then it's a part of me. It should be there!" I shake my head. "Maybe you didn't do it right, or you missed something," I quickly audit.

Daniel snorts. "Oh, I didn't miss *anything*." His tone is mean. "No, something you need to understand about the guys upstairs, Christa," he points at the ceiling, "is that they like to keep you guessing 'til the last possible moment and then drop a piano on you, just to see how you'll deal with it." He grits his teeth. "That's the cold truth."

I narrow my eyes. "Why are you acting like this? I don't understand." I cross my arms. "If anyone should be upset, it should be me." I scuff the dresser with the toe of my boot. "Did you… um… see something you didn't want to see?" Like me and Alden in the office at Trinity? I grip his jacket around me tightly.

He closes his eyes. "I just don't know what I'm supposed to do, how to even stop it. It's… it's all I can see, now," he whispers.

I moan and tug my hair. "God, Daniel—I'm sorry!" I exclaim. "What happened with Alden meant nothing! I hate that you even saw me like that with him… but there is nothing I can do about it now." I bite my nails. "It happened and it's over, and we just have to move past it."

Daniel furrows his brow and stares up at me. "What? No!" He shakes his head fervently. "This has nothing to do with him! I don't care about that. I barely looked at that." He sits up.

"Well then, what the hell?" I cry. "You're making me feel really bad. Ugh," I moan. "This was a mistake."

He twists towards me, his eyes sad. "Whatever you saw in there changed things… and not for the better." I put my hands in my pockets and look at the floor. "Like, you see me different now or something. You don't…" I sigh. "… *like* me anymore."

He exhales and rests against the wall. "That's not it at all,

Christa." He stares at me. "You did nothing wrong. I'm sorry." He hangs his head. "It's fine, none of this matters." I look at him, confused, as he gives me a small smile. "I'm sorry if I scared you earlier, when I was coming out of it. I was a little… disoriented." He scratches his ear.

I shrug. "It's okay," I murmur, eying him warily. "You obviously weren't yourself, and I get that it's an intense experience."

He nods and pats the bed beside him. I shuffle back over and perch on the edge. "So." I clear my throat. "I know there wasn't anything on being the Catalyst, but what *did* you see?" I pick at a small hole in my jeans. "You were in there for a while… Something must have happened." I take a breath. "I hope you didn't dwell too long on my middle school years. Those were pretty painful."

He takes my hand. "I saw a lot. I went back to the day you were born and worked my way forward. I saw you as a little girl with your parents, playing, growing up." He smiles. "I watched you start school with your friend Jodie, skin your knee when you fell off the jungle gym, almost miss school pictures in 6th grade when you couldn't get your locker open…" Tears sting my eyes. "Oh, wow." I clear my throat. "God, I was such a dork… Did you, um, see the one where I colored my nana's leather couch with permanent marker?" I wrinkle my nose. "I got in pretty big trouble that time."

He squeezes my fingers. "I saw… I saw the stuff about your dad—what happened…" he murmurs.

I pull my hand away, drawing my knees to my chest. "I don't know why that'd be worth looking at," I grumble. "Just a… shitty time with shitty memories." I clench my jaw.

"It was kind of a big deal, Christa," he whispers, touching my shoulder. I shrug away.

"Whatever," I snap. "None of that has anything to do with what's happening now."

He takes a breath. "Okay… I just didn't know if there was

anything *you* wanted to talk about, like what went down with your mom…" He fades off.

I spin around, my mouth twisted. "When did this turn into a therapy session?" I hiss. "The only reason I let you read me at all was to find out stuff about being the Catalyst, and there was nothing, so we're done!" He looks down at his lap. "I didn't let you in so that you could take a tour and play *This is Your Life.*" I shake my head.

Daniel leans back against the wall and folds his hands calmly. "Hey, I get it. I *know* this stuff's private—but let's remember who asked me to look in the first place." I roll my eyes. He sighs. "I just thought, if you *wanted* to talk about it…"

"He died, okay?!" I yell, my voice cracking. "It was a plane crash, and it was sudden, and I never got to say goodbye."

Daniel looks at me, his eyes soft.

"And he would've never been on that flight if it wasn't for my mom," I huff. "Three days before he was supposed to leave for Shanghai, he found out she'd been sleeping with some loser she met at Whole Foods." I pause to sneer. "They had this huge fight, and he was devastated and decided to take an earlier flight to give them both some space to think about stuff." I look down at the floor. "Next thing you know, there's a tropical storm over the Pacific and his plane is never heard from again." I pause and clear my throat. "In the beginning, I thought there was a chance that maybe he was stranded on a desert island like in *Lost* or something, but… it's been two years. He's never coming back."

"I'm sorry," Daniel murmurs. I shake my head and then look at him, my eyes suddenly growing wide.

"But… maybe…" I take a breath. "Maybe he did come back!" Daniel cocks his head. I jump up from the bed excitedly. "Like you! Maybe he's out, wandering around, saving the world—trying to find me!" I crouch down and take Daniel's hands.

He looks at me sadly. "Christa, that's not what happens…"

I let out a gasp, grabbing my hair. "No, really! He was a super great guy! He's probably saved like... a bunch of people and has been trying to work his way back to me to tell me he's okay..." I trail off as I watch Daniel's face.

"Christa..." he breathes, trying to pull me in.

I shake my head and slump back down. "No, you're right." I look away. "It's crazy."

He puts his hand on my back. "It's not crazy," he murmurs.

I bat him away. "No, forget it. I just want to believe every little kid dream I had for two years. It was a stupid idea." I wipe under my eyes with the back of my hand.

I hear Daniel sigh behind me. "No, it's not," he whispers. "It's just a highly unlikely one."

I turn to him, my face pinched. "Do... do you think he remembers me?"

Daniel smiles. "I can promise you that wherever he is, he remembers you." He loosely circles his fingers around wrist. "You are impossible to forget."

I nod and exhale. "God, I'm such a freak." I clear my throat. "Well, to finish a really crappy story, my mom totally spiraled after that. Burned through all of the insurance money, started drinking..." I breathe slowly. "She lost her job, we lost our house. Fortunately, my dad had all my school money in a trust, so I didn't have to leave Sacred Heart, but still... everything is just... jacked." I stare at Daniel. "And we've been at odds ever since."

He sighs and sits up. "She didn't kill him, Christa," he murmurs. "You have to forgive her."

I snort. "It's not that simple, is it, Daniel? Before I forgive her, I probably need to stop hating her. And I don't know if I can do that right now." I look away as he moves over to me.

"Maybe you don't have to do it all at once. Just start small." He sweeps my hair away from my face. "Not just for her, but for you, too." He shakes his head. "That kind of anger, it'll eat you alive."

I rest my cheek against his palm. "It's the only thing I have that's mine," I croak. "If it's gone… there'll be nothing left of me."

"That's not true." He grins, running his thumb along my cheekbone. "You're smart, you're brave, and you've got a killer right hook, that's for sure." He chuckles.

I shake my head and lay down. "I'm not brave. I just have a really strong sense of self-preservation." I take off his jacket and set it at the end of the bed, tucking the blanket back around me as Daniel lies down next to me. "Not like you."

He laughs. "Like me? What do you mean?" We snuggle together on the small bed, the blanket serving as a very weak barrier between us. I gaze into his eyes.

"Let's see… You've saved my life a couple of times now." I smile. "You went head to head with a vicious Demon without even thinking about it, brain-traveled on a maiden voyage through my messed-up mind… and you got stabbed by Zompocalypse earlier and didn't break a sweat." I shake my head. "I um… I didn't get a chance to say thank you for what you did for me at the hospital." I can still see Zompocalypse frothing at the mouth as he runs at me with that scalpel. I cuddle up and lay my cheek on Daniel's chest and listen to the soft thump of his heart beating against my ear. "He must have gotten you where it counts. There was so much blood…" I shiver.

He rests his hand on my hair. "Ach… just a flesh wound," he says, repeating the same stupid Schwarzenegger joke from the other night. I roll my eyes as he chuckles. "It's yours, anyway," he whispers.

I look up at him, my eyes soft. Daniel blushes. "I mean… it doesn't do me a whole lot of good to have a fully working heart if you're not okay. Part of the whole making sure you stay alive thing."

I nod and purse my lips. "I get it... the Guardian thing." I exhale. "Well, you're still the bravest person I've ever met, truly."

He stares at the wall. "I don't deserve that. I haven't always been—not when it really counted." The corners of his eyes crinkle.

I brush the side of his face with my fingers. "Looks like I'm not the only one who needs to do some forgiving," I whisper.

He nods. "Maybe." He exhales, his eyelashes fluttering. "Something to work on tomorrow."

I roll over and tuck my backside into him, his breath warm on my neck. We both fall asleep to the sound of the rain.

*

I wake to bright sunlight pouring through the window above us, tiny dust particles floating through the air like snowflakes, illuminated as they drift lazily around the room. I steal a quick peek at Daniel, still fast asleep. His mouth hangs open, and I can see his eyes moving behind his eyelids. He's dreaming. I smile and draw in a heavy breath, last night feeling like it's a million years away. It still doesn't feel real... I keep waiting to wake up and be back in my apartment, hitting the snooze button on the alarm. I lay back on the pillow and hold my hand out in front of my face, my fingers glowing in the backlight.

"No need to call Ripley's just yet," I sigh, glancing back at Daniel. "I wish I could see what you see."

I roll over and look down at the books on the floor, the one he was reading yesterday on top of the stack. I pick it up: Kurt Vonnegut's *Breakfast of Champions*. The pages are yellowed and frail, so it was most likely a bargain bin garage sale find. I flip through it for a minute before setting it back on the floor. I grab the next one off the pile and raise my eyebrows.

The leather cover is faded and peeling; I can just make out the words *See You in San Antonio!* embossed across the front with a weathered picture of a desert sunset. I open it.

It's some sort of travel journal, but instead of old pictures and captions, the pages are filled with people's names. The slant of the handwriting makes it feel very private. I check Daniel one more time, seeing that he's still sleeping soundly with his arm draped over his forehead. I wriggle into a sitting position, carefully holding the journal under my side in case he wakes up.

The first page is dated June 18th, 1982. It's a list of eight names: *Daniel, Oppa, Rita, Chef, Francois, Ramos, Jillian, Alden.*

The last one reads like a punch in the gut. I flip forward a few pages, trying to figure out the meaning of the names. The dates are sporadic, moving forward in time with no apparent pattern, the only constant being that they always begin with Daniel's own name. As the dates progress, the lists change. At first, he starts to lose names off of the original list, but then, in the 1990s, it begins to grow again, with new names added like Pete, Elenore, and Lena. The longest entry is on April 3rd, 2005 with 24 names. I flip to the most recent entry, dated November 14—three nights ago, the night of my accident. There are a bunch of names that I don't recognize, followed by the only ones that remain from the original list:

Rita-Jillian-Alden

At the bottom of the page, under Alden's name, is one that looks like it was quickly scribbled in: *Christa*. My breath catches in my throat, my heartbeat quickening at the sight of my name written in his handwriting. I trace the letters softly with my finger. I flip back to the front and see a series of numbers written on the inside cover. It's someone else's handwriting, more curved and flowery, and it lists seven numbers… a phone number.

I feel Daniel shift next to me and quickly drop the journal onto the floor. I pick up the Vonnegut book again and open to a random page.

"Morning," Daniel yawns, stretching his arms over his head. I rustle back around and snuggle into the crook of his arm, resting the book on his chest.

"Morning," I reply.

He sniffs drowsily and looks down at the paperback. "Oh man, how long have you been awake? Sorry, I don't usually sleep in." He sits up and rubs his eyes.

I smile and hold the book in my lap. "It's fine. Gave me a chance to catch up on my reading." I slowly readjust my back and wince as I try to work out a twinge in my neck. "You've got quite the library going." I gesture as I place the book back on top of the pile.

Daniel nods, sliding out of bed. "Yeah. They keep me company at night. Usually, I don't sleep very well." He stands and shakes his arms, glancing out the window at the early morning sunshine. "Oh, okay, well, it doesn't look too late." He crouches down and stares me in the eye, his brow crinkled.

"All right, looking pretty and blue... and officially done Haloing." He smiles and bites his lip, kneeling back on the floor.

I look at him expectantly. "Which means...?"

"Which means we can go out!" he proclaims. "You must be starving." He reaches under the mattress.

"Um, I could eat." I grin. "Like—a horse or two."

"I've gotcha covered." He smiles and reaches under the mattress to pull out a couple of crumpled dollar bills. "Little did you know that you were sleeping on a small fortune last night... Breakfast is on me." He laughs.

I shake my head. "Where does an Angel get cash from? Noah's Rainy Day Loans? Some special ATM with a crucifix on it?"

He laughs and taps his nose. "Ha. No... in between saving the world and hanging out with you, I work the line at a Chinese take-out." He shrugs.

I chuckle. "You *do* have mad cooking skills."

He gives a little bow. "Thank you. Can't let them go to waste!"

He shoves the money into his back pocket. "I never make much, but they pay in cash and don't ask too many questions. It's an honest living." He snags his hat from the dresser and grabs my hand, pulling me toward the door. "Come on, there's somewhere I really want to take you."

I twist back, scanning the room. "Yeah, just a sec…" He smiles as I grab his jacket from the end of the bed and shrug into it, tucking my hair back.

"Have you seen my bag?" I ask. Daniel shakes his head. I step over and check behind the bed. "Did I leave it in the cab?" I murmur, pursing my lips.

"I dunno. I'm sure it'll turn up." He drums his fingers on the doorframe. "Ready?"

I nod slowly. "Yeah, let's go."

We leave the factory and walk a couple of blocks before jumping on a bus, heading back to the coast. It's an early Sunday morning with no traffic, the sky crystal clear. When we pass Santa Monica Pier, I know we are on our way to the beach. The bus comes to a stop, and Daniel stands, taking my hand.

"This is us!" He thanks the driver and we get off, the cool ocean air ruffling through my hair. We take the bridge over Ocean Drive and head toward a bright yellow food truck parked a few feet from the beach. I smile at Daniel.

"Is this it?" I ask.

He nods. "You're gonna love it." He knocks on the side of the truck. "Hey, Benny!"

We walk around to the window. Inside is an Asian guy wearing a black baseball cap and working over a hot grill. His arms, neck, and face are covered in tattoos, and a cigarette hangs off his lip. He looks up and grins at Daniel, reaching out from the truck and high-fiving him in greeting.

"Hey, look what the tide dragged in! Daniel, my man! Howzit? Whatchu been up to?" the guy calls out, returning to the griddle.

"Oh, you know, little of this, little of that... Trying to stay out of trouble," Daniel replies.

"And failing, I'm sure," the guy laughs, his voice rough and gravelly. He glances down at me. "How'd you con this pretty little thing into hanging out with your sorry ass?" He smiles.

Daniel grins from ear to ear. "I told her I'd get her the best breakfast in town."

"Well then, you came to the right place." The guy nods in approval.

Daniel clears his throat and looks at me. "In continuing with your culinary education, Ms. Nichols, may I present to you, Master Chef Benny Woo, maker of the finest Hawaiian cuisine you'll find this side of Oahu. Benny, this is Christa. " Benny gives a short wave with his spatula. I nod shyly.

"You stayin' busy?" Daniel calls up to Benny.

"Oh, for sure. I've been parkin' the truck outside of Grauman's during lunch, and the tourists have been goin' loca over my stuff. Pretty quiet so far today, though— you guys are my firsts this morning." He lights another cigarette and pours a little more oil on the grill, looking over at me. "You like pineapple, Christa?" he asks.

"Sure," I answer.

"Good, cuz just about everything here's got pineapple on it. You want the regular, Daniel?"

"Yeah, thanks, man. She'll have the same."

"You got it, brother. Comin' right up." He turns away, and we lean against the truck, the metal warm from the grills going inside.

"So, you *do* have other friends." I giggle. "Not a total loner, apparently."

Daniel chucks me with his shoulder. "What can I say, I'm a

popular guy!" He cocks his head. "You should feel honored to be in my presence."

I raise my brows. "Um, yeah, okay." I snuggle close to his side.

After a few minutes, Benny whistles to us. Daniel reaches up and takes two cardboard plates, their contents steaming and crackling. He hands the food to me and then pulls out some cash from his back pocket.

Benny shakes his head. "You know the rules, *Hoaloha*. On the house." He grasps Daniel's hand and gives him a light fist bump.

Daniel bashfully looks down at his sneakers. "Thanks, Benny... That's really cool of you."

Benny laughs. "I'm a cool guy. You two *eat*, enjoy. Put a little meat on those bones." He starts cleaning the griddle with a wet washcloth. "Skinny cats!" He shakes his head. "It's un-American."

Daniel waves and points to Benny's cigarette as we start to walk off down the beach. "You know those'll kill you," he teases.

Benny winks. "It's *my* truck. Only place left you can still smoke in L.A."

We move toward the water and find a nice spot to sit. I hold my plate up to my chin, trying not to get sand in my food. Benny made us egg and pulled-pork breakfast burritos, garnished with grilled pineapple, avocado, and some kind of crazy red sauce. It's possibly the most delicious thing I've ever eaten. I glance back at the food truck.

"Does Benny know? About you, I mean," I ask in between bites.

Daniel wipes a little grease from his fingers onto his jeans. "No, but, every once in a while, I think he suspects something—particularly since he keeps getting older, and I... well... don't." He peeks over at me before going back to his food.

I stop eating and blink, processing what he just said. I stare at him in his tight blue jeans and surfer boy hair. I have no idea how old he really is.

"Anyway, I helped him out of a jam a few years back, and we've been friends ever since." He nods. "He's really cleaned up his act since I've known him. Went to culinary school, started his own business. He's a super talented guy." He takes a sloppy bite out of his breakfast, sauce running down his chin.

I relax and shake my head. "And the free burritos don't hurt." I laugh, offering him a napkin.

"One of the perks of the job!" he slobbers, pushing the rest of his food into his mouth.

I arch a brow and inhale mine in about four bites, practically licking the little cardboard plate clean. "That was insane." I sigh and stretch back on the sand, feeling happy to be fat and full. Daniel lounges next to me, propping his head up on his hand and looking down the beach.

"This is one of my favorite places to hang out. Good food, good views… Look, you can see all the way down to Malibu today." He points to the cliffs in the distance. I turn my head dreamily. It's a little overcast and cool, not uncommon for this time of year. I pull his jacket around me and sit up. We have the beach all to ourselves right now, like we're the only people that ever existed. I look over at Daniel, who is staring wistfully out at the ocean, his light hair blowing in the wind. It's a perfect picture, minus the red sauce he dripped on his shirt. I snicker and point to it. He glances down and clucks his tongue.

"Man, this is getting ridiculous!" He wets a napkin on his lips and tries to rub the spot away.

"Can't take you anywhere," I giggle.

"Guess not," he replies, giving up.

I raise a brow. "Looks like you'll have to make another trip to Good Will. Find another gem like that tea cozy on your head." I tug flirtatiously at his hat. "Where did you get this thing, anyway? Dumpster diving? Or did an old lady accidentally leave it on the bus one day, and you didn't take it to Lost and Found?" I purse my lips.

"Ha ha." He stops and squints out at the water. "Actually, it was my mother's."

I blanch, embarrassed, and clear my throat. "I'm sorry, I didn't know," I murmur.

He bumps me with his knee. "Hey, don't worry about it. It *is* pretty terrible," he says with a laugh, pulling it from his head. "But it's the only thing I got to keep from before, along with that." He jerks his head at me in his jacket while he picks a little lint off the cap. I glance down at the tarnished buttons. "Despite everything that's happened, I just can't bring myself to get rid of it." I watch his hands toss the ugly hat back and forth. Everything I know about him could fit inside of it.

"What was her name? Your mom, I mean," I ask quietly.

He puts his cap back on. "Rita."

A little bell goes off in my head: it's one of the names from the journal. I itch to ask more, but don't want to give away that I was snooping. "What was she like?" I say instead with a smile.

Daniel sits up and grins. "She was a ballbuster." He stares out at the water. "From what I can remember… she was really driven and didn't take crap from anyone. She knew what she wanted, and she went out and got it." He nods. "You would've liked her. The two of you have a lot in common." He waggles his eyebrows at me.

I grin. "Yeah?"

"Yeah. You actually remind me a lot of the girls back home— kind of tough, cool…" He smiles, pushing his hands down into the sand behind him.

Now we're getting somewhere. "And where's that?" I ask.

"New York. Queens, born and raised!" he exclaims, kicking sand on my boot. "You finally got it out of me."

I shake my head. "You don't sound like you're from New

York." I fold my used napkins and tuck them under the cardboard plate. "I mean, it's pretty obvious that you aren't from here, but I would have never guessed New York. Maybe Cleveland…"

He scrunches his nose. "What?!" he yells. "That somehow feels like a major dig!"

I smile wryly. "No, Cleveland's… cool. I think I've got family out there."

He chuckles. "Nice save. Well, it's been a long time since I've been back to the old neighborhood; been all over since then…" He turns and gawks at me. "And what do you mean, it's 'obvious' I'm not from L.A.?" He does his best De Niro impression. "Whatya talking about?"

I bite my cheek, trying to keep from laughing. "You just have a lot of… frenetic energy," I explain with a grin, looking over at the cliffs. "It's a little high stress for a local."

"Man," he whines, "I'm batting 0 for 2… So you think I'm a total spaz."

I tilt my head. "You said it, not me." I giggle.

He swats my hand. "Well, I strongly disagree," he scoffs. "I think I'm pretty laid back."

I roll my eyes. "Please. You are not laid back. *Benny* is laid back." I cock my head to the yellow truck.

"*Benny* is in a different time zone!" he jokes. "Stone cold! I can't believe you think I'm high stress… This coming from the biggest drama queen I've ever met." He sniggers and sits back against the sand.

"Hey!" I punch him lightly in the stomach, leaning over of him.

He grabs his sides and fake chokes. "Easy there, Mayweather! You know I can't handle what you're throwing down!" He feigns moving off, but then comes back quick and wraps his arms around my waist, gently grappling me. "Ahh, sneak attack!" he cries. I shriek and pretend to wriggle away, our legs tangling together. My heart beats out of my chest as I rub up against him.

"Oho, where you gonna go now?" he laughs, rolling me back and resting on top of me. "Come on, tough guy! Show me what you got!"

I dig my hand into the beach. "I've got a handful of sand and I know how to use it!" I crow.

He arches his brows playfully. "Ohhh, she fights dirty!" he pants, propping himself up. "Okay, I give, I give…"

He hovers over me and stares into my eyes. I lie still as he reaches down and brushes his hand across my cheek, holding my breath, every other part of my body begging to be touched like that, too.

"You blush when you get worked up," he murmurs, caressing my face. "Makes me want to do something crazy just to see it. It's like… the first day of spring." He smiles, resting his hand in my hair.

I arch my neck up, our mouths inches from each other. "Daniel…" I breathe, my eyes fluttering closed, lips parted and waiting. I feel his knees shift, his breath ragged. The tip of his nose grazes mine, and he hesitates.

I look up at him. "What?" I whisper. "What is it?"

He clears his throat and leans back. "I can't." He rubs his jaw, getting off of me.

I roll onto my side to face him. "I'm sorry, Christa," he says, gazing out at the water, his expression pinched.

I slowly sit up, confused. "I don't understand," I say after a minute. "I thought we were…" I fade off.

He sighs, drawing his knees to his chest. "I know. That's my fault," he mumbles, not looking at me.

I shake my head. "Wow, um, okay…" I brush sand off of my jeans. "No, I, uh… I must have just got my signals crossed." I wrap my arms around myself.

Daniel winces. "It's not like that," he whispers.

I look down at my lap. "No, it's fine. We've been through a lot together over the last couple of days, and I just…" I cough. "I just read more into it than was there. That's all." I clench my jaw.

He looks at me, his brown eyes pained. "Stop…" He leans towards me.

I hold up my hands. "Just… tell me one thing," I grit out. "Does this have anything to do with what Alden said in the alley last night?" I glare at him. "About me being… a *certain* kind of girl?"

Daniel shakes his head. "What— no!" he exclaims. "You remember that?"

I snort. "Yeah. I was out of it, but I'm not deaf." I huff. "And for the record, I know I'm not a 'good girl'… That's not a big goal of mine."

He attempts to touch my leg, but I push him away. "That's… that's not true," he sputters, his eyes wide. I sneer when he adds, "*I* think you're good!"

"That's not what I'm saying!" I tear at my hair. "I just know I'm not perfect… and I've never pretended to be! But I'm not… like *that*, either." I wince. "Everything I did… have done, I did because *I* wanted to." I look at the sky. "Not because I needed some guy to like me or because of peer pressure or whatever." I stand up. "So, if you're going to judge me or make me feel bad for who I am, then… I don't want to know you." I start to walk back to the bus stop, Daniel scrambling to keep up.

"Christa—wait!" he shouts. "Hey! Don't walk away from me again!"

I spin on my heels, my nostrils flaring.

He runs his hands through his hair. "I don't know what I'm going to have to do to prove it to you, but I'm on your side! I wasn't judging you or trying to make you feel crappy for stuff in your past," he continues earnestly, shaking his head. "I'm the last person to do that, okay?" He grabs my shoulder; I shrug away and cross my arms.

"Come on, Christa! After everything we've been through, do you really think that little of me?" He cringes.

I open my mouth to snap back, but stop. After a brief pause, Daniel continues. "Can you just quit and think for a second that maybe *this*," he gestures between us, "has nothing to do with you? Maybe I need you to cut *me* a break, all right?" He grimaces. "And just trust that I *want* to be with you, to know you…" He shakes his head. "… the only way I can."

I stare down at my boots. "That has to be enough, okay?" He wrinkles his forehead.

I nod. "Yeah, I get it," I mutter.

His shoulders sag. "You're still mad, I can tell." He sighs.

I shake my head. "I just want to go home," I grumble. "I'm tired. I want to shower and have some time alone." I look at him. "Can we do that?"

He nods and gestures weakly to the street. "Sure. The bus should be back any minute."

*

"Can you at least look at me?" Daniel pleads as we step into the front foyer of my building. I clench my jaw and stomp up the stairs. "I get that you're upset…"

"Oh, really?" I turn and glare at him wildly. "You get that?"

He sighs, stopping a few steps behind me. "You didn't say two words the whole ride back. I know 'upset' when I see it." The side of his mouth tugs up into a half-smile.

I shake my head and step onto the landing. "I'm… *embarrassed*, Daniel," I stammer.

He scratches his neck and looks at the floor.

"And hurt, and confused…" I continue, stalking over to my front door. "You know, I have no idea how any of this stuff is supposed to work with us now, especially after I put myself out there like that." I tuck my hair behind my ears.

"It's okay." He lightly rubs my hand. "I like that you did that…"

I roll my eyes and shove him. "God! Just stop being nice! And with the touching and talking!"

He crosses his arms as I glance at the door and slap the side of my thigh. "Crap, I don't have my key." I scowl, resting my forehead over the peephole. "Great…" I reach up and pound the door with my fist. "Mom? Can you let me in? I forgot my key…" I kick the bottom of the door with my toe, and it pops open.

I narrow my eyes. "That's weird. We never leave it unlocked," I murmur.

Daniel furrows his brow and steps in front of me. "Just hang back," he whispers. I nod as he pushes the door all the way open, revealing the inside of my apartment. "Stay here." He walks forward, leaving me waiting nervously on the threshold. I hear his footsteps in the kitchen, and then he comes back a minute later.

"It's all clear." He shrugs. "Place is empty."

I nod and step into the living room. Everything is exactly the way I left it, stacks of magazines on the coffee table and Mom's blankets tossed on the couch.

"She must be out. I hope she's not too pissed that I was gone last night," I mutter, resting my hand on the back of the easy chair.

Daniel flops down on the couch, staring at me. "I know you need some time to think about things," he sighs, "but I think we need to talk about what happened on the beach."

I shake my head. "There's nothing left to talk about." I spin the chair toward myself, about to take a seat. "You made it pretty clear how you feel." I look down at the cushion, and my eyes go wide.

"That's not the whole story, Christa!" he exclaims. "There's a lot more to it…" He watches my face and then looks down at the chair. "Ah, mystery solved." He points nonchalantly. "Guess your purse was here all along."

I glare at my bag, flawlessly displayed atop my leather jacket.

"No," I mumble, "this isn't right…" I pick up my bag and flip it upside down, shaking its entire contents onto the rug.

Daniel looks at me and sighs. "Christa, you need to stop avoiding me. I have to tell you something…" He exhales. "Something I saw last night while you were Haloing." He scratches the back of his hair and watches me as I kneel down and hold up a small box wrapped in light purple paper and a black satin ribbon. "What is that?" He shakes his head.

I hold my breath as I open the tag. In beautiful calligraphy, it reads: *Something 'Sweet' For You…*

My hands tremble as I set the box back on the floor. "Oh my God," I murmur, "he knows where I live."

Daniel purses his lips as I slowly rise and move toward the kitchen. "Who? Who knows where you live?" he asks behind me. I clutch my hair as I cross over to the stove.

"MOM!" I yell, feeling like the floor is dropping out beneath me.

"Christa, she's not here!" Daniel grabs my shoulder. "*Who* knows where you live? What are you talking about?"

I shrug him off and go back into the living room. "I have to call her. Where's my…?" I crouch to the floor, grabbing my phone from under the chair. My fingers quiver as I touch the screen, entering the passcode.

"She never picks up anymore… She just… has to…" I mumble. The missed text icon blinks in the corner of the window, bright and yellow. "Maybe this is her." I sigh, relieved.

"Hey, you gotta help me connect the dots here. I'm a couple of steps behind," Daniel calls from the kitchen door. "Who knows where you live?" he overenunciates.

I look down at my phone and feel the wind get knocked out

of me all over again. The caption reads: ... *And something 'sweet' for me.*

It's right below a photo taken a few feet away from me, on the living room couch.

"Alden," I answer, turning to Daniel and holding up my phone, revealing a grotesque selfie of Alden kissing my mother. "And he's got her. He's got my mom."

CHAPTER 6

"OKAY, CHRISTA, CAN you just sit down for a second?" Daniel cajoles. "And you need to stop looking at that thing."

I pace across the living room floor, my phone in hand. I stare at my mother's face. Her expression is drowsy and out of it, like she doesn't totally know what's going on. Alden leers back at me, his lips ghoulishly pressed to her cheek.

"Maybe he drugged her," I mumble. "He would've had to, to get her out quietly…" I trail off.

Daniel sighs. "Don't do this to yourself. We have no idea what happened." He crosses and stands in front of me, placing both hands on my shoulders. I gaze down at the screen. "Hey, gimme that." He gently pries the phone out of my hand and tosses it onto the table. "Now, let's take a deep breath and try to figure this out." He leads me over to the easy chair and I sit, poised on the edge.

"He was… he was in my *house*," I stammer. "Who knows how long he was here, what he did to her…" My throat tightens. "What he might *still* be doing to her." I put my face in my hands. "Oh my God."

Daniel sits across from me on the coffee table, our knees touching. "I know this is scary; I'm not going to lie to you, this is bad." He looks down at the floor. "But I also know Alden *really* well." He nods. "And there is motive in everything he does. His goal was never to kidnap your mom… This is all part of some bigger game." He brushes my leg with his fingers.

I look up. "A game?" I repeat slowly, staring at the wall.

Daniel sits back. "Yeah," he sighs. "So I have to believe that he's not going to hurt her; he still needs her for his next play." He takes my hand and gives it a squeeze. "And we'll find her before that happens, Christa. I promise." He stares at me.

I shake my head. "Should we… should we call the police?" I swallow. "That's what you're supposed to do when someone gets kidnapped, right?" I stare down at my lap. "We should. We should call them…"

Daniel cringes. "Not unless we want a bunch of dead cops added to the list." He rubs his forehead. "They wouldn't last a day on the case."

I grab my jaw. "Holy shit," I breathe. "I was so stupid." I look up at him. "Leaving all my stuff at Trinity… Of course he came here. I practically gave him an open invitation with my keys and license right there." I chuck my empty bag onto the floor. "I just wish it had been me instead of her."

"Come on, don't say that," Daniel murmurs.

I clench my jaw. "It's true. Whatever she's going through right now, she doesn't deserve it." I look down at my hands. "*I* did this to her."

"Christa!" Daniel exclaims. "No… I'm not going to let you talk like that."

My lower lip trembles. "I hate that the last time I spoke to her was us fighting. Things have been messed up between us for so long…" I try to breathe slowly. "I'll just never forgive myself if that was it, if she's…" I cock my head to the side. "Well, you know." I lean back in the chair and chew on my nails.

Daniel puts his hands on his knees and stands. "This is exactly what he wants: for us to freak out and lose our cool," he says, heading toward the kitchen. "I'm going to get you some water, and when I come back, we're going to come up with a plan." He nods affirmatively as I hunch comatose in the chair.

"Yeah, fine," I mumble. He looks at me and sighs, walking through the doorway.

I draw my legs to my chest, feeling about three inches tall. Did he have to force his way inside, or did she invite him in, totally unknowing? How long was he here before he took that picture? I stare at the couch, imagining Alden sitting there, casually picking up a magazine, glancing out the window, with Mom sedately nestled in the crook of his arm as he pets her hair. I shudder and look down at the floor. The contents of my purse are still scattered across the rug: old receipts, eyeliner, wallet, a Twix bar from the 7-11 with Riley, and the small purple box with black ribbon.

I lean down and pick it up, holding it in my lap. The paper is smooth and cool, its corners meticulously creased. I read the tag again: *Something 'Sweet' For You.* Asshole.

I run my fingers under the tape just as Daniel returns from the kitchen, water glass in hand. He looks at the gift and his eyes widen.

"What are you doing?" He puts the cup down.

I purse my lips. "I should open it, right?" I arch a brow. "It's obviously for me." I give the ribbon a light pull, and it slips onto the chair.

Daniel shakes his head and walks over. "I don't know if that's a good idea, Christa. Maybe after you have a chance to calm down…" He tugs at his sleeves.

"I am completely calm," I murmur, my hands quaking as I tear the paper away. It's a small ornament box, the top coming off effortlessly. I reach inside past the tissue paper and pull out a fragile glass orb.

Daniel's eyes narrow. "Is that… is that a *fish*?" He squints.

I hold it up in front of my nose. It's a snow globe filled with clear liquid, a stunning black and white fish suspended inside. It looks just like the one I saw in Alden's aquarium last night, its delicate fins swaying from the twitch of my hand.

"Yeah," I answer. "I think it's an angelfish."

Daniel leans in. "It looks so real…" He taps the glass.

The fish blinks.

"Oh my God," I gasp, almost dropping it. "It's alive." I give the snow globe to Daniel, bile rising in my throat. I collapse back into the chair as he scrambles to his feet.

"Okay, just hang on…" He clenches his jaw and looks around the room, holding the snow globe out in front of him like it's on fire. He sees the water glass and picks it up, fiddling with the orb before pouring everything into the glass. The fish darts around the cup, ramming its nose against the sides before settling grumpily at the bottom. Daniel exhales and moves the glass over to the end table by the window.

"Couldn't leave it in there." He sighs, gesturing back at the empty globe. "He's evil, but you gotta give the guy points for creativity." He turns back to me.

I clutch my stomach, my shoulders shaking. "The minute I think I have a handle on things," I rasp, trying to catch my breath, "or I think I'm okay, that I've got the whole picture figured out…" I gesture with my hands. "… something shifts, and I'm thrown back into a tailspin and don't know which way is up." I stare at Daniel in shock. "Is this how it's going to be for the rest of my life?! Now that I know everything—God, now that I'm a *part* of it," I spit, grabbing the back of my neck, "how is anything ever going to be normal again?!"

Daniel winces and closes his eyes. "I don't know," he murmurs. "I'm sorry."

"That doesn't help me!" I yell, bolting out of the chair. "You're the one who's been doing this forever—you're supposed to know what happens next!" I kick the coffee table with my toe.

"Like I said, I'm sorry. It doesn't work like that." He crosses his arms.

I let out a cold laugh. "Well then, enlighten me!" I bark. "Come on, earn your stripes! What are we supposed to do now?" I tear at my hair. "How are we going to get her back?"

Daniel opens his mouth, but is cut off by my phone vibrating against the coffee table. I jerk my head and glare at the screen: *Unknown Caller.*

"Well, for starters, we answer the phone," he mutters, picking it up and throwing it to me.

I catch it, my eyes wild. "I don't know what to say!" I cry. "Um, hi, is this the psychopath that took my mom? Would you mind bringing her back, please?!" I shake my head as the phone rumbles in my hand.

"You can do it, Christa." Daniel nods, his gaze locked onto mine. "Just take it a step at a time." The phone vibrates again. "I can't do it; he wants you."

I bite my cheek and rub my forehead. "Damn it!" I click the receive button. "Hello?" My voice cracks.

"Top of the mornin' to ye, darlin'!" Alden drawls into the line like a demented leprechaun. "How are my favorite lovebirds doing today?"

"Alden," I grit.

He chuckles. "So, I just wanted to check in, see if you'd gotten my message."

I exhale. "Oh, I got it." Daniel touches my arm, his face worried. I shake my head.

"Excellent, excellent. And you opened your present?" He holds, waiting for me to answer.

"Yes," I hiss.

"Wonderful," Alden purrs. "I saw you admiring her last night, and I thought, as a show of no hard feelings, that I would offer her up as a little peace offering—a token of goodwill." I can practically hear his smug grin. My fist tightens at my side.

"Are you kidding me?" I snarl. "You took my mother, you bastard! Where is she?!"

Alden sighs. "Calm down, Christa. Your mother is perfectly safe; I'm with her right now." He readjusts the phone. "She's settling into her new accommodations quite nicely." He clears his throat. "I have to say, beautiful women run in your family... I can tell she was something to behold, in her time. Too bad she's such a lousy drunk now. She's really gone to seed."

I bare my teeth. "I swear to God, Alden! If you touch her—"

"I wouldn't dream of it!" he scoffs. "No, dear, Julie is simply a means to an end." He pauses. "It's you I want."

I take a deep breath. "What do I have to do?" I ask shakily. Daniel juts out his chin.

"Meet me at Trinity later today, say, around 4 o'clock?" Alden croons. "I would prefer to discuss the terms of our arrangement in person." I hear a metallic clink in the background.

I furrow my brow. "What do you mean, 'arrangement'?" Daniel's eyes narrow. "I show up, you give me back my mom, and we leave. That's it!" I exclaim.

Alden laughs. "Oh, now... you think I went to all the trouble of wining and dining Mummy here just so you could walk out right before cake? No," he tuts, "it's a bit more complicated than that. But we'll sort it all out later today." He takes a breath.

"Oh, and if you could, leave old Danny Boy at home. I would greatly appreciate that." He sighs. "It's not that *I* mind, but my boys get a little... tetchy... with a Guardian on the premises. Wouldn't want to have another Emily on our hands!" He starts to chortle.

I shiver. "You're seriously twisted, you know that?" I sneer.

Alden clucks his tongue. "You flatter me, Christa, truly," he snickers. "So, do we have a date?"

"Yeah," I fume. "I'll be there." I hang up the phone, then look at Daniel and sigh.

"Well?" He motions with his hands. "What's the deal?"

I snarl and toss my phone onto the chair. "I'm supposed to meet him at Trinity at four to discuss our 'arrangement.'" I arch a brow. "Whatever that means."

Daniel crosses his arms. "No." He shakes his head.

I purse my lips. "What do you mean, *no*?" I bark.

He looks down at the floor. "I mean, no, you're not going. End of story." He exhales, leaning against the chair.

I snort, bending down to gather my stuff back into my purse. "The hell I'm not! Newsflash, you're not the boss of me," I reply peevishly, tossing an old lip gloss to the bottom of my bag.

Daniel's nostrils flare. "Yes, but I am your Guardian, and I am telling you that this is a bad idea." His voice rises. "This has 'huge ridiculous trap!' painted all over it! And the fact that you can't see that is more than a little disconcerting." He rubs his chin.

I slam my bag up on the chair. "What am I supposed to do, Daniel? He has my mom!" I get to my feet, my face reddening. "I'm sure if it were up to you, I'd be stuck here under lock and key taking a bubble bath and catching up on *Real Housewives*, but I can't do that!"

"No, you can't," he interjects. I glare at him. "You can't stay here anymore. It's not safe." He shrugs.

I glance up at the ceiling. "Wow, you are just Mr. Endless Possibilities right now! Can't go to Trinity, can't stay here... Well then, where to?" I snap waspishly. "Back to the factory to try on poodle skirts and practice duck-and-cover drills?"

He points back to my room. "Go pack a bag," he murmurs. "Bring enough for... I don't know... a couple days."

I roll my eyes. "You cannot be serious!" I huff.

He bites the inside of his cheek, looking around the room. "Like a heart attack," he grumbles, stepping over to the window.

I shake my head. "What about Trinity?" I glance at the SpongeBob clock. "Alden's expecting me in a few hours, and I'm not going to fuck this up!" I sling my purse over my shoulder. "She's counting on me!"

Daniel sighs. "I know. And we're getting her back—we just have to be smart about it." He scratches the back of his neck. "You guys have a car, right?" He checks the end table's drawers. "Any idea where your mom would have left the keys?" He starts digging through the couch, lifting up the cushions.

I watch him, my arms crossed. "They're probably in her purse..." I gaze around and find it, still smooshed against the wall from when she got home yesterday. I trudge over and pick it up, finding the keys inside. "Here. It's probably parked in the back— the world's oldest Toyota Corolla." I run a hand through my hair. "I still don't see the point of all this."

He smiles weakly and takes them from me. "I know, and you will." He jingles the keys. "This will be faster than the bus." He nods, moving toward the door. "Go get your stuff."

I groan, dragging myself back to my room. "You still haven't said where we're even going!" I yell.

I hear him sigh behind me. "To get help. I'll meet you down at the car." He quietly opens the door and steps into the hall.

*

"It's this one, right here." Daniel points from the passenger seat.

I frown and park in front of a small, inviting yellow house with a white picket fence, turning to him as I pull the keys from the ignition. "Okay... So this is totally random. Where are we?"

Daniel takes off his seatbelt and opens the door. "A friend's place... She'll know what to do next. Come on." He steps out of the car, grabbing my sleepover tote from the back.

"*She?*" I scowl, getting out and slamming my door. I sulk as

Daniel walks around and puts his hand on the small of my back, ushering me to the front gate.

He sees my expression and rolls his eyes. "Don't look so bent out of shape!" he snickers, tossing my bag over his shoulder.

I jut out my chin. "I just don't see why we need to be here. We already know what happens next," I reply sullenly. "I go to Trinity, tell Alden to eat it, and save my mom. I am so done screwing around." I shake my head as we step into a charming little garden. Rows of sweet-smelling herbs and desert flowers line the path, and bird of paradise plants stand sentinel on either side of the light blue front porch.

Daniel nods. "Okay, Tiger. Well, when that plan totally crashes and burns, you're going to be really happy to have backup." He clucks knowingly and hops up the steps to the door.

I scoff and step up next to him as he knocks. "*You're* my backup," I hiss, shoving my hands into my pockets. I still haven't taken off his jacket. "*You* can just wait outside, and if I need you, I'll… whistle, or something." I glare down at my boots.

"Cuz that works all the time in the movies," he teases, staring at the cherry blossom wreath on the door.

I turn to him and huff. "You know, for the record—" I stop as the door opens and almost fall backwards off the stoop.

Mary Carmen stands in the doorway, a long, emerald sundress hugging her curves. Her shiny black hair is pulled into a sloppy bun, with a pair of thick glasses holding it in place on top of her head. She stares at us, her mouth agape.

"Oh my gosh… Christa!" she finally stammers after a minute. "And… Daniel." Her eyes widen uneasily. "This is a surprise!"

"Yeah, no kidding." I glare at Daniel. He grins.

"What are you two doing here?" Mary Carmen asks, leaning against the doorframe. She has a cup of coffee in one hand and Sudoku puzzle in the other; we've obviously interrupted what looks like a very pleasant Sunday afternoon.

"We, um, we have a problem..." Daniel mutters under his breath.

Mary Carmen's jaw tightens. "What kind of problem?" she whispers, shifting her weight. Her eyes dart to my bag over Daniel's shoulder and back to me. "Does she *know*?" she asks tentatively.

I shake my head. "Wait—*she* knows?!" I shout. "About... everything?"

Mary Carmen glances at the house next door. "Please, keep your voice down," she mumbles, looking back at us. "Daniel?"

He rubs the bridge of his nose. "We have a situation," he sighs. "Involving... Alden."

Mary Carmen looks down and holds open the door. "Get inside, now—both of you," she says, her tone low. I wrinkle my nose as Daniel grabs my hand and pulls me in. Mary Carmen cranes her neck and checks the street before closing the door behind us. "Do you know if you were followed here?" she asks, locking the deadbolt.

Daniel turns and shakes his head, setting my bag on the floor. "I don't think so. I kept watch on the way over and didn't see anything suspicious. I think we're fine."

Mary Carmen nods, holding her coffee and newspaper to her chest. "Well, that's something." She exhales and stares at me, her eyes stopping on Daniel's jacket. She smiles tightly. I clear my throat, crossing my arms.

"Why don't you take a seat?" she gestures toward the front room. "I'll fix us something to eat, and you can tell me what's going on." She shoots Daniel a look as she moves down the hall.

He sighs and points to the faded pink couch. "Just take a load off," he says with a grimace, sitting down. "She'll be back in a minute."

I grit my teeth and plop down next to him, glancing around the room. It's a cozy space with bay windows looking out at the garden, the floral wallpapered walls lined with bookcases crammed to capacity. Next to the fireplace is a small, dusty TV that doesn't look like it gets a lot of use. The vibe screams grandma, but the couch is super comfy. If I were in a better mood, I'd think it was a great place to curl up with a hot chocolate and a good book.

Instead, I turn and glare at Daniel. "So, are you going to tell me why we're sitting in my sobriety instructor's living room?" I mutter, my jaw clenched.

He sighs and runs his hands through his hair. "Well, she's actually more than just a sobriety instructor," he says with a chuckle, "although she's pretty good at that." He picks up a lace doily from the couch and twirls it on his finger.

My eyes widen. "Wait, are you saying she's an…" I stare back into the hall. "She's an Angel too?" I whisper.

Daniel nods. "Yep. And a really good one, so try to be on your best behavior." He sets the doily back and smooths it with his palm. "She's been doing this for a long time, Christa. We need her help."

I sigh and sink back in the couch. "She knows about me," I murmur. "She knew I was the Catalyst yesterday and didn't say anything." I look out the window.

Daniel turns to face me. "She couldn't say anything to you about it. You would have thought she was nuts if she started rambling on about souls and Guardians and Demons," he scoffs. I roll my eyes. He taps my knee. "Anybody would! And you would've run off as fast as those leggy legs could carry you." He shakes his head. "We couldn't risk that."

I snort. "I just hate feeling like I'm the last to know. Late to the party, or something." I look down at my lap.

He sighs and props up his chin on one hand. "You know now, and you're with us. That's all that matters." He smiles.

"Yeah, I guess," I grumble, my brow furrowed. "So… how *do* you know each other? Guardian boot camp?" I smirk.

Daniel grins awkwardly. "Uh…" he stammers. He takes

a breath just as Mary Carmen enters with a huge platter of sandwiches.

"Okay, I've got ham and cheddar on the right, turkey in the middle, and lots of chips." She sets the tray down on the coffee table in front of us and hands me a napkin. "Christa, eat." She points at the food and jerks her head at Daniel. "You—start talking." She turns around, moves a stack of books off of a paisley print chair, and pulls it over. I grab a turkey sandwich and take a bite. Mary Carmen sits and nods.

"So..." Daniel leans forward and clears his throat. "I think it's worth noting, before we get into everything, that Christa—" He turns and smiles widely at me. I balk at him, my mouth full of food. "—is *safe*. Not a scratch or mark on her!" His eyes gaze up at the fading goose egg on my forehead. "No *new* scratches on her," he corrects, glancing over at Mary Carmen, who sits with her lips pressed into a thin line. "Totally, totally good..." he finishes mumbling, patting my leg. I roll my eyes.

"What is your point, Daniel?" Mary Carmen murmurs.

Daniel tugs at his ear. "I just want you to remember that, before I tell you that, um..." He looks at me and sighs. "... that Alden took Christa's mom last night." He looks down at the floor.

Mary Carmen shakes her head. "I'm sorry... *took* her? Took her where?" she asks, her face pinched.

Daniel scratches his arm. "Like, kidnapped. He showed up at their apartment and took her away. I don't know where," he mutters.

I put down my sandwich and tuck my hair behind my ears. Mary Carmen's knuckles whiten as she grips the arms of her chair. "How... how is that possible?" She glares at Daniel. "Even if he knew where she lived, you would have seen him before he got into the building if you were doing your job." Her voice rises. "Both Christa and her mother should have been home, safe, and *you* should have been out keeping watch!" Her eyes dart between the two of us.

I look at Daniel, who's nodding at the carpet. "Hypothetically, yes." He clears his throat and sits back. "That would make total sense if we, um—" He chuckles nervously. "—if we had been home, last night." He stares at Mary Carmen. She takes a deep breath and sucks her teeth. Daniel winces.

"So help me, Daniel…" Mary Carmen holds her hands up in front of her. "If you're about to tell me that you took her to that derelict rat trap, I am going to straight up lose it." Her face begins to turn bright red.

"That's a little harsh," he hems. "I haven't seen a rat in over two years." He glances at me. "There's a fat tomcat that hangs out, keeps them at bay."

"Daniel!" Mary Carmen barks. "How could you be so irresponsible?" She puts her face in her palms. "Spending the night there, completely exposed, anyone could have found her…"

"I was with her the whole time!" Daniel cries, sitting up straighter and tugging at his hair.

"And you left her mother unprotected!" Mary Carmen yells. "You're smart enough to know that this is a major liability!" Her nostrils flare as she leans forward. "Talk about a rookie move!"

Daniel hangs his head. "It wasn't his fault!" I interrupt. They both twist and stare at me. "I didn't want to be alone—not after what happened at Trinity!"

Mary Carmen glares at Daniel. "What happened at Trinity?!" she bellows.

I cringe as Daniel wraps his arms around his forehead and flops back into the couch. "Arrgh!" he groans. "You always do this!" He takes his arms away and gawks at her. "You go totally mental before hearing the whole story!" He sighs in defeat and looks over at me. "I'm sorry, Christa. I wasn't going to say anything, but the cat's out of the bag." He takes a breath. "Christa had her own run-in with Alden last night." I slump, trying to blend in with the upholstery. Daniel bites his tongue. "She accidentally left her purse with her keys and ID at the club, and that's how he knew where she lived. An honest mistake."

I exhale and slyly reach over, hooking our fingers together between the cushions, grateful that he left out the part about me freaking out and running off to Trinity by myself. He returns with a light squeeze.

Mary Carmen sighs. "What were you even doing there?" She shakes her head and clucks disapprovingly. "Of all the places to go, you take her to the largest Demon club in L.A.? What were you thinking?"

Daniel clears his throat. "I wanted him to," I lie before he can speak.

Daniel does a double take, and Mary Carmen glares at me.

"I didn't believe him when he told me about Demons. I... I made him take me," I mumble, putting on my ashamed face. Daniel stares at me, slack-jawed.

Mary Carmen nods, her lips pursed. "Well, now you know." She arches an eyebrow. "And I know it's hard to understand, since you can't see their true form." I look at her skeptically. She nods. "I figured it out during class yesterday, when you didn't approach me," she explains, gesturing to her eye and looking over at Daniel. He shakes his head.

She clears her throat. "Anyway... while you can't see them, I hope you *could* see that they are pretty much capable of anything." She frowns severely. "Anything except compassion."

I nod, staring at the floor. She sighs and leans over, patting my leg. "It's okay, Christa. Sometimes we learn these lessons the hard way," she murmurs. "All that matters now is how we move forward." She glances at Daniel. "Have we heard anything more from Alden?"

He sits up. "Christa got a call from him this morning." He rests his arm over my shoulder and nods.

I look up. "Yeah. I'm supposed to meet him at Trinity later today to talk about getting her back." My eyes dart between the two of them. "He, um, he wants me to come alone."

Mary Carmen laughs. "Of course he does! Would he like us to deliver you hogtied and blindfolded, too?" she jeers. She looks over at Daniel, who rubs his face tiredly. "Which is never going to happen... Right, Daniel?" Her tone is grave.

He sighs. "She really wants to go, Mary Carmen," he murmurs.

Her jaw tightens. "No. It's out of the question." She slams her fists down on the chair. "There is no way I am letting *the Catalyst* walk out of my house and into the hands of one of the most dangerous Demons in the western world. No." She shakes her head. "Over my dead body."

I glare at her. Daniel's mouth twitches, and Mary Carmen's eyes widen. "I mean it!" she exclaims, pointing at him. "And I am appalled that you would even consider it! I'm starting to believe that you are suffering from severely impaired judgement!" She blinks at me for a second before turning back to him. "Maybe there is something else you want to tell me about?" she fumes.

Daniel grimaces. "What?! No! What are you talking about?" He pulls his arm away from my shoulders.

Mary Carmen looks down at her lap and sighs. "Nothing. It's not important right now." She coughs. "We need to figure out how to get Christa's mother back without Christa going to Trinity." She reaches up and pulls her glasses down.

I shake my head. "Wait—no! He's expecting me!" I curl my feet under me. "If I don't show up, who knows what he'll do to her!" I stare at Daniel, my eyes wide. "Please, Daniel! You know I have to go!"

He clears his throat and crosses his arms. "I think..." He

pauses, looking down at the floor. "I think that we should at least hear other options."

I frown, leaning back on my heels. "Fine," I spit, turning to the window.

Daniel grazes my ankle with his fingers, but I kick him away. "Finally, something sensible!" Mary Carmen brays. Daniel cringes at her, but she sits forward. "Okay… It's plain to me that Christa shouldn't leave the house."

I narrow my eyes at that. "I'm sorry," she adds, pursing her lips. "I know you don't want to hear that, but it's the truth. This situation is far too precarious for you to be out and about. They have eyes *everywhere*." She glowers. "You will stay here until we can get your mother back and secure a safe location for you both."

I gawp between the two of them. "I don't even get a choice?!"

When Daniel does nothing but stare at his hands, I slap my thighs and get up. "No, this is crap! You can't make me stay here!"

Daniel startles as I step over his knees toward the front door. "No, no, no—Christa!" he calls, trying to catch my wrist. I shake him off and grab my purse.

Mary Carmen stands and adjusts her glasses. "Christa," she murmurs as I reach the hall, "if you want your mother to live, you will let us help you." I stop and grip the archway. "If you go on alone, they will capture you and kill her the first chance they get."

I bite my lip. "You don't know that," I rasp.

She sighs. "I do. I've been fighting them since before you were born." She slowly walks across the living room. "You can't even begin to fathom their complexity; they are designed for the sole purpose of decimating the human body and spirit." She stands behind me. "It makes any type of torture that you've witnessed or heard about look like a child's birthday party." She reaches out and rests a warm hand on my shoulder. I swallow, but don't shrug away.

"I know you are strong, but, please," she whispers, "this is what we are built to do. If there is any chance at all, it is with *us*." She gives me a squeeze.

I close my eyes and sigh. "I just want her back," I breathe. "I... I need her back."

Mary Carmen nods. "I know. Come." She leads me back to the living room. "Let's do this together." I grimace and let her guide me to the sofa. Daniel scooches over, making room on the couch, but I choose the paisley chair instead, still feeling raw from a minute ago. His face caves as Mary Carmen eases down into the empty seat, rolling her eyes at him.

"Okay, now that we're all starting on the same page..." She exhales, glancing at the two of us. "... I think we can agree that we need to go in with as much muscle as possible."

Daniel nods. "So, I'm definitely going."

Mary Carmen snorts. "Boy, are you about to pretend that you're tougher than me? I don't know who you think you're foolin'."

Daniel bolts forward and turns to her. "Oh, I am so going!" he snaps. "You know this crap with Alden isn't just about Christa!" He punches the couch. "There are things that need to be said, Mary Carmen, and I can't think of a more perfect time," he snarls.

She tucks a loose strand of hair behind her ear. "I don't know if *that's* accurate, but I can see that you're passionate." She sighs.

Daniel grinds his teeth. "Just give me ten minutes. I'll save her mom *and* send him screaming back to Hell with his tail between his legs." He looks over at me. I shrug, staring out the window. Mary Carmen takes off her glasses and rubs the bridge of her nose.

"All right, now that you've gotten that out of your system, we need to figure out who is going to stay with Christa." She takes a breath and glances at me. "You can't be here unprotected."

I purse my lips. "You just said you needed all the muscle you could get. It's not like we have any Guardians to spare right now."

Mary Carmen pauses and chews her lower lip. "What about Roger?" she asks after a minute, batting Daniel on the arm.

He scratches his cheek and looks at her thoughtfully. "Roger moved up to Portland after Tanya Ascended last summer. There's no way he could be here in time," he finally says with a sigh.

I stare at them. "*Ascended*?" I ask. "What's that?"

"To Heaven," Mary Carmen answers. "Tanya was a Guardian who completed her time on Earth. It's a really special moment when it happens. Big celebration." She beams.

I look at Daniel. "Is that what will happen to you?" I murmur. "When all this is over? You'll just be... gone?"

He takes a breath, but Mary Carmen interrupts. "Eventually." She glances at Daniel, who sits back heavily. "But not while he's still helping you. A Guardian never abandons his post." She gives a small nod for emphasis. "Now, back to the business at hand. What do you think about..."

Daniel stares down at his hands as she rambles on, listing other names that must belong to nearby Guardians. I quirk my eyebrows. "Man, that must have been a crazy *How I Spent My Summer Vacation* paper... for your friend Tanya," I grumble. No one is listening.

"Chi?" Mary Carmen asks, her eyes wide.

Daniel shakes his head. "He's racking up points in lockdown at Lancaster. It would be too complicated trying to get hold of him." He crosses his arms and gazes up at the ceiling.

Mary Carmen bites her lip. "I've got it!" she suddenly shouts. "Ellis! She's down in Long Beach now; she could be here in an hour." She looks over at me excitedly. "You'll love Ellis! She has the best stories, really funny." She scrambles to her feet. "I'm gonna call her right now!" She dashes into the hall.

Daniel watches me. I glare out the window like the rhododendron in front of the house is freaking Beyoncé, not wanting to meet his eyes.

"I wish you'd talk to me," he whispers.

I grip the armrests. "What is there to say?"

He sits forwards and folds his hands on his lap. "You could tell me what you're thinking, how you feel—"

"I don't want a babysitter," I interrupt. "I mean, wasn't it just a few hours ago that you were telling me how *brave* I was?" I give an angry snicker. "And now it's like I'm a little kid and the grown-ups are stepping in to fix the mess I've made." I shake my head. "It's not that I'm not... grateful. I know we need all the help we can get... It's just kind of insulting to be treated like a glass doll." I scowl.

Daniel sighs. "It's not like that, Christa. I meant everything I said last night: you *are* brave... and smart, and special..." He looks at his knees. "But Mary Carmen's right. You need to be protected, and Trinity is no place for you—"

"For the *Catalyst*, you mean," I interrupt. His face falls, and I immediately feel bad for saying it. "I'm sorry; I know you... *and* Mary Carmen—" I roll my eyes. "—are trying to help. I just want this to all be over." I slump down in my chair.

Daniel gets up and stands in front of the window, blocking my view. "I get that. And it will be, very soon." He puts his hands in his pockets. "And when it is, I'll still be here, if you... need me. If you still want me... as your Guardian."

I look down at my lap. "I know," I mumble. "And... I do."

I see him shift against the curtains. "Cool." He clears his throat. "Then we can go back to listening to awesome music and you ragging on my clothes." He smiles.

I bite the inside of my cheek. "They're not all bad." I tuck my hands into his jacket. "I just think, like, a couple more shirts without old man band logos on them might be good for you."

He mimes getting stabbed in the heart. "Ah! You're killing me!" He laughs, leaning against the wall. "But whatever you think is best, you being the prettiest person I know." He glances at me out of the corner of his eye. "Always looking like a million bucks."

I blush, my mouth curling, then sigh and look up at him. "I'm sorry I've been so… I don't know, pissed, freaked… blah." I twist my hair around my hand. "I'm really overwhelmed and worried about my mom." I clear my throat. "And it just felt like I was handling all of this a lot better when it was just you and me." I purse my lips, looking toward the hall.

Daniel nods and sits on the edge of the coffee table. "I know. Me, too." He leans in, his face a few inches from my own. I gaze into his eyes, noting the little flecks of gold around his pupils—almost the polar opposite of Alden's icy blue.

"Daniel," I murmur, furrowing my brow. "There was something… strange that happened at Trinity last night." I sit back.

He shakes his head. "Strange? Stranger than everything else?" he jokes.

I purse my lips. "No, really. They brought this… girl, woman, I don't know, into the office while I was there." I look up at him. "Her name was Emily. I think she was like you, a Guardian. She could see me…"

Daniel nods. "I did catch that last night, when you let me read you."

I fidget with my sleeves. "They beat her up pretty bad, Daniel—and she seemed really hardcore," I whisper. "I know you and Mary Carmen think you've got this whole thing figured out, but I'm worried it all goes deeper than even you guys are ready for." I tuck my hair behind my ears. "I don't want to lose you, too." I blush, staring down at my lap.

Daniel puts his hands affectionately on my knees. "You don't need to give that a second thought. Seriously, Christa, I appreciate you worrying about me, but believe me, I can win this one." He grins. "I've got moves you've never seen!" He laughs, whipping out a few karate chops.

I smile, and Daniel leans in, our foreheads touching. "I'll be back before you know it, *with* your mom."

I nod, feeling the warmth of his breath on my skin. I catch myself trembling again and quickly clear my throat before giving him a light slap on the cheek. He shakes his head, surprised. "Wha—?" he exclaims.

I flash my teeth. "Just keepin' you on your toes." I arch an eyebrow playfully. "Hey, you wanted to tell me something, earlier at the apartment." I look at him. "Right before the stuff with Alden—something else you saw while I was Haloing. What was it?" I sit back in my chair.

Daniel straightens up and looks at the floor. "Oh, nothing," he huffs, "just… um… that time in… uh… Mrs. Marthorp's class…" He starts to cough.

I roll my eyes. "Oh my God—that was so embarrassing!" I tug at my hair. "9th grade English? I was supposed to give a huge presentation on Hemingway in front of the whole class, and when I got out of my desk to do it, my skirt caught on Marco Geraldi's backpack and it tore all the way up the seam!" I groan. "Ugh. At least I had cute underwear on that day." I smirk. "Cried all the way to the school uniform exchange closet."

Daniel nods, coughs racking his body. "You did, pink," he rasps.

I scrunch my nose and slap his chest. "Pervert!" I laugh. "You told me you didn't look at any of that stuff!"

He keeps coughing. I narrow my eyes. "Hey, are you okay?" I reach over and put my hand on his shoulder. "Do you need some water or something?" I look around the room. He shakes his head, gasping for air. I move over next to him on the table, patting his back.

"Daniel! What's happening?" I stare at him as he catches his breath, holding his palm to his mouth.

"Nothing… nothing." His chest rattles. He takes his hand

away and quickly wipes it on his jeans. "Just got something stuck in my throat."

I tilt my head. "Looked like more than that. You've been doing that a lot," I murmur, watching him. "Do you have asthma or something? Can Angels have asthma?" I lean back.

He breathes through his nose, his face ashen. "Really, I'm fine," he pants, squeezing my knee. "Seriously." He smiles, but his whole body still shakes.

I nod, scratching my head. "Okay," I bite my lip and take his hand. "Cuz, if there's something you need to tell me, you can." I grin. "I mean, you already know pretty much everything there is to know about me—all my deep, dark crap." I look up at him. "You can tell me anything, too— if you want." I grip his fingers. "I um, I wouldn't… judge you, even the really bad stuff." Our eyes lock. "You can trust me."

"Okay," he whispers. He takes a breath. "Wow… um, yeah. Where to begin?" He chuckles, squeezing my hand. "So, the reason Alden—"

"She's coming!" Mary Carmen bursts back into living room. "Ellis—she's on her way." She looks at us, our hands clasped together. Daniel cringes and quickly tucks his hands between his knees. Mary Carmen crosses her arms and stares down at the floor.

"She said she'd be about an hour," she mumbles as Daniel stands up. "Should give us plenty of time to get ready." She watches him intently.

"Great," Daniel mutters, running a hand through his hair. "That's, um, really… great." He shoves his hands in his back pockets and steps into the hall.

Mary Carmen clenches her jaw and looks back at me. "I'm sure you'd like a chance to clean up," she sighs, putting on a smile. "Let's get you settled, and I'll show you where the bathroom is." I get to my feet as she adds, "You can have the first shower."

*

Damp and wrapped in a giant body towel, I step into the second bedroom and close the door behind me. Mary Carmen already moved my bag to the bed, and I pull out my hairbrush and the long-sleeve, forest green dress I brought from home, laying it on top of Daniel's jacket. I let my hand linger on the leather, soft and worn. I close my eyes and pick it up, pushing my nose into the lining and inhaling deeply. His scent is all over it: cinnamon and spice. I sigh and toss it back on the bed. What was he trying to tell me just now? The nickname 'Mystery Date' doesn't begin do him justice. I pick up my hairbrush. It had to do with Alden... maybe about their past? Screw Mary Carmen for butting in just as I was about to get some answers.

I shake my head and glance around the bedroom. It's a modest space, the only furniture being the bed, a nightstand, and an empty dresser. There's nothing on the walls except for a simple gold cross hanging over the light switch. I move over to it and trace my finger over the metal.

"Completely predictable," I mutter. I purse my lips as I walk back to the bed and lean against the satin blue bedspread, dragging my brush through my wet hair. I have to admit, part of me is relieved to have Mary Carmen around, bossy as she is. I look at my reflection in the mirror, noting my fading bruises.

"Let someone else take over for a while," I repeat, nodding to myself. "They've done this before; we're going to get her back." I smile and set my brush down on the dresser.

Absentmindedly, I turn and gaze down at a short stack of books on the nightstand. The top two are in Spanish, but the last one is an English translation of *Love in the Time of Cholera*. I plop down onto the bed and flip through the book. I remember having to read it for school last year, and it had been one of the few I actually finished. I find the section in the back where Fermina Daza and Florentino Arizo finally get together, scanning through the familiar passages. As I'm reading, something flutters from the pages, drifting to the floor. I close the book and crouch down.

It's an old black-and-white photograph of a baby in a christening gown. I pick it up and scrunch my brow. The baby has a sleepy, mischievous grin, a soft fringe of dark hair peeking out from underneath the bonnet. The baptismal dress looks old, but well-loved, and there's a pair of arms holding the baby, but you can't see who they belong to. I turn it over in my hand; there is a caption written in beautiful cursive on the back that reads *Miguel, 1962.* Apparently, someone had been using the picture as a bookmark. I slip it back between a couple of random pages and return the book to the nightstand, trying to make it look undisturbed. I quickly dress, slinging Daniel's jacket over my shoulders before walking out of the room.

"Having fun playing house?" I hear Mary Carmen murmur as I come down the hall. I peek into the kitchen and see her and Daniel standing at the sink, their backs turned to me. Very quietly, I sneak to the other side of the doorframe and tuck myself against the wall, curious.

"What's that supposed to mean?" Daniel scoffs, turning on the tap.

Mary Carmen clucks her tongue. "Come on, Daniel," she smirks. "Don't think I haven't noticed the way you look at her, how you are always touching her… whatever *that* was in the living room just now." She scrubs a pot with her sponge. "How you leap at the crook of her finger. I've never seen you like this before." She places the pot on the counter and thrusts her hands back into the soapy water.

Daniel laughs. "Yeah, okay. Don't get any ideas." He picks up the pot and starts drying it with a dish rag. "It's not like that. I just like being with her." Mary Carmen shakes her head, and Daniel sighs. "She's someone I can talk to. I think I could tell her every-thing, and, I don't know… it'd be okay." I feel my pulse quicken.

"You can talk to me!" Mary Carmen exclaims, pulling a sudsy plate out of the water. "We've been totally open with one another since day one…"

"I know." Daniel scratches his neck. "But it's not the same. There's just something about her."

"I'm sure there is," Mary Carmen snorts, turning off the water. "She's bold, reckless—bats her baby blues in those boots and you go running."

"Hey!" Daniel snaps. "Don't talk about her that way!"

Mary Carmen puts her hands up. "All right, *rendicion*! But I don't think I need to remind you that there is a lot riding on this girl." She sets her jaw, wiping her wet hands on her dress. "You know how long everyone at Home has been waiting for this…"

"No, I don't—it's not like I've ever been there," he replies hotly.

Mary Carmen sighs. "Please spare me your disenfran-chised Guardian routine," she drawls. "I can't go there with you right now."

Daniel huffs. "Just remember, some of us actually *have* to be here." He scrubs violently with the rag. "We don't all have the lux-ury of zapping back whenever we want."

Mary Carmen tosses her sponge into the water and puts her hands on her hips. Daniel sighs and pitches his rag onto the coun-ter. "I'm sorry, that was… uncalled for." He shakes his head. "You didn't deserve that."

Mary Carmen holds up her palm. "You are in the middle of a very dangerous game, *mi amor*," she hisses, staring down at the floor. Daniel stops and straightens up. "The entire Universe is up for grabs, and all you can worry about is if your new girlfriend thinks your record collection is cool."

"Oh, wow!" Daniel jeers, leaning back against the cabinets. "Why don't you tell me what you really think?"

"I think she's young!" Mary Carmen snaps. "And you are... not!" She glares at him.

When he rolls his eyes, she continues. "You may look it—but you're not! We both know that you're old enough to know that the stakes are sky high, and every move we make needs to be thought through from A to Z and properly calculated!" She shakes her head and points out the window. "I can promise you, that's exactly what they are doing across town! We are all working with the same prophecy..." She turns back to the sink.

Daniel's forehead wrinkles. "Wait—what prophecy?" He grabs her shoulder.

Mary Carmen jerks her chin up at him. "You *know* what prophecy!" she snipes, shrugging away. "The one that details the Catalyst's role in the coming Battle!"

Daniel stares at her, his eyes wild. "She picks Light or Dark, Daniel!" Mary Carmen shouts, her face reddening. "One is very good for us, the other is very good for them. Why do you think he wants her so bad?" She gazes down at the dishes and takes a breath. "Right now, it's too early to tell which way this thing is going... We need her to stay with us."

I feel all the air go out of my lungs as Daniel crosses his arms. "I didn't know about any of this," he rasps.

Mary Carmen sighs, her eyes softening. "Maybe if you spent a little more time on your homework and less on your hair." She reaches over and tucks a curl behind his ear.

He looks at her soulfully. "She's *good*, Mary Carmen. I know it with every fiber of my being," he murmurs.

She nods, grasping his arms. "I know you do, and I want to believe in her, too—but we don't have a crystal ball; all we can do is try to help her and hope that she chooses right when the time comes." She gives him a squeeze before stepping back. "But

Daniel, you must know," she adds, letting out a shaky breath, "it will fall on you if things don't go the way we want." She wraps her arms around her chest.

Daniel glares at her, his eyes narrowed. I wait with bated breath. "What are you saying?" he growls.

Mary Carmen closes her eyes. "Heaven is going to want to know where your... allegiance lies, in the event that the Catalyst goes Dark," she states heavily. "We need to know that your emotions aren't going to get in the way of our mission." She bites her lip, watching him.

"How you can you ask me that? Are you out of your mind?!" His voice cracks.

"Only in a worst-case scenario!" Mary Carmen holds out her hands. "Daniel, I'm sorry. This was always a possibility..."

He paces frantically in front of the oven, his face pinched. "Is this even something she has control over?" he cries.

Mary Carmen shushes him. I lean against the wall, suddenly dizzy, my hands trembling.

"No, it's just something that will happen." Mary Carmen shakes her head. "I can't tell you how, but we'll know it when it does." Her shoulders sag. "You're the Catalyst's Guardian, Daniel, and with that comes certain responsibilities..."

"Stop calling her that!" he yells, tearing at his hair. "Use her name... *Christa*." He rubs his jaw. "No... I can't... that's—that's not what we do!" he barks, his breathing growing ragged. "That makes us just as bad as they are... and I won't do it. I don't care *who* is on the other end of that command!"

I look around as he puts his face in his hands. Mary Carmen pulls him into a fierce hug, his back and arms shuddering. She holds him tightly, resting her chin on his shoulder. "Think about what you say next very carefully," she whispers into his hair. "They are always listening." Daniel exhales and nods. "You need to get a grip," she continues, her lips pressed to his ear. "I can see it all over you… It's not like you could ever be with her the way you want to be anyway." She closes her eyes. I feel my stomach drop. "That would mean throwing everything else to the wind, and I know you don't want to do that." She pulls back and smooths a hand over his face.

Daniel nods, his skin blotchy. "You're right, he mumbles. "I know." He takes a deep breath and picks up the dish rag, clearing his throat roughly. I squeeze my eyes shut before turning back to them.

"She's taking a long time." Daniel cocks his head back to the hall as he grabs a clean plate. "Think she's okay?"

"She's a teenage girl," Mary Carmen murmurs. "They take a long time to get ready."

Daniel slams the plate back in the sink, water splashing his shirt. Mary Carmen touches his arm, but he flinches away. "Don't," he says, looking down at the counter. "Just… not now."

Mary Carmen nods and goes back to scrubbing. I close my eyes and turn slowly, my movements hazy, but everything suddenly crystal clear in my mind.

I'm not safe here.

I pad down the hall toward the front door, knowing what I have to do. I move over to the couch and pick up my purse, holding the bag still so as not to rattle the contents inside. Painfully, I remove Daniel's jacket and lay it over the back of the chair, giving it a final squeeze before going over to the door and twisting it open. I only look back to the kitchen once, watching Daniel as he dries a dish and places it off to the side with such care.

"Bye," I mouth, closing the front door behind me and hearing the lock click into place.

CHAPTER 7

THE MID-AFTERNOON SUN beats down as I pull into the empty lot behind Trinity. I get out of the car and squint, the club looking like any other abandoned building you'd find a couple blocks down: desolate and quiet... too quiet. I shiver and walk quickly over to the sidewalk, not wanting to belabor this any longer than I need to. There's no velvet rope or crowd of party-goers to get in my way this time, so I march right up to the front doors and grab the patina-covered handles.

They swing open freely. Someone is expecting me. "Hello?" I call inside.

No answer. I take a deep breath and step toward the main room, where the service lamps are on over the bar.

Without the dancers and loud music, the hall feels more like backstage at a play instead of a dangerous Demon club. I glance around as I take a seat on one of the barstools, coiled on edge and waiting for something to jump out at me. Nothing happens. I sit for what feels like a millennia, spinning on my stool and rapping the countertop with my knuckles. I hear the heat go on, the pipes tinkering in the walls.

"This is stupid," I mutter.

I hop off my seat and walk behind the bar, the clomp of my boots echoing around the empty room. I grab a glass from behind me and fill it at the sink. I sigh and lean against the wine fridge, sipping my water. I wonder if Daniel and Mary Carmen have figured out that I'm gone already. They probably panicked and are on their way here… meaning I won't have a lot of lead time in front of them. I picture Daniel finding his jacket in the living room, his face crumpling as he realizes I've left without him. I frown; it's for his own good… and my own. I run a hand through my hair and check the small clock by the tap. It's time.

"Come on, where are you?" I grumble, tracing the rim of the glass with my finger. "Probably out in the parking lot hooking a bomb up to my engine." I roll my eyes and raise the water to my lips.

"That's rather pedestrian, don't you think?"

I sputter and spill water all down the front of my dress as I hear the voice, accompanied by footsteps coming from the hall. Alden enters the room, fastening the cuffs on a crisp white button-down, his shirtfront still undone.

"If I wanted you dead, I'd come up with something better than that," he chuckles. "Although the connection between automotive explosives and my heritage is not lost on me; clever, clever."

He taps the side of his nose and stops on the other side of the bar. "Glad to see you're making yourself at home." He looks at my drink. "I can fix you something a little stronger if you like." His mouth twitches.

I frown. "Only if I wanted to wind up passed out in a dumpster somewhere." I take another sip.

He arches an eyebrow. "Point taken—although you're living dangerously there." He juts out his chin toward the sink. "That's L.A. River water you're drinking. Imbibe at your own risk."

I sigh and put my glass down, looking around for something to mop up my dress with. Alden steps over and pulls a stack of napkins out from below the bar. "Looks like you got yourself again. Déjà vu," he simpers, handing me one.

"Just killing time," I answer with a glare, patting myself dry.

Alden nods, checking his cuffs. "You're early. I like that." He finishes with his sleeves and moves on to his shirt tails, glancing toward the main doors. "And it also seems that you followed directions. No Danny?"

I shake my head. "No." I look down at the bar. "I decided that I didn't want him to be part of this. It's not his fight."

"Bet that went over like a lead balloon," he snickers, fastening his lowest button. I watch him work his way up to the top, patches of his well-muscled chest peeking through the fabric. I glimpse some sort of scar over his heart and narrow my eyes.

"He doesn't know," I mumble, staring at the mark. "Or maybe he does, now. I dunno… I left without telling him." Alden's eyes widen, his fingers paused on the second button. "What is that?" I ask, pointing.

He looks down at his chest and smiles coyly. "You show me yours, I'll show you mine." He pulls his shirt front closed. I roll my eyes, leaning against the bar. "Kidding," he murmurs, tongue in cheek.

He clears his throat and slowly undoes a button and tugs his shirt aside, revealing a large, dark red burn in the perfect shape of a human hand.

I gasp and glare at him. "Is that… How did you…?" I lean in to get a better look. "Were you *branded?*"

Alden grins and quirks his eyebrows. "You wanna touch it?" I shake my head, taking a step back. "Come on, it's not contagious," he purrs, gently taking my wrist. He lays my palm over the mark, my fingers splayed across his heart, filling the handprint. It feels smooth and pliable, somehow stronger than normal skin. I quiver and look into his eyes.

"Perfect fit," he croons, his lips curling.

I wrench my hand away and cross my arms, saying,

"Whatever." I shudder, trying to keep my voice steady. "Enough flirting. Where is she?" My eyes dart around the room.

Alden sighs and finally finishes buttoning, tucking in his shirt at his waist. "She's not here. If you want to see her, we'll have to go to the Warehouse." He watches me as I glance back to the front doors and grins. "Expecting someone?"

I clench my jaw. "Time to start making some tough choices, Christa," he says, over-enunciating my name as he moves around to the other side of the counter. "Of course, you could wait for the cavalry to arrive and watch some silly drag-out barroom brawl go down," he clucks, sitting on a stool. "I'm sure Danny and whoever else he has helping you think they've got a pretty good shot." He rests his elbow on the bar and stares at me, his eyes bright. "They don't."

I draw in a sharp breath as he adds, "I'd have them flat on their backs before they even made it through the doorway." He cocks his head toward the front foyer.

I scoff and shake my head, springing to my feet. "Yeah right," I laugh. "There's no one else here. You'd be completely outnumbered."

Alden nods, looking down at his lap. "Don't be so sure about that," he calls down the hall. "Can we have the paperwork now, please?"

I jump as the waitress with pink hair from the other night emerges from the backroom. She's wearing a new black cocktail dress, but has the same pretty smile. She crosses over to Alden and politely hands him a manila folder. "Here you are, Mr. Alden," she demurs.

Alden nods, setting the file on the bar. "Thank you, Cameron," he murmurs, flipping it open. "Wait—"

Turning to leave, she gasps as Alden beckons her back with his finger. "Glasses," he states, not looking up.

"Of course, Mr. Alden." She pulls a pair of tortoiseshell frames from her dress top. I roll my eyes as she delicately places them on Alden's face. He shoos her away after that, and she gives me a nervous smile before scurrying off.

"Wow, she's super scary," I sneer. "Bet she's just vicious with a pair of ice tongs."

Alden chuckles as he scratches his cheek. "She serves her purpose," he mumbles, sorting the papers into two separate stacks. "We can't all be key players in the coming Battle; someone has to pour the wine and answer the door…" He glances up at me, his glasses balanced on the tip of his nose. "I'm assuming you know all about the Prophecy now?"

I cross my arms and clench my jaw. "Yes," I mutter. "Got the CliffsNotes version, anyway." I hop off of the bar, my lips pursed. "And in case you were wondering, I've already chosen; I'm going Light. As soon as this crap with you is settled, I'm taking my mom somewhere safe and we're hitting the straight and narrow, whatever it takes." I exhale, walking cautiously over to him. "So, now you're going to tell me exactly what you want and let her go."

Alden grins as he closes the folder and straightens his papers. "Your arrogance is intoxicating," he says, smirking up at me. "If only I had the same… *tenacity* when I was your age, to make such demands." He arches a brow and pats the seat next to him. "Please, sit. There's something I want you to look over."

I narrow my eyes as I perch on the stool. He sets one of the piles in front of me, the top line embossed in dark, black ink:

Affidavit of Ownership: Concerning the Deed and Title of Julie Nichols' Living Soul

"What is this?" I snarl, my eyes scanning down the page. I try to decipher the first block of legal jargon before tossing the papers aside. "Quit screwing around, Alden, and get to the point." I grit my teeth, looking back at the doors. Daniel and Mary Carmen should be here any minute.

"Of course," Alden replies beseechingly, reorganizing the papers. "Apologies for all the tiresome paperwork, but without sorting this out first, there really is no point in going any further." He wets his index finger. "We can just skip ahead to the last page…" He leafs through the papers. "Ah, yes, it's this section here." He places the document back on the counter.

I hastily read the last paragraph on the page.

*… wherein the grantor, **Julie Nichols**, cedes full custody of her living soul in its entirety to grantee, greater 5th-Level Demon, **Alden Murphy**. This includes all aspects of her physical, mental, and spiritual being and her past, present, and future selves in dreaming and waking states. Once pact is sealed, this transfer cannot be reversed, pending death or termination of contract by grantor.*

My mother's signature is scrawled on the line below, right next to Alden's.

I shake my head and shove the papers away. "This can't be real."

Alden adjusts his glasses. "It's legal and binding, I'm afraid," he breathes, picking up the pages. "We do love our red tape down here."

I gnash my teeth and glare at him. "What does that even mean? It's just a piece of paper!" I snatch the last sheet out of his hands, set to destroy it. It doesn't tear; no matter how I try to rip, crumple, or puncture it, the paper stays true to form. I huff and throw it back on the bar, my nerves completely rattled.

Alden blinks, a smile teasing his lips, before reaching over and placing the page back into the file. "Now, then," he chides, "are we ready to move on?"

I run a hand raggedly through my hair. "So, what? You own

her soul now?" I cry. "You type up some dorky little contract on magic Hell paper, and, all of a sudden, you have full control of her?" I bolt forward, knocking the stool over behind me. "No way. Just, no!" I get in his face. "That's not how the Universe works!"

He leers up at me. "Just keep telling yourself that, darling," he drawls. "Say it enough, and maybe it'll come true." He taps his fingers on the folder. "But I can promise you, this is not something you want to experiment with. If you try to take your mother away without my permission…" He chortles down at the bar. "Well, clean up on Aisle 4. You get it?" He leans back on his stool.

I cross my arms, tucking my hands away so he can't see how badly I'm shaking. "There is no way she'd sign something like that. You did something to her—threatened her, tortured her…" I scowl. "She wouldn't just throw everything away like that."

Alden laughs, standing up. "Getting her to sign was the easy part!" he crows, moving back around the bar. "Thanks to all the warm family memories I was able to glean from you last night while you were Haloing," he grins as he refills my glass at the sink, "I knew all of the right pressure points for poor Julie: bad wife, bad mother, failure at life…" He takes a quick sip and looks me straight in the eye. "She did it for you."

I gasp. "What?" I glare at him.

Alden shrugs and points at my mom's contract. "You glossed over it just now, missing the part where she signed her soul away to give you a better life." He bats his eyelashes and sighs. "The promise of a bright future for her only child was a very seductive offer to someone drowning in guilt over tearing apart a once happy home." He clucks his tongue. "She picked quite the package for you: Ivy League school, successful career, gobs of cash and a hot hubby… dying in your sleep at the ripe old age of 93…"

"Shut up." I shake my head. "None of it was real. You can't do any of that stuff."

He smirks. "Oh, we can—and more," he murmurs, running

his finger around my water glass. "But it's expensive, and Julie was ready and willing to pay the price. It was sad, really." He wrinkles his nose. "And not exactly exciting for me, either. It was like shooting fish in a barrel." He finishes off the water.

I stare at the ground, wishing the floorboards would just fall apart and suck me under now. "You're a monster." I whisper.

He rolls his eyes. "If the horns fit."

He sighs, smoothing the bar with his palms, then moves the second stack of papers in front of me. I glare at it, then back at him. "What's this?" I rasp.

Alden grins maliciously. "Why, it's *your* contract, Christa," he purrs, leaning against the prep counter. "It's the reason we're here! Go on, give it a look." He crosses his arms, assessing his cuticles.

I glance down, reading my own name written in dark script. I furrow my brow and flip through the papers, my eyes unable to focus on the contents. "Just tell me," I finally mutter, pushing the stack back at him.

He smiles and straightens up. "Three days," he replies. "I want you to come and stay with me for three days."

I narrow my eyes.

"No funny business!" He raises his hands yieldingly. "You'll have your own room, your own bathroom." He pushes himself up onto the counter. "And best of all, you'd earn your mother's freedom!" He stares at me, his eyes bright. "You'd be completely safe. No harm would come to you or your loved ones while you were in my care, you have my word."

I shake my head. "You actually think I'd agree to that?" I cross my arms, remembering the alley last night. "After what you did to me?"

He looks at his lap. "Considering your other option is to let your mother rot for the rest of her short, miserable life..." He gazes up at me. "Yeah, I do."

I flare my nostrils and glare at the contract. "*If*," I bark, "if

I stay with you, you'd let her go? My mom?" I stare at him. "No more pact, agreement… whatever?"

"Null and void," he answers, taking off his glasses. "She'd be free to go live her life as she chooses, soul intact—" He takes a breath. "—*after* your three days with me. I have to know you'll hold your end of the Deal, Christa. She stays under my control until you fulfill your agreement." He arches an eyebrow. "That's just smart business."

I glower and trace my finger over my name. "That's all this is to you, business?" I hiss. "We're talking about my mother's *soul…*"

"Which she traded away of her own volition," Alden corrects. "Think about it, Christa." He clears his throat. "What an invaluable learning opportunity for you. Light versus Dark… Shouldn't you know where both sides stand before you make such an important decision?" He swings his feet airily.

I exhale. "That's not why I…" I shake my head. "I'd be doing it for her."

He snorts and hops off the counter. "Like mother, like daughter," he snipes. "Well, whatever your reasoning, your three days would start immediately." He looks at me seriously. "No going back to your place to pick up your toothbrush, no running off to a certain towheaded Guardian to say goodbye. Once you sign, you're mine."

I gasp at his severity.

"For three days, anyway," he adds with a grin.

"I—" I close my eyes. "I…"

I jump as someone pounds on the front doors, the whole hall reverberating. Alden faces me, his eyes manic. "Ding dong! Should we see who it is?" he exclaims.

I shake my head as the pounding grows even louder, like the person outside is throwing himself against the wood. "No— he can't be here!" I yell, looking toward the entrance. Visions of Emily collapsing to the office floor rush through my mind.

I turn to Alden. "Okay, but I'm not signing anything until I see her!" I shout.

Alden nods, gathering up the papers. "That can be arranged." He quirks his eyebrows, tucking the contract into his pocket before taking me by the arm. "Come on, this way."

He drags me down the hall to the fire exit, the walls quaking from the assault up front. When he shoves open the backdoor, we run out into the bright afternoon. I shade my eyes, spying my Toyota down the alley in the lot, eclipsed by a shiny black town car idling at the bottom of the stairs. I glare at Alden.

"Your chariot awaits, Persephone," he says with a smirk, gesturing to the car.

I turn back, the whole club shaking. "How... how did you know I'd—?" I stammer. He winks. I shake my head and take the stairs two at a time, Alden's hand on my elbow as he opens the car and we both slip into the backseat.

"Home, Frank," Alden calls to the driver, slamming the door closed behind him.

"Very good, Mr. Alden." The driver pulls deftly onto the road, leaving Trinity shrinking in the rearview mirror.

We're only in the car for a few minutes before we park in another empty lot behind an old warehouse. I look out the window and recognize the main road: we're not far from Daniel's place. The driver gets out and opens my door.

"Here you are, Miss." His large frame blocks the way before he steps aside and offers his hand; I cautiously accept, his mammoth palm cradling mine. His skin is calloused, but smooth.

"Thank you," I mumble, getting out. He holds open the door for Alden.

"Thanks, Frank." Alden puts a hand on the driver's shoulder.

"Stick around for a second, would you?" Frank nods and steps back against the car. Alden turns to me.

"This next part is slightly embarrassing, and I hate that I even have to ask—but I need to check to see if you're armed before we can go in." He tilts his head back toward the warehouse. "Security reasons."

"Or a reason to cop a feel," I mutter, crossing my arms.

Alden grimaces. "Apologies for not having a woman present to perform the search, but here we are." He scratches his temple. "Frank can do it instead, if you like. He's both honorable *and* human… and it's just a pat down."

I glance at Frank who looks back shyly. "Fine." I motion to the big guy. "Let's just get this over with."

Alden nods at Frank. Frank steps behind me and clears his throat. "Please lift your hands level with your chest and spread your legs." he murmurs kindly in my ear. I roll my eyes as he checks my boots and pats my arms and thighs, barely grazing his hand up my skirt. He coughs and moves back.

"She's all good, sir. No weapons." He looks at the ground.

I arch my neck back toward the driver. "You're a gentleman, Frank. I picked the right horse." I grin, lowering my arms, and see him smile down at the pavement. I glare back at Alden, who's staring at me intently. "He said 'all good,'" I jeer.

Alden purses his lips. "He really didn't give it to you. Curious…" He shakes his head.

I shrug. "What are you talking about? Who didn't give me what?" I bark. "What does this have to do with my mom?"

Alden snaps to attention. "Nothing." He claps his hands. "You can just take it around back, Frank. Hold off on any dinner runs for now, just in case we need a pick up." He pats the driver's back. "I'll give you a call if anything else comes up."

Frank tips his cap. "Of course, Mr. Alden. I still have my birthday present." He looks over at me bashfully. "Stephen Tyler

biography, books on tape. Mr. Alden gave it to me for my breaks."
He shakes his head and snorts. "That guy lived a *crazy* life…"

I smile. "That's cool, Frank."

Alden clears his throat and takes my wrist. "That will be all,"
he grumbles. Frank nods and gets back in the car. Alden glances at
me out of the corner of his eye as he drives away.

"Good man, that one, but he will talk your ear off if you show
the slightest interest." He leads me toward the building, over to
the heavy steel doors shadowed against the wall. "Which isn't the
worst thing in a driver, unless you're looking for some bloody peace
and quiet." He puts all of his weight against the door and grunts,
shoving it open. "It's right through here." He gestures inside.

I exhale and step into a hallway as he hauls the door shut,
pitching us into absolute darkness. I gasp and feel Alden run his
fingers through mine. "Just walk. Go on." He gives me a little
nudge with his shoulder. "There's nothing to be afraid of."

"Easy for you to say," I grit out as I shuffle forward, Alden's
shoes clacking on the hard floor next to me. We take about fifty
paces before he stops.

"Just need to get the lock." He lets go of my hand and steps
forward. I hear the jingle of keys and tumblers turning. I count in
my head: there are seven, altogether. Alden pushes open the doors,
bright light flooding the hallway.

"Paranoid, much?" I mutter at the locks, now visible on the
door. "Who are you afraid is going to get out?"

Alden snickers. "More like who's going to get in. Demon-
grade security… only the best for our little detainees." He grins
and points into the room. "She's in there."

I stare and charge through the double doors, but quickly stop
on the threshold, my breath caught in my throat.

There are people. People in cages. Thirty, fifty… maybe more;
I can't count them all. All of them are crammed into narrow dog
runs, complete with chain-link fences and heavy padlocks on the

gates. I cover my nose with my hand, the stench overwhelming. The hall is lit by a row of windows lining the ceiling, sunlight glinting dully through the grimy glass. A group of men covered in what looks like their own filth watch us silently from the cage closest to me, their faces dark and gaunt.

I blink and glare at Alden. "This… this is…" I gulp and choke on the smell. "… barbaric!" My voice bounces off of the walls. The quiet in the hall is disturbing.

Alden sighs. "I can assure you that their basic needs are being met." He leans against the doorframe. "The occasional shower, three square a day, a roof over their heads…" He purses his lips. "I know the accommodations may not be up to *your* standards…"

"Oh, please!" I snap, motioning back to the prisoners, who are lying listlessly in the runs. "You can't keep them locked up like this! You have to let them go!"

Alden puts his hands in his pockets, propping a brick in the door behind him with his foot. "I do not, thank you very much," he huffs. "Besides, that would be the height of impropriety, as they are not all mine." He glares down at the man closest to the gate, whose eyes are trained on the floor, his whole body shivering. "I'm not about to go stepping on everyone else's hands just because you've got a bad taste in your mouth." He gives the door a light kick with his shoe as he moves away. The prisoner inches back from the gate and swallows, his eyes closed.

"They're innocent people…" I reply.

Alden rolls his eyes. "Don't be naive, Christa; no one is innocent." He jerks his chin down the aisle. "You should find what you're looking for in the last cell on the left."

My eyes widen, and I spin around, spying a ruffle of red hair poking through the chain links at the end of the hall. I run and crouch down on the cold cement next to the cell, tossing my bag off to the side.

"Mom?!" I cry, grasping the fence. Her eyes are closed, her face tucked against her chest. She looks so small, curled up into a ball like a five-year-old who fell asleep after a long day at the beach. I push my fingers through, trying to touch her head. "Mom—can you hear me?"

Her eyes stay shut. I turn to Alden, who's slowly making his way down the hall. "What did you do to her?" I snap.

He stops at the gate and looks down at her. "I gave her a light sedative to help her sleep after we arrived last night." He shrugs. "Should be wearing off any time now."

I shake my head and slam my fists against the fence. "MOM!" I shout. She doesn't stir. "Open this," I command Alden, getting to my feet. "Open the fucking door—NOW!"

He crosses his arms. "That is not what we discussed; you just said you wanted to *see* her." He gestures down at her unconscious body. "Well, there she is."

I lunge forward until my face inches from his. "Motherfucker!" I snarl, my fists tightening. "You open that gate this second, or I'll—"

"What?" He grins, clutching my raised hand. "You'll hit me? Isn't that, like, second base with you? Everything's moving so fast," he purrs, brushing my hair with the tip of his nose. I shove him away, stalking back to the cage.

"You know what you need to do, Christa. You want her out of here, all you have to do is sign." He pulls the contract out of his back pocket. "It's simple."

I cringe and bend down by her head again. "Mom," I whisper, gently tapping the fence. "Mommy, please…"

Her eyelids flutter. "Christa…?" she breathes, her voice raw. "Christa, where… where am I?" She lifts her head feebly.

I grab the chain links and press my face to the gate, my throat tightening. "It's okay, Mom. I'm here, I'm right here—"

She licks her lips. "I can't… I don't think I can move." She sweeps her hand over her hip, patting it repeatedly like she's afraid it's going to disappear.

I quickly wipe away a tear. "Don't worry—you don't have to move right now. Just rest." I strain at the chain links, trying to get my hand through to her. "Everything is going to be okay…"

She winces, her expression pained. Alden clears his throat and taps his toe impatiently. I glare up at him. "Don't you dare," I growl.

He sighs. "As touching as this little reunion is…" He pulls out his phone, checking the time. "… I'm on a tight schedule today. So if we could think about wrapping this up, that would be great for me." He puts his phone back into his pocket and pulls out a pen.

I stand, my face cold. "I don't really give a shit *what* works for you right now!" I shout, motioning at my mother. "Why can't she move—what's wrong with her? What the hell did you give her?"

Alden exhales and scratches his head with the pen. "I *may* have upped the dosage slightly… given that I knew she had a history with pills and alcohol. I wanted to make sure it worked." He starts to pout. "But I have to admit, I'm a little surprised she's still so wonky. Hm." He shrugs, clapping his hands. "What can you do? I'm sure sensation will return to her legs very soon."

Mom moans from the floor. "Christa, it hurts…" She holds her thigh tightly. "It's burning…" I watch her, panicked, as she begins to writhe on the concrete.

Alden grins. "Ah—right on cue!"

"Why is she doing that?!" I ask shrilly. "She's in pain—"

"That's a good sign," he murmurs. "It means there's no permanent nerve damage."

Mom lets out a low wail. I grip the fence. "It's okay, Mom! It's okay… I'm…" I sigh, bowing my head. "I'm not going to lose you, too."

My lower lip quivers as I cross over to Alden, who has a bemused expression on his face. "All right." I scowl. "I'll do it."

He breaks into a huge smile. "Fantastic." He beams, squeezing my arms warmly. "I knew you'd come around."

I glower. "How do I know you'll keep your end of the Deal?" I narrow my eyes. "Let her go now, so I know you're not lying—"

I gasp as his gaze turns steely and he pulls me roughly to his chest, pinning me against the wall. "The whole defiant, pissed off Lolita shtick was cute, in the beginning," he spits, clenching my shoulders, "but you really need to learn when to shut that pretty mouth of yours—"

"Ow! Let go of me!" I try to wriggle free, but he holds me firmly, pressing his lips to my ear.

"Let's be very clear," he whispers. "I *always* keep my part of the Deal. When there is nothing else left in this crappy little world, I will still have my word." He steps back, his jaw tight. "Don't ever call me a liar again. The Deal was that she stays until your three days are up. Take it or leave it."

I look down at the floor, rubbing my arm tenderly. "Just..." I shake my head. "Just show me where to sign."

He nods and flips through the pages. "Here, at the bottom—next to mine." He points, then watches eagerly as I wrench the pen from his hand and scribble my signature on the line.

When I'm finished, I chuck the pen back at him. "Okay, that's it," I snap, jerking my head at the cage. "Can you help her?"

Alden nods, carefully tucking the papers back into his pocket. "Almost. There's just one more thing." He holds out his hand. "We shake on it."

I shrug, my face pinched. "Fine, whatever..."

His eyes glow as our fingers brush, his skin hot. "Do we have a Deal?" he murmurs.

Just as I'm about to grasp his palm, the double doors at the end of the hall burst open. "CHRISTA—NO!" Daniel howls, sprinting toward us with Mary Carmen following close behind. "DON'T TOUCH HIM!"

Alden shoves me back, stepping between us. "Danny!" he booms, plastering a big grin on his face. "I was wondering when you'd stop by…" He makes a show of craning to look around Daniel's back. "And I see you brought a friend! Ah, Mary Carmen!" He holds out his arms. "*Hola, mamacita*! Long time, no see. What a treat. I thought you'd have run Home for dinner by now."

Mary Carmen glares at him before glancing over at me. "Let her go, Alden!" Daniel shouts, stopping a few feet in front of us. "You have no right to keep her here!" He stares at me, his face alarmed.

I push against Alden's arm, desperately wanting to run to the Guardian. Alden rolls his eyes. "No one is being held against their will; this isn't your niece's dance recital."

He finally takes his hand away, and I stumble as I dash over to Daniel. I throw my arms around his neck as he pulls me into a giant bear hug.

I hear Alden tut behind us. "Can't say I've ever seen a Guardian do *that*, but there's a first time for everything." He pulls out his phone and puts it to his ear, turning toward the wall and muttering, "Yeah, can you send Vince and Tony down?"

Daniel, meanwhile, stares down at me and tucks my hair over my shoulders. "You're okay," he murmurs anxiously.

I nod. "Yeah," I breathe, "and I'm sorry I left like that. I know you must have been worried."

Daniel bites his lower lip. "Did… did I do something wrong? Or say something…?" He grimaces at the floor.

I shake my head. "No—no!" I cry, gripping his jacket. I glance over at Mary Carmen, shift uneasily, and clear my throat. "I just didn't want you to get hurt, any more than you already have." I cringe. That's true, but I keep my mouth shut about the whole

'Mary Carmen and Heaven want me dead if I don't play their game right' drama.

He looks up at me. "Christa—what are you talking about?" He touches my cheek. "I told you—I *can't* get hurt. If anyone should be going up against a Demon, it's me."

I nod, pressing my face further into his palm because his touch feels so nice. "I know, but..." I look at Alden, who is finishing up his call. "I don't know. I think we're missing something... important."

Daniel furrows his brow. "Like what?" He puts his hands back on my waist. "Did he tell you anything?"

I shake my head and lean into him. "No... Just, I need you to trust me." I sigh, then reach up and graze his chin with my fingers. "I care about you too much to have you be a part of this."

"Christa, you're the only one who matters to me! You know that, right?" he exclaims, grasping my hips.

I nod. "Okay," I whisper. "It's not *you* I'm worried about." I can feel Mary Carmen's eyes burning holes into my back.

Daniel runs a hand through his hair. "Now, I get that you left because you were trying to fix things on your own, but that isn't the answer. I can't let you go through with whatever scheme he's cooked up. I mean, have you seen this place?" He gazes around the room. "It makes the Gulag look like a 5-star hotel—come on!" He stares at me, his brown eyes pleading. "Let's go home."

I sigh. "I can't do that, Daniel. My mom..." I tilt my head toward the cell. "She's here. He's got her."

Daniel shakes his head and storms over to the cage. "Well, come on! What are we waiting for!" he yells, slamming his hands into the fence.

I grab his shirt and pull him back. "Wait—no! There's a contract!"

He stops and glares at me. Alden puts his phone away and

leans against the wall. "We can't take her yet," I finish, "not before—"

Daniel spins and grabs Alden, pulling him up by the collar as a small smile creeps across the Demon's face. "You think this is real funny, don't you!" Daniel spits, shoving him against the brick. "Bet you were just sitting back laughing last night, like you were on the goddamn Johnny Carson show!" He presses his knuckles into Alden's throat.

"Language, Danny," Alden gurgles. "You wouldn't want to get in trouble with the folks upstairs."

Daniel squeezes tighter. "Shut up!" he yells in Alden's face. "Now, I know you can end this whole thing whenever you feel like it, and that's what you're gonna do." He grinds his wrists as Alden sputters, his cheeks purpling. "You're gonna tear up or blow up whatever you've got on her mom and let everybody go home." Daniel loosens his grip and sets Alden, sputtering, back onto the floor. "We all get out alive, no big choices are getting made, and we fight another day, all right?" He looks around wildly as Alden smooths his rumpled shirt.

"That's something to consider. Hmm..." We all watch as Alden straightens his cuffs, rattles his pockets, and checks the bottom of his shoes.

"What are you doing—?" Daniel sneers, taking a tentative step toward me and placing his hand protectively on my arm.

Alden silences him with a raised finger. He then readjusts his neck and takes a deep breath. "I've thought about your suggestion, and I'm afraid I'm going to have to decline," he sighs, resting against the chain links. "Christa and I already have another Deal sorted out."

"Son of a—" Daniel charges forward, but I grab his elbow and pull him back. Mary Carmen rushes to his other side, tugging him by his jacket. "Are you crazy?!" he still manages to bellow at Alden. "If you think I'm gonna let you come anywhere near her..." He struggles against us. "If you even *look* at her, *think* about her, I'm gonna rip your head off!"

Alden nods and rolls his eyes. "Stop embarrassing yourself, Danny! It's done," he jeers.

"Nothing's done until I say it's done!" Daniel roars, swinging his arms. "Come over here and say that to my face!"

"Daniel, enough!" Mary Carmen shouts, straining against his shoulder.

Daniel shakes us off and steps away, running his hands through his hair. "Daniel," I murmur, walking over to him and placing my hand on his back.

He turns around and looks at me, his face grim. "What does he have you doing?" he pants.

I cross my arms and take a breath. "He wants me to come stay with him," I sigh.

Daniel shakes his head. "No." He puts his hands on his hips, staring down at the ground.

I rub my palm against my face. "Not forever!" I cry, moving over to him. "Just for three days, and then this will all be over!" I look up at him anxiously. "And then we can go home, together! Please, Daniel," I beg.

He shakes his head. "It's not going to be that easy, Christa! It never is with this joker!" He waves at Alden. "He has a million tricks up his sleeve."

I take his hand and squeeze it, hard. "I need you to be okay with this so *I* can get through it," I whisper. "Please."

He glares up at the ceiling, then exhales and pulls me close, bending his neck so that our foreheads touch. "You know I would do anything for you," he rasps, gripping my fingers. He looks at me, and my heart melts as he nods and steps back. "But I'm not letting you go that easily."

My eyes widen. "Wait, Daniel—" I stammer.

He gives my hand a squeeze and pulls away. "You didn't shake on it, right?" he asks.

When I shake my head, Daniel chuckles and turns to Alden. "Hey, take me!" he calls, holding out his arms unabashedly. "Take me instead."

Alden tilts his head.

"What? No!" I scream, looking at Mary Carmen.

Her mouth hangs open. "Daniel!" she cries.

Daniel shakes his head, his eyes locked on Alden's. "Now, why would I want to do that?" Alden murmurs, popping off of the fence.

Daniel steps right in front of him. "Because it's all you've wanted since the day you stopped breathing!" he answers grimly.

Alden considers, tapping his mouth. "True," he nods. "I do look forward to the moment I can watch you bound and gagged in agony, rotating over a barbecue spit." He grins. "It's a favorite little daydream of mine."

Daniel shrugs and bats Alden's arm. "Well, now's your chance! Come on: hang me up by my thumbs, bleed me dry into the next century—I don't care." He sticks out his chin and looks back at me. "Just leave her out of this. Leave this one alone."

I shake my head. "Daniel, no!" I moan. Mary Carmen moves over and takes my hand. I look at her skeptically, but don't pull away.

Alden furrows his brow. "It's tempting—really, Danny." He takes a deep breath. "But my answer is still *no.*" He grins and rocks back on his heels.

Mary Carmen lets out an audible sigh. "Thank God," she whispers, rubbing my arm. I glance at her, and she gives me a small smile.

I nod and turn back, straightening my spine. "Don't sound *too* relieved," I mutter.

"How can you say that?" Daniel is yelling at Alden and pacing tempestuously. "After years of chasing each other back and forth across the country, with the resentment, the rage—" His voice shakes. "All the pointless loss—"

"Oh, what do you know about loss?" Alden snarls suddenly, pounding his fists into the chain link fence. "You've never known a day of loss in your whole life! Until now, maybe." He cocks his head at me. I wrap my arms around my chest and gaze down at the floor.

"I've lost things I can't even remember I had!" Daniel roars, his face turning red. "If you think you're the only one who's been suffering, well, you need to get your head out of your ass and take a good look around!" He motions to himself. "Do you have any idea what it's like to wake up every morning with that kind of guilt—"

Alden bursts out laughing. "*Now* I've heard everything! A *Guardian* lecturing a *Demon* about guilt—that's just too much!" he crows, clapping his hands. "Must be a full moon or something. Whew!" He snorts and catches his breath, wiping a tear away. "Thanks, I really needed that."

Daniel crosses his arms. "Are you through?" he mutters.

Alden goes quiet and glares at him icily, his eyes piercing. "Not even close," he hisses. "The fun's just beginning." He steps over to me deliberately. "I've got big plans for Christa and myself." He turns and arches a brow at Daniel. "Plans that don't include you, Danny."

I hold my breath as he rests his palms on my shoulders. Daniel flinches. "Stay," Alden orders, tightening his fingers at my collarbone. Daniel freezes, his eyes on me.

"You see, I've decided that the best way to make you truly suffer is to take away everything that—" Alden puts his hands around my throat and looks up at Daniel impishly. "—*matters* to you. Word choice, word choice is the name of the game! If you don't say it out loud, it never really happened!" Alden sing-songs, stroking my neck.

"You have no idea what you're talking about," Daniel grits out with a scowl.

Alden rolls his eyes. "Right." He caresses my skin and whispers, "Relax," into my ear as I twist my shoulders. "Anywho," he adds, "Christa stays with me, comes to her senses when she sees how the world *really* works, and all you can do is stand by with your fingers in your mouth watching as I take her to the next level." He looks smugly up at the ceiling. "Brilliant, if I do say so myself." I exhale as he pets my hair and moves back.

"Deal or no Deal, she'd never choose your side," Daniel grimaces, taking a step toward me. "She's too good for that." I stare at him, my lips parted.

"I don't think your moral compass will be serving as our guide anytime soon, Danny," Alden snickers. "Not with your track record." Daniel takes a few more steps and wraps his arms around my waist, grasping my hands tightly.

Alden watches us, his mouth twisted. "You know, sometimes I actually feel sorry for you." He hooks his fingers into the chain links. "With your past completely torn away from you and barely a memory to hang your hat on. This herculean task set before you… a coward asked to become a hero overnight; it's unfair, really." Alden shrugs.

Daniel rests his chin on my shoulder, his jaw clenched. "I'm not a coward," he growls.

"The hell you're not," Alden scoffs. "No, I think the word I'm searching for is… *feigling?*" He arches a brow.

Daniel glares at him quizzically. "What is that, German?" When he looks down at me, I shake my head.

"You tell me," Alden whispers, his eyes bright. *"Sie zerstört Ihre familie, sie selbst zerstört."* He ticks off on his fingers. *"Du hast mich zerstört."* He stares at Daniel, who looks back at him blankly. "Nothing? Really, *mein wildes ding?*"

Daniel shrugs. Alden clucks his tongue. "That's depressing.

Time really is the cruelest master." His head jerks as the doors at the end of the hall bang open, two men in dark suits flanking the entrance.

"Finally!" Alden brays, beckoning them inside. "You boys certainly take those smoke breaks seriously." He saunters past us, waving them down like an air traffic controller. "There will probably be a bit of an outburst when she goes," he mutters, patting one of the men on the back. The goons nod and head towards us.

"Hey!" Daniel yells, positioning himself in front of me. "You can't take her! You know the Rules—the terms haven't been set!"

Alden massages his temples wearily. "I really need you to take a breath, Danny; they're not here for Christa." He rolls his eyes and jerks his thumb back toward my mother's cage. "Yeah, right there on the floor, guys."

The two men step past us and open the door to the cell, lifting my mother up by her arms and legs. My eyes go wide. "Wait—where are you taking her?" I cry, glancing between Alden and the men. Daniel holds me firmly as they walk back again, hauling Mom out like a Persian rug.

"Christa..." she rasps, her head drooping as they pass.

I reach out to grab her, but Alden holds up his hand. "Ah-ah," he chides, waggling his pointer finger. "Hands off my stuff." He pats Goon 1 on the arm as he shuffles by. "Move her to the Green Room; I'll deal with her later." The guys nod and walk swiftly back toward the double doors.

"Stop!" I shout. "Bring her back!"

Daniel squeezes my hand. Alden shrugs. "Deal or no Deal, she's still mine. I can do what I like," he replies.

I spin around and stare at Daniel. "Do something—make them stop!" I yell, my voice shrill. I glare at Mary Carmen, who is just standing by with a stunned look on her face. "Someone, help!" I cry.

Daniel hesitates, looks over at the men, and takes a step

forward. Alden shakes his head. "*You* know the Rules," he chuckles. "Try to touch her, and she will go to goo before you can say 'Here I've Come to Save the Day!'"

Daniel sighs and looks down at me. "I'm sorry, Christa. There's nothing I can do."

I turn and watch in horror as the doors swing shut behind the men and my mother. "No…" I breathe.

Alden exhales and steps forward, scratching his jaw. "Now that that messy bit is all cleaned up…" He turns back to us and rubs his hands together. "… it's back to business." He hones in on me. "Tick tock, Christa. It's time to make that Deal. My patience is running thin, and, as you can see," he motions back toward the doors, "I'm very busy. I don't want to keep Mummy waiting long."

"What are you going to do to her?" I hiss.

Alden rolls his eyes. "That is not your concern. If you want to see her again, you know what you have to do." He holds out his hand. "Three days, that's all it is. She'll be fine." His gaze turns dangerous. "Let's finish this."

I look at the doors and then back at Alden. "All right, fine." I nod and step forward.

Daniel grabs my wrist. "No, no, no! You don't have to do this!" he pleads.

I shake my head and gently pry my hand free. "Yes, I do," I whimper. "She needs me—and for once, I can actually *do* something for her." I take a deep breath and look into his eyes. "It's my turn to be strong, like you."

Daniel cringes. "If I'm strong at all, it's only because you make me that way," he whispers, closing his eyes. "I just found you, and now I'm losing you."

I reach over and squeeze his arm. "That's not true. Don't listen to him." I jerk my head at Alden. "It's three days. I'll be back making you crazy in no time."

Daniel sighs, defeated. "And I'll be waiting," he murmurs. "Close by!" he calls to Alden.

"Of course you will," Alden says with a snigger.

Daniel's fists clench aggressively. I put my hand on his chest. "Let it go. Look at me," I murmur. Daniel huffs and stares at me. "Let's end this, okay?" I press my fingers into his t-shirt.

He nods. "Yeah, okay." He steps back.

I smile weakly and walk over to Alden. "I'm ready now," I exhale, holding my head up.

Alden arches his eyebrows and puts out his hand. "Do we have a Deal?" he asks again.

I grip his palm and shake. "Yes, we have a Deal."

A bolt of electricity shoots up my arm. I gasp in pain and grip my wrist. "Christa!" Daniel cries out behind me.

I twist and squint at him, my vision blurry. "What the…" I breathe. I hold tight to my hand, which is still tingling. It almost feels like I stuck my finger in an outlet. I blink, the shock subsiding.

"It's done!" Alden shouts. I glance around the room, dazed. Everyone is still standing in their exact same spots, but I see little bits of burning paper blowing across the floor, the smell of smoke in my nostrils.

"What's that?" I ask blearily. Alden puts his hand on my shoulder.

"Your mother's former agreement; her contract has been voided." He reaches over and pops open the lock on her door. "And yours is now beginning." He motions inside the cell, his eyes trained on Daniel. "You can say goodbye, if you like."

I step in and watch as Daniel and Mary Carmen slowly walk over to the cage. Mary Carmen reaches in and pats my arm. "What you did, Christa… is very brave." She nods. "I… I don't know if it means anything, but I am proud of you." She smiles.

I sigh and nod back at her, forgetting for a moment what she said in the kitchen earlier. "Thanks, Mary Carmen," I whisper.

She gives me a squeeze and steps away from the cell. "Take care. We'll see you when you get out." She exhales, and Daniel moves in.

"I guess this is it," he sighs. Alden steps behind him, lingering by the cell door. I clear my throat.

"Yeah, guess so." I look up at the Guardian. "Um, will that Link thing you have still work while I'm in here?" I ask nervously. "Like, you'll know if I wind up at the bottom of the ocean or something?" I wince.

Daniel nods. "Yes," he rasps. "No matter where he tried to take you, I could find you. I *would* find you—don't worry about that."

I exhale and smile. "Okay, good," I sigh. "That makes me feel a little better."

Daniel skims my wrist with his finger. "Christa…" he murmurs.

Alden clears his throat. "No touching—she's on my clock now," he snaps, holding open the door. "And visiting hours are over." He jerks his chin toward my purse on the floor. "Take that with you, Danny, along with any cash, credit cards, phone." He leers at me. "No sneaky pillow talk past curfew."

Daniel glares at him coldly as he picks up my bag. "You're unbelievable, you dirty piece of sh—" he mutters as he steps out of the cage.

"See you in three days, Danny!" Alden grins, patting him heartily on the back as he passes.

Daniel turns to face me as he moves down the hall. "I'll see you soon. Promise!" he calls from the double doors. "Don't forget about me."

I scoff. "Impossible."

Daniel smiles and steps out of the hall, the doors swooshing closed.

I cough and look at Alden, watching Daniel's body be blocked by the gate. "So... now what?" I murmur, gripping the cell wall.

Alden turns to me. "Now..." he sighs. "We play." He grins and offers his hand. "Come on."

I glance around, confused. "I'm... not staying here?"

Alden laughs. "Oh no! Unless you want to use the hole in the floor for a toilet?" He shakes his head, leading me out of the cage. "No, this was all for show. You'll be staying upstairs with the rest of us." I flush angrily as he slams the cage door shut behind us. For a minute, I debate pitching a fit and demanding to stay down here just to prove a point, but then I take a final look around the room and see all of the empty eyes staring back at me. I shiver.

"They never said anything." I look away from the prisoners. "Never cried out, begged to be saved." I clutch my arms. "That's... weird, right?"

Alden shrugs. "They know there is no point in wasting the energy. For them, this is the end of the line. There is no promise, no salvation, no pretty Guardian coming to save the day." He raises a brow as he leads me out. "Prepare yourself, Christa: you are now living amongst the Despairing and Condemned. Hope you enjoy your stay."

CHAPTER 8

"THIS IS YOU: lucky number 13."

Alden raps the gold-plated number with the key before opening the dark mahogany door. It swings open, revealing what looks like a very expensive hotel room. I arch my eyebrows in surprise as I step inside, fighting the instant desire to take off my boots for fear of destroying the lush white carpet.

"It's... nice." I blush at my understatement as I look around the room. The walls are painted a sleek navy blue, highlighting the giant canopy bed in the center of the room with its bright white linens. There is a large picture window on the main wall that's framed by sheer curtains, with a soft, powder blue chair positioned underneath it along with an end table and a small reading lamp. Above the bed is a sprawling abstract painting, bold strokes of purples and blues striking across the bare canvas. It makes the room downstairs feel like it belongs on a distant planet.

"I like the colors," I mumble.

Alden smiles. "That's not surprising," he chuckles.

I glance back at him oddly.

"Just seems like blue is your... preferred shade." He tilts his head and steps over to the wardrobe across from the bed, opening the cabinets. "The TV's in here, along with any intimates you might need while you're visiting." He gestures to the drawers. "All of your other clothes are in the closet." He motions back to the wall by the door.

I bite my cheek. "*That* should be interesting," I whisper.

He purses his lips. "I had some help from our resident fashionista. I have to warn you, she got a little carried away." He rubs his neck. "There's an outfit for just about any type of occasion in there, but no need to panic—I can assure you that you can leave the fur-lined ski suit tucked away. Don't think we'll be hitting the slopes this trip."

I wince and look down at the floor. "It's like you knew I was coming," I murmur, gathering my hair over one shoulder. "I don't know if I should be grateful or horrified."

Alden scratches his ear. "Why don't you check out the shoe selection first, and then you can decide." He smiles awkwardly.

I cross my arms and glance around the room. "Um, bathroom?" I ask, casting my eyes to the floor.

He nods and steps back into the hallway. "Right here." He flicks the light on and off. "Should be fully stocked, but if there is anything you need, just let me know, and I'll have someone run out and fetch it." He clears his throat and steps over to the nightstand. "The phone is here." He taps a beautiful, old-fashioned rotary dial telephone with his fingertips. "You know how to use one of these?"

I nod.

"It only makes internal calls. Dial 23 to reach me or 15 for Housekeeping. They can bring you anything you like, day or night," he murmurs.

I glance toward the window. "How about a ladder?" I grumble, looking out. I squint, expecting a not-so-picturesque glimpse of the parking lot, but instead see rows of palm trees and sand framing crystal cool water. It would be an amazing view, if we were anywhere near the beach.

I cross over and pull back the curtain, tapping the glass with my hand. "What is this?" Trying to find where the screen meets the window frame, I find the open latch and force the window as far as it will go; it's only a few inches, but the image doesn't alter. I gasp and step back.

"How—?" I narrow my eyes and put my face to the opening. I can hear seagulls and smell the ocean air. After I push my fingers out and feel a warm breeze, I can't help but turn and stare at Alden, wide-eyed.

"It's a full sensory mirage," he states, stepping over to me. "All of the windows and doors are controlled by the building's mainframe. You can change it with the TV remote if you like…" He finds the controller and aims it at the window. In an instant, the beach is gone and replaced with a series of different images: a bucolic meadow, a rainy-day forest, and a sunset view of Hollywood and Vine, complete with traffic noises.

"That's amazing," I admit.

Alden shrugs and tosses the remote on the bed. "Beats the alternative," he replies, checking his phone.

I sit on the edge of the bed. "So, where do you sleep?" I gaze back at the huge mattress, smoothing my palm over the duvet. "I mean, um…" I look up at him uncomfortably. "This isn't your room too, is it?" My voice is small.

The corners of his eyes crinkle. "My room is down the hall. A deal's a deal, Christa… Unless that's an invitation?" He raises his eyebrows.

I look at my lap and blush. "No, I was just curious," I mutter.

He smiles at the floor. "Well, then, I think that about covers it." He puts his hands on his hips. "There is business that requires my attention downstairs, so I need to leave you for a while. Will you be all right on your own?"

I look up at him. "Yeah, sure." I shrug, leaning against the bedpost. "Is there anything I'm supposed to be… doing?" I pick at a loose thread on my dress.

Alden puts his hands in his pockets. "Take a load off!" He smiles. "Seriously: rest, watch a movie, get cleaned up. I'm sure you wouldn't mind a few hours to yourself after everything that's happened." He pulls the keys out and jangles them. "But, as you're still new around here, I'm going to hold onto these and ask that you stay in your room." He puts them back into his pocket.

I tuck my legs underneath myself. "I get it," I mumble. "Wouldn't want the inmates out of their cages, wandering around." I glance back at the painting on the wall. "Lovely a cage as it may be."

Alden nods at the carpet. "Something like that," he sighs. "I'll come by a little later and see how you're doing. Again, if you need anything, you can dial out." He points back at the phone. "15 for—"

"Housekeeping, I know," I snap. "You just told me, like, three seconds ago."

Alden grimaces awkwardly. "Right, okay. I'll leave you to it, then." He turns and walks toward the door.

I bite my lip and sigh. "Alden," I call. He spins back on his heels. "What is all this? The gorgeous room, the fancy tech." I wave at the window. "And you being so… *nice*." I sneer and shake my head.

"Would you rather I wasn't?" he whispers. "Would that make it easier for you?" He stares at me, his eyes blazing.

I pull my knees tightly to my chest. "I don't know…" I mumble.

"Because there's still an empty cell downstairs, if that would be more to your liking," he finishes aloofly.

I glare at him, my cheeks reddening. "This is fine."

"I thought as much." Alden pinches the bridge of his nose, his eyes closed. "So," he exhales, "if that's all, I'll see you later."

I nod and cluck my tongue. "Yep, that's all." I stare at the dark TV screen across the room.

Alden watches me for a minute, then nods. "'Til then," he mumbles gravely, closing the door behind him. I hear the lock click into place, and his footsteps fade down the hall.

When I can't hear them anymore, I fling myself onto the bed. "Fuck," I rasp, punching the pillow angrily with the back of my fist. "This is going to be a long three days."

I look up at the smooth plaster on the ceiling. I don't know what I expected—waterboarding and electrodes hooked up to car batteries? I guess I should be relieved that I'm not tied up in a basement somewhere, but that doesn't get rid of the enormous pit in my stomach. How did I get here? A few days ago, I was trading jabs with Riley and Tom over stolen candy bars, and overnight I've become the cornerstone to some massive battle between Heaven and Hell. I close my eyes and breathe through my nose, really wishing that Daniel was here. I already miss his stupid jokes and goofy grin, waxing poetic about bands from half a century ago, and the way the sound of his voice instantly calms me down. I wonder what he's doing right now. He's probably with Mary Carmen. I wonder what Mom is doing. I sigh and sit up.

"That's why you're here, idiot," I murmur. "You did it to save her." No matter what Alden throws at me in the coming days, at least I know that Mom's going to be all right in the end—and that should be enough. "A deal's a deal," I mumble, my hands between my knees. "Suck it up and handle it… and stop talking to yourself, you've only been here an hour. It's too soon to be cracking up." I shake my head. Maybe I should have taken Alden up on his offer to move down to the Dog Run Room; at least there would be other people there, although those guys didn't seem very chatty. I exhale and glance down next to me, the remote wedged under my hip. I pick it up and point it at the TV.

"Let's try this…" I mutter as I press the 'on' button. A bright pinprick pops up in the center of the screen, and a series of chimes go off like something out of *Close Encounters of the Third Kind*. The light expands, revealing a white screen, followed by a green circle that coils around itself. I squint and watch the graphic; it's a snake eating its own tail—an ouroboros, I think it's called. The image fades, and the face of an attractive young Asian man takes its place.

"Welcome to Serpentine," he says with a smile, "your personal interactive operating system. Using your remote control, please choose your selection from our main menu." His eyes dart to the right side of the screen, where several user options pop up. The list includes *TV Guide, New Releases, Local Time and Weather, Information*, and *Settings*. Serpentine's face stares back at me, his expression neutral. I crinkle my forehead and point the remote.

"Serpentine? Weird name," I grumble, shifting under the TV's gaze. I click on *TV Guide*, and a full channel listing comes up, exactly the same as we have at home.

"Standard," I murmur, exiting out. I go under *New Releases* and get a bunch of movies that are still out in theaters, just like you would find in any hotel room—except these are free.

"Sweet," I cluck, although it would have been fun to rack up a huge bill and make Alden pay it. "You are such a nerd," I chide myself. "Way to really stick it to him." I sigh and select *Local Time and Weather*.

"Local time in Los Angeles is 6:18 p.m.," the face declares evenly. "Sunset was at 4:53 p.m.; the current temperature is 58 degrees Fahrenheit. Tonight's low is 52, with clear skies." Another menu bar comes up at the bottom of the screen with other cities listed: New York, Rio, Moscow, Tokyo, and somewhere called Porticullis. I purse my lips and click on it.

"Local time in Porticullis is 3:18 a.m.," Serpentine replies. "Weather undetermined." He doesn't say anything else. I scrunch my nose.

"3 a.m.? Where is that... northern Africa?" I sit back. "Never heard of it." A little note blinks under the face: *DIAL 3 TO CONNECT.* I take a deep breath.

"Yeah, not going to do that." I smirk, getting off the bed and stepping closer to the TV. "We'll save prank calling sleepy Demons for my last night here." I set the controller on the wardrobe shelf as I cross the room and make my way to the bathroom, feeling the need to pee. I turn on the light and gasp.

"What the…" My whole apartment could fit inside this bathroom. There's wall to wall white marble and a huge Jacuzzi tub with a gas fireplace next to it that flickers to life as I enter the room. A separate, dual-headed shower stands adjacent to the expansive vanity, complete with about a million shiny bottles of perfume, cosmetics, and lotions covering the countertop. I run a hand through my hair and find the toilet.

"Okay, this is kind of luxe," I admit, glancing around before I flush. I step over to the sink and wash my hands, catching a glimpse of myself in the mirror.

"You are less so," I tell myself with a grimace, turning off the water. I look absolutely exhausted, my face thin and haggard, my skin uneven. While the bruises from the accident are just about gone, they've been replaced with heavy bags under my eyes. I push my hair back and cringe.

"Someone needs a nap," I mutter, before glancing down at my dress. It's wrinkled from where I spilled water earlier and starting to smell a little funky from all the running around. I sigh and unbutton it, finding a stick of deodorant.

"Gonna have to start playing the game at some point," I sigh, tossing my dress on the floor and kicking off my boots. "Now's as good a time as any." I put on a fresh coat of deodorant, splash some water on my face, and walk out to the closet.

I scrunch my lips hesitantly as I roll open the door, expecting something in horrible pleather, but am pleasantly surprised when I'm presented with rows of beautiful dresses, sweaters, and tops in every color imaginable. I look down and see a stack of designer jeans and leggings and about thirty pairs of corresponding shoes, from heels to sneakers.

"Guess they decided to leave the straps and bondage gear at home," I croon, pulling a soft, light gray sweater dress with a cowl neck off the rack. Instinctively, I close my eyes and rub it against my cheek; the wool is so fine, I feel like I could melt into it. I quickly clear my throat and reach down to grab a pair of leggings.

"Way to get emotional over a dress, loser," I scoff. I start to put it on over my head, but notice that Serpentine is still on, his big face staring out into the main room. I readjust the cabinet doors to cover him up, not wanting an audience while I get dressed. I tug the dress down; it fits perfectly, accentuating curves I don't really have. I pull on the leggings and go back into the bathroom, applying a little lip gloss and concealer and twisting my hair into a bun on top of my head. I nod at my reflection.

"Slightly more human." I shrug, rubbing my forehead, then switch off the light and pace back into the bedroom. I swing my arms and look at the bed; I'm tired, but I don't really want to sleep yet. I step over to the wardrobe and rifle through the drawers, finding nothing but silky lingerie and nightgowns. I sigh and slam them shut.

"Death by boredom." I glance around the room, unsuccessfully trying to find a clock. I open the TV cabinet back up, Serpentine's face gazing placidly at me. I click on *Local Time* again.

"Local time in Los Angeles is 6:23 p.m." He blinks. "Sunset was at 4:53 p.m. Current temp—"

"Arrgh!" I snarl, chucking the remote at the bed. "Could this be going any slower?!" I reach up and clench my bun irritably. "Of course he puts me up here… Why bother bringing out the heavy artillery when just making me wait is enough! Christ!" I exhale and lean against the bed.

"Okay, I really need to chill out… Can't totally lose it on the first night." I rub my face and bend over, picking the remote back up.

"All right, let's see what's going down here…" I clear my throat and go back to the main menu. "Information," I recite, clicking on the link. "I am ready to be informed."

Serpentine nods and smiles. "Information," he repeats. "Please select one of the following options from the menu screen."

I scan the new list that materializes next to his head. "Calendar, L.A. Attractions, Frequently Asked Questions…" I read aloud, pausing at the last item. "FriendFinder? What's that?" I click the remote.

"FriendFinder." The face grins, his white teeth glimmering. "Please stand in front of your screen and clearly state the name of the individual you wish to locate. All subjects must be residing on the mortal plain," he adds matter-of-factly.

I turn and furrow my brow. "Seriously? I just… say their name? This can't be for real."

I hold the remote up like a microphone. Serpentine gazes back, unfaltering. "Right, now I'm talking to a load screen; that's not crazy at all…" I smack my lips together and sigh.

"Friends… Okay, um, Jodie. My best friend, Jodie Phan." The face dissolves, and a new window pops up. My jaw drops when I recognize the familiar pink butterfly bedspread. "Oh my God, that's her room," I breathe, leaning against the bedpost. Jodie walks in and sits down at her desk, carrying her favorite mug.

"Jodie!" I yell. She doesn't respond, just blows the steam off her cup and flips through the large textbook in front of her. "Jodie!" I cry again, running over to the TV. She keeps her head down, focused on her reading.

"Oh my God," I gasp, my eyes welling up. "That's amazing… Holy shit, I'm so happy to see you!" I touch the glass, running my thumb over her image. She picks up a pencil and writes something in the margin of her book.

"I don't think you can hear me… That makes sense." I wipe my face and smile. "Still, that is so cool." I clear my throat. "I want to do another one!" I step back, Serpentine's face returning at my call. "Um, Tom… Tom Wyndam—"

The screen dissolves before I can finish saying his name, and a new window appears, this time showing the hospital room I visited yesterday. Tom is lying quietly in the bed. A nurse is in the process of changing his IV. I sigh.

"He's the same." I nod to my empty room behind me. I wait for a moment, watching the nurse move around the bed, checking his vitals and making sure that the sheets are tucked in properly. I stand up straight.

"Okay… one more, I guess." I tongue my cheek thoughtfully. "I don't even know if this will work."

Serpentine's big face fills the screen once more. I take a deep breath. "Daniel. Can… can you show me him?" I scratch my neck. "I don't know his last name."

Serpentine blinks and disappears, the screen going dark. I wait, watching for a new window. Nothing comes up.

"Crap," I mutter. I sigh and step back, tossing the remote dejectedly. As I turn to crawl onto the bed, though, I hear a scuffing noise behind me. I twist and see my Guardian in his jacket on TV, his hair blowing in the wind.

"Daniel!" I cry. He's outside, the night sky his backdrop, standing on what looks like a roof. He kicks bitterly at a layer of gravel, spraying stones all over the stucco. The shot pans out, and I recognize the building.

"Oh my God… he's here!" I exclaim, looking up at the ceiling. I stand up on the bed and stretch, pushing my palms to the plaster. "Daniel! Daniel! I'm here! Daniel!" I scream at the top of my lungs, pounding with my fist. I glance back at the screen to see if he can hear me, but he stares forlornly out at the skyline. I plop back down on the comforter, out of breath.

"Damn it," I sigh, shoving a pillow in my lap. I watch him pace along the rooftop, his hands in his pockets. "Well, I guess it's better than nothing."

I slump against the headboard and watch him take a seat along the edge of the roof, his long legs dangling over the side of the building. He sighs, his head bowed. I snuggle into the pillows, finding solace in knowing that he's only a couple of layers of metal and paint away. He reaches back and picks up a handful of gravel, looking out at the city.

"You'd like this," he murmurs.

I jerk my head to the screen. "Daniel? Can you hear me? I'm right here—"

"As soon as you get out," he talks over me, "I'm taking you up to the Hills, and we're just gonna stretch out and count the lights." He motions with his arm. "This is nothing compared to what we'd see up there. You're gonna love it."

I bite my lip. "That sounds nice," I whisper. "I wish we could go right now."

"I wish we could go right now," he echoes with a sigh, tossing a couple of stones over the edge. "That'd be heaven."

I shift my hand under my cheek, my pillowcase damp. "Daniel…" I breathe.

There's a knock at the door.

"What? Uh—hold on…" I call as I scramble off the bed, feeling like I've been caught in the middle of doing something dirty. I step over to the TV.

"I'll see you soon," I murmur to Daniel on the screen.

There is another impatient knock. "Come on already!" a high-pitched voice snaps through the door. I cringe and hustle across the room.

"Sorry…" I shake my head and close the wardrobe cabinets on the TV as I make my way to the door. The pounding turns into an irritated kick. I rest my hand against the wood.

"Um… who is it?" I call. The kicking stops, and I hear the clank of silverware.

"Dinner service!" the voice shouts back. "Are you decent?"

I glance down at my dress. "Uh, yeah." I try the knob, but it's locked tight. "I would open the door for you, but… I… I don't know how." I rub my forehead, still feeling a little warm from seeing Daniel.

The voice sighs. "Duh. Just get out of the way!" he barks, a set of keys jangling on the other side of the lock. I blink and step back, the door bursting open. I press up against the wall, almost getting run over by a large cafeteria cart that's stacked high with trays and dishes. Driving the massive thing is a small boy with a shock of bright red hair and a super pissed-off expression on his freckled face. He shoves the cart into the center of the room.

"Took you long enough!" Freckles grumbles, putting the wheel locks down on the cart. He gawps up at me. "Were you taking a dump or something?"

I stare at him, taken aback by his rudeness, but feeling overwhelming relief to have another person in the room. "Uh, no," I mumble, glancing back at the bed. He looks me over, his arms crossed.

"*You're* what everyone's talking about? You're just a girl," Freckles sniffs. "And a pretty dumb-looking one, too."

I stand there, my mouth agape. "Uh, thanks?" I clear my throat.

He sighs and moves around the back of the cart. "I mean, you're glowing and all, so that's something." He unhooks a cabinet near his knees. "But it's not like *that's* all that special."

"Wait—you… you can see me?" I ask, surprised.

"Of course I can see you!" Freckles shouts. "I'm not blind." He pulls out a white tablecloth and snorts. "But I thought you'd have, like, x-ray vision, super muscles, or at least look more like Mystique! The way everyone is freaking out over you." He shakes his head. "Talk about not living up to the hype." He crouches down and opens a drawer, banging around in it noisily.

I chuckle, massaging the back of my neck. "Sorry. I guess I'm just a little behind the curve," I sigh. "Looks like everyone, including ten-year-old boys, knows more about me than I do."

He shoots me a withering glare. "I'm twelve!" he snipes. "God, you're stupider than you look." He selects a fork and knife from the drawer.

I purse my lips. "Wow, nice to meet you too, grumpy little kid I've never seen before!" I hold out my hand. "I'm Christa, Huge Disappointment; and you are—?"

Freckles looks up at me and rolls his eyes. "Not Interested in Talking to Wastoids," he smirks, stepping in front of the cart and pulling out a table extension. I tuck my hand back behind me and bite my tongue, trying not to laugh.

"Now move so I can set up your food," Freckles grunts. "You wanna eat, right?"

I nod vigorously and sit on the edge of the bed. "Yes, sir. Don't let me stop you." I hold my hands up in surrender, then watch him lie the white cloth over the tabletop before setting out a pretty red flower in a glass vase. He hastily throws out the silverware and a napkin and pushes the table closer to me, going out of his way not to touch me.

"Such service!" I giggle.

His mouth twists petulantly. "Okay, so we have vegetarian and non-vegetarian."

"There are choices? Really?" I perk up, my stomach rumbling.

He glowers. "You look like a vegetarian: skinny and weak. You probably just eat salad all day and cry whenever you hear about cute baby cows being slaughtered. So lame."

I blink. "You've got me all figured out. How about you just give me whatever has the most food, okay? I'm starving." I lay the napkin in my lap.

Freckles crosses his arms and stands behind the cart. "That would be the rib eye. But I bet you can't eat the whole thing," he huffs.

I arch a brow. "Is that a challenge?" I grin. "How about this: if I clean my plate, you tell me your name. Deal?"

He narrows his eyes. "I don't make Deals," he growls. "Even with loser Mortals like you... or whatever you are." His face twitches as he pulls out a plate covered with a silver dome.

I clear my throat. "I'm sorry. I was just messing around... I didn't even think—" I look down at my lap. "I'm just happy to have someone to talk to." I smile up at him hesitantly.

Freckles sighs. "It's Trevor," he mutters, setting the plate in front of me. "My name. But don't go thinking we're friends now, cuz we're not." He takes off the lid. "Now shut up and eat."

I inhale the warm aroma of the meal. A huge steak sits before me, garnished with mashed potatoes, cheddar biscuits, and butter-soaked green beans. "Oh, yes..." I breathe, my mouth watering as I pick up my knife and fork. "I have big plans for you." I sink the blade into the steak.

"You're weird," Trevor sneers.

I cut hastily, glancing at him out of the corner of my eye. "It's not poisoned, is it?" I ask. "Maybe I should make you try the first bite." I hold out my fork, a smile teasing my lips.

Trevor huffs. "It's not like I would tell you if it was," he snipes, adding another, "Idiot!" for good measure.

I nod. "Okay. Looks like I'll just have to trust you." When I put the fork in my mouth, I close my eyes and moan, the steak melting down my throat. "Mmm... that's awesome." I chew happily, quickly trimming away with my knife.

Trevor rolls his eyes and steps over to the TV. "Whatever," he clucks, opening the cabinet. My eyes bug out and I almost choke as I lurch forward, afraid that it's still stuck on FriendFinder and Daniel.

"No!" I mumble, my mouth full of cheddar biscuit. "Don't open that!"

Trevor looks back at me like I have two heads. "You don't want music? I'm supposed to put on background music!" he snarls.

I shake my head. "I'm good, really. Just leave it shut." I motion with my hand.

He sighs and bangs the cabinet closed. "So annoying," he hisses, going back to the cart. "I can tell you're one of those girls who likes everything 'just so.'" He scrunches his shoulders. "High maintenance, or whatever." He reaches down and pulls a glass of water from the shelf and shoves it towards me.

I nod and take a gulp. "Thanks." I set the glass down and wipe my mouth with the back of my hand. "You have a lot of experience with 'high maintenance' girls, Trevor?" I wink. "What's your girlfriend like?"

He wrinkles his nose, his angry little freckles becoming more prominent. "Gross! I don't have a girlfriend! All the girls at my school are total nerds." He shakes his head. "And Human. Sick."

I shovel mashed potatoes onto my fork, considering. "I didn't realize that was a bad thing." I look up at him and squint. "I mean, since you look pretty human, too."

He crosses his arms and scoffs. "You would say that, but no, I'm not. Jeez, you don't know anything." He purses his lips contemptuously. "For your information, I'm an Amalgam."

I stare at him. "What... like mercury?" I murmur, flashing back to 10th grade chemistry.

Trevor sighs. "No, idiot! Like, half-Demon, half-human. It means that I'm tougher, stronger... just—" He scrunches his face. "—way more awesome than you!"

I furrow my brow. "How does that work, exactly?" I clean the back of my mouth with my tongue. "Being an Amalgam?"

Trevor's face turns bright red. "The same way it works everywhere else!" His voice cracks angrily. "Demon and human get together, and there's a half-Demon baby nine months later! God, why do you need everything explained to you like a little kid?"

I watch him while I chew. "You're not dead," I state between bites. "And one of your parents is a Demon…"

"Yeah," he mutters. "My dad."

My eyes go wide. "Wait—Alden's your dad?" I sputter, spraying bits of green bean.

Trevor puffs out his cheeks. "No way! That jerkwad doesn't have kids!" he screeches.

I swallow, blotting my mouth with my napkin. "No, Vesper's my dad," he continues. "He's in charge of this station."

I nod slowly. "I've met him," I mutter. "Scary dude."

"You know it!" Trevor exclaims. "One time, he tortured this huge UFC fighter for like—four days straight! The guy had to be three times his size!" His eyes brighten. "But my dad had him screaming for his mommy the whole time. It was so cool."

I shake my head. "I bet." I push back from my plate, my appetite gone.

Trevor grins. "He brought a Guardian in yesterday. She was all messed up." He wrinkles his nose. "They've had her down on three since she got here… I'm not allowed on that floor. Full Demons only, with special access to Level 4s and above." He frowns.

My ears burn at the mention of Guardians. "What did she look like?" I mumble, pushing potatoes around with my fork.

Trevor sighs. "The usual: dirty, homeless, crazy… This one was black." He shrugs.

I close my eyes. Emily. "Well, it sounds like you guys are pretty busy here at this… station?" I try to sound casual.

Trevor nods. "We're the biggest in the country! But not the world." He takes away the silver dome and starts wiping it down with a dishcloth. "That's Moscow."

I bite my lip. "So we're not actually *in* Hell," I comment. "This is just an outpost or satellite office."

Trevor laughs. "Of course this isn't Hell! Your feeble body would disintegrate the second you tried to set foot in there." He shakes his head. "Only the dead can go to Hell. Everyone knows that."

I sigh. "And you said you're not allowed on the third floor unless you're a Level 4… What does that mean?" I ask.

Trevor rolls his eyes, taking my plate away. "There are seven Demon grades. Usually, when someone first becomes a Demon, they start down at level 1. They don't have any powers and get bossed around by the higher levels." He gestures to himself with the rag.

I smile tightly. "Hence dinner detail," I say with a nod. "Gotcha."

Trevor takes a breath. "As you go along doing more Demon stuff, you gain more powers and graduate to different levels, the highest being 7." He wrinkles his mouth. "Level 7s are too strong to leave Hell, so the highest you're going to run into is a 6." He grins. "Like my dad."

I remember how my mother's contract said that Alden was a level 5. "So Alden must be pretty powerful, being a 5." I arch a brow.

Trevor scoffs. "And he'll be the first to make sure you know it. Dillweed." He snickers.

I let out a small laugh and look at him. "So, you're literally like… Demonspawn," I chuckle.

In an instant, Trevor's face turns bright red. "Hey, don't you call me that! Stupid human!" he spits out, kicking the cart.

I startle and sit back. "I didn't mean…"

"And stop laughing all the time!" he shouts. "I don't know what *you* think is so funny, being locked up here! You're the last person who should be happy about anything!"

I look down at the tablecloth. "That's probably true," I murmur. "But it's the Deal I made, and now I have to live with it." I brush away a few crumbs with my palm.

Trevor rolls his eyes and grabs the vase. "Boohoo, it's three days." He jerks his head at me. "We've got bodies downstairs that have been rotting in the walk-in longer than that." He glances around the room. "You should know all this. Didn't you come through the Kennel Room?"

I nod slowly.

"Then you're just spoiled." he sniffs, breaking down the table.

I pull my knees up to my chest and watch him. "You must know your way pretty well around this place, cruising with your crash cart, feeding everyone," I murmur, leaning over the edge of the bed.

He scoffs. "Um, yeah. I was born here." He shakes his head haughtily. "Of course I know this place, better than anyone else!"

I rub one of my earlobes. "So you know what… *where* the Green Room is?" I haven't forgotten the name of the nebulous pit where Alden sent my mother.

Trevor blows a raspberry. "Of course I know where the Green Room is! I'm in there, like, three times a day to fix *something*. Junk's always falling apart in there." He glares at me suspiciously. "Why?"

I sigh and pretend to be fascinated with the state of my nail beds, trying to hide my nerves. "No reason." I shrug. "I just figured, since you're the guy who knows this place inside and out, you could…" I clear my throat. "… show it to me." I glance at him slyly.

Trevor shifts from right to left. "You're not supposed to leave this room," he mumbles. "Alden said so—"

I scoff. "You always do what Alden tells you to do? I thought you just said he was a total dillweed."

Trevor glares at me. "He is! And no… I don't always do what he tells me! Last week, he told me to fix the restraints on one of the cruciation tables, and instead I went up to my room and played

X-Box all afternoon! What do you think of that?" He puffs out his chest.

I nod appreciatively. "Impressive." I keep the quiver out of my voice. "So what difference does it make if we sneak out for a few minutes? He'll never know." I have to see Mom, make sure she's okay.

Trevor sighs and bites his lip. "I dunno. If they caught us, I'd be in really big trouble…"

I sit up and look him in the eye. "Come on, Trevor. If anyone can bust me out, it's you." I pout, crossing my legs seductively. He blushes as his beady little eyes scan down to my knees.

"All right, fine. For, like—five minutes!" he shouts.

I grin and clap my hands, hopping off the bed.

"And you better keep your mouth shut and do exactly as I say!" he huffs, the top of his red hair just brushing my shoulder as I whisk past him to grab my boots. "Hey! I mean it!" he barks. "This is life or death!"

I nod placatingly, stepping towards the door. "Of course, Trevor." I arch my brows as I mime zipping my lips.

He rolls his eyes. "Yeah, right. Something tells me it's impossible for you not to say something stupid." He sighs, opening the door and dragging the cart out after him. "Just, if you tell Alden I did this, I will make your life *miserable*. Got it?"

I stand up straight and fold my hands behind my back. "Promise. Which way?"

He slumps and points down the hall. "First floor elevator. Don't clomp your boots!" he growls as I step behind him. "You look like you're ninety freaking pounds, but you sound like a horse! So annoying!"

We step out of the elevator and walk down a brightly lit corridor, the floors tiled a sterile hospital white. Trevor stops in front of an unmarked door and turns to me, his face stone cold.

"Okay, so the big rule for this room is that you don't touch *anything* with your skin." He looks down at my bare arms and sighs. I nod and square my shoulders. "Just keep your hands to yourself, and stay in the aisle. You don't want any of the pollen to get on you."

I look at him, confused, as he puts his key in the lock. "Pollen? Like… with plants?"

He rolls his eyes. "Yeah, genius. Why do you think they call it the 'Green Room'?" He pushes the door open.

I feel my pupils constrict in response to the hot, blinding light that radiates from inside the room. I follow Trevor as he steps past the threshold, a heavy wave of humidity passing over us as we enter a sea of lush, tropical greenery with UV lamps lining the walls. Bright yellow flowers burst through the waist-high leaves like shining pearls. I gaze around in wonder.

"They're beautiful," I whisper, walking further in.

Trevor nods and reaches around the doorframe. "Hang on, let me get the clock." He picks up a kitchen timer that was sitting on a shelf and sets it, the soft ticking echoing behind us.

I walk down the small path that cuts through the center of the room, reaching my fingers out to brush the flowers on either side of me. "Hey!" Trevor dashes over and slaps my arms down. "What did I just say?!" he yells. "DON'T TOUCH ANYTHING! Jeez! I knew this was a bad idea!"

I wince and grip the hem of my dress. "Sorry," I bluster. "They're just so pretty…"

Trevor sighs. "That's why they're so dangerous!" He shakes his head and looks out at the rows of plants. "They're from the Amazon. The flowers put out a pollen that makes people sleepy. If you get it on your skin, you instantly pass out." He clenches his jaw. "And I would be in so much trouble if I had to drag your skinny butt outta here! We'd get caught for sure!"

I look down at the floor.

"We can't be in here too long, or they'll start to get to us just from standing next to them. I set the clock for five minutes." Trevor nods back at the timer and takes a few steps forward, grabbing a water bottle off of the floor and spraying one of the plants. I watch him, my hands plastered to my sides. He glances back at me.

"Someone has to come in here a couple times a day to spray. The plants have to stay moist; the room is also rigged with special humidifiers." He jerks his head toward the wall. "They break ALL THE TIME, and who do you think gets called the minute one of them shuts down?" He aims the bottle at the flowers in the back. "They like it really wet in here. Keeps the plants happy, so they keep making more pollen." He grimaces. "Like I don't have anything better to do than sit around playing in the dirt. So dumb."

"Why do they need so much pollen?" I ask quietly. "Do they harvest it for drugs or something?"

Trevor exhales. "I forgot who I was talking to," he mutters. "You have to be the dumbest person who's ever lived; I don't know how they didn't catch you sooner."

I wince, but I'm distracted from my embarrassment when he adds, "They use it to keep *them* asleep. Duh!" Trevor shakes his head.

I narrow my eyes. "Who?" I wet my lips. "Who are they keeping asleep?"

Trevor smacks his forehead with his palm. "God, it's right in front of your face! THEM!" He reaches over and angles my chin toward the ceiling. "You really want those to wake up?"

My eyes scan upward, and I choke back a scream. There are bodies suspended from the vaulted ceiling, swinging upside down like long, flesh-colored bats. They all have the same sleepy faces, their mouths hanging open slack-jawed and their eyes half-lidded. Each individual is wrapped in sheer linen, lifeless acrobats swaying back and forth from the inertia of their own slumbering breath. The occasional drop of condensation drips down off of a nose or fingertip.

I cover my mouth with my hand and look back at Trevor. "W-w-why are they up there?" I stammer.

Trevor shrugs. "Low-level stuff. Mouthed off to a Demon, messed up one of their plans…"

"Or was part of their plan all along," I interrupt, spinning around frantically, looking for Mom.

Trevor shakes his head. "I guess. This room's mostly just a holding area—kind of like being grounded." He places the spray bottle back on the floor. "They send the guys who really screwed up to 3." He glances down at his sneakers. "I wanna go up there so bad."

I hug my arms over my chest. Trevor sighs and points at one of the bodies. "Rope would slice right through them, since it's so wet in here. That's why we have to use the cloth." He gives one of the bodies a light push.

"How thoughtful," I breathe, "but hanging there like that can't be good for them… Just being upside down for too long could kill someone, right?" I start honing in on each of the bodies, trying to spot my mother's face.

Trevor sighs. "We're not allowed to kill humans, stupid! It's against the Rules, death being too much intervention, throwing off the balance… or something." He scowls. "So we have to check and double-check everything, like, a million times. Most of the bodies in here are Demons anyway." He shoves past me, almost knocking me into the plants.

One of the cocoons starts to squirm. "*Hiiissssssttttt…*" it gasps, like someone letting air out of a tire. I stumble backwards, my hand brushing a leaf. Trevor's eyes go wide. I shake my head and straighten up, still conscious.

"God, it's like you want to get found out! What's wrong with you!?" Trevor yells, glancing at my hand. I wipe it against my dress.

He exhales and looks up at the hanging body. "They make noise every once in a while. Happens all the time." He looks back at me, probably noticing that my face is ashen. "Stupid *and* afraid?" he sneers. "You're useless."

He sighs, stepping back down the path. "Come on, our time's almost up."

I follow him, my legs wobbly. "How... how long will they leave them up there?" I mumble. Maybe there's some sort of time limit and Mom will get lucky.

Trevor cocks his head. "As long as they want, 'til they're not mad anymore… It depends on the Demon." He looks over his shoulder. "The ones in the back have been here the longest. I think they've had one guy hanging around since the late '90s." He scoffs. "Loser."

He opens the door. I shuffle toward it, stifling a yawn. One of the bodies hovering over me sways as I step next to Trevor. I look up and shudder as I spy a flash of red hair poking through the linen. I stop and turn the cocoon toward me.

"What are you doing?!" Trevor shouts.

I shake my head. "Mom!" I rasp. Her eyes are rolled back and empty, and I can make out the fillings in her molars.

"Are you crazy?!" Trevor wrenches my hand away. "We're not supposed to touch them! They're covered in the stuff—"

Brrrinnng! We both jump as the timer goes off.

"Please—we have to get her down!" I beg, trying to pull my wrist away from him.

Trevor holds firm. "No way! Do you have any idea how much trouble we'd be in?!" He twists behind me and shoves me toward the door. "Come on, before you fall asleep—"

I stop struggling and lock eyes with Mom one more time before he closes the door behind us, securing it tight.

"You didn't tell me your mom was in there!" Trevor finally says with a glower. "That would have been important information to have!" He starts to pull me down the hall.

I shake my head, little shapes and stars pulsing in my vision from the blinding lights inside. "I'm sorry. I had to know where she was," I whisper. "Now I kind of wish I didn't. That was truly horrible." I shuffle forward, my stomach sinking.

Trevor clucks his tongue as we make our way back to the elevators. "Well, get used to it. This place is all about new ways to mess with people." He taps the up button on the wall. "I've been trying to get them to try this awesome water submersion torture I saw in a video game, but Dad doesn't think it would be 'cost effective,' or whatever his lame-o accountant said." He scoffs. "The tanks would take too much to upkeep, I guess… but it would be so cool." He sighs, the doors opening. "When I'm in charge, we are definitely doing it." We step onto the elevator together.

I bite my nails. "Do they know they're up there?" I tuck my hands into my elbows. "In the Green Room. Are they… conscious at all?"

Trevor shakes his head. "I dunno. I've only seen them take down and wake up one before. A girl." He wrinkles his nose as the elevator starts to ascend. "She screamed for, like, a week after that—until she lost her voice." He shrugs. "Who cares?"

"That's awful," I exhale. I cross my arms, wondering if Mom will do the same thing in three days.

Trevor snorts. "It's not supposed to be fun, idiot! Maybe they shouldn't have screwed up in the first place. Did you ever think of that?"

I jerk my face toward him. "My mom didn't screw up," I hiss. "She doesn't deserve to be up there!"

Trevor looks away. "Then she's, like, the only one." He smirks as the doors open on the 4th floor. "The rest of them aren't a bunch of sweet little schoolteachers, you know!"

He waves me out of the elevator, and we head back to my room. "They all did something to get up there, and it's our job to make them pay." He nods confidently. "Just because you can't handle it doesn't mean it doesn't still need to get done. Besides," he sniffs, looking down at the floor, "it was your idea to go anyway. *You* asked *me*."

We stop in front of my door. I sigh and put my face in my hands. "You're right. I'm sorry." I look back at him. "I wanted to know what happened to her, and now I do." I take a deep breath. "At least I know she's alive."

Trevor chuckles. "Barely. Sucks to be you right now." He grins.

I bite the inside of my cheek. "Yeah, it does." I clear my throat, polishing the *13* with my index finger. "I don't know... It all seems like it's pretty clear for you, black and white—but the whole deciding who's good, who's bad scenario... it's not really my thing." I stare at the floor, thinking.

Trevor crosses his arms. "You *would* say that—but you'll probably have to get over that soon." He snorts, reaching to turn the key in the lock. "Because that's part of what you do, right?"

I eye him warily. "I'm not sure." I sigh, then offer my hand. "Well... thanks. It's been an education."

Trevor huffs and bats my hand away. "Whatever. It was something to do." He flushes. "You're pretty dumb, but... not boring."

I give a small smile as I push open the door. "I'll take whatever I can get. Later."

"Yeah, fine," he replies, dragging the cart back toward the elevators.

I walk in and close the door behind me, the room pitch black. I feel around for the light switch.

"Left side, by the bathroom door," a voice drawls from the darkness. I reel back and slump against the wall, gasping for air.

"Never mind; here." The small table lamp by the window clicks on. Alden sits relaxed in the blue chair, grinning wickedly. "Enjoying yourself?"

CHAPTER 9

"*D*O YOU ALWAYS sit lurking in the dark?" I hiss, catching my breath. "It's kind of creepy."

Alden chuckles and edges forward. "Helps me think," he murmurs, staring me down. "I like the quiet of it. I'm sorry I missed dinner." He clears his throat. "I was tied up with work."

"I bet," I whisper, thinking about Mom hanging downstairs and wondering if I'm in for a room upgrade. "Well, I hope I didn't keep you waiting too long." I shrug and move into the room, hopping onto the end of the bed.

Alden snorts and glances up at the ceiling. "*That's* rather cavalier, coming from someone who just got caught red-handed!" He taps his heart. "Please forgive the pun."

I take a deep breath, waiting for the other shoe to drop. "So, what? Am I in trouble?"

Alden stands and puts his hands in his pockets. "I don't know, Christa," he sighs tiredly. "You disregarded the one instruction I gave you before I left, which is a blatant sign of disrespect." He frowns. "Normally, I would have to do something about that, but that would put a major damper on the night I had planned for us." He bites his lower lip and looks at me.

I shift. "I'm sorry... It won't happen again?" It came out as a question.

He laughs. "And the sky is only blue on Tuesdays and Thursdays!" He shakes his head. "Tell you what," he tuts and crosses toward the hall, "I'll let you choose: either Door Number 1, which would be a... penalty befitting your crime." He chooses his words carefully. "I'm sure you encountered a few of those on your tour with everyone's favorite prepubescent ginger." He rolls his eyes, and I look down at my lap. "Or, you could go with Mystery Door Number 2, the original activity I had set for us this evening." Alden smiles widely and crosses his arms. "It's your choice, my darling. I'd be happy as a clam either way. Never a dull moment." He quirks his eyebrows at me.

I scowl down at the bed. "Well, I'm obviously not going to pick the first one," I grumble. "Who would sign up for that?"

Alden rubs his jaw. "Some people might find comfort in the certainty that comes with Door Number 1. You can pretty much expect that it will be... unpleasant, for a period of time, but then it's over and done. Door Number 2 has a bit more inherent risk." His eyes brighten. "Risk of the unknown, risk of danger, risk of possibly having fun." He grins. "I think you can tell where my bias lies." He shrugs. "But you're the guest, so it's up to you."

"Whatever... fine. Door Number 2," I answer waspishly.

Alden does a little victory dance. "I knew there was a reason I liked you!" He motions with one hand. "Come on; we're already running late."

I furrow my brow and get off the bed, slouching over to him. "Where are we going?"

"No spoilers!" he caws, taking me by the elbow. "But I'll give you a hint: it combines several of my favorite pastimes."

I smirk. "What, arson and listening to yourself speak?"

He taps his nose and ushers me out the door.

We take the elevator back to the first floor and walk down past the Green Room to the far end of the building. We stop in front of a set of double doors that are similar to the ones going into the Kennel Room, except that these have small porthole windows and no apparent lock. I stand up on my toes and squint through the glass, but it's too dark inside to see anything.

"What's in there?" I snap.

Alden sighs and rubs his face. "The Loch Ness monster, the headless horseman, and Godzilla playing five-card draw with Death," he simpers. I roll my eyes and cross my arms. "Seriously, Christa! Can't you let your guard down for five minutes and just go with it?"

I shake my head. "Um, no, I can't," I bark. "Let's review." I hold up a hand and start to count on my fingers. "You manipulate me, attack me, invade my private thoughts, kidnap my mother—" I close my eyes, catching myself before I say *and hang her upside down in a flower-induced coma*. "—and do God knows what to her! You threaten my friends—"

"I did no such thing!"

I glare at him. "—hold me hostage, and take away all of my personal freedom." I glare. "Does that about cover it?"

He scoffs and looks away. "I know the circumstances aren't ideal…"

"Ha! Understatement!" I mock, leaning against the wall.

Alden closes his eyes and exhales. "… but I did all of that because you *need* to be here." He purses his lips. "You need to see it, feel it, smell it." He reaches over and grabs my forearms. "To understand what it truly means to be…" He gazes into my eyes and speaks with relish. "… damned."

I stare back at him, breathless. He arches a brow and steps back.

"Otherwise, what's the point? Of you being the Catalyst?" He shrugs. "Everything is so clear-cut on the other side; they're the good guys, we're the monsters. Let's all go out and fight the good fight and sleep sweet and sound in our beds at night. Must be bloody peachy knowing that everything you do is right and just."

"I don't think it's that simple," I admit, pushing off of the wall.

Alden snickers. "You're right. It's not." The corners of his eyes crinkle. "And if that's the only thing I can get you to see in the next three days, I've won."

Not knowing how to answer, I rub the side of my neck. "So," I cough, breaking the silence, "are you going to show me what's behind Mystery Door Number 2?" I nudge the door with my boot.

Alden wrinkles his nose and nods. "Why don't you go inside and find out?"

I chew my lip and push the door open with my hand. It swings freely, revealing a dark hallway. As it closes again, I hear laughing and... *singing*? I glance back at Alden and shake my head. "What—?"

"Go on." He gestures like a mother duck coaxing her chicks into the water. I take a deep breath and step inside.

It takes my eyes a minute to adjust to the track lighting on the carpet. I walk a few cautious steps forward, and the laughter grows louder. I turn a corner and smell... popcorn? "It's a movie theater," I exhale, the hairs on the back of my neck going down.

Alden comes in behind me and laughs. "My favorite pastimes: movies, munchies..."

"And lurking in the dark." I twist toward him, my eyebrows arched. Alden tilts his chin and motions for me to go forward again.

As I enter, I'm overwhelmed by a wave of stadium seats that rises up on my left, jam-packed with people. The crowd lets out a roar at something funny. I turn to the screen, and my jaw drops. "*Moulin Rouge*?" I sputter, watching a mile-high Nicole Kidman dancing in a can-can skirt.

Alden lets out a low chuckle. "It's one of our favorites. Surprising, I know... such a polarizing film." He shakes his head.

"But I think it's a black heart indeed that cannot relate to such a classic tale of true love, art, and loss." He sighs melodramatically, then grabs my hand and pulls me up the theater stairs. "Plus, the music's fantastic! Come on—let's get some snacks!"

I follow, bewildered, and take the steps two at a time as we pass the other movie-goers. A few of them turn and stare as we make our way up to the neon-lit concession stand at the top of the embankment. Alden grabs a pack of Red Vines off of one of the racks and gestures to the guy behind the counter. "Do you want popcorn?" he asks me, like we're on a first date.

I shake my head. "No, I'm still full from dinner."

I glance over at the audience. Everyone seems thoroughly engaged in the movie, singing along with the musical numbers, bursting into raucous laughter whenever something funny happens, and quieting down at the romantic parts. I squint down to the front row and recognize Vesper, his silver hair glimmering as he holds court with several other people dressed in black suits. I feel a shiver go down my spine and take in the rest of the crowd. I lean into Alden's shoulder.

"Is everyone here a… a Demon?" I whisper.

Alden nods, tucking his candy under his arm and picking up a soda. "For the most part; there's also a couple of Pets to gather up the trash and make extra snack runs." He points to a pair of empty seats in the second-to-last row. "Those look free."

We make our way over to them, carefully stepping over two guys with shiny shoes. Their eyes widen as they let me pass. "*That's* not distracting at all," one of them snickers. "Worse than an iPhone."

Several other Demons in surrounding seats spin around to watch us as we get situated. Alden flips one of the crushed red velvet cushions for me, and I plop down hastily, slouching in my seat and feeling like I showed up to school without my clothes on.

"Why does everyone keep looking at me like that?" I hiss, tucking my hands between my knees.

Alden shrugs, his eyes on the screen. "You're new, and everyone wants a peek. They'll get over it." He offers the package of Red Vines. "Want one?"

I push them away. "No thanks, I'm okay." I crane back toward the concessions stand. "I would never have thought this was here…" I narrow my eyes. Hiding behind the candy display, I spy Trevor angrily shoveling Gummy Bears into his mouth. He glares at me and puffs out his freckled cheeks before running away. "Such a spaz," I mutter, crossing my arms. I shift back and wriggle in my seat, trying to get comfortable.

Alden squints at the screen. "Who's such a spaz?" he murmurs, fully engrossed in the film.

"No one." I gaze around the theater. "So, does everyone live here? How many rooms are upstairs?"

Alden nods. "For the most part. Some are just visiting from other cities, and there are a few Demons who choose to live on their own, but we're… encouraged… to live together." He pulls another Red Vine from the plastic. "The building mainframe expands to accommodate however many we have staying here at a given time. There's always enough room." He breaks into a huge smile. "I love this song."

I roll my eyes. "This is so weird," I grumble under my breath.

"What?" Alden tilts an ear toward me.

"Um, the theater full of Demons watching a movie musical? Shouldn't you all be out causing chaos and destruction?" I ask skeptically.

Alden gnaws on a piece of licorice. "We can't work all the time, Christa. Everyone needs to blow off a little steam now and again." He smiles crookedly. "And even mass murderers can appreciate a great score and book." He breaks away and laughs as one of the characters takes a prat fall.

I purse my lips. "It's like the freakin' *Twilight Zone*," I murmur.

Alden sips his soda. "Mmm, we screen the marathon on New Year's Eve. Oho, that's rich!" he crows, kicking the seat in front of him as he watches the movie.

"Unbelievable." I shake my head.

"Hey, quiet in the cheap seats!" a tall, stunning black woman giggles, twisting around from the row in front of us.

Alden smiles and rests his chin on his palm. "Hello, Mandisa," he croons lazily. "Enjoying the film?"

"Yes, more so if I could *hear* it over all this chatter from behind!" She grins, her teeth big and white. She turns to me and her eyes light up. "Ah! You're here! How wonderful!" She reaches over and taps my knee. "It's Christa, right?" Her voice is musical and foreign.

I nod slowly, taking in her closely shaved head and white cashmere sweater, the dipping V-neck showing off her dark, supple skin. "Um… yeah," I mutter.

Alden sits up and clears his throat. "Christa, this is Mandisa." She holds out her hand and I take it, her grip confident and inviting. "She's the one who picked out all your clothes. Makes Anna Wintour look like a second-rate nobody."

Mandisa smiles and tucks her face bashfully into the seatback. "Always the charmer!" she purrs, glancing up at me. "Ah! And I see you went with the Badgley-Mischka… I love that one!" She holds out her arm so as to get a better look at my dress. "And it fits you like a dream. Oh, I am so pleased!"

The guy next to us shushes her. She bites her lip playfully and shrinks down in her seat. "Sorry!" she mouths to him, staring back at us. "Aww, just look at you both." She arches a brow. "The two of you look magnificent together! So dashing, so classic—total power couple."

I blush and hunch down. Alden rolls his eyes. "Easy, Mandisa. She's only just arrived. We don't want to scare her off."

"Too late," I smirk.

Alden sips his drink and jerks his chin. "Taking Bernie out for a walk, I see." He nods at the short, chubby white guy with horrible acne sitting next to Mandisa.

She smiles and lovingly scratches the back of his Spiderman t-shirt. "I thought a little socializing would be good for him!" She pats Spiderman on the cheek. His eyelids flutter as he leans into her touch. "He's still so clingy from his time on the container ship that it's hard for me to leave him now." Spiderman nuzzles her shoulder with his head.

"Maybe you should invest in a doghouse. Tie him up before you go out so he doesn't pee on the rug," Alden replies dryly.

I glare at him, appalled, but Mandisa only laughs. "Yeah, maybe…" she snorts, Spiderman pushing into her like a housecat begging to be groomed.

"Mandisa… Mandisa…" he groans, flopping her arm on top of his head. She sighs and authoritatively grabs him by the scruff of his neck.

"Bernie, please don't interrupt! I'll be with you in a moment," she scolds. He settles into his seat, sullen. She turns back to Alden, her eyes wide. "Hey—have you been over to 3 today?" she asks excitedly.

Alden shakes his head.

"They're really making progress," Mandisa enthuses. "I think we're going to have some answers by Thursday Meeting!" She scrunches her shoulders.

Alden nods. "That would be something." he murmurs, his eyes back on the film.

Mandisa smiles as Spiderman starts whining and anxiously pawing her thigh. She rolls her eyes and pushes up the sleeve on her sweater. "All right, all right! Mama hears you!" She gives me a wink. "Have a nice night, Christa. Please let me know if there's anything I can do to help you settle in."

"Thanks," I grumble. She spins back around in her seat, and I can make out a bright scar flashing against her skin on the back of her neck. It's the top of a circle, a ring—another branding. I grimace and turn to watch Spiderman. He's started clawing at his own legs, his jeans ripping under his fingernails.

"Please..." he rasps. Mandisa sighs and calmly places her elbow on the armrest between the two of them. He bows his head and suckles the soft side of her arm, starting off restrained, but quickly beginning to tear away at her like a wild animal. Mandisa sits back and watches the screen.

I gasp, recognizing the crazed expression in his eye: he's just like Zompocalypse. I shudder and look back at Alden, who is happily munching on his candy. I curl my knees up to my chest, trying to make myself as small as possible, and I keep my eyes closed for the rest of the film.

*

A while later, the lights come up, and everyone starts to file out of the theater. Alden turns to me and stretches.

"You know, I've probably seen that flick a hundred times, but it only gets better every time I watch it! What did you think?" he asks with a yawn.

I shake my head. "Um... you know—bright, loud," I mumble.

He sighs. "Wow—quite the review. You should be writing for the Times." He stands up and smooths the creases out of his pants. "We should get going. Just leave it." He gestures to the empty soda and candy wrapper.

I get up and follow him down the steps. We walk back into the hallway, everyone saying goodnight to each other and heading toward the elevators. I see Mandisa standing in line, Spiderman sulking at her side and trying to hold her hand. She casually brushes him off like he's no more than an ant interrupting a summer picnic and continues chatting with a woman in a black dress. I feel myself starting to shake again and cross my arms.

Alden takes one look at the long line and sighs. "Wanna take the stairs?" he mutters. "It'll probably be faster."

I nod, relieved not to have to have to spend another minute with a million Demon eyes checking me out. Alden takes my hand and opens a door, leading me to the fire stairs.

I clear my throat. "So, what was wrong with that guy? Spiderman—I mean, Bernie," I correct myself as I clomp up the concrete stairs. "With Mandisa?"

Alden glances back at me. "Was he bothering you?" he asks.

"Yes… I mean, no." I frown. "Didn't you find it a little disconcerting, the way he went all Kujo on her arm?" I grab onto the railing.

Alden sighs. "He's a Pet, Christa. In essence, he's Mandisa's whipping boy, running errands for her, performing odd jobs. A Pet can be a very useful tool when trained properly." He smirks. "I'm not sure how useful Bernie is, but I'm sure Mandisa has her reasons for keeping him around. In return for his service, she shares her blood with him—a fairly common transaction."

I furrow my brow. "So he's… Smudged?" I murmur, remembering the word Daniel used for Zompocalypse.

Alden chuckles. "Someone's been doing her homework! Yes, he is Smudged through and through. It's how we lure most of our human help—first with the promise of blood, then with the heady aspiration of someday becoming Demons themselves." He turns to me on the landing.

I cringe. "People *want* to become Demons? Why?"

Alden tilts his chin. "The sheer power that comes with being Damned is very attractive to a lot of people." He purses his lips. "A surprising number of people. They witness the acts that we're able to perform on the mortal plane, and they want to possess that power." He sighs and arches a brow. "But the majority of them spend the rest of their eternities toiling in the lower realms, never seeing the light of day again. I imagine that dear Bernie signed up for a similar fate, whether he knows it or not—no matter how much of Mandisa's blood he consumes." He holds open the fourth floor door for me.

I walk through. "I still don't get how they can make themselves drink that stuff…" I grimace down at the floor. "So gross."

Alden closes the door behind us and guides me down the hall. "Along with its natural healing properties and the fact that it provides a major high, it also allows the drinker to see the Divine World. As I'm sure you already know, Demons, Angels, and even you look… different." His expression grows stony. "But the Mortal eye cannot perceive it, keeping us hidden—which is probably for the best. Unfortunately, Demon blood is also incredibly addictive. Coming off of it is excruciating, which is what you caught a glimpse of tonight."

I nod. "Looked familiar," I whisper at the floor. "So, if I were to drink *your* blood, I'd see everything, too?" I stop and turn to him.

Alden narrows his eyes. "In theory… yes," he murmurs.

I stare at my hands where they're folded across my dress front, plain and unyielding. "Would I become a Pet, like Bernie?" I breathe.

Alden throws his head back, laughing. "I don't think *you* could ever be a Pet, even if you bled me dry!" He pats my arm and guides me back to my room. "No, that job requires a very specific disposition: submissive, obedient, a lack of purpose." He grins. "All qualities that you are severely lacking in." He stares at me, his expression turning serious. "But you *would* be Smudged: see the Unseen, your vision forever altered." He stops in front of my room.

I bite my lip and stare at him. He sighs and pulls out his keys. "I can tell you're thinking about it, Christa, and I understand why," he adds softly.

I look away.

"But that's not something I'm willing to do." Alden crosses his arms. "If you were meant to see us, you would. Justice is blind, I suppose." He looks down. "For whatever reason, this is how things are supposed to be, and I'm not going to get in the middle of that. Too much is at stake."

I exhale and shake my head. "That's what everyone keeps telling me. I just wish there was a manual, or something. A little more to go on than, 'You're super important and you have to do this major thing… except no one knows anything about it.'"

Alden nods and pushes open the door. "You've had a very long day. Get some rest, and I'm sure things will look differently in the morning," he murmurs.

I snort. "Easier said than done." I step into the room. "Goodnight, I guess." I turn to close the door, but the Demon reaches out and takes my wrist. "Goodnight, Christa." He traces his thumb over my palm. I gasp, a small shiver shooting up my arm. "I am glad, you're here," he whispers, letting me go.

I shrug, pulling my hand back. "It's, um… it's not like I had much of a choice."

He nods slowly, leaning against the doorframe. "There's always a choice, for the living."

His eyes crinkle. I watch the hallway lights reflect in his dark hair. He's so close that I can make out his burnt-paper smell mingled with something clean and soapy. He must have showered while I was out with Trevor. My legs quake at the thought of it.

"What does that mean?" I ask, my tone breathier than I intended.

Alden shrugs and leans in a little more. "Just that you still have full control of your destiny," he replies. "You can decide what you want to do, who you want to be, who you want to be with…" He reaches up and gently strokes my cheek. I close my eyes at his touch, my heart beating so hard it feels like it will escape from my chest. "It must be so… liberating." He pulls his hand away.

I open my eyes and clear my throat, taking a step back. "Uh… yeah, I guess." I cross my arms over my chest, mostly to keep myself from doing something stupid. "So… I'll see you tomorrow?" I wince. That came out more as a question than a statement.

Alden smiles. "First thing. You sure you'll be all right on your own tonight?" He motions into my bedroom. "Not that I'm implying…" He looks down and puts his hands in his pockets.

I wrinkle my nose. "I'll be fine, thanks," I giggle.

He nods and bites his lip rakishly. "All right, until the morning." He quirks his eyebrows. "Sweet dreams."

I blush. "Okay, sure. You, too."

He nods as I shut the door. I sigh, resting against the wall, listening to his footsteps fade down the hall. "What was that?" I gasp. I close my eyes and rub my face, trying to gather my bearings, my hand and cheek still tingling where he touched me.

"He's a Demon. Remember that," I grit out.

I exhale and step into the room, kicking my boots under the bed and flopping down onto the pillows. I look over at the window. More stars are crammed into the frame than seems physically possible, like I have a front row seat to a private viewing of the Milky Way galaxy. I shake my head.

"This place has a monopoly on the beautiful and disturbing." I turn to face the wardrobe. The cabinet doors are open, and the TV is off, its dark screen staring blankly back at me. I sit up and furrow my brow.

"I thought I closed you." I climb off the bed and step over to it, picking up the remote. I study it, considering going back into FriendFinder to see Daniel one more time before bed. I let out a yawn and rub my temples, feeling a small headache coming on.

"I need to crash… So I'll do it tomorrow." I set the controller down and close the doors, pressing them firmly shut. I crawl back across the bed and smash my face down into the pillows, waves of exhaustion rolling over me. I fall asleep instantly.

Strange dreams play in my mind all night, the kind you don't remember when you wake.

*

Morning arrives with the sound of a seagull squawking off in the distance. I let out a groan and peel open my eyes, my muscles still asleep. I crane my neck back toward the window and see that the original beach scene is back on screen. I prop myself up and try to swallow, but my throat is completely raw. I mash my palms into my eyes and scrunch my forehead.

"What time is it?" I mumble, instinctively looking for my phone before I remember that I don't have a phone anymore. I scrunch my face and look around the room. "Is there a clock somewhere?" I rasp.

No. I grunt and roll over, slowly stretching out my arms and legs. "God, I feel like I've been hit by a bus." Despite sleeping through the night, I still feel totally wiped out. Scratching my head, I drag myself out of bed and step over to the wardrobe. The doors remain shut this time. I open them and take out the remote, giving the 'on' button a quick swipe. Serpentine's pleasant face materializes instantly on the TV.

"I need the time," I murmur, scanning down the menu with the remote.

"Local time in Los Angeles is 9:16 a.m.," the head replies. "Sunrise was at—"

"Fine," I mutter. He stops talking.

I blink tiredly and cough as I glance at the bottom of the screen to the city listings. New York, Rio, Moscow, Tokyo… Porticullis is still at the end. I raise my eyebrows.

"Porticullis," I state, pushing the button.

"Local time in Porticullis is 3:16 a.m.," Serpentine answers. "Weather undetermined."

"That can't be right." I huff and shake my head. "Yo, HAL, 'Error,' or whatever," I call to the face. He stares back at me blankly. "You've got your signals crossed; it was 3 a.m. in Porticullis last night. Update your clock." The *DIAL 3 TO CONNECT* banner blinks softly. I watch it for a moment before shaking myself.

"I don't have time for this. He'll be here any minute. Thanks for the info," I scoff at Serpentine, pressing the power button.

"My pleasure—" he starts to answer before getting cut off as the screen goes black. I pause and bite the inside of my cheek, setting the remote back slowly.

"Yeah... It's time for coffee." I nod to myself, stepping down the hall. I take a breath and slouch into the bathroom, afraid to look in the mirror. The fear is justified: huge dark circles underline my eyes, my remaining bruises are now an ugly yellow, and a very fashionably placed zit is forming right over my top lip. I roll my eyes and sigh.

"Better get to work," I murmur, searching the vials on the vanity for some concealer and eyeliner. I wash, brush, and preen myself quickly, then haphazardly pull clothes out of the closet. I grab a black dress that closes up in the back and am struggling with the zipper when there's a knock at the door. I walk over to the threshold.

"It's unlocked," I hear Alden's muffled voice call.

I take a breath and open the door. He stands in the hall, dangerously dapper as usual, a pair of designer sunglasses perched on his nose. He takes them off and gives me a onceover.

"Morning." He crinkles his forehead sexily as he looks me over. "Nice dress."

I can feel my skin flushing under the silk fabric. "Thanks... I didn't know what we were doing, so I just picked something." I hold open the door.

"Your instincts were dead on." He nods and steps inside. I walk backward, attempting to hide my exposed back.

He grins at my odd movements. "You all right?" he asks, tilting his head.

I grimace and turn around. "Just trying to get this." I motion over my shoulders, standing in front of the closet mirror.

He arches a brow and steps behind me, our reflections gazing back at each other. "Allow me." He slowly pulls up the zipper and rests his hands on my bare arms. I flinch ever so slightly, my breath catching in my throat. "There," he whispers in my ear. "Very Audrey. All you need now is…" He reaches into the closet, pulls out a pair of large black sunglasses, and hands them to me. "You'll want these for breakfast."

I look at him and scrunch my forehead. "Are we going out?"

Alden smiles. "Unless you want to stay here and have breakfast in bed with Trevor," he chuckles. "Although the place I'm proposing makes much better eggs."

How do you like your eggs? I hear Daniel's voice asking in my mind. I blush guiltily as I stare at Alden, standing before me. I haven't thought about Daniel all morning.

"Christa?" Alden asks, taking a step closer. "You okay?"

I shake my head and snap back to attention. "Yes," I answer hastily, taking a quick breath. "Going out would be… good. I just thought I wasn't allowed to leave." I glance around the room.

Alden tilts his chin. "Unescorted by yours truly, yes." He grins. "But I thought we could dine together this morning, if that's all right with you."

I smile weakly and find a pair of heels. "Sure. Girl's gotta eat," I joke.

Alden snickers and opens the door. "You are lucky I think so highly of myself, or that might have stung a bit." He waves me out.

I set the sunglasses on top of my head. "You can take a little abuse," I tease as he locks the door. I close my eyes and cringe at myself. Stop flirting.

He purses his lips and turns to me. "I'm better at giving than receiving," he purrs, patting his pockets. His brow furrows, and he clucks his tongue. "Damn, I think I left my wallet back in my room." He takes my hand and leads me down the hall away from the elevators. "Hang on. This will only take a second."

I glance around the corner. Unlike my room, all of the doors in this hallway have little fingerprint sensors instead of a lock and key. We walk down the corridor and stop in front of Room 23. Alden puts his thumb up to the door, and it unlocks. He guides me in and leaves me standing on the threshold.

He crosses over to a large wall closet. "It should be in my pants from last night."

I walk forward hesitantly, curiosity goading me on. There isn't much in the way of furniture. A modern, low platform bed with a gray duvet laid across it sits center. Two simple nightstands on either side of the bed boast angular glass lamps, and the walls are painted powder gray. There are no decorations on them. The only other noticeable thing is a large, old-fashioned camera sitting on the nightstand. I move over and lift it carefully, surprised by how heavy it is.

"Thought the only pictures you took were selfies with your captives," I say with a smirk.

Alden turns and grins, still hunting through his closet. "Ha. I found that little gem at an antique store in Bakersfield last week. The refractor mirror is cracked inside, but I think I found a replacement for it. Should be able to fix it..." He reaches into a pair of pants and feels around.

"Hm, pretty handy," I answer with a nod, placing the camera back on the table and sitting on the edge of the bed. I see a glimmer peeking from around the other side of the lamp and find a small, tarnished Celtic cross on a silver chain.

"This is pretty." I smile, holding up the necklace. "Kind of girly though, even for you. Doesn't the cross burn every time you put it on?"

Alden snatches it out of my hand. "Careful, that's very fragile!" he snaps, cradling it in his palm.

I shrink away. "Sorry. I didn't know," I mutter.

He sighs and shakes his head, putting it back on the nightstand. "It's fine. I usually wear it everywhere, but I have to get a new chain. The clasp is broken." He scratches his one of his ears.

I look up at him and purse my lips. "May I?" I reach slowly for the necklace. "That's happened to me a couple times, and I know there's a little catch, right here." I squint and point to the fastener. "Ah, here you go." I smile, releasing the clasp. "Good as new." I hand it back to Alden.

He looks at it before clipping it around his neck. "Thank you," he says curtly. "Guess you're pretty handy, too."

"Not totally useless." I tilt my head, looking up at him.

He stares at me strangely. "It would seem so." He clears his throat, glancing down at his chest.

"I, um, didn't think you'd be religious," I murmur, gesturing to the cross. "You know, being a Demon and all."

He lets out a small noise. "Oh, more than ever," he says, tucking the cross under his shirt collar. He smiles and holds up his wallet. "Found it. We're good to go."

He ushers me from the room.

The black town car is waiting for us downstairs in the lot, Frank in the driver's seat. He sees us and quickly reaches over to the radio before stepping out.

"Morning, Mr. Alden," he says with a smile. Alden gives him a short nod. "Ms. Nichols." He tips his cap at me.

"Hi, Frank," I murmur. He holds open the door and I slide across the leather backseat, Alden following close behind.

"Where to, Mr. Alden?" Frank asks as he climbs back in the car.

"Le Petit Dejeuner in Beverly Hills, Frank. Thanks." Alden settles into his seat and takes out his phone, his finger lightly grazing the screen. I turn and stare out the window, the abandoned lot almost immediately replaced by shops and restaurants, everything over-saturated and incredibly light compared to the Warehouse. The world is already awake, people out shopping, talking, and eating at sidewalk cafes. Everyone looks so happy and carefree. I sigh and twist back to Alden.

"So, are you missing work today?" I ask. "You know, since you're... with me?" I try to sound normal.

"You are my work," he replies, not looking up from his phone.

I clear my throat. "I mean, what would you be doing if I wasn't here? Would you be at Trinity?" I tuck my hair behind my ear. "Or out terrorizing the elderly? You know... what do you do every day?"

He smiles and puts his phone down. "Are you trying to get to know me better, Christa?"

I shake my head and look away. "I don't know, I'm just talking," I mumble. "You don't have to answer."

"No, I think it's charming." Alden sits back and exhales. "I would probably be doing just this, actually. Out, driving around with Frank, making calls." He chuckles. "The whole Demon gig isn't as glamorous as it seems. Lots of planning, waiting—and when something *does* happen, you have to act fast. Missed opportunities are severely frowned upon here."

I nod. "Were you in big trouble the other night when I left you at the club? It seemed like Vesper thought I'd be coming back with you." I shiver.

Alden shrugs. "He didn't really notice. Maybe if I had been a lower level, he would have been more vigilant, but I've been at this game for a while, and he knows I get the job done." He glances over at me. I fold my hands in my lap.

"It's weird that he's Trevor's dad... It' doesn't seem to... I don't know, fit." I purse my lips.

He nods slowly. "That's a pretty sad story, one that Vesper doesn't like to flash around." He grimaces at the back of the driver's seat. "But he wouldn't really be one of us without the tragic past, right? He takes care of the boy better than you'd think."

I rub my neck. "Where is Trevor's mother?"

"Dead. From childbirth. That's what happens to all of them," he clips out, staring through the window.

"That explains... a lot." I mutter.

Alden clenches his jaw. "You'd think by now they'd stop playing with fire, save everyone the heartache." He shakes his head.

I narrow my eyes. "What? You mean stop raping human women? Yeah, that *would* be a good thing."

Alden glares at me. "You think that's the case in every one of these relationships?" he growls. "Unlike *other* immortals, we're not required to completely sever our natural emotions and impulses." His face flushes. "I can assure you, Vesper loved that woman, and she loved him back."

I slump and look away, embarrassed.

"I know that probably goes against everything you thought you knew about us, but it's the truth." Alden smooths back his hair.

I shift in my seat, focused on the power window lock. Alden sighs. "I'm sorry if I've made you uncomfortable." I can feel him staring, trying to read my face. "That was not my intention."

I take a breath and gaze back at him. "No, you're right," I murmur. "I made an assumption, and it was rude of me. I'm sorry." I curse myself immediately; he is the last person I need to apologize to.

Alden sits back, his eyes wide. "Well… you're forgiven." He coughs, looking out his window. "Get your things. We're here."

The car stops in front of a white stucco building, its roof covered in clean Spanish tile. Café tables line the street, diners chatting happily over plates of pancakes and fruit. Alden opens his door and takes my hand, leading me toward tall pots filled with red geraniums. He calls back to the car, "Just take it around, Frank. I'm guessing we'll be about an hour."

"Yes, Mr. Alden." Frank nods through the window, pulling away.

We walk past the flowers and up to the hostess stand. An edgy, pretty girl with a pinup-style hairdo looks up and squeals. "Ah! Jamie! How fabulous!" She saunters around the desk and embraces Alden, kissing him on both cheeks.

I watch him skeptically as he smiles at her. "Hello, Natalie, my darling. How are you?" He pats her warmly on the arm and steps back to me.

"Amazing, now that you're here!" She glows, glancing over at me. "Two this morning? Usual table?" Her gaze lingers on me for a moment, eyes narrowed, before she breaks into a large, fake grin.

"That would be lovely," Alden agrees, guiding me by the arm. Natalie puckers her lips and takes us over to a table right by the sidewalk, perfect for people-watching. She sets two menus down and watches as Alden comes around the table and pulls out my chair. "Lucky girl," she mutters under her breath. I wince and put on my sunglasses as Alden sits opposite me.

Natalie clears her throat and clasps her hands together. "Today's specials include Chef's award-winning pumpkin panna cotta and our three-cheese Parisienne omelette. Jacque should be over shortly. Please let me know if you need anything else." She rests her hand on Alden's back and gives his shoulder a little squeeze. "Enjoy."

Alden nods, then removes his sunglasses from his shirt collar and puts them on. I open my menu and shake my head.

"So… *Jamie*." I tilt my head. "What's good here?"

He smiles wryly. "Due to my line of work, I sometimes need to employ the use of a fake name." He sets his napkin in his lap primly. "I hope you will do me the kindness of not blowing my cover."

I shrug. "Your secret is safe with me." I glance down at my menu and see that I can't read a word of it. "It's all in French," I grumble.

"Oui," he replies coyly with a grin. "Guessing that was a class you slept through?"

"I took Latin." The mention of school reminds me that it's Monday, and I would usually be in Bio right now. Mr. Trundi is probably pissed that I got suspended and haven't emailed him a finished term paper yet. I wonder if Jodie is starting to worry that she hasn't heard from me recently, or if anyone's noticed that I'm gone. And the one person who *has* noticed that I'm gone and has been fighting to get me back ever since, I have no problem forgetting in the presence of a hot bad boy. I sigh, feeling my mood start to slip. The events of the last few days are cascading down on me.

Alden looks up. "I'll order for you. Don't worry, you'll love it." He smiles.

I grimace and fuss with my silverware. "It's fine. I'm really not all that hungry." Girls who betray their Guardians don't deserve to eat.

Alden sits back in his chair and frowns. "You said that last night at the movies as well." He narrows his eyes. "I hope you're not planning to go on a hunger strike while you're here, Christa. I won't have that."

"I'm not." I scowl. "It's no big deal."

He clears his throat. "Is this because of what happened in the car just now?" he says under his breath, leaning in.

I set my jaw. "No," I answer. *It's because you took me away from my life and made me your prisoner, and I should hate you—a lot.* "Just order me whatever. I'll eat it, okay?" A waiter passes by and sets a basket of pastries in the center of the table. I grab a muffin and shove it in my mouth. "Happy?" I mumble.

Alden rubs the bridge of his nose. "Are you going to tell me what's bothering you, or am I going to have to play a round of *20 Questions?*"

I toss the muffin onto my bread plate and slump in my chair. "Why would you think something's bothering me?" I reply petulantly.

He glares at me, my reflection in his aviators. "Because you're suddenly more sullen than usual." He snickers, taking a croissant. "And that's saying a lot."

I cross my arms. "Did you ever think it's because you're holding me captive?" I burst out. "I would think that would put anyone in a crappy mood."

He sighs as he picks up his spoon, dipping it in a little pot of strawberry jam. "It just seemed like, after last night, you were a little more... I don't know, open to the whole arrangement." He smears jam on his roll. "Something's obviously changed. Tell me what." He glances over at me.

I grit my teeth. "Nothing's changed... and talking was never part of our Deal," I sneer. "If you're feeling chatty, why don't you call Betty Page back over here?" I motion to the front of the restaurant. Alden looks at me, confused. "The hostess!" I bark.

He stifles a laugh. "Is that what's putting you off?" I roll my eyes and stare out at the intersection. "Come on, Christa. Don't give it another thought."

"Whatever," I murmur, watching a pair of window shoppers across the street. "I'm just tired. I... I didn't sleep well last night. That's all." I glower, taking another bite of my muffin.

Alden chews the inside of his cheek. "We have ways of abetting that, for tonight," he states. I drop my food and glare at him, repulsive images of my mother's unconscious form hanging upside down in the Green Room running on repeat through my head. He raises a hand. "Nothing weird! Relax."

I rub my neck tensely and look back at the shoppers. They've crossed the road and are making their way right past us. They gawk at Alden and I, awestruck, and start to giggle.

"Wasn't she on that show—the one with the zombies... or was it fairies?" I hear one of them whisper.

"No—*Vampires Suck!*" The other squeaks. "Yeah... totally! She looks just like Catalina! Oh my God, I love L.A.!" They shriek and clutch their shopping bags as they scurry down the sidewalk.

I look at Alden and sigh. "Better get used to that," he grins, tilting his head. "And they aren't even getting the full effect; they have no idea what a big celebrity you *really* are." He arches a brow.

I cringe and shake my head. "I would pay them to trade places with me in a heartbeat," I mutter.

I glance at Alden out of the corner of my eye. His smile is gone. "You have no idea how truly wretched things could be for you—"

He stops himself as the waiter stands by our table. "So sorry to interrupt, sir. Are you ready to order?" the man simpers in a French accent.

Alden takes a breath and nods. "*Bien sur, Jacque,*" he says, switching into perfect French. "*Je voudrais l'omelette parisienne...*" I slouch, my hands folded in my lap, until he's finished ordering. The waiter nods and leaves.

Alden spins in his chair to face me. "It's three days, Christa. That's it!" he hisses. "You're being put up in a beautiful room, given beautiful clothes to wear—"

"Still a cage and an orange jumpsuit," I interject.

He rips off his sunglasses. "No one has threatened or harmed you in any way, right?" He looks me over. I nod begrudgingly. "Or forced you to do anything you didn't want to do?"

I shrug. "Only be here," I mumble.

I jump as he slams his palm on the table. "You did that!" He coughs and lowers his voice. "That was your choice, your signature at the bottom of the contract!"

"Be serious, Alden!" I spit. "You put me *and* my family in an impossible situation—I did what anyone with an ounce of moral fiber would do."

"So why not make the best of it?!" he crows, sitting back. I flush and look around at the other diners. "Day 1 is almost done; by the time you wake up tomorrow, you'll be halfway through." He sighs. "It's pretty much a waiting game for you. You can either pout for the next 48 hours, which I really hope you don't—" He shakes his head. "—or you can use this time constructively and *experience* something." He scoffs. "What have you got to lose?"

I clench my jaw and slouch further down in my chair. "Why do you care so much that I see what your life is like? Doesn't it go without saying that it's awful and full of torture and horror, and all you do is ruin lives?" I jerk my chin up at him. "You're a Demon; what else is there to know?"

Alden sits forward quietly, his hands folded on the table. "You yourself said it wasn't that clean cut last night," he whispers, his lip curling. "Did you mean that?"

I cross my arms and shrug. "I dunno," I mumble. "Maybe." Honestly, nothing feels clean cut anymore.

Alden looks down at the tablecloth. "I just thought..." he murmurs, keeping his gaze averted. "I thought you would understand, that I could make you see..." He shakes his head.

I glare at him. "See what?" I snap.

He looks up at me, his eyes crystal blue. "That we're more human than you know." He smiles sardonically. "Than anyone knows."

I draw in a sharp breath. We sit and stare at each other, the sounds of clanking silverware and small talk all around us.

"If you're so *human*," I rasp after a moment, "then how you can you do all the terrible things that you do? Torture, manipulate…"

Alden snickers. "I think you just answered your own question." He arches a brow and nods towards the back of the restaurant. "Here we go."

The waiter returns with a large tray full of colorful cups and dishes. He sets a mug of coffee in front of me, along with what I can only assume is the award-winning pumpkin panna cotta. As he moves around and serves Alden, I lean into my plate and inhale, the spicy cinnamon aroma enveloping me. My stomach rumbles hungrily, but I push it away and pick up my coffee instead, the warm smell reminding me too much of Daniel.

Alden glances over as he cuts into his omelet. "Everything all right with your breakfast?" he murmurs.

I sip my coffee and quirk my eyebrows. "It looks great," I mutter. "I'm just a slow starter in the morning."

He nods and chews his food. He's about to say something else when a small, well-dressed older woman with short silver hair comes up behind him, a smile stretched across her face. "Jamie!"

Alden turns and grins up at the woman, standing to give her a hug. She embraces him tightly and kisses both of his cheeks. "Hello, Muriel," he murmurs, his expression warm.

She pulls back and looks him over. "Natalie said you were back. I just had to come out and say hello." Her voice carries the slightest hint of a French accent. "You were gone so long this time—we were starting to wonder what had become of you!"

She glances over at me. "I'm sorry, I am keeping you from your beautiful friend." She nods kindly, her hand fluttering to her silk scarf. I blush. She turns back to Alden and beams. "We are all so glad you're back."

His eyes crinkle. "Me, too. Thanks," he replies.

She smooths out his collar, her touch motherly. "Ready for battle," she sighs, pulling away. "I can't explain it, but every time I see you, it just fills my heart with such joy." She arches her eyebrows at me. "I'm going to send out something special for you two. Please, eat! And be happy." She winks at Alden before walking back to the kitchen. He exhales and sits back down.

I arch my eyebrows. "Someone's popular this morning," I snort. He picks up his coffee cup. "It's nice," I continue, looking around. "This place... Seems like you come here a lot."

Alden nods and taps a short rhythm on the table. "I do. Almost every day when I'm in town." He straightens his shirt sleeves. "I was in Asia until the middle of the week last, so this is my first time coming by in a while."

I tut approvingly. "Asia? Wow, that's a hike. Business or pleasure?"

He looks toward the kitchen and puts his napkin in his lap. "Always business," he whispers, pointing with his fork. "Eat your breakfast, Christa. You don't want it to turn to mush." He cuts into his egg.

I grimace and pick up my spoon. "Right." I sigh and jab a piece off the corner, the custard jiggling on the silver. I stick it in my mouth and force myself to swallow. "Mmm..." I groan, trying not to breathe through my nose. "Yummy."

Alden clenches his jaw. "If not for me, do it for our lovely hosts." He looks away. "I know it's probably not as good as whatever Danny put together for you." He glances back, his eyes dancing. "I saw he presented you with quite the spread the other day back at your apartment. He's very talented. Cooks with his whole heart." He snickers.

I bristle and put down my silverware. "What's with you two, anyway?" I shake my head. "Why do you hate each other so much?"

Alden takes another sip and sits back. "What did he tell you?" he mumbles, gazing into the mug.

I exhale and shift in my chair. "Just that you guys knew each other... before." I shrug.

He lets out a low chuckle. "That *is* true; we did know each other, quite well," He scowls. "It never ceases to amaze me, how the people you hold in the highest esteem are always the ones who... disappoint you the most."

"What were you like back then?" I ask quietly.

He puts down his fork and sighs. "Tragically sincere. Young." His mouth makes a moue shape. "And very impressionable. And Daniel... wasn't. At least, I didn't think he was." He scratches his cheek. "He was everything I had ever dreamed of becoming: confident, popular, daring. For a time, I tried very hard to be just like him." He shrugs darkly. "But our true natures won out, in the end."

I cross my arms. "What happened?"

Alden grimaces and tilts his head. "Aww... I don't think I should be the one to regale you with *that* tale, Christa. You'll have to ask Danny when he picks you up in a couple of days." He rolls his eyes. "If he can remember how it goes."

I bite my lip. "Yeah, maybe." I pick up my spoon and dunk it back into the panna cotta, pulling out a huge bite. I shovel it into my mouth, gagging on the heavy cream.

Alden arches a brow. "It's meant to be savored. Really, we're in no rush." He delicately takes another bite of his eggs.

I sigh and lean back. "So what are we doing today? Besides the obvious loathing each other."

Alden gazes up, his expression pained, but quickly recovers. "I actually thought we could go up to Runyon and get some fresh air." He looks up at the sky. "It's a beautiful day. Nice stroll through the canyon."

I shrug. "Sounds fine. Boring, but fine."

The waiter returns with a small plate. He sets it in the center of the table. "Compliments of Madame." He smiles before walking away.

I look at the plate, and my breath stops. Encircled by a delicate twine of caramel sit two apple slices that are carved into perfect hearts—just like the ones Daniel made for me the other day. I look up at Alden and see recognition flash across his face.

I push back from the table. "I can't do this." I start to get up.

Alden reaches out and grabs my wrist. "Christa—I had no idea…"

I shake him off. "It's fine. I just want to go." I throw my napkin on the table.

He sighs and runs a hand through his hair. "You barely touched your food—" he murmurs.

I shake my head, looking around. "I'm fine. We should get a doggy bag and bring it home for the inmates downstairs," I jeer. "It's been a blast playing pretend, but I'll be up front."

Alden closes his eyes and shakes his head. "I guess I'm done, too," he mutters, pulling out his phone. "Let me just call Frank and have him bring the car around."

"I can get that for you…" Frank reaches across and pops the car door open. I nod brusquely and get in.

Alden sighs and hands Frank a to-go carton. "If you're feeling peckish," he grumbles, sliding into the back.

Frank's eyes light up. "Cool," he grins. "Uh, where to, Mr. Alden?"

"Back to the Warehouse, just to change." Alden slams the door shut. Frank nods and moves around to the driver's side.

"Of course." Frank sidles in and turns on the car. "Oh, you have a message, sir…" He spins to addresses us.

"Yes?" Alden furrows his brow.

Frank clears his throat. "Scartoni got a call from one of the street scouts. Looks like they spotted that vet you were looking for around La Cienega and Westmount. Was just by there earlier today." Frank looks at him complacently.

Alden narrows his eyes. "That's not far from here…" He stares out of the window, lost in thought.

I cross my arms. "What? You've got a sick cat or something? What's going on?" I tease.

Alden turns to me and blinks. "Hmm," he replies. "Okay, new plan." He taps the seatback and puts on his sunglasses. "Frank's going to take you home, and you can get changed. Think exercise clothes." He opens his door. I watch him disbelievingly as he gets out of the car and back onto the sidewalk.

"Wait—you're leaving?" My voice cracks. "Can you do that?"

Alden nods and looks back through the door. "Frank will take care of you. I'm just going to walk." He starts to leave, but stops. "The contract still stands, Christa. It would be very unwise for you to give into any capricious urges you might have." He glares at me through his dark lenses.

I scoff and slump into my seat. "It's like, impossible for you to talk like a normal person," I retort. "Just say 'don't run away.'"

He smiles. "Don't run away," he calls. "I'll be back soon." He shuts the door behind him and jogs out into the traffic.

I sigh and turn to Frank. "Is he always like this?" I mumble.

Frank smiles in the rearview mirror and pulls onto the street. "Like what?" he asks, focusing on the road.

"Infuriating." I take off my sunglasses and glare out the window.

Frank chuckles. "Aww, he's not so bad. Give him a chance. He's a really nice guy." He grins back at me.

I arch a brow. "Yeah, you're going to have to try harder than that," I snicker. "You know what he does, right?"

Frank tilts his head. "Sure, but that's just his job. You wanna be defined solely by what you do for a living?"

I wrinkle my nose. "I'm in high school. I don't *do* anything yet."

He laughs quietly and clicks his turn signal. "Well, someday you might do something, and even if that something's really great, I bet you're gonna want someone in your life who puts all that aside and likes you just for you." He turns the wheel. "It's pretty special."

I look down at my lap. "I thought I *had* found something special." I grip my fingers. "Or at least the start of it." I sigh and gaze out at the freeway.

Frank watches me in the mirror, his face pinched. "Hey," he says after a minute. "You feel like hitting a drive thru? I mean, I know we've got the fancy leftovers." He holds up the take-out container. "But I'm more of a Big Mac guy, myself."

I blush awkwardly and giggle. "Um, is that allowed?"

Frank shrugs. "I won't tell if you don't." He smiles. "And Mr. Alden said I'm supposed to take care of you, and you look like you could use a chocolate shake."

My stomach growls in agreement. "Yeah, sure... okay." I nod. "But I don't have any money."

"I got it." He waves and scrunches his nose happily as he pulls off at the next exit. We stop at a McDonald's, and Frank orders at the window.

Once we have our food, he parks in the lot. "Here you go," he says, handing my shake back to me.

I take it and grimace. "This is weird," I murmur. "Would... would it be okay if I came up there with you?"

He looks at me and grins. "Only if you're okay with listening to Stephen Tyler." He points his thumb back toward the radio. "It's getting really good." I nod earnestly, and he gets out to open my door. Once settled in the front seat, I take a long, satisfying slurp off my shake.

"Oh my God, that's just what I needed," I moan, my eyes rolling back in my head. Frank chortles and pulls a large French fries out of the bag.

"Dig in." He sets them in the cup holder between us and turns up the stereo. He takes a Big Mac out, the lettuce and sauce dripping off the back. "I know it's, like, a million Weight Watcher points, but sometimes you just can't worry about it, you know?" He glances over at me nervously.

I snicker. "I get it, Frank. No judgement." I reach over and stuff a bunch of fries in my mouth. He smiles and takes a big bite out of the burger.

We munch away contentedly, listening to the life and times of Aerosmith. The CD ends just as I make it to the bottom of my shake. "That was really good, thanks." I stretch my arms out in front of me and readjust my back. "So, are you married, Frank? Kids?"

He chuckles and swabs his jacket with a napkin. "No... I'd like a family someday, just haven't met the right person." He scratches his temple. "I've still got my dad, though. He lives up in Santa Barbara at this really great rest home Mr. Alden helped me get him into. I always go and visit on my day off." He gathers up the trash in the bag, holding it out to me for my cup.

I smile and wedge it in. "That was nice of him," I murmur.

Frank nods and pulls out of the lot and back onto the main road. "I told you he wasn't a bad guy." He takes a draw off his soda. "You know, we've all made mistakes, done things we wish we could change." He turns onto the freeway. "And sometimes, you gotta make up for the stuff you did; that's all Mr. Alden's been doing—serving his time." He looks over at me. "It's a broken system. He's not that bad. Nobody really is."

I shrug. "I guess. The BTK killer had a wife and daughter, right?" I arch a brow. "So maybe there's hope for Alden yet."

Frank let's out a huge roar. "Oh man! Tough cookie... I can see why he likes you." He smiles.

I roll my eyes and lean toward the radio. "So is there another disc in this set? What happens next to dear old Mr. Tyler?" I grin.

The corners of Frank's eyes crinkle. "Glove compartment, disc 3. Hook us up."

I get the disc, and we sit and listen the rest of the way back.

CHAPTER 10

ONCE BACK IN my room, I strip off the black dress and head over to the wardrobe. Someone has been in to clean: my laundry is gone, the pillows on the bed fluffed up. I open the lower dresser drawer, rifling through for a minute before pulling out black workout pants and a light blue running shirt. I dress and pull my hair back in a tight ponytail, grabbing a pair of sneakers from the closet. I stand in front of the wardrobe, ready to go.

"Now what?" I mumble, glancing around the room. My eyes settle on the closed TV console, and I arch a brow.

"He probably won't be back for a while." I purse my lips, opening the cabinet doors. I pick up the remote and point it at the TV. "Sneak a little peek at the other side." The green Serpentine logo crosses the screen, and his face appears shortly thereafter.

"Welcome to Serpentine—"

I point the remote and click a few buttons. "Yeah, we can skip that part," I sigh, accessing FriendFinder. I straighten my shoulders and clear my throat. "Show me Daniel," I state clearly, butterflies going off in my belly. Serpentine blinks, and a new window appears. I recognize the location immediately from the large bird of paradise flowers: Mary Carmen's front garden.

"I don't know how you can do that with everything that's

going on." Daniel glowers from the porch, sulking on the front steps. Mary Carmen kneels in the middle of a flower patch with a trowel in one hand, the hot sun beating down on her back.

She sighs. "These beds won't weed themselves, and it's not like there's a whole lot else we could be doing right now," she grunts, tugging on a particularly nasty dandelion. "All we can do is wait it out."

Daniel gets up in a huff. "That's not true! We could be trying to get her free!" he shouts, crossing over to her.

Mary Carmen stares up at him. "And how do you propose we do that, hm?" She stands, wiping the dirt off her knees.

Daniel shrugs. "I don't know... We could call the Gray! There has to be a loophole we missed, what with everything moving so fast yesterday—"

Mary Carmen shakes his head. "I can promise you that Alden made sure his i's were dotted and his t's crossed before he made his play." She mops her brow carefully to avoid getting soil on her face. "Trying to outmaneuver a Demon in legalese is a fight you will never win."

Daniel paces cat-like in front of her. "Then we play by our own strengths!" he exclaims. "There's an open ventilation shaft on the roof—I saw it last night when I was over there." He looks at her wildly. "I bet it goes all the way down into the heart of the building. I *know* I could fit in there—"

I let out a gasp, clutching my stomach hopefully. Mary Carmen holds up a garden-gloved hand. "And do what? Find her, kick down the door, and go riding off into the sunset?" When Daniel narrows his eyes, she barks, "You know what would happen the second you tried to take her out of there. You can't risk it!" She tightens her fists. "And what if *you* got caught? Huh? You seem to have forgotten what happened the last time a Guardian trespassed on their property..."

Daniel looks away. Mary Carmen's nostrils flare. "You gonna

give *me* the pleasure of finding and putting all your pieces back together again?"

"Hey, come on!" Daniel shouts. "This isn't at all like what happened with T.J."

"No, it's worse!" she interrupts. "Because that... that *animal* has got it in for you personally." She shakes her head and exhales, staring at her feet. "I would never see you again, Daniel."

He sighs and takes a step toward her. "Hey, M.C., don't talk like that." He smiles weakly and rubs her arms. "It's just hard for me to be sitting around doing nothing. Every part of me is aching to go help her—"

Mary Carmen looks up. "I know, but she signed a contract, Daniel. They both did."

Daniel puts his hands on his hips. "She didn't know what she was doing. We should have stopped her, tried harder..." He gazes down at the ground.

Mary Carmen's shoulders droop. "You have to give her a little more credit than that, Daniel," she replies softly. "Christa is a smart girl, and she did what she thought was right. She's trying to save someone she loves, and that in itself is virtuous." She looks up at him. "It's a step in the right direction. I know you're worried about her, but look at the bigger picture."

He scratches the back of his neck. "Don't get started on that again—I've had enough Catalyst talk for two lifetimes," he grumbles, waving her off bitterly.

Mary Carmen purses her lips. "Well, get used to it! If you're as deep into it with this girl as it seems," she sneers, "then pretty much the rest of your existence is going to be Catalyst talk."

Daniel scowls. "Whatever," he huffs, kicking a pebble across the sidewalk.

Mary Carmen shakes her head and pulls off her gardening gloves. "Yeah, whatever..." she mutters, walking up the steps. "I have to get cleaned up for work."

"Wait—you're going to work?!" Daniel squawks.

Mary Carmen gives a frustrated groan. "*Dios mio, tienes que estar bromeando!*" She shouts. "Yes, I am going to work! I don't think *I'll* be squeezing through some ventilation shaft anytime soon, you think?!" She motions to her large chest.

Daniel blushes and stalks down the walk. "Fine! I'll figure it out myself!" He slams the gate closed behind him.

"You do that!" she yells, opening her front door. The both disappear out of the frame, and the screen goes black.

I take a step back and lean against the bed. "Whoa," I mumble, trying to gather my thoughts. So Daniel's found a way in, and he still wants to fight for me... be with me. I smile coyly and hop up on the end of the bed. Things, surprisingly, are looking up; even Mary Carmen had nice things to say about me.

"She thinks I'm smart," I twitter to no one in particular. I lay back on the bed and grin up at the ceiling, imagining Daniel crashing through and down on top of me. Forget trying to escape— even if he could just find me here, alone... I close my eyes and exhale, my breath growing hot.

"Oh my God, get a grip," I mutter to myself, rubbing my face. I sit up and look at the TV. "What time is it anyway? Alden should be back soon..." I clear my throat and grab the remote, clicking to find the time.

"Local time in Los Angeles is 1:22 p.m.," Serpentine states. "Predicted sunset for 4:51 p.m...."

"Cool story," I breathe, clicking around with the controller. I go back to the city listing. "Let's see if you fixed your bug," I murmur, selecting Porticullis.

"Local time in Porticullis is 3:22 a.m., weather undetermined," the face reports.

I tut. "That is starting to get annoying," I grumble. "Who do I call to change that?" *DIAL 3 TO CONNECT* flashes across the bottom of the screen.

"Yeah, okay," I scoff, rolling over to the bedside telephone. I lift the heavy black receiver from its cradle and put it to my ear, tracing my finger in the number 3 slot. "I'll do that."

I laugh, thinking of Daniel charging away from Mary Carmen in a huff as the rotary clicks back and then is replaced with a dial tone. "Thank you for calling Porticullis, home office," a woman's voice answers. "This is Sheri. How may I direct your call?"

"Uh… yeah," I mumble, surprised that a real person answered. "I'm… calling to file a complaint?" I motion at the TV, but then remember she can't see me. "There's a problem with my TV. It keeps giving me the incorrect time for… you guys." I wrinkle my nose; I must sound completely insane. "Is that something you can fix?"

I can hear Sheri breathing on the other end. "What time does it have listed?" she asks after a minute.

I look back at the screen. "Uh… 3:22… No, 3:23 a.m.," I reply. "It's just said the same thing since I got here."

"That is the correct time," Sheri answers, "give or a take a few second delay." I look around the room, dumbfounded. "Now," Sheri continues calmly, "do you have your party's extension? If this is a call regarding Collections, our menu options have changed…"

I clear my throat. "No, no. I don't even know what that is…" I stammer. "I'm sorry. I shouldn't have even—" I take a deep breath. "What is this… Porticullis? I've never even heard of anywhere called that."

"If you don't know your party's extension, I can take your name and current location and leave a message," Sheri interrupts.

I can't help but laugh out loud. "Yeah, sure, I'll leave a message. My name is Christa Nichols, and my current location is trapped in some cracked out version of *Demon Night* called the Warehouse. But if you try to spring me before my three days are up, apparently I'll internally combust or something." I shake my head. "My mom decided to sell her soul to the Devil to get me a better life, and now I'm trying to make it right." I roll my eyes. "You got all that down, Sheri?"

The line is quiet. "Sheri?" I repeat hesitantly.

"Yes, Ms. Nichols," she answers after a minute. "I will put in your message, and an Agent should be with you shortly."

She hangs up, the phone going dead. I glare at the receiver before setting it back in its cradle.

"This place gets weirder by the minute. Just call me Alice." I sigh and look at the door. "He's taking forever." I get up and circle around the room before settling into the blue chair by the window. I rub my face tiredly and snuggle into the cushions.

"Best to use this time constructively…" I yawn as my eyelids flutter closed, deciding that a nap is the best idea ever.

*

"Hey." I startle as someone lightly taps my knee and swivel around like a frightened meerkat. Alden is standing before me.

"Hey." I clear my throat. "How long was I out?"

Alden shrugs. "I don't know. I just got here." He paces aggressively in front of the bed. I look up at him and see that he's still dressed in the same clothes from breakfast, his shirtfront sweaty.

"I thought you said workout stuff," I mutter, sitting up.

He scratches his head and glares at me. "What?" he barks. "Oh yeah…" He glances down at his clothes. "I'll be fine." I stand and watch as he stalks into the bathroom. He curses as he knocks over a couple of the glass vials on the vanity.

"What's with you?" I call. "You seem kind of amped up." I stretch my arms over my head and twist a crick out of my spine. "Something happen at the vet?"

"What are you talking about?" he snaps, stepping out of the bathroom, patting his face and neck dry with a towel.

I roll my eyes. "Your cat, remember?" I laugh. "Whatever was so important that you went bolting out into oncoming traffic."

He tosses the towel onto the floor behind him. "It was nothing," he mutters. "Dead end." He sets his hands on his hips.

I sigh and swing my arms. "Okay, well, you ready for that hike?" I try to sound enthusiastic. "Got on my spiffy new Nikes and everything." I smile and gesture down at my feet. "You should relish this moment; I'm not exactly an athletic person."

Alden snorts. "You didn't seem particularly keen on it at breakfast. Why are you all gung-ho now?"

I take a nervous breath, recognizing that glint in his eye. "Just trying to take your advice and make the best of our situation," I murmur. "No one likes a whiner, right?" Seeing Daniel on FriendFinder being so… motivated had given me that boost that I needed to get through the next two days.

I watch Alden's mouth twist. "How big of you," he breathes, taking a few steps back. "Sure, fine, let's go for a walk. But on one condition." He looks at me crossly. "If I agree to take you, you have to promise that you'll do exactly as I say for the rest of your time here."

I blink. "Where is this coming from?" I grumble, crossing my arms.

He shakes his head at the ceiling. "I'm sick of your attitude! The eye rolling, the muttering under your breath." He shrugs. "If you're going to behave like a child, then I'm going to treat you like one."

I draw in a breath.

"So, if you want to go out, I want things to be different," Alden finishes. "I mean it." He holds out his palm. "I want you to shake on it."

I glare at his hand. "Another Deal?" I whisper.

His jaw tightens. "Take it or leave it," he snaps.

I sigh and catch myself rolling my eyes. "Fine, whatever." I take his hand and wince as the small electrical charge buzzes up my arm. He lets go, and I shake out my wrist.

"Wonderful. Now, let's go have an amazing time," he huffs, holding open the door. I tentatively step past him, and we walk down the hall. We take the elevator down to Level 1, but head the opposite way from the parking lot. I look at Alden questioningly.

"Are we not meeting Frank?" I ask.

Alden shakes his head. "I gave him the rest of the afternoon off." He glances over at me. "I thought we might drive ourselves." He opens a door to his left and pulls me through, revealing a cavernous garage filled with exotic cars in every color imaginable.

I take a deep breath. "Wow. I can't say I was expecting this." Just add it to the list.

Alden grins. "Beats your mom's old Corolla, I bet," he purrs. "Go on, take your pick."

My eyes widen as I look around. "I wouldn't even know where to start," I giggle.

He arches a brow and grabs my wrist. "How about: fast—or really fast?" He gestures to a cherry red Ferrari, followed by a silver car that I don't know the name of.

I blush and smile. "Um, that one's... pretty," I mumble, pointing to the silver one.

Alden nods. "The Bugatti. Excellent choice." He opens up the driver's side and takes out the keys. "Will you be taking the wheel, or should I?"

I guffaw. "Uh, yeah, that's all you," I chortle. "I don't even want to think of what I would have to agree to if I crashed that thing." I cross my arms.

He tilts his chin with a crooked smile. "Suit yourself."

He opens the passenger door for me, and I watch him cautiously as I get in. He closes my door and walks around the hood, climbing into the car himself before putting the key in the ignition, the engine roaring to life.

"Buckle up." Alden grins as he puts on his sunglasses. "This isn't a Volvo." He stares sexily through the windshield as he shifts into gear, speeding out of the garage.

We hop onto the freeway for about a minute before he gets off on Mulholland, the trees growing thicker as we accelerate up into the Hills. I white knuckle the bottom of my seat like I'm riding the space shuttle; we're so close to the ground that I can feel the road rumbling underneath us.

"Hey, take it easy!" I call over the thrum of the car, a list of Hollywood celebrities who've perished on this road ticking off in my brain.

Alden looks over carelessly. "Come on. You don't take the top thoroughbred out of the stable just to go for a hayride." He shifts into fourth as we pass a Hazardous Turns sign. "Live a little!" He jerks the steering wheel to the right, drifting the first switchback.

I shut my eyes and wedge my fist against the roof of the car. "Quit it, Alden! That's not cool!" I cry, staring anxiously out the window. When he does the same again for the next turn, our tires skidding noisily, I yell, "Hey, I mean it!"

He lets out a whoop. "Should've known you'd be a total back-seat driver!" he laughs, twisting the wheel. "I thought you liked it fast and dirty." He reaches over and tickles my knee.

I slap his hand. "What is wrong with you?" I say with a glare. "Slow the fuck down!"

He rolls his eyes and drives us up a very steep hill, his foot grinding against the accelerator. I hold my breath, dreading the oncoming mountaintop drop that awaits us on the other side.

"Brakes!" I scream, locking my legs as we crest the hill. He takes the car back down to first, gliding effortlessly, my organs mashing against my ribcage from the velocity.

"I want out... Lemme out!" I moan, reaching for the door handle.

His eyes widen as he glances at me and shakes his head. "Stop! We're almost there!" He points. "Look!"

I see the sign for Runyon at the bottom of the slope and exhale. "Pull over, now!" I bark.

Alden sighs and moves over to the shoulder. Before he's turned off the car, I'm out on the side of the road, my hands on my knees, gasping for air.

"Hey, relax!" he chuckles, checking the car and coming over to me. "You all right?"

He tries to touch my back, but I bat him off. "That was really jacked up!" I shout, clutching my stomach.

He grins at me, disbelievingly. "Come on, Christa!" he laughs. "I thought you'd get a kick out of it…"

"Well, clearly you don't know shit about me!" I snap, trying to catch my breath. "Why would you think I'd like that—after what happened to me?!" I point up to the fading bruise on my forehead. "God! Did it even register that I was in a near fatal car crash, like, less than a week ago?" Hot tears prickle under my eyelids. "Seriously, Alden… you say you want me to be in a better mood, and then you pull this crap—what the hell?"

He looks down at the ground. "I didn't even realize… I totally forgot about that," he murmurs, clearing his throat. "I'm sorry—"

"Yeah, really!" I straighten up and smooth my hair. "You know, people die all the time in cars, buses, planes… even when they're *not* being stupid!" I pace in a tight circle, kicking pebbles under my sneakers. "Don't ever do that to me again!"

Alden nods. "Okay. I'm really sorry, truly," he whispers, tossing the keys to me. "I promised no harm would come to you, and I never go back on my word." He looks up solemnly. "You can drive back right now, if you want."

I sigh and shove the keys into my pocket. "No. I mean, we're already here." I motion to the sign. "And I don't know if I'm ready to get back in that thing, anyway." I tug on the hem of my shirt and start heading toward the path.

"Damn it," Alden curses behind me, his steps crunching on

the gravel. He keeps a few paces back as we make our way into the canyon. The landscape quickly changes from deep woods to sagebrush and looming sandstone, the hot, late afternoon sun peeking through the rocks as we walk. We pass a few other walkers who are out with their dogs, getting in that last workout before heading home for the day. I jump a set of craggy steps with ease and turn back to Alden, who's struggling down the path, slipping in his dress shoes.

"You okay?" I call, shading my eyes.

He nods, grasping a branch as he stumbles down the steps. "I'm good," he pants. "Just probably should have changed before we left." He stops and straightens his back.

I roll my eyes. "Yeah, no kidding." I take a lunge stance. "We can go slower."

He gives me a look. "I don't need you to do me any favors," he chides. "And what happened to you not being an 'athletic person'?" He jerks his chin at me. "You look pretty sporty right now."

I shrug. "Mom and I used to come up here every Saturday and do the trails." I look out at the canyon. "Just to talk, be outside. It was fun." I tighten my ponytail. "It's been a couple years since I've been back, but it's all pretty familiar."

He scrunches his forehead. "That's the first nice thing I've heard you say about your mother," he remarks, sidling up to me. "Interesting."

I sigh. "It wasn't always super crappy between us." We start walking again. "We used to have a nice life, I guess…" I glance over at him. "Don't read too much into it."

"Just said it was interesting." He mops his brow with the back of his hand. "Christ, it's hot out here."

I let out a small laugh. "I would think you'd be used to that, being a Demon and all." I reach down and pick up a twig from the side of the path. "Hell's gotta be worse."

He stares out in front of him, his eyes glassed over. "It's, um, it's not what you think," he murmurs after a moment. "Not like what they tell you in the stories." He shakes his head as I turn to him, adding, "All fire and brimstone, people wailing in agony. It's actually quite… still." He shudders. "Quietest place I've ever been."

I shred the stick apart. "Is it… horrible?" I murmur, looking at my feet.

"Yes." He nods matter-of-factly. "That part they didn't make up. Not what I'd call a vacation destination." He looks up and smiles at a pair of other hikers passing on the trail.

I toss the pieces of twig away. "Do you ever go back?" I ask. "I mean, how do you get there, from…" I clear my throat. "Here? Do you have to sacrifice a virgin or something?"

Alden arches a brow. "What? Nervous?" he teases. I smile sardonically, and he adds, "No, it's closer than you think."

We come to a fork in the trail, the main path continuing in front of us while a windier, more rugged path goes up the hillside to the right. Alden points up and grins. "What do you think? Game for a little off-roading?"

I purse my lips. "I don't know, Alden," I sigh. "I've only done the off-shoot hikes a couple times. They can get rough." I glance at him. "We didn't bring any water, and you're *really* wearing the wrong shoes for this…"

He laughs. "Excuses, excuses!" He shrugs. "If you're not up for it, just say so."

I snigger. "Yeah, it's not me I'm worried about." I motion to his soaked-through button down. "I don't think *you're* up for it."

He puts his hands on his hips. "Already dead, darling. Nothing to lose." He looks at me puckishly. "Except maybe my pride."

I sigh and scratch my temple. "Okay, fine. I guess we can go up a little ways, see how it goes."

Alden grins and claps. "That's my girl!" he crows, stepping up on a rock. "Onward and upward!" He tromps into the brush. I look up hesitantly and follow.

The main trail disappears behind us as we make our way up the steep grade. The path quickly narrows, and soon we're walking single file with Alden in the lead. I glance at the clear sky, the sun starting to make its way toward the horizon. Sunset will be coming soon. Alden wheezes in front of me, the back of his white shirt tinged pink.

I stop. "Hey—what's up with your back?" I call.

He turns, getting whacked by a tree branch. "Ow—what?" he snaps, pushing aside the bramble.

I step over and pull out his shirt tails. There's a six-inch slash running along the crest of his left hipbone, oozing through a sloppily applied gauze dressing. I wince and place my palm over it. "Jeez, Alden! No wonder you're going so slow... What *is* this?"

He twitches away and tugs his shirt down. "Nothing—just a flesh wound." He grins, catching his breath. He reaches over and holds back the branch blocking the trail. "Should've brought my machete," he jokes.

I glare at him. "Don't give me that. What happened?" I gesture to his side.

He runs a hand through his hair. "Like I said, it's nothing! Let it go, please."

I look down at the path. "This was a bad idea," I mumble. "We're underprepared, and you are in no condition to be out here. We should turn back."

Alden snorts and motions me forward. "Nonsense. Come on, there's got to be a great lookout point or something at the end of this thing. They wouldn't make you work so hard otherwise." He takes a few steps and trips over an exposed tree root, falling backwards.

I cross over and take his arm. "What are you trying to prove?" I grunt, helping him up. "I don't care if we're out here or not..."

"We're out here because I say so!" he shouts, wrenching away from me, his face red. "I'm glad you're enjoying your false sense of freedom, but let's remember who's really in charge here, all right!"

He presses tightly against me. "You're going to keep going, because I'm *telling* you to keep going, got it?" His breath is on my face.

I glare into his eyes, my expression cold. "Got it," I mutter.

He huffs and clears his throat. "Now, why don't you take point for a while?"

I say nothing as I slip past him, navigating the rugged path. I hear him suck in a breath behind me before he starts moving again. We walk forward in silence, the sky beginning to turn orange and pink. I shake my head and look out in front of me, only seeing more thick brush.

"It's going to be dark soon. We should call it." I run my tongue around my dry mouth, really wishing I had thought to bring a water bottle—or twelve.

"We're fine. Keep moving," he replies dully.

I grit my teeth. "You're ridiculous," I mumble under my breath.

"What was that?" he calls.

I roll my eyes and trudge on. "I said, what could do that?" I cringe as a bit of bramble clips my arm. "To your back... Don't you guys heal instantly? Or is that just Guardians?"

The Demon chuckles. "Well, no one takes a beating quite like a Guardian—but yes, we do heal quickly." He stops and exhales heavily. "But these were special circumstances today. I went in expecting apples and got kumquats instead."

I shake my head. "What does that even mean?" I sneer, turning back to him and seeing that his face is pale and ashen. I stop. "You look really bad."

"I told you, don't worry about me." Alden cringes. "I just need to rest for a second."

I twist around and squint ahead. "I think there might be a clearing up there. Do you think you can make it?" I step over to him and slowly reach out my hand. He nods and takes it, giving my fingers a light squeeze. I come over to his side, and we walk the last fifty feet arm-in-arm, Alden stumbling to stay upright. The path opens up onto a small cliff, the edge looking out at an amazing sunset framing the Hollywood sign and the canyon below. I guide Alden over to a large rock and help him sit. He gasps painfully as he rests his head against the stone.

"Thank you," he breathes, gazing out at the sky. "I hate to admit it, but you were probably right." He purses his mouth. "We should have never come up here... Although, we would have missed all this if I hadn't been such a cocky bastard." He motions to the view and laughs, breaking into a cough.

I smirk. "Yeah, guess so," I say, then sit down next to him and sigh. "You're not the first person to underestimate Mother Nature—but next time, we could probably just hop a tour bus up to the sign and wait it out."

He grins. "You and the bus." He turns to face me. "Every guy I've put on you in the last couple days has come back complaining about the bus." He chuckles to himself.

I wrap my arms around my knees, looking down at the dirt. "You've been following me?" His creep factor just went up about a million percent.

Alden tuts. "Well not me, personally... but yes, I've been keeping an eye on you—since the other night at Trinity." I shake my head as he bats me lightly on the arm. "Don't act so shocked, Christa! Daniel was doing the same thing."

"That's different," I snap.

Alden rolls his eyes. "It shouldn't come as any surprise that we all want to keep tabs on the Catalyst." He rests his head against the cliff wall. "Don't take it personally."

"Whatever," I mutter. "Sorry if I put you out, having to buy multiple bus passes."

He laughs. "Yeah, possibly the worst way to get around this town." He pauses and watches me. "But you love it."

I smile begrudgingly. "Gotta get out somehow," I explain with a shrug. "I wouldn't say I love it, but it's the most... *reliable* ride

I have." I look down at my sneakers. "Can always count on L.A. Public Transit to be consistently late; it's comforting, always knowing what to expect."

Alden nods and inhales. "So destructive. It's awful how it completely destroys people, steals their lives, their families' lives." He swallows. "Turns them into shells of their former selves…"

I glance at him. "I'm assuming we're not talking about the bus anymore," I whisper.

He shakes his head. "No." He grimaces, brushing my hand. I inhale, but let him hook his fingers with mine. "We're not." He looks back at me knowingly.

I feel my throat tighten and pull away. "So you've got a messed up family, too? That's something else we have in common, along with our striking good looks and sunny dispositions." I snicker.

He leans his head back again. "I *used* to have a messed up family; they're long gone," he murmurs. "Good riddance."

I wrinkle my forehead. "Was it hard? Dying, I mean. Losing everyone?" I blush and look away. "Sorry if that's too personal…"

He sighs, clearing his throat. "I had already lost everything, everyone that I cared about." He winces as he sits up and stares out at the hills. "Dying was the easy part."

I sit up. "Shit, Alden, I'm sorry…" I sigh. "I don't know what else to say."

Alden shrugs. "Don't worry about it." He shakes his head. "At this point, I've been dead for longer than I was ever alive. Seems kind of silly to be sad about it now." He leans forward gingerly. "Besides, if I had known what kind of glorious afterlife awaited me, I would have done everything differently." He smirks and stands, strolling over to the cliff's edge. "Guess that's a bit of an advantage that you have, going forward: really knowing that whatever kind of person you are now matters." He glances down at the canyon below.

I shrug. "I guess… I always thought it mattered, even if there wasn't anything after this." I scratch my neck. "You know, for the people here and now. Although, I'm sure I haven't been the nicest or most well-intentioned girl out there… for anyone who's keeping score." I watch him sharply.

"Survival tactic." He grins, his feet dangerously close to the edge. "Only the good die young." He dangles a leg over the canyon.

I narrow my eyes. "Hey, don't do that," I call.

He looks at me and gestures toward the Hollywood sign. "You should come over here. Look at that!" he brays.

I shake my head. "I don't like heights," I reply. He arches a brow and holds his arms out like a tightrope walker. I inhale. "Seriously, that's a really steep fall."

Alden chuckles and takes a step back. "You actually look concerned. I didn't realize my health was one of your top priorities."

I roll my eyes and get up, dusting off my butt. "I wouldn't say it's a top priority." I walk over and stand behind him at the edge. "I just don't know if I'm ready to watch you go splat at the bottom of a cliff."

He nods. "Even after I kidnapped your mother?" He smiles. I cross my arms as he adds, "Guess I'm not working hard enough."

"You realize that I'm less than an arm's width away, right?" I put my hands on my back and glare out at the view, the sky turning purple. "Let's not kick the hornet's nest too much."

Alden rubs his neck. "You got it," he murmurs, staring at the mountains in turn. "It really is something."

We stand in silence for a minute, taking it all in. Finally, I turn to him. "I'm not trying to step on your toes or anything. I know *you're* in charge…" I twitch my head. "… but we're about to lose our light. We really should go down. Are you feeling better?"

He nods and pats my arm. "I'm good." He points back to the path. "I'm following you."

I twist my mouth. "Yeah, right. That'll last for about five seconds." I step toward the trail, pushing aside an angry-looking sticker bush.

I hear a scuffle behind me and then a thump. I sigh and spin back to the cliff's edge. "I told you to stop screwing around—"

He's gone. I freeze, my breath catching in my throat. "Alden?!"

A faint wheeze comes from the cliff's edge. "Holy fuck... ALDEN!" I rush over and crouch down to see Alden dangling over the side.

"What goes up, must come down," he grunts, grasping an overhanging rock. "You were right again, about the shoes." He gazes up at me. "That's twice today. You have to know how much I hate that."

I reach forward and grab his wrists. "Oh my God, just hang on!" I cry, trying to hoist him up. I grit my teeth and pull.

He stares back at me, his jaw tight. "This certainly is an interesting predicament we find ourselves in," he pants, digging his toes into the cliff. "I am curious how you will tackle this one."

"W-what?" I sputter, letting go with one hand to tug at his collar.

He grins. "I mean, I know what *I* would do." He narrows his eyes. "And I know what Danny would do—but I'm anxious to see what the *Catalyst* will do when posed with a true moral dilemma." He grimaces.

My grip slackens. I let go and sit back on my haunches, watching him cling to the side. "What the hell are you talking about?" I rasp.

He rolls his eyes. "Think about it, Christa. You have just been presented with an easy out." He struggles and readjusts his hands. "Of course, we both heard what you said a few moments ago about not wanting me to go splat... You could do the 'right thing' and pull me up." He bites his lip. "I'd brush myself off, we'd exchange some witty banter, and then we'd head home, contract still in place, everything exactly the same as when we first came here." He arches a brow. "Or... you could let me fall."

I suck in a breath.

He clears his throat. "Tempting, isn't it?"

I gasp, finally finding my voice. "That is so messed up. I… I would never do that," I mutter, focusing on a pile of pebbles next to me.

Alden smiles. "No one would blame you if you did, what with me being your captor after all." He wrinkles his nose. "They'd probably call you courageous, pat you on the back." He groans, his forehead dripping with sweat.

I bite my tongue. "What about the contract?" I ask, leaning over him.

He gives a small shrug. "I don't know. We're off-property, and there isn't a whole lot of precedent to work from." He grins cunningly. "Might be neat to find out."

I shake my head and look away. "You're insane," I grumble, shifting back on my heels.

"And you're conflicted," he whispers. "Admit it. The thought of running off back to Danny and your little God Squad is more than appealing: it's downright seductive."

I flush at the mention of Daniel, and Alden tilts his head to the side. He watches me and chuckles. "There it is—that flicker of doubt. Creeps in every time." He swallows and looks down. "That is one hell of a drop off."

I gaze past his shoulder and instantly feel dizzy, taking in the trees and rocks hundreds of feet below. "I… I don't know…" I reply breathlessly, my arms and legs wanting to bolt while some other, deeper part of me says to stay.

Alden clucks his tongue. "I don't know if we have time to make up a pros and cons list just now. Might want to make a choice in the next nanosecond…" He claws his fingers into the ground next to me, his nail beds starting to bleed. "Come on, Christa, I know you want to—I can smell it on you!" His eyes shine brightly. "Let me fall. Prove my point."

I glare at him. "Which is what?" I snap.

He gives a dark chuckle. "That we're more alike than you

thought," he grunts, slipping a little further down the cliff. "Beyond our striking good looks and sunny dispositions."

My face tightens, and I dig my nails into my palms. "I am nothing like you," I growl. "Not even close." I reach out and grab his wrists, lunging backwards with all of my weight and hauling him up. He scrambles up the cliff, and we both tumble onto our sides, gasping for breath.

"Good girl!" Alden pants, getting to his knees. "And full of surprises. The minute I think you're gonna go left, you go right. Intriguing! Looks like Danny's just going to have to wait." He holds out his hands to help me up.

I hit him away and get to my feet. "Don't," I grit out, wiping dirt off my pants.

Alden laughs. "Come on, you just saved me from grizzly catastrophe! We're bonding," he crows.

I shake my head and take a step back. "I didn't do it for you. I just didn't think the pleasure of watching you break every bone in your body was worth me losing a piece of my soul." *I* may not think that my soul is worth much, but I do know at least one person who would disagree. I shiver and glare at Alden, adding, "Survival tactic."

He arches a brow. "Well… whatever your reasoning, I'm grateful." He readjusts his neck. "Growing cartilage back is *so* time-consuming."

I roll my eyes. "Whatever." I reach into my pocket and throw him the car keys. He stares at me, taken aback. "I can't drive stick, so looks like you're back in the driver's seat," I snap.

"Right then, back again," he whispers.

I grind my teeth. "Just don't pull any of that crazy crap like you did on your way here." I stalk back toward the path. "Or next time you find yourself dangling from a cliff, I'll push you myself… How's that for witty banter?"

He breaks into a large grin, and I really wonder if I made the right choice.

*

297

"Home again." Alden slips the key into the lock and lets me into my room. I march right into the bathroom and put my face under the tap, guzzling mouthful after mouthful of icy water. When I'm satiated, I wipe my lips and turn to him.

"Are you hungry? Do you want to get a bite to eat or something?" he asks coolly.

I rub my jaw. "Is that a thinly veiled order or an actual request?" I say with a glower. "It's hard to tell with you."

He scrunches his mouth and puts his hands in his pockets. "I guess I deserved that," he murmurs. "No, it was just a question. I want to make sure you're... all right, after our little excursion." He looks toward the door. "I can have Trevor bring you something if you want to be alone, which I would understand."

He watches me as I cross my arms and glare at the floor. "You're angry," he states when I don't answer.

I tug at my hair. "Well—yeah, Alden!" I glare up at him. "One minute you're all nicey-nice, cutting up my breakfast for me, and the next you're driving down Mulholland like a madman while my life flashes before my eyes!" I shake my head. "Let's be clear, schizophrenia is *not* hot. I'm just... so ready to get off this rollercoaster." I lean against the wall.

Alden sighs. "I'm sorry... There!" he says heavily, slapping his thigh. "Does that make it all better? It was a happy accident, and I never meant to put you in a difficult position..."

I roll my eyes. "That was the most sincere apology ever," I snort. "Thanks, I feel so much better." I jerk my face away.

Alden puts his hands on his hips. "Well, what do you want me to say, Christa? Please, baby, please forgive me for not caving to your every emotional outburst and teenage whim?" he scoffs. "I'll leave that to Danny, thanks."

My cheeks redden as he crosses his arms. "Say that you're messing with me!" I spit out. "Tell me the truth, that you wanted me to let you go, kick-starting my twisted path towards the dark side." I stare across at him. "You can bet your ass I'm not going to let that happen. I…" I pause. "I promised."

Alden's eyes narrow. "You have no idea what I really want," he whispers. "If you did, we'd be playing a very different game."

I shudder. "Well then, enlighten me," I rasp.

He takes a breath, considering. "Not tonight." He looks down at the carpet. "I can see that you're tired and need to rest. Are you sure I can't get you anything, send out for dinner?"

I sigh and rub my face. "No, I don't want anything," I mumble, jerking my chin at his back. "You should probably get that thing looked at. It was pretty nasty out on the trail."

He winces and touches his hip tentatively. "Should be right as rain after a good night's sleep." He glances up at me, his eyes soft. "I appreciate your concern. It's a rare thing, around here."

I sigh. "I think we both know that if I wanted you hurt, I would've let you Wiley E. Coyote all over the canyon."

He looks at me and takes a step closer. "Thank you for that," he murmurs, stopping in front of me. "Even if you did just do it for yourself, or for Daniel… I am grateful." He reaches out and grazes my chin with his fingers.

My eyelids flutter, tingles running down my neck. "Did you mean what you said back on the cliff?" I breathe. "About doing life differently, if you had known how things were going to turn out?"

His gaze softens, and he lowers his hand. "Yes. This is never a path I would have chosen for myself." He looks at me, steely-eyed. "The violence, the nightmares, the regret. Every day I wake up dreaming I'm somewhere else, only to come crashing back to…" He sighs and gestures around the room. "… whatever *this* is. Yes, I would have done everything differently." His voice cracks, and he turns away. "I would have focused on what was important and become the man I wanted to be, the man I was *supposed* to be. I would not have let petty emotions get the best of me." He clears his throat. "And more than anything, I would have known when to walk away. Does that answer your question?"

I shift. "Yes," I exhale. "Yes… and I accept your apology."

He gazes back at me, our eyes locking. "Okay," he murmurs. We stare at each other for a moment, until he coughs and looks away. "Will you be okay tonight? I know you mentioned earlier that you have a hard time sleeping."

I cross my arms. "The room is fine, the bed is fine…" I sigh. "I'm sure I'll doze off at some point."

Alden furrows his brow. "Like I said at breakfast, we have ways of helping you sleep." He brushes my arm.

Violently, my mind flashes back to Mom in the Green Room, and I shake my head. "Yeah, I got that!" I exclaim, louder than I intended.

He freezes. "I, um…" I sigh and look at the floor guiltily. "I've seen the Green Room, with Trevor."

Alden nods and scratches his head. "I figured. I wasn't planning on hanging you up by your toes," he teases, "unless that's something you're into."

I roll my eyes. Despite that, his expression is serious when he continues. "No—I thought I made it clear that I had an alternative to drugs. It's perfectly safe and noninvasive." I pause and lean into the doorframe as he adds, "You can trust me—"

I shake my head and laugh. "Yeah, and global warming is totally not a thing."

Alden grins. "It's true. I'm a terrible liar, always have been." He shrugs. "Well, not as obvious as some, I suppose."

I look at him and shake my head. "What does that mean?"

He arches a brow. "Danny, Mary Carmen, *all* Guardians," he scoffs. "Didn't it seem strange to you?"

I straighten my back and try to sound cool. "What?"

Alden snickers. "The coughing, choking, practically going into anaphylactic shock any time they tell a fib."

I shift my weight. "Yeah, what about it?" I ask, acting like I've known about it the whole time, while mentally I try to retrace any time that Daniel had one of his fits with me.

"Personally, I find the whole thing rather Shakespearian… suffocating on ash whenever they lie, pieces of their own insides burning away." Alden runs a hand through his hair as I inhale sharply. "I get that they're supposed to be held to a higher moral standard, but, really, they're losing a certain defense mechanism, right?" He narrows his eyes at me. "Always needing to be so straightforward, never getting to keep anything to themselves, *for* themselves…" He watches me as I glance down at the floor.

"I don't know. I guess it's just part of who they are," I mumble.

He nods. "Guess so." He sighs and steps toward the threshold, opening the door. "I've kept you up later than you like. I'll leave you to it."

I lean toward him achingly as he walks through the doorway. "Wait," I murmur.

He turns back slowly. I take a breath, part shocked, part forgiving for what I'm going to say next. "Maybe we could… try… whatever it is you can do to help me sleep."

Alden's eyes crinkle. He steps back into the room, closing the door. "Of course. Are you ready now?"

I nod. He gestures back to the bed. "All right, lie down." When I look at him warily, he shakes his head. "Unless you sleep standing up, come on." He points. "Nothing unseemly is going to happen."

Damn, a little voice in my head breathes, the rest of me quickly shutting it up. I sigh and move into the room, jumping up on the duvet. I kick off my sneakers and shake my hair out as Alden pulls the blue chair over to the side of the bed. I ease into the pillows as he turns off all of the lights in the room before sitting down. He clears his throat.

"Is this some kind of hypnosis thing?" I mutter, folding my

hands over my stomach and staring up at the ceiling. "Am I going to wake up quacking like a duck?"

He chuckles. "Nothing that New Age, no." He leans forward in the chair slightly. "I'm going to sing to you."

I blush, embarrassed. "Um, okay…" I stammer. "I'm not big on serenades. It's, like, the most awkward thing ever when people burst into song in public."

"We're not in public," he cuts me off quietly. "And this isn't a serenade, it's a lullaby—one my mother used to sing to me."

I shrink into the comforter, remembering what he said about his family back in the canyon. "Fine… Well, it's worth a shot, I guess." I shrug. "Beats tossing and turning all night."

He nods. "Just, close your eyes and try to relax."

I exhale and shut my eyes. We sit silently for a moment before he starts to hum. It starts out soft, barely audible, but grows slowly into a gentle melody. I feel my eyelids instantly grow heavier, every muscle in my body going slack, and I fight to stay awake, longing to hear the next part of his song.

Alden goes through the melody one time, and then opens up, clear and sweet, singing the lyrics.

Rest tired eyes a while
Sweet is thy baby's smile
Angels are guarding and they watch o'er thee
Sleep, sleep, grah mo chree
Here on you mamma's knee
Angels are guarding
And they watch o'er thee

The birdeens sing a fluting song
They sing to thee the whole day long
Wee fairies dance o'er hill and dale

For very love of thee

Dream, dream, grah mo chree
Here on your mamma's knee
Angels are guarding and they watch o'er thee
As you sleep may Angels watch over
And may they guard o'er thee.

The primrose in the sheltered nook
The crystal stream, the babbling brook
All these things God's hands have made
For very love of thee

Twilight and shadows fall
Peace to His children all
Angels are guarding and they watch o'er thee
As you sleep
May Angels watch over and may they guard o'er thee

I hear him exhale when he's through, sitting back. My head lolls to the side, and I spend any energy I have left to open my eyes. He starts to get up to leave.

I let out a little groan. "Stay…" I breathe, reaching my arm out.

"What?" He looks at me, shaking his head.

I clear my throat. "Stay," I repeat.

He chuckles, gripping the arms of the chair. "Afraid of the dark?" he murmurs. "I didn't think the big, bad Catalyst was afraid of anything."

I tilt my head up at him. "You know that's not true."

His gaze softens, and he settles back into the chair. "All right," he sighs, crossing his arms over his chest. "I can stay for a little while. You're lucky I cleared my calendar for you…"

I shake my head, and he stops. "No... stay *here*." I pat the bed next to me.

Alden stares at me before letting out a low laugh. "Christa," he moans, "be serious."

I exhale and put my hand under my pillow. "I am serious... Just sleeping," I whisper. "And you said I could trust you. Prove it."

I watch him shift in his seat. "Why?" he asks after a minute, looking at me out of the corner of his eye. "Why me?"

I shrug. "Because I don't want to be alone in this place," I reply. "And I don't think you want to be alone, either."

He clucks his tongue. "I've been alone for so long that I don't remember being any other way." He takes a breath. "All right." He climbs onto the bed, and we watch each other as he hovers over me, his mouth inches from mine.

"Just sleeping," he breathes. I nod, his shirt collar brushing against my cheek. He lingers for a moment before settling down next to my side.

"Hope you don't hog the covers," he grunts, folding his hands over his chest as he closes his eyes.

I watch his face muscles relax and curl around him, resting my head on his chest. I feel his breathing stop. "Is this okay?" I ask quietly, listening for his heartbeat.

He swallows and nods. "Of course," he snickers, the corners of his mouth turning upwards. "In the absence of Angels, I'm the next best thing."

CHAPTER 11

WHEN I WAKE in the morning, Alden's gone.

I sit up and gaze down next to me to where the bed sheets still hold his imprint. I smooth my hand along the indent and press my face into his pillow, his burnt paper scent lingering in the fabric. This time, I don't get nauseated.

"What time *is* it?" I mutter, glancing over at the window. There is a pretty alpine sunrise scene on screen. I get up and stick my face into the opening, closing my eyes as I inhale cool mountain air. Feeling refreshed, I grab the remote and turn on the TV.

"Welcome to Serpentine…" the face says, beginning his opening shtick. I look at him suspiciously. I swear there's a glint of knowingness in his eyes now, like he got a front-row seat to a really good show last night.

I wrinkle my nose. "You can just keep *that* to yourself," I murmur, clicking on the time. It's 8:54 a.m.… plenty of daylight left. I sigh and play around with the menu options, debating opening up FriendFinder to check on Daniel, but I change my mind as an overwhelming wave of guilt crashes into me. I glance back at the bed.

"I'll catch up with him later." I shrug, opting instead for some crummy reality show rerun on cable. I pitch the remote on the chair and walk into the bathroom, noticing that I'm still wearing my exercise clothes from yesterday. I take my time getting ready, enjoying the endless supply of hot water in the shower and trying on six different perfumes before settling on a spicy fall scent from Dior. After I dry my hair and put on my makeup, I step out to the closet and open it, considering my options.

"What am I feeling today?" I flip through the dresses, thinking that Mandisa really did an amazing job putting my wardrobe together. I pause on a hot little red number. I can tell it's a traffic stopper just by looking at it on the hanger. I hold it against myself and mosey over to the mirror. The color is stunning with my hair and eyes.

"Might be a little much…" I bite my lip, arching my neck back. "But if you can't wear a sexy red dress while you're stuck in Hell, when can you?" I run my hand over the material, seductive to the touch. I grin and tug down the zipper.

"I'm totally doing it." I smirk as I step into the dress. "Alden's going to lose it when he sees me in this—"

I gasp and look up at my reflection, a small smile still teasing my lips. "Don't talk like that," I quickly chastise myself. "That's not you." I straighten and zip up the side, the silky fabric hugging my body. I look… dangerous. I take a deep breath and shake my head.

"This isn't you, either…" I start to unzip, but stop at the sound of a knock at the door. I jerk my chin around, adding, "But it's going to have to be, for now." I readjust the dress and scurry across the room, standing in front of the doorway

"Come in," I call, resting my hands at my sides. The lock clicks, and Alden lets himself in.

"Hi," he breathes, his eyes going wide as he looks me over.

I feel the corners of my mouth twitch. "Hi." I blush, glancing down at my bare feet.

He takes a step closer. "You look…" He shakes his head and

blinks. "Unstoppable." He reaches out and brushes my skin, sending shivers down my arm. I smile and hold my elbow where he touched me, looking up at him shyly.

"Thank you," I murmur. I notice that he has taken time to clean up as well, since he smells of soap and is wearing a new, black dress shirt and charcoal gray pants. His blue eyes gleam back at me. "You look nice, too."

"Well, I've got a big day planned for us," he replies, arching a brow. "I hope you're well-rested."

My cheekbones burn as I try to hide my smile. "Slept like a baby. You?" I rest against the wall.

He scoffs, leaning into my ear. "Pretty well," he whispers, "although you kept me up a bit, talking in your sleep." The tip of his nose grazes my hair.

I flush. "Hope I didn't say anything too incriminating." I clear my throat, not able to tear my eyes away from his.

He grins. "Secrets, secrets." He pushes off of the wall. "You ready to go?"

I nod. "Yeah, just let me get my shoes."

I trot back into the room and grab a sexy pair of heels from the closet, making a quick decision to take a leather jacket as well. I shrug it on and switch off the TV before dashing back over to Alden, stopping by the door to put on the heels. I position myself to give him a generous view of my backside, lazily fastening the little straps over my arches. I peek over my shoulder and see that he's grinning.

I pucker my lips. "Ready now," I purr.

He steps forward, offering his arm. I take it.

"Don't know if *I* am, but we'll give it a go," he chuckles, whisking us out of the room. Arm in arm, we stalk down the hall like a pair of ravenous tigers, ready to devour the world.

I start to turn the corner, thinking we're heading to the

elevators, but Alden holds firm and guides me toward his room. I glance at him. "Where are we going?" I murmur, my pulse quickening.

Alden smiles. "I have something to show you." He tugs lightly at my arm as we walk. "A gift, if you will."

I tense, remembering the last time he gave me a present. "I hope whatever it is doesn't have gills…" I sneak a peek at him out of the corner of my eye.

He laughs. "No gills, fins, or fish lips this time. Promise." He squeezes my arm. "You'll like this."

I hold my breath as we approach his room, the gold 23 shimmering on the door, and look at him expectantly. He shakes his head and keeps moving. "No, not in there… Here." He leads me across the hall to another door, Room 27. He stops and quirks his eyebrows. "Ready?"

I inhale. "I guess."

He nods and opens the door. I follow him inside, half of me dying of curiosity, the other half completely terrified. Alden places his hand on the small of my back and ushers me into the room. It's almost identical to mine, with the same furniture and big white bed—but the wall color is different, a serene, provincial yellow with a vase full of dried flowers on the nightstand. A light breeze blows through the window curtains as I step in and see who's curled up on the pillows.

"Mom…" I gasp, rushing over to the side of the bed. There is a young Indian woman in a white doctor's coat standing next to her. She smiles up from her clipboard as I approach.

I jump on the bed and take Mom's hand. "Mom, I'm here!" I exclaim, squeezing her fingers. Her eyes are closed and she doesn't respond, but I hear her snoring quietly.

"She's going to be in and out of consciousness for the next day or so," the Indian woman explains, her voice soft, "as the drugs leave her system. Should be ready to go home very soon." She nods warmly.

I look up at her and then back at Mom. She's been cleaned up and dressed in white satin pajamas, her red hair brushed back. She looks very comfortable, not at all like the frothing, post-Green Room psychotic mess Trevor described. I turn and stare at Alden, who is leaning against the wall.

"You did this? You brought her here?" My voice is full of emotion.

He straightens up and walks over to me. "I thought you might like to have her a little closer, know she's being properly looked after," he answers, putting his hands in his pockets. "She still needs to stay until the terms of our agreement are fulfilled, so I've enlisted the expertise of Dr. Bahati here." He blinks at the Indian woman. "She's been very helpful."

Dr. Bahati nods at both of us and then addresses her clipboard. "Your mother has not suffered any other injuries while she's been here," she states, reading her notes, "but she did have extensive internal damage from years of previous drug and alcohol abuse." She looks over at me, the corners of her eyes crinkling. "I've given her a restorative, but she's going to need longer treatment once you leave here. I would be happy to give you a referral to a fantastic program when you're ready."

I stare at the floor. "I don't know how we'd pay for that..." I mutter.

Alden clears his throat behind me. "Don't worry about that."

I look at him, before turning back to Dr. Bahati. "Thank you. That would be great," I whisper. Dr. Bahati smiles as she puts her head down and goes back to writing up her report.

I exhale and turn to Alden. "I... don't know what to say," I sigh.

He reaches out and rests his hands on my shoulders. "*This* is where she belonged from the start, Christa." I tremble as he rests his forehead against mine. "She needs to be somewhere that she can get healthy. I'm sorry I didn't move her sooner."

My breath catches in my throat. "No, you didn't have to do anything... I know that." I bite my lip. "I'm just so... relieved, I guess?" I look over at Mom in the bed. "This is the most peaceful I've seen her in a long time. Like, maybe this was the best thing that could have ever happened." I shake my head. "I know that must sound crazy!"

He brushes his hands down my arms. "I understand." he murmurs, giving me a gentle squeeze.

I run my fingers through my hair. "She's finally on her way to getting better... I've been hoping for that for so long." I stare up at him. "She's going to get better, right?"

Alden nods. "Yes," he whispers.

I smile. "Thank you," I breathe, leaning into him, pressing my face into the hollow of his neck. He slowly wraps his arms around my waist and pulls me close. "I don't know how I'll ever repay you."

He chuckles throatily. "I'm sure I'll think of something." He pulls back and tucks my hair behind my ear. "Now, how about we leave Dr. Bahati to her work, and you and I go find your next present?" He arches a brow.

I shake my head. "What do you mean—there's *more*? How does it get any better than this?" I giggle and check behind his back. "You got a pony hiding somewhere?"

He laughs and takes my hand. "Next time. Come on, we're supposed to meet him at noon." He starts to point me toward the door.

I shake my head. "*Him?* Hmm... curiouser and curiouser..." I grin, then glance back at my mother. "Is it okay to leave her? Will she be all right?"

Alden weaves his fingers through mine. "She'll be fine. Dr. Bahati will stay with her, and you can visit for longer later tonight."

He nods at the doctor and guides me into the hall. "You do *not* want to miss what's coming," he says, shutting the door securely and walking us back to the elevators.

*

"The airport?" I stare in confusion out of the backseat window, the sign for LAX cruising by. I turn and turn at Alden where he's sitting next to me. "Are we… going somewhere?" My stomach does little flip flops.

He smiles. "Only lunch." He shifts in his seat, pulling out his phone. "And it looks like we're going to be right on time." He leans forward and taps Frank on the shoulder. "Just drop us at the west entrance. You should be able to park in the cell phone waiting lot."

Frank gives a small nod. "Sure thing, Mr. Alden." He spins the wheel and turns into a wide, circular drive.

Alden glances back at me. "We're going to be meeting a new human acquaintance of mine," he states, pulling at a loose thread on the armrest. "While he knows my name and that I am a successful businessman with many connections, both above and below ground…" He gazes out the window. "… he has no knowledge of the Divine World. You are part of that now, Christa." He looks at me, his eyes serious. "And the one rule that we're *all* expected to uphold is that we don't talk openly about our world with the mortals, pending a Pet/Master situation. Do you understand?" He tilts his head.

I nod. "It's as much to protect them as ourselves," he continues. "The Afterlife is a hot topic amongst the living; knowing too much would severely throw off the Balance—the thin string that keeps the Universe together." He sits up. "At its worst, revealing ourselves would cause instant and devastating chaos on an apocalyptic scale." He snickers. "At best, you come off as completely insane, and men in white coats whisk you away to spend the rest of your days in a padded room."

"Can't have that," I chuckle.

"I should hope not," he agrees. "Feel free to ask him anything you like, as long as you keep our golden rule in mind." He opens the car door and looks to the front. "See you in a bit, Frank."

"Of course, Mr. Alden. Ms. Nichols." Frank smiles over his shoulder.

We get out, and Alden steps around to the trunk, taking out a small, black wheelie suitcase. I arch a brow.

"Would seem a little strange to be at an airport with no bags, don't you think?" His gives a half smile and takes my hand.

"I suppose. Where are we going?" I ask as we stroll past a family of five with all their luggage and car seats and enter through the automatic doors.

"We're looking for Terminal 4…" Alden mumbles, glancing at the overhead signs.

I take in the long line at Security and clear my throat. "Quick question… How, exactly, are we going to get in without tickets?" I quickly look away as a very stern TSA agent gives me a onceover from his desk.

Alden smiles and reaches into his back pocket. "Who said we didn't have tickets?" He hands me a dark blue envelope; I look inside and pull out a U.S. passport and airline ticket. I snort and give it a quick read.

"A one-way ticket to Paris? You know my French is horrible."

Alden quirks his eyebrows and leads me over to the line of waiting passengers. "Go big or go home," he says with a grin, coolly watching the same young dad from before struggle to fold up a super awkward stroller. "Check out your passport."

I sigh and flip the little blue booklet open. The photo is the same as on my normal passport, but I do a double take when I read the name listed underneath it.

"*Nicki Crystal?*" I grimace. "What is this, Alden?"

He gives a shrug as the line moves forward. "Couldn't have any record of you showing up here—so I called a guy and had him whip this up for you." He smiles crookedly. "I hope you like it."

"Um… you couldn't come up with a name that sounded a little less porny?" I ask as I wrinkle my nose.

He wraps his arm around my hips. "It's your name—Christa Nichols—but reversed." He makes a twirling motion with his finger.

I can't help but laugh. "Yeah—I got that!" I exclaim, smacking my thigh with the passport. "Whatever… This whole ordeal is getting more elaborate by the minute. There better be a major payoff in the end."

"We shall see." He tilts his head toward mine. "If you want, we can just skip this whole thing and hop on the flight…"

He stops and smiles at the security officer who is taking our paperwork. She blushes and stamps our tickets. "First line on your left," she mumbles, eyeballing me as we step over and take off our shoes.

"Oh, not on your life!" I crow, slamming my heels onto the conveyor belt. "Whatever you've cooked up is way better than the Eiffel Tower and a city full of stinky cheese."

Alden laughs. "Suit yourself." He steps through and holds up his arms inside the security scanner. I do the same, and we meet up on the other side.

"Okay, so we're looking for the Chili's Too…" He glances around the terminal uncertainly.

I smirk at him as I re-buckle my shoes. "*That* is a sentence I never thought I'd hear coming out of your mouth," I snigger.

Alden rolls his eyes and points down past several gates. "I see it up on the right. Let's go… We don't want him to skitter away before we've had a chance to talk." He takes me by the arm, and we walk briskly to the restaurant.

Once inside, Alden looks around, his eyes narrowed as he surveys the dining area. "He's not here yet," he mutters. "Come on, let's get a table." We walk over to a four-top and sit down.

A moment later, a young, blonde waitress bounds up to us. "Hi, welcome to Chili's Too!" she exclaims a little too cheerfully. "Can I get you something to drink? Maybe put in an order of our world-famous jalapeño poppers—"

"I'll take a coffee, thanks." Alden nods at me. "You want anything?"

I shake my head. "I'll just have water…" My stomach rumbles under the table. I realize I haven't eaten anything yet today, but I'm too nervous to think about that right now. "That's all for me."

The girl nods, her smile slipping a little. "Okay, well I'll put that coffee and water in, and if you change your mind…" She grins again and gives us a thumbs up. "Just holler!"

Alden cringes. "Fine. Thank you." He watches the entrance as she skips away.

I look around the empty restaurant. The only other patron is an older man in a dark suit sitting across the way from us, a black leather briefcase resting against his leg on the floor. He reads a newspaper while tenderly cutting into a large steak and mashed potatoes, keeping his head down as he chews. I notice that he holds his knife and fork like he's from Europe, a smooth, efficient way of eating. He only pauses to flip his paper over.

I sigh and turn back to Alden. "So, this is kind of anticlimactic," I murmur.

He smiles as the waitress returns with our drinks. She sets them on the table and goes back to the kitchen.

"What… or *who* are we waiting for?" I ask.

Alden puts a sugar in his coffee and gives it a stir. "Patience, grasshopper…" He arches a brow. "He'll show."

I huff and rest my elbows on the table. "Who is this guy, anyway? How do you know him?" I pick up my glass and take a drink.

Alden clears his throat. "I'm not one to ruin a surprise…" He pauses and takes a quick sip of his coffee. "… but I don't think it would be saying too much to tell you that he's someone who had a major impact of the course of the world's collective destiny. He's a game changer, whether he knows it or not." He sits back and folds his hands, staring out at the terminal.

I shake my head and sniff. "Okay… vaguebooking much? That has to be the worst hint ever—"

"He's here," Alden mumbles, not moving a muscle.

I straighten up and crane my neck. A tall, young guy wearing a white, short-sleeved button down and black slacks hovers by the hostess stand, his greasy hair slicked back like he thinks he's a member of the Rat Pack. His eyes dart anxiously around the restaurant, a faded navy blue messenger bag slung over his shoulder.

I furrow my brow in surprise. "That's him? He doesn't look like a game changer."

"Quiet, Christa," Alden whispers, staring down at his coffee cup. Wannabe Dean Martin sees us and scuttles over to our table, hunching down in the seat next to me.

"Hello, Kyle," Alden croons, taking another draw from his mug. "Pleasure to see you again."

Kyle Dean Martin glares at me. "You didn't say there'd be two of you," he snivels, leering at me from across the table. "Who's she?"

Alden opens his mouth. "Nicki," I interject, offering my hand. "Nicki Crystal." I see Alden's lip twitch out of the corner of my eye.

Kyle Dean doesn't reach back. "What is she doing here? I thought you'd be alone, like last time…"

Alden sighs. "Ms. Crystal is my trusted associate. She's here as a courtesy to me; I wanted another set of ears on this to keep everyone honest." He tilts his head. "Is that going to be problem, Kyle?"

Kyle Dean slouches and crosses his long, skinny arms. "That depends—do you have the money?" He eyeballs us both.

Alden smiles and reaches back, pulling out his wallet. "Here is the amount we agreed on," he murmurs, taking a check out of the front pouch. "I believe that everything should be satisfactory now." I can't read how much the check is made out for.

Kyle Dean's face goes red. "I said cash! I was very specific about that!" he retorts.

Alden sits forward in his chair and motions with his hand. "You picked the location. I couldn't very well walk through Security with a suitcase full of unmarked bills, could I?" He smirks and points to the check. "I assure you, it's legitimate. I'd be happy to go with you to any bank of your choosing after this, and they'll say the same." He stares at Kyle, his eyes cold. "Now, are we ready to move forward?"

Kyle Dean sighs, his downturned mouth making him look like a grumpy frog. "Fine. I've only got ten minutes... The 1:20 from Phoenix is running early today," he sulks.

I sit forward, my tight dress stretching across my waist. "You work here?" I ask.

Kyle Dean shakes his head at Alden. "I thought you said the bitch was in on this!" he grits out.

Alden blinks and sits forward. "I said she was here as a courtesy to me," he murmurs, arching his fingers on top of the check. "And if you can't mind your manners and keep a professional tone, we're going to take our ball and go home." He starts to pull the check away.

Kyle Dean's eyes go wide as he stares at Alden's hand. "Okay, okay! I'm sorry," he mutters, licking his lips.

Alden arches a brow and takes his hand away. "Now," he continues, "did you bring what *I* requested?"

Kyle Dean glances at the man at the table next to us, finishing up his steak. "Yeah, I got it," he whispers, reaching into his messenger bag. "They'd kill me if they knew I took it…" He sets a small white box in the center of the table and hastily grabs the check in its wake, tucking it into his shirt pocket.

Alden furrows his brow at the box. "That's all? Are you sure?" He glares at Kyle Dean.

Kyle Dean snorts. "Yeah I'm sure! There wasn't much left… The whole main cabin smoldered like the inside of a pizza oven." He jerks his chin at the box. "Seat 9A, right? Business class."

I clear my throat. "I'm missing something," I murmur, resting my hands on the table. "Seat 9A? Like on an airplane?" I look at the box, then back at Alden, who is watching Kyle Dean.

Kyle Dean rolls his eyes. "Yeah. Flight 9538 from two years ago," he jeers.

The bottom of my stomach drops. I know that number. "That wouldn't have been on its way to Shanghai, would it?" I rasp, my hands trembling.

Kyle Dean nods. "At least you know something," he says with a scowl. "Except it never made it…"

I lean forward. "Got lost during a tropical storm over the Pacific," I interrupt. "That's what everyone said—TV, the airline…" I remember two suits showing up at our front door to give us the news. Worst day of my life.

Kyle Dean sits back in his chair and chuckles. "That's just the story they told the networks. That bird never left the runway!" He swings an arm over his chair, clearly feeling more relaxed.

I sit back, my mouth agape. Alden glances over, trying to read my face.

"So…" I take a shaky breath. "What… what *did* happen?"

Kyle Dean shrugs. "I guess the technical term is 'mechanical failure,' but I don't know if that does it justice." He snickers and smooths his hair back with two fingers. "There was a malfunction in the air supply, and the inside over-oxygenated. When they flipped the switch for the main engines… BOOM!" He puffs out his cheeks and mimics an explosion with his hands.

I spin toward Alden, who is now leaning back in his chair, focused on Kyle. "The external skeleton of the plane held the explosion in," Kyle continues, "so we didn't know what had happened until they sent a traffic controller out to the runway to check it out. It was a frickin' horror show…" He gazes around the restaurant. "Does anyone work here? I wanted to get a sandwich."

I lurch forward. "So why didn't they just say there was a problem with the plane? Why make up all that shit about the storm?!" I bark, trying to keep my voice steady.

Kyle shakes his head. "Because the insurance payout would have been astronomical!" He sneers. "Blaming it on an act of God was way more cost-effective for the airline." He grins. "The part about the typhoon over the South China Sea was my idea… Radar was riddled with weather that day. I got a big fat bonus for that," he adds with a gloat.

My knees rattle together under the table. Alden reaches down and rests his hand gently on my leg.

"All those people… their families," I hiss, staring at the salt shaker. "Holding out hope that maybe they were still alive, or that they'd at least find the plane, get some closure." I glare at him. "But that was just a load of crap—something *you* made up."

Kyle Dean shifts uncomfortably. "Well… yeah," he scoffs, furrowing his brow at Alden. "What's her problem?"

Alden clears his throat. "She's trying to get a clear picture of what happened. We appreciate your cooperation." He smiles and turns back to me. "Do you have any other questions?"

I close my eyes and take a breath. "What happened to the plane? And all of the… passengers?" I whisper.

Kyle Dean shrugs. "They stripped the plane for scrap. The engines were completely shot." He glances over at the man across the way, who is now carefully stacking dollar bills on top of his tab.

"There wasn't much left inside. Hope those guys had planned to be cremated!" He chuckles, but it turns into a cough when Alden and I don't join him. "Whatever remains were left were stored and inventoried in our south field warehouse." He nods at the box in the center of the table. "That's all that's left of the poor bastard in 9A. There are a couple hundred of those sitting on a bookshelf."

I focus on the box now, a tiny *9A* written in the lower left hand corner.

Alden sighs and slowly moves it toward me. "Go ahead," he murmurs.

My lip quivers as I take the sides and pull off the lid. I know what's inside before I even open it. I glare at it in my hand. It's now smaller than its twin, the fire having melted away the gold fastener and chain, and its fur is charred and blackened.

"Unlucky rabbit," I mumble, putting the misshapen rabbit's foot back into the box. I exhale and push it over to Alden, sitting back in my chair.

Kyle Dean sniggers. "Well, this has all been really weird…" He checks his watch and stands. "… but I gotta get going. Let's, um…" He scuffs his shoe on the chair leg. "Let's never meet up again, okay?" He shakes his head at Alden.

"Of course. You fulfilled your end of the Deal. We're done," Alden replies. I keep my gaze trained on my hands where they're folded on the table top. "Thank you for your time."

Kyle Dean snorts and crosses the strap of his messenger bag over his chest. "Whatever…" He rubs his arms like he's cold. "Just forget this ever happened, that you ever met me." He narrows his eyes at us. "It would probably be best for everyone."

He turns and walks quickly toward the exit. I look up, catching Alden bat his eyelashes, his blue eyes glowing. The man across the way in the dark suit blots his mouth with a napkin and gets up from his table, leaving the restaurant, briefcase in hand. Alden watches him go before turning to me.

"Are you all right, Christa?" he whispers. "I know this all must be very upsetting for you."

I sit up, looking at the wall. "I'm fine," I answer after a minute. "I'm ready to go." I glare down at the box where it's wavering on the table like a mirage.

Alden's eyes follow mine. "Do you want to bring that with you?" he asks softly.

I shake my head and look up at him. "No." I stand and smooth my dress. "I'm ready to move on now."

He nods and gets up, tossing a five-dollar bill on the table. "Very well." He cautiously offers his hand, which I take without even thinking. "Let's move on."

We walk silently from the restaurant and out of the airport.

"Let me call Frank," Alden murmurs, taking out his phone as we wait on the front sidewalk. I nod and look up at the sky. The clouds are suddenly clearer, the sun brighter. I don't know how long I stand there, staring up at the blue—but I startle when Alden taps my elbow.

"Car's here," he mumbles, ushering me over to the curb. He opens the door, and I crawl inside. Alden follows and taps the driver's seat.

"Let's head home for a bit, Frank." He faces me. "Unless you want to go somewhere else?" I shake my head, so he nods and repeats, "Just home."

"Yes, Mr. Alden." Frank pulls away from the airport.

I stare out of the window, watching shops and parking lots go by. "Christa…" Alden murmurs after a while. "Do you want to talk about what happened?"

I sigh and grip the seat leather with my fingers. "Stop the car," I rasp.

Alden's head jerks to the side. "Frank, stop the car," he calls.

Frank pulls into an empty Taqueria lot. Alden turns to me. "What is it, Christa?" He furrows his brow.

I look at him. "Why was he a game changer?" I bite out. "Kyle... What's so special about him?"

Alden exhales. "He's special because of you," he answers. "His role in your father's death and the mismanagement of it ultimately led to you becoming the Catalyst."

I glare at the seat in front of me, my chest heaving. "So... he's the reason all of this is happening to me? I was normal before, and now, because of his lies, I'm... *not?*" I blink back tears.

Alden sighs. "He can't take sole credit, but yes, he was part of it." He leans toward me. "Christa..."

"That—" I gasp for air. "That lying... son of a bitch!" I kick the seatback. "He ruined my life! They killed my dad and made me think there was a chance..." I put my face in my hands, heavy sobs wracking my shoulders.

"Christa!" Alden grabs my arms and pulls me close. "Christa..." I struggle as he puts his mouth to my ear. "Hey—hey! Calm down! I know he hurt you, and he'll pay! He'll pay..." he coos. I stop and stare at him, his gaze warm. "I promise..."

"He'll pay," I repeat, searching his face. "You promise."

Alden nods and closes his eyes, his breath quickening. "Yes. I've taken care of it. It's already done," he breathes, our foreheads brushing together. He touches my cheek with his fingers, wiping my tears away. "You don't have to worry."

I let out a little whimper, his scent burning my nose. "Just... just stop..." I shake my head and crush my lips onto his, sucking the breath out of his lungs. He kisses back hungrily, pulling me out of my seat and onto his lap. I straddle my legs over his hips, and we tear at each other, our mouths searching desperately. He moans and pulls back.

"Frank, take a walk!" he yells.

Frank nods and gets out. "Yes, Mr. Alden."

The door closes, and we slam back together like magnets. Alden shoves his hand up my dress and tears at my panties, tugging the lace down over my hip. I gasp and press against his chest, nipping his neck and the silver chain with the cross hanging off of it. I work the buttons on his shirt open, revealing his chest and the bright handprint over his heart. He lets out a sharp hiss and rips my underwear away as I dig my fingernails into it.

"Christa…" he groans, tangling his hands in my hair as I kiss my way back to his mouth. I push up and arch my spine as I fumble with his belt buckle, both of us panting and watching my fingers. I get his belt free and start working the top button on his pants, feeling him get hard underneath me. He swallows and sits back.

I'm just about to get his zipper open when the phone rings. "Fuck…" he grunts, his pupils flashing. He licks his lips, gripping my waist with his hands and pressing me down, my thighs rubbing against him. He moans, and the phone rings again.

"Goddammit!" he curses, sitting up. I perch back on his knees, my breath ragged. Alden sighs and pulls his phone out. "I'm sorry… I have to take this." He clears his throat and stares at me as he answers.

"What?" he barks. He stops and listens, his eyes narrowed. "And you're sure this time? I can't have any more mistakes." He waits. "Fine. I'm on my way." He hangs up and sighs.

"What is it?" I murmur, running my hand through my hair.

He smiles sardonically up at me. "Duty calls, I'm afraid." He purses his lips and looks at his belt, then back up at me. I nod and awkwardly crawl off of him.

"Oh… okay." I tug my dress back down and sit on the edge of my seat. He clears his throat and quickly pulls himself back together as well. "Where… where are we going?" I rasp.

He straightens his back. "I have to make a quick stop, not far from here. *You* will be staying in the car with Frank." He glares out the window. "Where *is* Frank?"

I shake my head. "I don't understand. Why can't I come with you?"

Alden sighs. "I don't think so, Christa. This one could get messy. It's not exactly ride-along material."

I bristle. "What? You don't think I can handle watching you be the bad guy?" I laugh. "Um, hello? I think as both emancipator and your captive, I have a pretty good idea of what that looks like." At least, I think I do.

Alden sighs and finishes buttoning his shirt. "It's not just that," he huffs. "You're going to have questions and want to know about every little thing that happens, and I can't go into it all with you…" He looks out the window and rubs his face. I sit back in my chair.

"I have to go find Frank," he exhales before opening his door. "I'm sorry. This shouldn't take long."

I bite my tongue and glance around the car. "Secrets, secrets…" I arch a brow sullenly. "Whatever."

He sighs as he steps out, slamming the door behind him.

*

"Where are we?" I ask quietly. We've driven out past Trinity and the Sunset Strip, going the same way as if I were coming home after a night of partying. Frank parks at a shadowy underpass, turning off the car. I glare out of my window at the desolate street, dim sunlight filtering in through cracks in the bridge, then furrow my brow. "This looks… familiar."

Alden scoffs. "It should: this is where Boyfriend crashed his car last week, where you got that nasty bump on your noggin."

I gasp as he gets out of the car. "Wait, what are we doing here?" My voice quivers.

Alden sighs. "*You* are going to wait in the car." He nods at the front. "Frank will keep you company."

I shake my head. "No offense, Frank... but I'm not staying here." I open my door and scramble out. Alden's jaw tightens as he slams his door. I tut. "You're obviously keeping something from me—"

"I keep a lot of things from you," he simpers, his eyes thin slits.

I jut out my chin. "Yeah... but you get a phone call, and then all of a sudden we're back at the scene of the crime—where all *this* began..." I exhale, Daniel's face flashing in my mind. "No... I'm coming, too."

Alden grits his teeth. "I don't have time to argue with you." He taps on the driver's side window. "Glove compartment."

Frank gives him something, and he tucks it behind his back. He walks around the car and takes me by the hand. "All right, Christa. Unlike our last meeting, I am going to insist that you keep your head down and your mouth shut. This is business." He stops and glares at me. "I mean it."

I glower. "Yeah, I got it." I glance around as he leads me down the abandoned road. I try to remember anything from that night—the graffiti, the wall-to-wall concrete—but everything comes up blank. I can make out homeless people sleeping, even though it's only late afternoon, tucked up underneath the bridge and clutching dirty blankets around themselves. A few of them stir as we walk past, but no one calls out or tries to stop us. We make our way to where the road dead ends and stand in front of a streetlamp, a huddled mass covered in an oversized brown trench coat dozing beneath it. Alden clears his throat and gives it a swift kick.

"Fuck!" the mass cries out, shifting to the side. A young man with thick glasses and a large, full beard emerges from a pile of old clothes and stares, shaking himself awake. When he takes one look at us, his eyes grow wide.

"How… how did you find me?" he stutters, backing up against the wall.

Alden shrugs. "I won't say it was easy, but you're not Jimmy Hoffa, Pete." He laughs. "A couple carefully placed scouts led me right to you; it just took a little longer than I would have liked. The sneak attack from the pair of Archs you arranged the other day didn't help my mood either." I watch as he steps onto the sidewalk.

Pete smirks. "Bet they got you good." He holds out his hands as Alden moves closer. "Hey! Stay the fuck away from me!" he shouts, pushing his glasses up his nose.

Alden chuckles. "Beware fair-weather friends… They always let you down, in the end." I look at the man's olive-colored jacket and see a name stitched into the front pocket: *Cpl. P. Highland.*

I close my eyes and sigh. "You're the vet," I murmur to myself. "Not vet, like veterinarian, but veteran. I'm such an idiot."

Pete glares at me. "What are you doing here?" He winces, shaking his head. "You're supposed to be with Daniel."

I almost fall over. "You know Daniel?" I breathe, moving forward. Alden holds me back with his arm.

Pete nods. "I was here, the night of your accident." He sighs and looks between the two of us. "You probably don't remember me… I couldn't… I…" He puts his head in his hands. "The blast was too much for me, from the wreck, so I hid—over there." He gestures back to the bridge. "Dan ran right for you, though; I watched the whole thing." He smiles weakly. "I'm sorry I couldn't do more. I wanted to, I tried…" His voice fades. "That other guy with you, the one trapped in the car. Is he okay?"

I shake my head. "Tom? I don't know. He's still in the hospital…" I trail off.

Alden sighs. "This is all very emotional, and you guys should totally friend each other on Facebook," he twitters, "but I think we know why I'm really here." He eyes Pete menacingly.

Pete straightens up, cornered against the wall. "I don't have it," he spits, staring at the sidewalk. "Dan took it back, last time I saw him."

Alden puffs out his cheeks and exhales. "*Why* has everyone been so difficult lately?" he tuts, rolling up his sleeves. "It's, like, twenty extra steps to get anything done—really sucks the joy out of it." He clears his throat. "Okay, Pete. You're lying, obviously." Pete shifts, his fingers gripping the brick behind him. "What's it going to take to get you to give me what I want? Money? Blood?" Alden holds up his bare forearm.

Pete's nose twitches before he recoils back against the wall. "You've got nothing I want, Demon!" he shouts.

I stagger behind Alden, taken aback. "I would never sell him out like that!" Pete continues vehemently. "Not for you, not for anything! He's my fucking brother!" He tears at his hair.

Alden sighs. "He has that effect on people. You're not the first to express such admiration." He pulls his keys out of his pocket and runs them along his soft, exposed underarm, raggedly cutting into the skin. A few drops of bright red blood well in the scrape. Pete's eyes hone in on them.

"But blood is thicker than water, or so the expression goes," Alden continues, holding up his arm. "Are you sure we can't work something out?"

Pete paces in front of the wall. "I've been clean for three weeks. I'm not going back to that," he mutters, keeping his eyes down.

I watch him, my brow furrowed. "You're... Smudged?" I murmur. "So you can see him?" I jerk my chin toward Alden. "And me?"

Pete looks up at me, his face haggard. "Yeah, I see you both. Surprised you can stand so close to that ugly mug." He chuckles darkly, reaching into his jacket. I feel Alden tense next to me, but relax when Pete pulls out a cigarette. He puts it to his lips.

"Mind if I smoke?" he asks as he lights it, taking a puff. Alden grins.

Pete goes on. "When I got back from my last tour, I was all messed up. I was trying to get my life back together, living with my parents over in Pasadena. I had a job at my uncle's car repair, and I even started seeing this really pretty girl I knew back in high school." He shakes his head. "But I couldn't settle. I got in with the wrong crowd. A few months later, I found myself waking up in some fleabag motel in Studio City with a syringe full of Demon blood hanging out of my arm." He glares at Alden. "I came back to civilian life empty and feeling like I'd left a piece of myself over there, and these bastards were more than happy to fill that hole with a bunch of garbage."

Alden rolls his eyes. Pete looks back at me. "I ran into Daniel a little over a year ago. We knew each other from the war. He…" He purses his lips and sighs. "It's not important. Anyway, he looked… *different* than the last time I'd seen him, as you know." He motions with his cigarette. "It was the first time I'd met anybody from the other side." He stops and clears his throat. "And it blew my mind. Dan's been helping me ever since, trying to get me cleaned up so I can live a real life." He bites the inside of his cheek. "That's why he was down here the other night, trying to get me to go to a shelter, to get outta the rain." He gazes at me. "Guess it's good he was, more for you than for me."

I nod, my eyes glassy. Pete clenches his jaw. "Where is he? Does he know you're running around with this asshole?" He points at Alden.

I wrap my arms around my chest. "He knows," I mumble.

Pete shakes his head. "Well, I'm sure he's not happy about it." He scowls, taking a drag off his cigarette. "Especially after everything he did for you." I stare down, shamefaced, at the pavement.

Alden steps forward. "Enough," he interjects. "Where is it, Pete? I don't like having my time wasted."

Pete leans against the lamp post and flicks his cigarette away. "Like I told you, I don't have it," he sighs.

Alden scrunches his face and reaches behind him, pulling a gun from his waistband. I gasp and stumble back. "Alden—what are you doing?" I squeak.

He aims the gun at Pete, who holds up his hands and freezes. "Time's up, Corporal! Looks like this party just got a whole lot more exciting!" He tilts his head. "Now, are you going to give me what I want, or are we going to shut it down with a bang?"

Pete swallows and takes a tentative step forward. "Just finished my last smoke, now I get my last words," he whispers. His voice is shaking, but he glares stonily. "Fuck you, Demon. And... I'll be seeing you soon."

The corner of Alden's mouth twitches, his gun arm rigid. Pete quirks his eyebrows and draws an X on his chest. "Okay, do it." He juts out his chin. "Shoot me, cuz that's the only way you're getting anything—from my dead body."

Alden crinkles his brow and continues holding the gun.

"Do it, come on!" Pete snarls. "Fuckin' shoot me already! What are you waiting for?!" He looks up, his eyes wild.

Alden watches him, a smile teasing his lips. I hold my breath as he cocks the hammer and aims. "All right, but I'm not gonna do it; Christa is," he replies, lowering the gun.

I stare at him, speechless. Pete's face falls. "What? No! You can't do that!"

Alden shushes him as he walks over to me. I shake my head. "Alden—I can't... I don't..." I stammer.

He smiles. "Come on," he murmurs, snugging me against his side and wrapping his arms around me. I rock back and forth in a daze as he places the cold gun in my palm. "Just point and shoot."

I shudder as he wraps my knuckles around the trigger, keeping his fingers firmly over mine. I shake my head and look at Pete, his eyes like saucers. I look back at the gun, heavy in my hand. "I've... I've never fired a gun before," I mumble.

Pete shifts his weight. "Don't do it, Christa," he snaps, his whole body trembling. "I don't give a shit about my life—it's been over for a while." His pupils dart back between Alden and I. "But for your own sake, don't do it... It—it will destroy you, inside and out." He cringes. "I know. Take it from me, okay?" He lowers his hands slowly. "Just put the gun down."

My breath quickens. Alden's grip tightens, keeping me in check. "You and I made an agreement yesterday," he whispers in my ear, "that you would do *exactly* as I say, remember?"

I nod shakily. Alden clears his throat. "Now, I am telling you, *ordering* you to shoot him."

My arm spasms, and I gulp for air. "No," I choke. "I won't do it."

I gasp and buckle in agony as stabbing pains course through my stomach. "Gah...!" I clutch my belly, feeling like my organs are being ripped out one at a time. I sway and bite my tongue as Alden hoists me back up, pressing me securely against him. I exhale as the pain subsides.

"Alden—why are you doing this?" I whimper. "You're hurting me."

His face hardens. "That's the Deal; the pains will only get worse if you refuse." He sets my arm in place and cocks the gun again. "Christa, shoot him." He aims the barrel with his hand. Pete takes a breath. "Don't listen to him. Fight it!" he shouts, standing tall.

I wince and bow my head, tightening my finger on the trigger. "No," I rasp. "I can't... I can't kill a person." I howl as the pains come back, now in my arms and legs too, twisting and wrenching like I'm a wet towel being wrung out. "STOP!" I scream into the street.

Alden clucks his tongue behind me. "I'm so glad Danny's not here to see her like this; it would utterly devastate him." He sighs, his eyes ticking over to Pete again. I pant and stare at the lamp post, my vision blurry.

Pete shakes his head. "I promised him, Christa! I'm sorry!" He grabs onto the post. "I'm sorry... I'm so sorry..." He looks away.

I inhale and try to find my feet, my legs like jelly. Alden holds me up and props the gun in my hand. "You can make this all go away," he breathes into my hair, reaching up with one hand and jerking me by the chin. "Come on, look... *LOOK* at him, Christa... This is an intimate act, and you owe it to him to see his face." I wince and try to look away, but Alden holds my head in place. Pete frowns back at me.

"You can make all this go away," Alden continues, "by following instructions. Do as I say and shoot him."

My finger wobbles dangerously on the trigger, sweat breaking out on my brow. Daniel's face flashes in my mind again, and I close my eyes, keening back against Alden's shoulder.

"Leave her alone!" I hear Pete yell. "Get out of her head!"

Alden laughs. "Give me what I want, and it's over!" he exclaims. "Come on, soldier! How many more rounds do you think she's got before she turns into pink mist? One? Maybe two?" He adjusts his arm under my waist. "Just wait 'til Danny hears all about how your obstinacy got his best girl killed." His teeth gleam. "What I wouldn't give to be a fly on the wall for that conversation."

Pete steps forward. "There's no way you'd risk that!" he shouts. "She's the goddamn Catalyst! The fact that you've let it go this far is crazy!"

Alden laughs. "Oh, try me! You should know by now that I only play for high stakes... So, out of the two of us, who do you think is going to be the first one to stand down? Hm?" He presses his cheek to my temple. I hang limply in his arms, barely able to stand.

Pete wavers across from us, his face hard. He shakes his head.

Alden sighs. "Okay, next hand." My chest heaves as he lifts me up and puts his mouth to my ear. "Shoot him."

I grit my teeth, the gun rattling in my palm. "Nn... nn... no." I rasp. I double over when what feels like a million needles pierce my skin down to the muscle and bone, infusing pain into places I didn't even know I had. I crouch on the ground and wail, clawing with my hands at my eyes and mouth, smashing the gun barrel against my cheek. When Alden pulls me back to my feet, I kick and yelp like a wild dog.

I hear Pete gasp. "Stop! You're killing her!" he cries. "All right, here! Just take it!" He pulls something from his pocket. "Take it— take it! Just stop!" He clutches the item in his hand.

Alden grins. "Thank you, Corporal," he simpers. "Now, that wasn't so hard, was it?"

He lifts my arm and cocks the gun with his thumb. Pressing his finger over mine, we pull the trigger together, Alden embracing me tight as the gun kicks back.

Pete staggers into the lamppost and falls to the ground, his mouth forming a perfect O. He lies still as a bloody rose blooms across the front of his jacket. There is silence at the underpass.

"No," I whisper, standing by, motionless.

Alden lets go of me and takes the gun, wiping it down before putting it back into his waistband.

"No... no... that didn't just happen..." I moan.

He turns to me, flecks of blood dotting his arms. "Yes, it did. I warned you this wasn't going to be an easy job." He reaches into his shirt pocket and hands me a cotton handkerchief. "Here, for your face."

I blink down at the cloth, not quite sure what I'm supposed to do with it. My hand shakes as I tuck it into my dress.

"He's dead." My tongue swells in my mouth as I say the words and glare at the body. I catch myself as I start to hyperventilate, sucking large gulps of air in through my nose.

"Calm down, Christa." Alden sighs, stepping toward Pete's body and bending down next to it. "It was just business—nothing to get worked up about."

I stare at him, aghast. "You… you killed him," I murmur, thoughts and emotions flooding my brain.

Alden looks back at me and grins. "You helped." He snickers as he pries Pete's fingers open. He holds up the object and inspects it, gold glinting in the sunlight. He stows it safely away in his pocket.

I shake my head and step toward him. "No, I didn't," I gasp as I almost trip over Pete's legs. "You were the one who pulled the trigger! It was you!" I look at him wide-eyed. "How could you do that?"

Alden shakes his head. "You had no problem pulling the pro-verbial trigger on dear Kyle a little while ago." I gape at him as he reaches down and picks up the old trench coat. "Just the mention of ending his pathetic little life got you all hot and bothered."

I cross my arms and hold myself protectively. "That… that wasn't the same! He killed my dad! He deserved it—" I stop, doubt creeping in.

Alden looks up and tilts his chin. "*Sort of*," he clarifies. "He sort of killed your dad. Which is enough for me!" He motions down at Pete. "How do you know *he* didn't deserve it?" He looks back up at me. "Ah… I see. It's not the same when *it suits you*. Typical mortal," he tuts.

I shake my head. "He gave you what you wanted, and you still killed him! Why?" I shout.

Alden sighs and throws the trench coat over Pete's body. "He stole my girlfriend, he ran over my dog with his truck, I didn't like his beard—what difference does it make?" he barks, moving over to the road. "He was an addict and a loser, and now he's dead. No use crying over him now." He turns back toward the car. "Are you coming?"

I shake my head. "How can you say that?" I hiss. "Wake up, brush your teeth, get a sandwich… shoot someone dead?" I twist toward him. "Is that seriously your life?"

Alden clenches his jaw. "You thought it was something else?"

I wet my lips. "And you're okay with that?" I shout. "Callous, thoughtless… That's really who you want to be? Some lame-ass muscle for Hell?" I sniff. "God, I thought you were better than that."

Alden glares at me. "You talk as if I ever had a choice in the matter!" He marches over and grabs my arm, shaking me violently. "Not everyone is the ruddy Chosen One," he jeers, getting in my face. "Here you stand, one of the most powerful beings in the Universe, yet you're exactly like everybody else—experiencing, *living* the bare minimum. You're someone who just lets things happen to you instead of grabbing destiny by the horns and making it your own. What a waste." He lets go and stalks back to the street, sneering.

I grit my teeth. "Daniel was right about you," I call.

He stops.

"Shame on me for thinking any different," I add. "He's good, and you're… not."

Alden turns back to me and balks. "Is that what you really think? Seriously? Oh wow… He has been working you, Sweet Girl!" He lets out a hollow laugh.

I cross my arms and shift uneasily as he steps back over and puts his mouth to my ear. "I could tell you stories that would make your toes curl," he breathes, brushing my hair back. "About him and so many pretty girls that look just like you… what he did… why he's still here…"

I push him away with a glare. "At least he's something you'll never be."

Alden straightens his back. "And what's that?" he rasps.

"Repentant."

He takes a step back. "What do you know about penance?" he hisses.

"Enough to know that you don't have it. I'm a fool for thinking you were different." I clutch my arms, thinking about last night in my bed. "Guess you showed me. You really are evil, and I really am an idiot."

He glares at me for a moment before his face softens. "Christa, I can explain..." he sighs. He tries to touch my hand, but I hold him back.

"Stay away from me!" I snap. "You tortured me—used my suffering to get him to give up." I nod back at Pete's body. "I thought you said no harm would come to me while I was in your care."

He looks down at the ground.

"Twist it however you want," I continue, "but we both know what you did. You went back on your word. All for some stupid knickknack." I jut out my chin toward his pocket.

He snorts and looks up at the sky. "I can't help it if you're going to tear yourself apart over some cracked-out war hero!" he yells. "Did you see me lift a finger, lay a hand on you?" He shrugs. "You did that all to yourself. Take responsibility!"

He starts to walk off, but spins back. "And mind you, it was a stupid knickknack he was willing to die for. So put that in your pipe."

I narrow my eyes. "Who are you trying to convince, Alden—me, or you?" I whisper.

He exhales and kicks the lamppost. "Christ!" He winces and shakes his ankle, then sighs and puts his hands on his hips. "Come on, we have to get out of here. An Agent should be here any minute." He turns and glances down the alley.

I shake my head. "What? Agent?" I look at him, confused.

Alden furrows his brow. "For Collection! We don't have time for this, Christa!" He waves toward the car. "Let's go!"

"Wait…" I exhale and crouch down next to Pete's head, smoothing his hair off his face. His glasses sit askew on his nose. I reach over and gently remove them, tucking them into his jacket.

"I've never seen anyone die before," I murmur, looking down at him, his mouth now relaxed, his eyes open and dull. "Is there something we're supposed to do now?" I swallow. "Should we close his eyes?" My fingers tremble over his face.

Alden groans. "Buy him a bloody new suit and take him down the shore for all I care!" he cries. "But if we hang around any longer, you're going to be doing that from the sheriff's office… or worse, all right? NOW!"

I swallow again and stare down at Pete. "I'm sorry." I close his eyes before Alden wrenches me away by the arm.

*

"Do you need anything—" Alden barely gets the words out before I slam my door in his face.

"Fine," he sighs from the other side of the door. "I have some work to take care of, but I'll check in on you after that. Try to sleep."

I slump against the wall as I hear his steps fade down the hallway. I slide to the floor, resting my head on my knees. My shoulders heave as the sobs come one after another, until my face is a smooshed-up mess of snot and tears. I arch my neck back and try to catch my breath, sniffling as I pat my cheeks dry with my palms. I look over at the dark room, the window still displaying the alpine sunrise, its red sun peeking from behind snowcapped mountains.

I stand and walk into the bathroom, flicking on the light. The fireplace blazes to life, heating the room and illuminating the glass bottles on the vanity. I step over to the mirror and look at myself, seeing dark circles under my eyes and gaunt cheeks that are splattered with blood—Pete's blood.

"Dammit." I pull Alden's handkerchief from my dress top and pick at the spots until they're all gone, my fingers trembling. I toss the cloth away and sigh.

"Fuck," I mutter, staring down at my hands. There's more blood all over my knuckles. I gnash my teeth and turn on the sink, blasting hot water and scrubbing my hands until they're raw and pink. I stop the water and walk out into the room, heading straight to the TV and quietly opening the cabinet doors.

"I need to see him," I whisper as Serpentine materializes. "Please... show me Daniel."

Serpentine nods, and a new window appears. The sun is just beginning to set on the roof. I break into a smile when I find Daniel huddled in the corner, trying to wrench a heavy piece of sheet metal away from a large vent.

"Daniel! Oh, thank God..." I breathe, pressing my fingers to the screen.

He shakes his head and stands, putting his hands on his hips. "Come on, there's gotta be a way to get in there," he mumbles to himself. He puts his finger to his lips and starts pacing in front of the vent.

Tears trickle down my cheeks. "Daniel, I... I need you," I cry softly, watching him move along the roof. "Everything's gotten really messed up, and I don't know what to do." He walks over to the edge and stares out at the sky. I sigh. "This super bad thing just happened, and I need to see you... Please, can you come down now? There's so much I have to tell you, and... and say I'm sorry for..." I wipe my nose and watch him run his hands through his hair in frustration.

"And I need you to tell me it's okay... that I'm okay! That I'm not..." I mash the heels of my wrists into my eyes. "That I'm *good*! Please, Daniel! I need you... I need you..." I break into a fresh set of sobs and collapse on the floor as he steps toward the center of the roof.

"Hey!" he shouts. I jolt, thinking he's yelling at me, but he spins around and jumps back, his teeth bared.

"Hey! I see you!" he shouts to someone off-screen. "Come out here and—"

He gets cut off, the screen going black. Serpentine's wide face looms in front of me.

"What? What's happening? Where's Daniel?" I sit up, alarmed.

"Connection lost," Serpentine explains. "We are experiencing technical difficulties. Please enjoy a complimentary showing of *Meet Me in Saint Louis!* while we attempt to remedy the problem. Thank you for your patience." He nods as the screen changes over to the image of a robust Judy Garland, singing her heart out from a Hollywood soundstage.

I scuttle to the end of the bed and grab the remote. "Wait—no! Hey, come back!" I yell, punching a bunch of buttons at random. "Stop!"

Judy alters on the TV from black and white to full technicolor, the sound shooting up to full volume. "HEY!" I scream, holding my ears. "Turn this off—NOW!"

The room falls silent, and the screen goes back to its original pinprick. After a moment, Serpentine reappears. I sit up very straight. "Okay," I rasp, my voice shaking. "Now, I don't know *what* just happened, but I want to see Daniel. Show me Daniel!"

Serpentine blinks. "We are experiencing technical difficulties. Please enjoy—"

"No!" I interrupt. "Something was about to happen up there, and you didn't want me to see it!" I stare Serpentine square in the eye.

"We are experiencing technical difficulties—"

"Enough!" I jump off of the bed and stalk wildly in front of the TV, jabbing the controller. "FriendFinder—now!"

Serpentine nods, and the FriendFinder menu comes up. "FriendFinder," he repeats. "Please stand in front of your screen and clearly state the name of the individual that you wish to locate. All subjects must be residing on the—"

"Daniel!" I shout. "Show me Daniel!"

"We are experiencing technical difficulties—"

I scream and throw the remote at the screen, Serpentine goes silent. I huff and step over to the window, the curtains blowing back from the mountain air.

I bite my lower lip and slam my palm against the window. "Just show me the fucking parking lot!" The image wavers slightly from the force of my hand. I cock my head and hit it again, harder. It statics around the edges, little sparks of green electricity peppering the screen. I wind my fist back to punch it, and it flickers almost defensively before switching to an image I haven't seen before: L.A. at night from above, the city lights laid out like a beautiful, glowing carpet. It's the exact view that Daniel described from the roof the other night. I lower my arm and sink into the blue chair, the wind knocked out of me.

I narrow my eyes. "Stop messing with me, you piece of shit!" I hiss, stalking over to the TV again. Serpentine waits patiently. "I know there's more to you than meets the eye… Show me Daniel!"

Serpentine blinks. "You know that's not possible, Christa," he replies.

I gasp and stagger back at the sound of my name. "You… you know who I am," I rasp. "And you can talk." I slump against the end of the bed, my face frozen in what I'm sure looks like a grotesque Joker grin. I start to laugh hysterically.

Serpentine smiles. "Why is that so funny?" he asks, tilting his big face.

I snort. "It's not." I hiccup, my eyes watering. "I'm going insane! Oh my God, I'm going insane…" I gasp and let out a hyena-like shriek, then smash my fist into my mouth.

The face rolls its eyes. "Get ahold of yourself, Christa," he orders.

"Stop saying my name! Can you see me?!" I grab my knees and rock back and forth, my breath coming out in spasms. "You're just a computer. This… this can't be happening!" I shake my head and crawl back against the bedpost.

Serpentine sighs. "Would you like me to call Housekeeping and have them bring up something to help you relax?" he murmurs.

I shake my head fervently. "No… NO!" I scream. "Just stop talking to me!" I jerk my chin and try to push myself under the bed, clawing like a rat at the carpet. "I'm afraid. Please, I'm afraid…"

Serpentine's head starts to quake, his eyes turning red. "CHRISTA!" he shouts. "ENOUGH!"

I shudder and clamp my hands over my mouth, monkey speak no evil. The face exhales and goes back to normal. "Now, like I've been trying to explain, I cannot find Daniel; he is out of my reach." He glares at me.

I slowly come out from under the bed and inch toward the screen. "How is that possible? He was just here a minute ago. I… I need to see him!" I stammer.

Serpentine shakes his head. "What you need is to rest, Christa. You're having an episode," he answers. "Now, go take a nap."

I stare up at him feebly. When our eyes meet, and he puffs up his cheeks, blowing at me like I'm a silver dandelion in spring.

The ground sinks beneath me as I slump backward to the floor, falling into a heavy sleep.

CHAPTER 12

SOMEONE IS KNOCKING at my door.

My eyes open, and I find myself sprawled across the floor of my room, the TV screen dark. I sit up and rub the back of my head, wondering how long I was out. The knocking comes again, and I look over at the door, my forehead scrunched. I get to my feet and glance around. The bed is still made up, and all of the lights are off. The window background is one that I haven't seen before, and I go over to take a closer look. It's raining; the sky is gray, and tiny rivulets of water are coursing across the glass. I squint and put my nose up to it, realizing that the liquid isn't actually water, but blood. I stretch and let out a yawn and am moving to turn on a lamp when the knocking continues.

I blink, remembering why I got up in the first place. I walk over to the door, my steps weightless, and answer.

There's no one there.

I glance around the hall, searching for a minute before shutting the door again. I hear the faint sound of water running and turn to see a cloud of steam billowing out of the bathroom. The door is open just a crack, small, flickering lights coming from within. I turn and step inside.

White candles of varying heights greet me as I cross the threshold. They cover the vanity and the floor, creating a path to the shower. The glass is all fogged up. Hesitantly, I wipe my hand across to see who's inside.

Daniel turns and smiles, slicking his wet hair back before opening the door. "Took you long enough," he laughs. "Come on; I warmed it up for you."

My eyes scan down his tan, naked body, lean muscles glistening in the candlelight. I look away shyly.

"What's the matter?" he asks, holding out his hand. "Figured you'd want to clean up, after today." I nod. He watches me as I glance down at my clothes, my dress smeared in something dark and sticky. I shrug out of it and toss it on the floor behind me. I look back at him as he holds open the door for me.

"You're beautiful," he murmurs. I smile, taking his hand and joining him inside.

The hot water courses down my arms and legs, steam pouring out over the top of the stall and making the air heavy. I turn and face the showerhead, closing my eyes and opening my mouth to drink. Behind me, Daniel's strong hands massage my shoulders, break away to comb back my wet hair, trace down the length of my sides. The soft spots under my ribcage tingle as his fingers brush over them, my skin reddening from the intensity of the heat. I twist around to look at him, running my palms over his arms and into his damp curls. He smiles and leans down, pressing his lips to mine. We kiss—at first soft and gentle, but then deep and crushing, like we're going to swallow each other whole.

"I've wanted you so bad," he pants into my ear, his mouth finding the secret place behind my jaw. My eyes flutter shut, and I moan, raking my nails down his tattooed back. He lets out a sigh and kisses me harder. "You have no idea what it's been like, waiting for you."

I gasp and tilt my face back under the water stream, his mouth hot and inviting on my neck. I bring my hand to my face to push back my hair and notice that it's covered in blood. I startle and pull away, turning Daniel around to see five deep, horrible gashes running down to his tailbone, slashing across his tattoo like a ripped painting. I open my mouth to scream, but he spins back, smiling, and wraps his arms around my waist.

"It's fine…" he whispers, nuzzling into my ear. I close my eyes and melt into him again, desperate for closeness. He licks the edge of my collarbone and pushes me firmly up against the wall. I gasp as he presses his body to mine, feeling the light hairs on his chest against my bare skin. He traces his tongue back up my neck, his hands now on my hips, pulling me to him. I lean back and stare into his eyes.

"You know, I never stopped believing in you." He grins, smoothing hair off of my forehead. "You're the one."

I smile and graze his jaw with my fingertips, his slick skin falling away like tissue paper to reveal a layer of bright red muscle. I lean in and kiss his smooth lips, the taste of cinnamon and copper swirling around my mouth. He shudders and kisses down my sternum, his tongue lapping at my navel. I sigh as his hands grasp my ass, tugging me closer. I rest my foot on the soap tray as his mouth finds me, warm and full. He kisses me again and again, getting a steady rhythm going. I swallow and splay my fingers against the wet shower wall, trying to savor this moment as long as possible.

Daniel pauses and looks up at me, his face almost completely torn away, the nerves around his eye sockets exposed. "I love you, Christa," he utters, lacing his fingers through mine.

I smile at him longingly. "I love you too, Daniel," I reply. He goes back to me, and I throw my head back, lost in ecstasy, feeling like gold is running through my veins. As the swelling crests and turns to a dull ache, I reach up and touch my neck, feeling a soft powder raining down on my skin. Still panting, I open my eyes and stare at my hand, now covered in a wet dusting of ash.

The water turns off.

I hyperventilate as I frantically look around. Daniel's gone, replaced by a thick paste of wet ash running down the drain. I get on my knees and frantically scrape around the grate, pieces of him getting caught under my nails and spraying across my legs like black paint. I claw at the edge of the filter, my fingertips bleeding as I let out a hysterical wail. I can hear twisted, maniacal laughter coming from the other side of the shower door. I get to my feet and slouch against the back wall, still bathed in Daniel.

"Right, then left, then back again, round and round we go," Aiden sings, pressing his face to the glass, distorted and terrifying.

"Ashes, ashes, we all fall down."

*

A light rapping at the door jolts me awake, releasing a gasp that was caught in my throat. I'm back on the bedroom floor, a thin film of sweat covering my chest. I glance around wildly, the window displaying the familiar beach scene and lighting up the room. I grab my chest, still trying to catch my breath. Another knock. I get up and stare at the door.

"Come... come in," I rasp. The door opens, and a large black man who I've never seen before walks into the room, the color of his tailored suit matching the gray at his temples. His eyes smile behind a set of wire-frame glasses. I stare at him blankly.

"Good morning, Ms. Nichols." He nods, offering his hand.

I stagger forward and take it, his palm warm. "Hello," I manage.

He steps back and folds his hands. "I received a call from our main office yesterday that you were in need of an Agent; is this correct?" he asks simply.

My jaw hangs open. "I... I guess. I did call..." I shake my head, yesterday a blur. "Porticullis?"

He nods. "I apologize for my tardiness; there were extenuating circumstances." He clears his throat.

I sit on the edge of the bed. "Its... fine," I breathe. "How did you get in here? Are you a Demon, too?"

He shakes his head. "No—but there are very few barriers in this universe that Agents cannot cross." He nods in a friendly manner. "Otherwise, shuttling souls from this world to the next would be a very tricky proposition."

My pulse quickens. "So you can get me out of here?" I rasp. "We can leave? Can you help my mom, too?"

The man shakes his head. "I can't take you or your mother off-property, Ms. Nichols," he replies gravely. "That would violate your Deal with Mr. Murphy, which would be breaking the Rules."

When I sigh, dejected, he clears his throat. "But maybe there's something else I can help you with."

I shrug. "I doubt it—not unless you have a Guardian tracking system squirreled away in that suit." I stare at him. "My... my friend, my Guardian... he's missing." I close my eyes, trying to remember what Serpentine had said about Daniel.

He's out of my reach.

The man chuckles. "No better than the one you have in place right now." I look at him quizzically. "Your Link," he explains, motioning at me and taking a seat in the blue chair. "The one you share with your Guardian. It works both ways, you know. Haven't you felt the pull since you've been apart?" He folds his hands over his paunch.

I blush; I just thought those were my butterflies.

"If the situation presents itself, search within and come what may," he continues, tilting his chin.

I frown. "That sounds... ominous," I huff, pulling my knees up to my chest. "How do you know so much about this stuff? Are you an Angel?"

He shakes his head. "No, I am not one of those, either." He smiles kindly. "Porticullis remains a neutral third party that is responsible for the distribution of souls post-mortem as well as arbitrating any negotiations between Heaven and Hell." He settles into the cushions. "Our Agency is comprised of delegates from both sides to ensure absolute integrity." He nods, glancing around the room.

I narrow my eyes. "But... you're dead, right?" I tuck my hair behind my ears. "I mean, not... alive."

He chuckles. "I am dead. The majority of the world is, when you get down to it." He grins. "You'll get used to it."

He grunts and gets up, stepping over to the TV. "Nice room," he says with a nod, brushing his hand over the top of the screen. "You get cable in here?" He picks up the remote.

I lurch forward. "Yeah—but don't touch that!" I jump off of the bed and slam the cabinet doors closed. The man watches me, nonplussed.

"Sorry." I gesture at the TV. "He's... temperamental."

The man nods and walks to the center of the room, his hands in his pockets. "Okay." He smiles back at me. "Well, Ms. Nichols... I'm not exactly sure why I was summoned here. No negotiations to arbitrate or Dead to harbor." He arches a brow at me and checks under the bed. "Are there?"

I shake my head. "Not here, no..." I smile tightly, thinking of Pete in the alley. "Sorry. I didn't mean to waste your time."

His eyes brighten. "The time, yes!" He points over to the bedside telephone. "That's why you called the Home Office..." He looks at his wrist and starts removing his watch. Unlike the rest of his attire, it's old and tarnished, the face yellowed, the leather strap cracked. He motions for me to come closer and takes my hand.

"What's this?" I ask, staring as he buckles it around my wrist.

"I may not be able to help you directly, but this might help make the rest of your stay here go a little smoother." He steps back and admires his work. "Looks nice on you."

I give a small smile. "I *have* been wondering what time it is..."

Like, since the moment I got here. I look up at the man. "Thanks."
He nods warmly.

I stare down at the watch, checking the time. I sigh. "It still says 3:15." I shake my head.

The Agent grins. "It'll sync up on its own. Just give it a couple of minutes. It's a good watch."

I skim the band with my finger. It's a little big, and I'm able to flip the face over, finding a small engraving on the silver back that says, *Thank you for your service.*

I grimace. "Wait, I... I can't accept this. It looks... important." I start to take it off.

The Agent presses his lips together and holds up his hand. "You're *more* important, Ms. Nichols." He jerks his chin toward the watch. "That old ticker there has served me well, and now it'll help you on your journey."

I stare at him, then look back down at my wrist. "Why are you helping me?" I ask quietly.

He clears his throat. "Our Agency's number-one priority is to maintain the Balance in the Universe." He looks out in front of him. "Over the last 48 hours, that Balance has shifted severely... We're still trying to figure out why. Currently, all signs are pointing to a very strange triangle that's taken form in the heart of Southern California." He turns to me and grins. "A Guardian, a Demon, and the Catalyst... There's gotta be a good walks-into-a-bar joke there somewhere."

"You know about me being the Catalyst?" I whisper. "Can you tell me what I'm supposed to do?"

He takes a breath, but is interrupted by a pounding on the door. "Hey! You awake?" I hear Trevor yell.

The man turns and shrugs. "Looks like my time is up." I stare at him, crestfallen, as he points at the watch. "You hold onto that—and good luck, Ms. Nichols." He steps toward the hall. "I'm sure we'll meet again soon."

I shake my head as Trevor kicks the door. "HEY!" he screams.

"How are you going to get past him?" I whisper, motioning to the door.

The man smiles. "Oh, I'll just show myself out." He opens the closet, then steps in amongst the shoes and dresses and closes the door behind him.

I cringe and dash over. "Wait—that's the closet...!" I open it, and he's gone, the hangers undisturbed. I blink, utterly confused.

I hear Trevor kick the front door with his sneaker again. "Come on, get up!" he barks. "I don't want to hear that you don't like your pancakes because they're cold—that's all on you!"

I shut the closet and scurry over to the door. "Um, yeah, I'm here," I call. "You can come in now."

Trevor sighs as he puts the key in the lock. "It's like you think I don't have anything better to do than wait around all day for you," he gripes as he pulls in the cafeteria cart behind him. "I *know* the world revolves around you, but I have stuff I want to do today, too." He glares at me, taking in my now-weathered red dress. "What are you wearing?"

I clear my throat and sit on the edge of the bed. "Just haven't had a chance to change." I look at him tiredly. "What's on the menu this morning?"

He twists his mouth and pulls the lid off the plate. "Pancakes, bacon, apple slices, and coffee." He exhales and slouches. "I also have freshly squeezed orange juice if you want it—but if you do, than I have to make it right in front of you, and it's really annoying for me."

I sit back on the bed. "Coffee is fine."

Trevor nods and starts setting up the table. "So... thanks for not telling Jerkwad about the other night—us sneaking out," he mutters, pulling a table setting from the cart and offering it to me. "Looks like you *can* keep a secret."

I flush and look down at my lap. Apparently, it's Alden who

is the better secret keeper. I'm sure he's saving it all for just the right moment.

"You bet," I sigh, taking the napkin. "I didn't want you to get in trouble." He pushes the plate toward me, and I start shoveling food into my mouth, my appetite finally catching up with me.

"So what did you guys do yesterday?" Trevor asks, moseying around the room. "Not that I care."

I glare at my food, sticking a piece of apple in my mouth. "Oh, you know, out and about," I reply slowly. "Went to eat, drove around, took a walk." I sigh and blot my lips. "Boring, normal stuff." I push through a little wave of nausea, thinking of what happened at the Underpass... and then Daniel disappearing.

Trevor snorts. "He is so lame. If I could drive, I would have totally taken you somewhere awesome, like the House of Secrets or Lucky Strike. You like bowling?"

I smile and nod. "I do. Something to keep in mind, the next time I'm being held hostage."

Trevor looks at the window. "I guess." He scratches his neck. "So was he... nice... to you?" I glance up at him as he scuffs his sneakers on the carpet. "Or a major douche like he is to everyone else? Alden, I mean," he clarifies.

I shake my head. "I don't know what he was. For a while, I thought I had him figured out, and then, I don't know... it all got chucked overboard." Yesterday's events flit through my mind. Trevor watches me, his freckled face pinched. I cough and put my fork down.

"Thanks for breakfast, Trevor, but I think I just want to be alone for a while."

He blushes and lets out a big huff. "Fine, whatever." He throws the leftovers onto the cart. "I was going to ask you if you wanted to get out of here for a while, but if you want to be alone, then that's just hunky dory." He slams the table legs down.

I sigh and run a hand through my hair. "I don't know if I can handle another Green Room right now," I breathe. I don't know if I can handle just existing right now.

Trevor's lip curls. "Well, I wasn't going to take you there… or to any of the torture rooms," he grumbles. "The halls are totally empty, and it would have been a perfect time to go down there, but if you don't want to hang out, then I can just go do something else… I have tons of other stuff to get done." He shrugs. "You're the one who's locked up, not me."

I lean back on my elbows and consider. "All right, you've piqued my interest," I admit. "What is this mystery location you want to take me to?"

He grins impishly. "It's a surprise, but I'm sure you'll love it." He raises his eyebrows and steps over to the door. "I'll meet you out in the hall." He snickers. "Get changed. You're starting to smell."

I sigh and get off the bed. "Ouch, powerful burn." I look around for my boots. "If that's coming from a twelve-year-old boy, I must be pretty rank."

I emerge from the room dressed in a clean pair of jeans, a white, long-sleeve t-shirt, and my own boots. It feels comforting to be back in clothes that I would normally pick for myself. Trevor nods, and we walk to the elevators.

"We're going to 2. It's mostly a lot of meeting rooms and boring stuff, but there is one room I know you're going to freak out over." He bounces on the balls of his feet as we get into an elevator and head down.

I eye him suspiciously. "Good freak out or bad freak out?"

"You'll like it! I promise!" He grins, slapping my arm.

The doors open, and we walk out onto the floor. The hall is set up exactly the same as Level 1, with white doors on either side of the corridor. We quickly move down, and Trevor puts his hand on a door to the left. He stops and stares at me.

"Okay. So you need to walk into this room *slowly*. They're really hyper, and if they don't know you, they'll go crazy and bite your face off. But they like me, and since you're with me, they'll *probably* like you, too. But just BE COOL!" He points his finger at my nose, his tone grave. I look back at him and nod. He dips his chin and turns the knob.

They start barking the minute we walk in—four oversized pit bulls with jaws the size of bear traps that bound over to us and maul Trevor, putting their paws on his shoulders to lick his face and hair. Trevor laughs and pushes them off playfully.

"All right, guys… take it easy! Take it easy! I have a new friend for you to meet. You have a lot in common—you're kind of stupid and drool a lot." He grins and glances over at me.

I roll my eyes. The dogs stand at attention, tails wagging, tongues lolling out of their giant heads. "You can try to pet them now," Trevor says, gesturing to me.

I tentatively reach out and place my hand on top of the nearest dog, scratching behind his ears. He shoves his nose into me and sniffs. The other dogs cross over to give me a whiff, one by one allowing me to pet them. I crouch down and laugh as their smooth tongues lap at my face and neck. The black and white one even rolls over and lets me rub his belly.

"What are their names?" I ask.

"That's Auggie, Rudy, Dashie, and Mark," Trevor lists, pointing. "Christa, meet the Hellhounds."

I look up at him, noting that this is the first time he's ever called me by name. "Hellhounds?" I ask.

Trevor nods. "Yeah, Guardians of Hell. It's an old legend that dogs used to guard the gates of Hell, keeping the good people out and the bad ones in." He bends down and starts scratching Dashie's head. "These guys just work down on Level 1."

I abruptly stop petting, which is not tolerated by Auggie, who lays down on top of my knees and starts begging for a rubdown.

"I'm sorry, *work*?" I murmur.

He looks at me matter-of-factly. "Of course. When someone's worst nightmare is to be attacked and torn apart by animals, who do you think they get? Bunny rabbits?" He thoughtfully purses his lips. "That might be kind of cool, I guess." He shakes his head at me. "Get a clue! If you're here, you're either being tortured or the one doing the torturing. We've been over this… This isn't Disneyland." He sits and starts scratching Dashie's belly.

I wince and look down at Auggie, who is pressed against my side. I run my fingers over his short fur and feel little raised scars all along his shoulder blades down to his back shanks: lash marks. Auggie whines and cranes his jowls back against my chest.

"I can't imagine this guy tearing anyone apart," I coo, stroking his chin softly. Auggie yawns and stretches out his big paws, getting comfortable on my lap. Mark moves over and pushes my other arm onto his back. I giggle and start in on him, too.

"Believe it." Trevor shakes his head, still petting Dashie. "If any of the upper levels were in here right now, they'd be totally different dogs. It's scary." His eyes go wide. "They *really* lose it when Alden's in here."

I snort. "Yeah, he seems to have that effect on everyone." I rest my back against Rudy, who is snoring behind me. "This is nice," I sigh. "I wish we could stay here forever."

Trevor juts out his chin and grins. "I knew you'd like them," he gloats. "Chicks dig animals."

I let out a big laugh, waking up Rudy. Dashie looks up at Trevor lovingly, lounging across his lap.

"They're crazy about you," I say with a smile. Trevor turns red and goes back to petting the dog, so I add, "Look how she's giving you the eyes! Like you're the only person in the whole world." I nod at Dashie. "She loves you."

Trevor smirks and softly strokes her ear. "Someone has to," he whispers. I stop petting Rudy and look at him. "I sometimes sleep in here with them… so they don't get lonely." He massages her neck. "Big babies."

"That's cool," I murmur, tracing the inside of the dog's paw. "So have you brought your friends here? I bet they'd think these guys are the best."

Trevor shakes his head. "I told you, all the kids at my school are idiots." He pulls his knees up. "Why would I want to do anything with them?"

I nod. "I get it. I used to have a bunch of friends, back when I first started high school." I run my hand along Rudy's smooth side. "But after my dad died, most of them just faded away… like I was toxic or something." I shrug. Trevor stares at me. "Guess it was just too sad, or too much."

He clenches his jaw. "Your dad died?" he asks.

I look at him and nod.

He turns his face toward the door. "My mom died, when I was a baby." He glares back at me, challenging.

I'm about say *I know*, but catch myself in time. "It sucks," I reply.

Trevor bites his lip and nods. "Yeah, it does." He shakes his head and gets up, crossing to the crates in the back. "We, um, we have to feed them before we go, or they'll go crazy when we leave."

All four dogs get up and follow him, tails wagging furiously. Mark goes over to Trevor's side and nudges the bag of dog food. "Cool it, you big pig," he teases, scratching him behind the ear. He pours kibble into all of the bowls, and the dogs start munching hungrily. "I'll be back later, guys," Trevor calls before turning to me. He motions toward the door.

"Come on, before they notice you're gone," he whispers. I nod and get to my feet. We step out, and he closes the door behind us. We begin to walk back down the hall.

"Thanks for letting me meet them. They're really sweet." I smile sadly. Daniel would have loved them.

Trevor looks at the floor. "Yeah. They get a bad rap, but they're really just a couple of dorks…" He stops in front of the elevator and punches the up button. The doors open, and we get on.

"I still remember when those guys were puppies… They were too busy chasing each other's tails to think about gnawing someone's arm off." He taps the button for Level 4.

I stare at the panel for a minute, the Level 3 button glaring back at me. It suddenly seems larger than the others, glowing bright against the metal. I close my eyes and feel an overwhelming desire to push it, just push it. Before I realize what I'm doing, I reach out and smack it. The doors close, and Trevor glares at me.

"What do you think you're doing?!" he shrieks. "We're not supposed to go there!"

I take a breath and lean against the wall, feeling the upward pull as the elevator starts to move. "You said that's where they take the guys who really screw up, right?" I rasp, thinking of Daniel on the roof. Someone else was there with him last night, and I have a pretty good idea who.

Trevor shakes his head. "What's that got to do with anything? Only 4th Level Demons and above are allowed—there's a reason for that! It's a portal that leads directly to Hell, you idiot! All of the satellite offices are linked to it!"

My eyes widen. "We're going to… Hell?" I breathe.

Trevor grits his teeth. "I'm an Amalgam, and you're just a Mortal… We're gonna fry! I can't believe you just did that!" He winces at the doors and slams himself against the opposite wall.

I straighten up and position myself in the middle of the floor, balling my fists and bracing for some invisible impact. "It's okay… I've got a hunch, Trevor." I bite my lip and look down at the Agent's watch, the time now reading correctly at 10:23 a.m. "Search within and come what may."

"Just cuz you've got a hunch means I have to roast like a marshmallow?" he squeaks, clawing up the wall. "I am never trusting human girls ever again!" He squeezes his eyes shut and curls up into a ball.

I turn and hold my breath, the doors opening up to Level 3 with a polite ding.

I gasp.

CHAPTER 13

I HOLD MY BREATH and stand in the center of the elevator, waiting for something to happen... an alarm, an explosion, a rain of fire. But nothing comes—just... silence. I take a step forward and look out into the corridor, which is painted the same off-white as the rest of the warehouse. There's a small placard on the wall just outside the doors. I clear my throat.

"Trevor," I whisper. "Trevor, get up."

His little freckled face pops up from his arms, and he squints ferret-like into the hallway. "We're not dead," he breathes, shakily getting to his feet and stepping over to me. "Are we?"

I smile down at him. "No, we're fine. Totally fine," I repeat, nodding at the doors. "Come on, let's check this place out."

Trevor stares dumbstruck at me for a second before gnashing his teeth and tearing at his red hair. "Are you crazy? Don't you get how lucky we are to be alive right now? No!" He reaches over and frantically taps the 'Door Closed' button. "I am taking you back to your room, and we're going to pretend this never happened!"

I lurch forward and hold the doors open, my feet straddling the threshold. Trevor's eyes widen. "STOP! Get back in here!"

I shake my head. "I can't do that, Trevor. Daniel needs me, and I'm not going to let him down." I look out into the hall. "I *know* he's here; I can feel it." My urge to go sprinting down the corridor grows stronger by the second. It's the Link, I know it.

Trevor glares at me. "What are you talking about? And who's Daniel?" he spits.

I turn to him and exhale. "My Guardian. He's been trying to help me this whole time, but now he's in trouble, and I'm the only one who knows…" I sigh. "It's my turn to keep him safe."

Trevor tuts and crosses his arms. "Are you kidding me? You want me to risk my neck for a *Guardian*?" He snorts. "No way. Those guys are total choads."

I shoot him a frustrated glare. "Whatever, Trevor—stay, go, I don't care."

He gasps as I step off of the elevator. I grin and hold out my arms. "Look, still in one piece!" I exclaim. "I'm saving my Angel." I stalk over to the placard.

Trevor moans and scuttles behind me. "You have got to be the dumbest, most pigheaded human that's ever existed—and that's saying a lot!" he grumbles. He huffs and stops by my side.

I smile at him. "You don't *have* to come with me, Trevor; I get it if you're too scared…" I bite my lip, not wanting to let on that I'm pretty terrified myself right now.

"I'm not scared!" he screeches. "Whatever happens next is going to be ten times better than what would go down if I came back without you and that asshat found out!" He shakes his head. "You are going right back to your room after this is all done."

I smile and turn back to the sign. We both go quiet as we read it.

WARNING

This facility is currently operating at a LEVEL 6 SECURITY rating. All branded personnel will be subject to random screenings per REGULATION 3801Q.

Agents and all other visitors must check in at the main desk located at the east entrance before gaining access. Be advised that no mortal should enter beyond this point. Permanent death will result after 14 MINUTES* exposure.

*Further information regarding exposure data sites and future testing dates can be obtained from the Level 2 mainframe.

The green Serpentine logo gleams underneath the text. I turn and smile weakly at Trevor. "Well, things are looking up. The sign says we've got, what, fourteen minutes inside before we turn to dust? That's something!"

Trevor rolls his eyes. "We are so eff'd."

I sigh and look around, my eyes searching the empty wall. "Now, how do we get in?" I mumble. The hall ends abruptly about thirty feet away, and there are no doors or windows.

On the floor next to Trevor's shoe sits a small wooden box. I stare at it and kneel down. "What's this?" I ask, opening the lid. Inside is a set of silver scissors, a book of matches, and a rather menacing-looking pair of rusty pliers. I look over at Trevor, who crouches next to me.

"Why are these here? Are we supposed to do something with them? *Build* a door?" I grab the pliers and whack them against the wall. Nothing happens.

Trevor exhales. "It's old blood magic. My dad's told me stories about this stuff." He jerks his chin at the box. "I'm guessing that, to get the door to appear, you have to... give... a part of yourself using one of these tools." He shrugs. "Pick your poison."

I glance at the pliers in my hand and quickly drop them back into the box. "You mean, we have to—to *hurt* ourselves to get in?" I whisper, staring around the hall.

Trevor rolls his eyes and picks up the scissors. "What happened to 'It's my turn to keep him safe' and 'I'm not going to let him down'?" he mocks. "You're such a wuss."

Swiftly, he reaches up and clips a lock of my hair off with the scissors, letting it waft featherlike down to the floor. As the hair touches the tile, a heavy metal door with a glass window at the top materializes on the wall.

I stagger to my feet, beaming at Trevor. "You're a genius!" I cry, patting him on the back.

Trevor gets up, his ears turning red. "Yeah, okay," he mumbles, gesturing toward the door. "Don't get too excited. You've still gotta go in there."

I nod and take a deep breath, pushing the door handle down. The lock releases with a gentle *click* and pops open.

I pause to look at Trevor. "Here goes nothing," I whisper.

He scrunches his mouth and points to my watch. "Fourteen minutes... starting now."

I nod in agreement, and we both step inside.

I blink. It's a hallway, white and bright—just like every other floor in the building. I move in and let the door shut behind us, the handle click echoing down the quiet corridor. I exhale and stare in front of me.

"Shit." What feels like miles and miles of white doors line both sides of the wall, fading off endlessly like an Escher illusion. I bite my lip and glance down at the watch: it's 10:30 a.m. on the nose.

"We do not have time for this..." I mutter, glaring around at all the doors.

Trevor shoots me a look. "I thought you said you knew where he was!" His squeaky voice is amplified by the silence.

I shake my head. "I said I knew he was here, on 3... but I didn't expect this!" I snap, stepping over to a door on my left. I open it and look inside: it's an empty room with a large dentist's chair set in the middle.

I slam the door shut and walk across the hall to another, wrenching it open. Nothing, except for about three inches of water flooding the entire floor. I shake my head and open another door and another after that: empty, empty.

"Fuck!" I curse, my voice reverberating down the hall.

Trevor shifts nervously. "We should just go. We're never going to find him in here. It's like looking for a needle in a haystack!" he yells.

I tug at my hair. "No—I'm not stopping! Not until I find him!" I wet my lips and try another door. This time, there's a white bunny perched in the center, twitching its pink little nose.

"Enough with the funhouse tricks!" I slam the door shut. "Where is he?" I pace farther down the hall.

"Who are you talking to?" Trevor opens a door on his right. He looks inside, then hastily closes it. I stop and check my watch: it's 10:34.

"Okay... I'm going about this all wrong." I sigh and rub my face. "Search within and come what may, search within and come what may..." I close my eyes and slow my breathing, counting backwards from ten.

"You're meditating now?" I hear Trevor bark, slamming another door. I let my mind drift over the last few days... Pete, in the car with Alden, seat 9A, the cliff, panna cotta... breakfast on the beach, Van Morrison, red hat, cinnamon... holding my hand...

"Daniel," I murmur, my eyes flashing open. I turn to my left and glide down the hall, Trevor stumbling to keep up.

"What? Did you find something?" he squeaks.

I don't answer. Instead, I move about two hundred feet and stop in front of a door on the right side of the corridor, resting my hand on the knob. Trevor looks up at me expectantly.

"He's here," I breathe, pushing it open.

Trevor peeks past me and lets out a gasp. "What the—" he

exclaims, staggering in the archway. I feel my knees buckle also, and I grab the doorframe for support.

The windowless walls are boarded up with driftwood planks, the floor a hard concrete. Standing near the west wall is Daniel, shirtless, beaten, and bloody. "Daniel…" I exhale and run to him, putting my hands on either side of his face. He moans at my touch. "Daniel, can you hear me?" His eyes are swollen shut, and his head lolls between his shoulders.

"Christa…" he rasps, his mouth barely moving. "No… It can't be…"

I close my eyes as I press my forehead to his. "I'm here! I'm really here…" I croon, smoothing his hair back. "It's okay. I'm getting you out—"

He shakes his head. "No, no… You can't be here." He licks blood off of his cracked lips. "It's too dangerous…"

"That guy is messed up." Trevor whistles from the doorway. "I've never seen anything like it!"

I shake my head and stare at Daniel. "I don't care if it's too dangerous—there's no way I'm leaving you again!" I run my hands down his arms where they hang heavily at his sides. "I'm sorry I didn't come sooner. I didn't know…"

I stop and grab my stomach, a sharp pain coursing through my abdomen. "Crap," I exhale, memories of last night's torture fest flashing in my mind. I check my watch: 10:38. Daniel raises his head listlessly.

"Christa, you have to get out. Go." He cringes away from me. "You'll die in here."

I gulp and straighten my back. "I'm fine. Don't worry about me." I grimace and take his wrists. "Come on… This has to end the Deal with Alden. Not hurting anyone else was part of it." I smile and pull him gently. "Let's go home."

He throws his head back and lets out a bloodcurdling scream.

I drop his hands and stare at him in horror. "What? What is it?" I exclaim.

Daniel pants, frozen in place. I glare back at Trevor. "What's happening?"

Trevor looks on, wide-eyed. "He's stuck! He can't go!" He gestures at the wall. "Can't you see that?"

I shake my head. Daniel winces and forces his eyes open. "I'm sorry, Christa..." he slurs. "Get out of here..."

I look around wildly. "How? How is he stuck? I don't see any chains or ropes... Daniel..." I touch his face again. "What can I do?" I feel down the rest of his arms to the legs of his jeans.

He winces and tilts his chin. "Leave." His voice cracks. "Please."

I glance up and see four wooden posts jutting out of the wall and forming a large trapezoid behind him. Thick, dark ichor drips from each of them. "Trevor, what is this?" I narrow my eyes and walk over, touching the stains. Dried blood. I follow one of the drips down to the floor and see Daniel's feet, still in his Converse sneakers and suspended off of the wall at a very unnatural angle.

"They're his wings," Trevor replies, awestruck. "Can't you see them?"

I shake my head, all of the air going out of my lungs. "He... he *pinned* you," I gasp, staring at the empty space between Daniel and the wall. He's hanging by invisible appendages that I cannot see. "That son of a bitch. I'll kill him."

Daniel looks up at me. "No, Christa," he sighs. "It... it wasn't Alden."

My jaw drops as the door flies open. "Christa! Get away from him!" Alden barks from the archway, shoving Trevor aside.

Trevor stares at us before bolting back down the hall. I spin around to face Alden, my lips pulled back from my gums. "You bastard! What have you done!?" I march over and reach up to slap him across the face.

He grabs my wrist and holds me in place. "Get out of here, now!" he shouts, thrusting me back through the door.

I struggle, my teeth bared. "I knew I couldn't trust you this whole time!" I screech, beating my fists into his chest. "You're a liar and a cheat and a monster! You won't get away with this!"

He wraps his arms tightly around me as I try to wriggle back to Daniel. "You have to leave right now, Christa! Stop!" he yells into my ear. "Before it's too late!"

He lets me go as I push away. "Not without him!" I pant, grasping my side as the pain returns. "You can't keep him here—that was part of the Deal!" I wince and stumble backwards. "After everything that's happened, you can't take that away from me!" I glance back at Daniel. "Let him go—now!"

Alden sighs, exasperated. "That's what I'm trying to tell you, for God's sake! I'm here to help! I've been looking all over for you for the last hour!" He tears at his hair.

"Christa, listen…" Daniel groans, lifting his head.

I let out a whine and run to him. "I don't care if I die! I'm staying with you—no matter what!" I cry.

Alden sighs and steps over to the wall with the stakes. "What are you doing?" I shout, wrapping my arms around Daniel tightly.

Alden clenches his jaw. "We have to pull these out—like taking the pin out of an insect." He reaches down and grits his teeth, wrenching the post from the wood. "Ruddy piece of shi—" he grunts as he tosses it with a clatter onto the floor, moving around to the other stakes.

Daniel looks at me wearily. "I told you I'd stay close," he murmurs.

I touch his chin. "Next time, let's skip the trip to Hell and just go to the movies instead, okay?" I joke, stroking his ear.

He nods into my hand. "It's a date."

Alden rolls his eyes. "Oh Christ, spare me…"

He removes the final stake, and Daniel slumps into my arms,

wincing up at me. "Now who's the superhero?" he chuckles. When I blush, he adds, "Keep this up, and you're gonna start making the rest of us look bad." His face tightens as he gets to his feet, laying an arm around my shoulder.

"Can you walk?" I ask, steadying him against myself.

He nods. "Yeah... I should be okay any minute now." He clears his throat and looks at Alden. "Thanks," he says tersely, "for getting me down."

Alden frowns. I look between them both, my vision blurring around the edges. "So... it wasn't you, really." I clear my throat. "You didn't put Daniel in here."

Alden shakes his head. "Wish I could take credit, but, sadly, no." He smirks. "But someone who obviously knew what they were doing did; this room hasn't been used properly in almost a decade. It's a special treat." He arches a brow. "If it had been up to me, I would have let you stay there a while longer, tell a few jokes, trade a couple of barbs, maybe take an embarrassing photo for SnapChat." He steps toward the door, adding, "Raincheck."

He turns back to us, and his eyes widen as I fall to the floor. "CHRISTA!" Daniel yells next to me. My hand trembles, and I grab his arm, wheezing as my throat starts to close up. I glare at my watch: 10:42.

"I... I can't..." I gasp, clawing at his skin.

Daniel shakes his head. "No, no, NO!" he screams, embracing me.

Alden smacks him on the shoulder. "We have to get her out of here! Come on—this way!" He pulls Daniel up, and they both start running, Daniel trying to hold me against his chest.

As soon as he staggers out of the room, however, he falls to the floor. "I'm sorry... Hold on..." Daniel rasps, clutching me tightly. "I'm still regenerating..."

Alden turns and runs back to us, pulling me out of Daniel's arms. "No—what are you doing?!" Daniel cries, grabbing my wrist.

Alden flashes his teeth. "Don't be a fool! I'm faster than you right now! If she dies here, she stays here. Is that what you want?"

Daniel stops and lets me go. "Fine, just get her out of here." He cringes as I gasp for air, my eyelids fluttering. Daniel stares into my eyes, adding, "I'll be right behind you."

Alden stands and cradles me against him, and then we're passing door after door as we dash down the hall. When we get to the end, Alden holds me with one hand while he wrenches the heavy metal door open with the other, both of us crashing through to the safety of the elevator bay. The door slams closed behind us, and we fall to the floor. I choke and sputter as my airways reopen.

"Daniel—where's Daniel?" I rasp once I can speak.

Alden pants and motions back toward the door. "He's coming. He's a little off, since he's still regenerating—but he can take his time. You're the one we needed to get through."

I sit up and breathe in and out, checking my watch: 10:44.

"Puny mortal," I say with a relieved smile, looking up at him. "Thank you... for saving me." I slowly climb to my feet. "And Daniel. I'm sorry about what I said back there." I stare at the wall. "Thinking it was you that... did *that*."

Alden shrugs and looks at me. "It wouldn't be too far a stretch," he sniffs, "if the circumstances were different."

I shiver. "Guess so... You make it so easy to forget who— *what*—I'm talking to."

I watch Alden tense. "You're still upset about last night. I get it..." he murmurs, taking a step toward me.

I shake my head. "No, you don't." I sigh and gaze around the space. "Where's Trevor?" I stop and check the empty elevator car. "Did he take off?"

Alden furrows his brow. "I saw him run once I got to the room. I figured he was out already." His eyes flash down to the wooden box on the floor. "Didn't he make a sacrifice when you first arrived?"

I shake my head. "No, we used *my* hair." I glare at him. "Why? Does that matter?"

Alden stalks back to the door. "Uh, yeah." He stares through the little glass window. "Unless you offer a sacrifice, you can't leave."

I gasp. "Then he's still in there—Alden!" I shriek.

He crouches down and fumbles with the box, quickly grabbing the pliers and jumping back up. "Dammit, I see him over by the Flood Room." He shoves the pliers back to his molars. "I have to go back."

I cover my face with my palms, waiting for the grating sound of metal on bone.

"Wait..." Alden murmurs. I take my hands away and see him at the window again. "Danny..." His eyes widen. "Shit. Okay— he's Altering..." Alden twists toward me and waves me away from the wall. "Get back—get back, Christa!"

I stagger to the elevator. Alden rushes over and covers me with his body, pushing me to the floor. "Stay down! He's gonna blow the door!" he shouts in my ear. "Whatever you do—don't look!"

I hear a thin wail like the sound of a teakettle going off somewhere, right before the metal door explodes off its hinges, taking half of the wall with it. Alden crushes me with his shoulder, bits of rebar and brick raining down on his back.

We huddle together, frozen, until the hall goes silent again. As the dust settles, I blearily look up.

It's not really a person standing above the rubble—more like a burning white ball of light. I shake my head and see Trevor, unconscious and cradled warmly against it. I squint my eyes and try to focus on its face.

"It's... you," I breathe. "You're..."

"Christa—NO!" Alden yells. He jerks my head down, but the damage is already done. I choke on froth and foam that starts coming from my mouth as Daniel's visage shines back at me, bold and familiar.

I manage to give him a small smile before my entire body seizes and the world goes dark.

*

When I come to, my head is resting against something firm and strong, the warm scent of cinnamon filling my nose. I try to move my arms and legs, but everything below my neck feels numb. My eyes drift open, and I stare up at Daniel, who has stopped glowing. He is looking at someone to his left, his face imploring.

"Please, Alden, she needs it! Please, I'll do anything..." Daniel begs, placing his hands gently on either side of my head. I smile at his touch.

Alden grunts. I tilt my head and see him in the corner by the elevator, he shirt sleeve rolled up, hovering over Trevor. I watch Trevor wake up, a ring of red around his mouth. He shakes his head and crawls into the elevator. Alden leans up and pushes a button for him, sending him on his way. He turns back to us.

"It might be too late for her," Alden sighs, stepping over. "After you went all Akira on us. Is she even still alive?"

Daniel stares down at me, worried, but soon breaks into a relieved grin. "She's waking up!" He presses his fingers lightly to my temples. "Christa, Christa! Can you hear me?"

I open my lips to speak, but no words come out.

"You're lucky you didn't burn her eyes out of her skull with what you just pulled," Alden murmurs, sitting down next to us.

Daniel glares at him. "I had to save that kid! Couldn't just leave him in there!" He gazes back at me. "I'm so sorry, Christa... You have to know I would never do anything to hurt you."

I try to nod, but the best I can do is bat my eyelashes. Daniel's brow crinkles. "Why can't she talk?"

Alden shrugs. "You would know better than me—it's *your*

freaky superpower," he snaps. "Little reminder of what happens when mortals play with Gods. Catalyst or not, she's still human." He frowns at me. "I didn't want to, earlier—but we might not have a choice."

"Please," Daniel rasps, still holding me against his bare chest. "I'll do anything. Just... help her."

Alden glares at him. "You sure are fighting for this one a lot harder than... others," he whispers. "It's unfortunate that this new courageousness is a recent development." He looks away.

Daniel sighs heavily. "Alden... we both know I can't take back what happened—but I've been trying to be better ever since." He swallows. "To make my second chance count... make it count for her."

"You don't speak of *her*!" Alden hisses, his eyes growing violent. "Like you really *knew* her—what she would have wanted..." He composes himself as he stares down at me. "And don't you dare mention second chances to me. You don't get to insult me in my own house."

Daniel closes his eyes. "I'm sorry," he says, running his fingers over my jaw. "Please—just give her back to me." I blink, a tear trickling from the corner of my eye onto his hand. He reaches up and gently wipes my cheek.

"Fine." Alden sucks his teeth and takes a deep breath before leaning over me. Using the scissors from the box, he carefully traces a line down the soft part of his wrist, bright red droplets of blood rising to the surface of his skin.

"Drink up, Christa, and get ready for the ride of your life," he mumbles. I glance back at Daniel, questioning, my lips parted. He looks down at me, pained, but nods and gently lifts my head to Alden's wrist.

"I don't know if you can understand me, but just pretend you're one of those vampires on that stupid TV show," Daniel jokes, his voice quiet. "You only need a little. Try not to think too much about what you're doing." I blink, and Daniel pushes my mouth to Alden's skin.

At first taste, the blood is foul, like rotten fruit. After a few draws, though, it changes and becomes smooth and sweet. I suck harder, the blood filling my mouth; I'm now able to lift my head on my own, and I stretch hungrily, wanting more. I sit up and grab Alden's arm, lapping and gnawing like a dog at a bone. I look up and see Alden watching me, his eyes half lidded, his mouth twisted.

"Jealous, Danny?" He grins. "Finally realizing that there is so much I can give her that you can't?"

I feel Daniel tense behind me. My head rolls in delirium, pure energy coursing through my body. I pull back, releasing Alden, and lean against Daniel again. My eyes are closed, my whole body throbbing and feeling more alive than I've ever felt before.

I open my eyes and look at Daniel. He looks exactly like he did before, but now I can see that his pupils are lined in gold, constantly shimmering. They match the perfect pair of golden wings that are floating behind him, so fragile and complex-looking that, when I exhale, I worry that I'll blow them away.

"Daniel," I breathe. "I can *see* you."

He smiles at me. "Hope I'm not too disappointing."

I stare at him in wonder. "No," I sigh. "You're beautiful."

Alden clucks his tongue, disgusted. I turn to him and gasp. Protruding from the top of his head are two great ram's horns, gnarled and horrible like twisted tree roots. He stares back at me, his eyes hollow. I swallow and clear my throat.

He chuckles. "From your expression, I'm guessing you can now see me, too. How do *I* look?"

I shake my head and sit forward, smoothing my jeans. I look at my hands and stop. I'm glowing, truly *glowing*—bright blue. I hold my hands up in front of my face and stare at myself in awe.

"Oh my God—Daniel, I see it! I see… me! I'm—I'm *blue*." I start to laugh.

Daniel grins and rubs my shoulders. "Yes, you are very blue. Have been since the first day I met you." He gets up and pulls me to my feet. I wobble a little as he wraps his arms around my waist. Our eyes meet, and I can count the tiny gold flecks around his irises.

"Are you okay? How do you feel?" he asks.

I stare up at him. "Do you think we'd make green?" I mumble unintelligibly. Daniel laughs and rests his forehead against mine. I smile and caress his chin, hearing Alden snicker behind us.

"Well, I think it goes without saying that Christa and her mother are now free to go," he murmurs. Daniel and I turn to gawk at him. "The terms of our Deal were clearly breached—by no fault of my own, I might add," he explains with a sigh. "But you did almost die on my watch, twice—and while this is all very embarrassing, I never go back on my word." He stares at me coolly. "Although I am sorry that I didn't get to find out the final verdict on whether you choose light or dark."

I snort. "Isn't it obvious?" I shake my head, leaning into Daniel.

Alden's mouth twitches. "Maybe on the surface, but we both know where you *really* live, when the lights go off," he purrs, crossing to my other side and tucking my hair behind my ear.

Daniel hits his hand away.

"All right—relax, Danny!" Alden shouts, moving over to him, his sharp horns just grazing Daniel's ear. "I know that right now it feels like you've won, walking away alive with your girl by your side," he whispers, just loud enough for me to hear, "but long after you forget why you're here, Danny, why you're *really* here… I'll remember. I'll remember for the both of us, and you *will* burn. I can promise you that." He laughs and slaps Daniel on the arm, stepping back. "Enjoy the fall. Should be fun to watch."

Daniel glares at him and takes my hand firmly. "Come on, Christa." He pulls me toward the elevators.

I stop and turn to Alden. "What about my mom? You'll let her go, too?"

Alden shrugs. "Of course. Dr. Bahati will move her to Westside as soon as I make the call; you can meet her there." He takes out his phone.

I glance back at Daniel. He nods. "She should be okay, Christa," he murmurs.

I turn again toward Alden, who is running his thumb over the phone's screen. "So... that's it," I call, finding it difficult to look at him. "It's over."

"Yeah, yeah... Get outta here before I change my mind." He turns back to his phone, holding it up to his ear. "Yes, doctor, we're ready to make that move..."

I gasp and spin, throwing my arms around Daniel.

"Lock up your boys... She's free and on the prowl!" He grins, clutching my waist, then motions to the busted up wall behind us. "And all we had to do was blow up Hell to do it."

I shake my head and press my face into his neck, inhaling his scent. "I'd do it again," I sigh.

I feel his arms tighten around me. "I know," he murmurs, leaning back. He takes my hand. "Come on. Let's go home."

CHAPTER 14

"*O*OMF! UM, HI…" Jodie grunts as I pull her into the world's tightest bear hug. "What are you doing here? I thought you were still suspended until tomorrow." She pulls back and smiles at me. "Don't get me wrong—I'm really happy to see you!"

I shake my head, glancing down at her textbook on the desk and smooshing into the seat next to her. "Uh… I guess I am, technically—but I thought Trundi's afterschool study group was safe." I look around the classroom, watching the other kids working at lab stations.

Jodie nods. "I doubt anyone here would rat you out." She leans in conspiratorially. "Although *everyone* has been talking about what happened."

I stare back at her. "What? What happened?" I ask, my mind racing. Did they find out I'm the Catalyst? Did Demons come looking for me while I was gone?

Jodie scoffs and giggles. "Um, the whole running into the boys' locker room thing? Did you forget about that?"

I breathe a heavy sigh of relief. "Oh, right." I quirk my eyebrows. "Well, you know me—completely unpredictable."

She laughs and picks up her pencil. "I'll say. I still can't believe you did that." A little blush creeps up over her collar. "I mean, they were like… naked, and stuff."

I chuck her on the shoulder. "And all their boy parts were putting on clothes and stepping into shoes, leaking testosterone out of their ears." I smile. "I missed you."

Jodie tuts. "Yeah—more like you missed making fun of me and my humiliating virgin ways." She pauses and glances over at me. "How's your mom? You didn't say much in your text last night, just that she was in the hospital, but everything was okay…?" She shakes her head in confusion.

I take a breath. "Yeah… She went on a really rough bender over the weekend and had to get checked in." I tuck my hair behind my ear, looking down at my lap. "I don't know what happens next, but I'm going back to see her after this. Her doctor thinks she'll be ready to go home tomorrow." Wherever that is.

Jodie nods and pats my leg. "She'll be all right. She just needs time." She runs her pencil eraser along my sleeve. "Is… this what you're wearing to go visit?"

I look down at the oversized plaid shirt I fished out of a bin at Goodwill with Daniel last night after we were done at the hospital—seeing that all of my clothes are still back at our old apartment, which is super unsafe now that every Demon in Southern California knows where I live. I matched the flannel with a pair of cutoff denim shorts and black fishnets.

"What? I'm keeping it casual." I shrug. "Figured, since it was after school, I didn't need my uniform."

"I guess." Jodie chuckles and furrows her brow. "Are you sure you're okay? You seem a little… distracted." She watches me, concerned. "More so than usual."

I slouch and run a hand through my hair. "Oh, you know—I've got lot on my mind…" I play with the buttons on her calculator. "With… school…"

Jodie laughs. "And maybe your new friend?" She arches her

brow toward the front lab table, a smile teasing her lips. I sit back and follow her gaze.

Daniel stands next to Mr. Trundi, lab goggles in place, adjusting a microscope. "Hey, Christa—check this out!" he calls to me, grinning. "I'm gene-mapping! Totally Asimov or what?" He pats Mr. Trundi on the back excitedly. Mr. Trundi lets out a long sigh and points back to the slide. I cross my arms and chuckle, watching him.

Jodie clucks her tongue. "I know *that* look." She winks, rubbing her neck. "Something to make your recidivism a little sweeter?"

I blush. "It's nothing like that," I mumble. "We're just friends, that's all." I look up at him longingly.

Jodie lets out a snort. "Yeah, really good friends!" She smacks my knee. "And if you're not yet, you will be soon." She glances back at Daniel. "That poor chump doesn't stand a chance."

I scooch down in my seat. "Come on, it's not like that." I wrinkle my nose and grin.

Jodie looks between the two of us. "Okay, whatever you say." She taps her notes with her pencil. "But he *is* pretty cute... in a kind of surfer, grunge, Kerouac sort of way." She laughs. "Little weird, but... so are you."

I bite my cheek and peek up at him, now listening intently as Trundi instructs on how to properly clean petri dishes. "Couple of weirdos," I murmur, glancing at the golden halo around him and back to my blue hands, glowing in my lap. "Sounds about right."

*

"You're just in time! She woke up about ten minutes ago..."

I startle as Mary Carmen greets us downstairs at the ER entrance, two cups of coffee in hand. I'm still getting used to her face, last night being the first time that I ever saw the long red slash that runs through her right eyebrow and all the way down to the corner of her lip. It's the Mark of the Seraphim: someone who has been to Heaven and seen the face of God. Daniel tried to prepare me for it on the way over from the Warehouse, but calling it a "shiny happy people scar" doesn't do it justice.

"Here, these are for you." She smiles, handing one cup of coffee to me and the other to Daniel. "She's going to be so happy to see you, Christa." She motions us toward the elevators. "You were the first thing she asked about when she came to."

I cringe. "I was afraid of that," I mutter, glancing at Daniel. He sighs as we follow Mary Carmen up.

We go to the 12th floor and step into my mother's hospital room. It's a bit cramped, but it has a nice view of the pier. Mom lies in the bed, perched on a mound of pillows. She turns and sees me in the doorway. "Christa," she breathes. "You're here."

I look between her and Daniel. He places his hand on the small of my back. "I'm gonna talk to Mary Carmen in the hall, give you two some time," he murmurs. "I'll be right outside the door."

I nod. "Okay," I whisper, crossing over to the bed.

Mom looks up at me hazily. She's been switched from her white pajamas into a standard hospital gown. She must have gotten a bath last night.

I exhale. "I'm glad you're up," I say with a smile. "You've been pretty out of it for the last couple of days." I try to replay all of the possible cover stories that Daniel, Mary Carmen, and I hashed out, quickly throwing out gas leak and alien abduction in favor of a slightly altered version of the truth. "Do you remember… anything?" I ask.

She sighs and rests her head back on the pillows, her red hair feathering perfectly. "I remember that… boy… coming to the apartment," she rasps, looking up at me. "The one with the dark hair and… those eyes…" She clears her throat, folding her hands over the sheet. "And I let him come inside, and we talked for a while. But everything after that is a blur… I remember, at one point I was with a lot of other people, but I couldn't describe any of them to you…" She coughs. "And then I remember being in a bright yellow room, and it smelled nice, like…" She narrows her eyes. "Like jasmine, maybe? Or maybe that was another place?… God!" She shakes her head at me. "Is that even important?"

I take a seat on the stool next to the bed and nod. "Of course it is. Anything to help you piece together what happened," I sigh.

She nods and grips the bedrail. "Do *you* know what happened to me?" she whispers. I shift uneasily, and she adds, "I keep having these memories—or maybe they're dreams—of you, of your voice being there…" She chews the inside of her cheek. "That's crazy, though, isn't it? He didn't get you too, did he?" She stares at me.

I swallow and shake my head. "No, Mom. He didn't get me."

She exhales, glancing up at the ceiling. "That's something. Even though I can't remember *my* last three days, at least I know you were safe." She nods and reaches out for my hand.

Tentatively, I reach out and take it. Both of us turn at a knock at the door.

"It's just me," Mary Carmen says with a wave. Daniel pokes his head around the corner. "And Daniel, too. Can we come in?"

Mom smiles and nods. "Sure. The more the merrier." She sits up and squints at Daniel. "I know you… from before." She looks at me and grins. "This is your friend from school, right? History class?"

I nod and grin back at him. "Yep, History." I arch a brow. "Hopefully not doomed to repeat itself."

He winces and gives me a wink. Mom looks between us, confused. "Man, I feel like there's so much I've missed," she murmurs, giving my hand a squeeze. "I want things to be different now, Christa—whatever it takes." She stares at me. "I mean it. I don't care what I have to do. I want to be there for you."

My throat tightens. "I know, Mom." I smile and take my hand away.

Mary Carmen clears her throat. "I actually wanted to talk to you about that, Julie." She steps next to the bed. "There are a couple of great rehabilitation programs down the coast, and I know several of the directors..." She's interrupted by yet another knock at the door.

"So sorry to bother you, but we heard Mrs. Nichols was awake!" a cheerful voice calls from the threshold. We all turn to see a small bald man in jeans, a white sweatshirt, and flip flops. Mary Carmen looks at him, her mouth agape.

"Harold?" She shakes her head. "What are you doing here? I was just about to talk about her options, Transitions being one of them..." Her eyes crinkle. "How did you know?"

Now, it's Harold's turn to look confused. "I thought Mrs. Nichols had already *chosen* Transitions." He furrows his brow. "Being that her payment for full treatment cleared last night. I was coming to sort out her transportation... Huh." He scratches his neck. "This is awkward."

Mom looks at Mary Carmen. "What is he talking about?" she asks.

Mary Carmen shakes her head and looks at me. "I don't know," she breathes, searching my face. "Do you know anything about this?"

I sit frozen on the stool. "No," I lie after a minute. "I don't."

Everyone looks back at Mom—everyone except Daniel, who leans against the window with his arms crossed, staring at me.

"So... let me get this straight." Mom leans forward and puts her hands on her knees. "I've got a free trip to rehab, if I want it?" She stares at Harold. "Is that what you're telling me?"

Harold nods quickly. "Well, yes!" he blusters. "It's certainly one of the more mysterious ways I've seen someone get treatment... but if you want it, we're ready to have you." He tilts his head. "Someone out there must really care about you and your family."

I watch Mom smile and turn back to Mary Carmen. "And it's a good program? Will... will it work?" she asks.

Mary Carmen nods. "If you do your part, it's one of the best." She turns to Daniel, awestruck. "I still can't believe..."

He shrugs, his eyes glued on me. I exhale as Mom takes my hand again. "What do you think, Christa? Should I do it?" She looks at me expectantly.

I break away from Daniel's gaze and smile at her. "You should. Your health is the most important thing right now," I murmur, standing up. "Don't worry about anything else... I'll be fine."

She watches me for a moment before nodding. "Okay. Yes, I'll go." She smiles, turning to face Harold. "What happens next?"

*

"So, how long did he say she's going to be gone?" I ask, taking a bite out of my sandwich.

"Mmm... I think five months? It sounds like a really great rehab program down near Del Mar." Daniel picks at his plate. "Mary Carmen couldn't say enough good stuff about it while you were in the bathroom... lots of celebrities, huge wait list." He stares at me as he pops a pepper in his mouth. "It's some kind of miracle that she got in so fast."

I shrug, all of a sudden completely fascinated with the folds in my paper napkin. "Stranger things have happened," I murmur.

Daniel exhales and tilts his head. "Hey, I'm happy for her... and for you!" He nods, placing his hand on top of mine. "I'm just glad your back."

I smile shyly. "Me, too." I glance down the pier at the carnival rides and crowds of tourists wandering around in the early evening twilight, cotton candy in hand, some of them even jumping onto the Ferris wheel right across from our picnic table. Daniel smiles and crams the rest of his burrito into his mouth. It's another Benny Woo creation, his yellow truck only a few yards away. I look back at Daniel and sigh, his warm, golden brown eyes burning like dying embers.

I smile when he catches me staring. "What? Did I get myself again?" He glances down at his shirt, mouth full of food.

"No, you're fine," I chuckle. "I'm still getting used to you... like this." I motion to his wings, floating in the ether behind him.

He nods, sitting up straight. "It *is* an adjustment; I've been like this for a while now, and I still think it's weird every time I see myself." He grins, picking at his teeth. "I see you checking yourself out... mmm, pretty much any chance you get!" He laughs. "At the hospital, at Goodwill... What do you think?"

I sigh and look down at my plate. "Guess I'll never need to be afraid of the dark again," I mutter, taking one last bite of my food. "Which is probably a good thing, cuz I think I'm going to have nightmares for weeks to come." I shudder, thinking about everything that's happened.

Daniel leans in and takes my hand. "Do you want to talk about it—what happened?" he asks quietly.

I shake my head. "I don't know what there's left to say. I already told you... everything," I whisper. Almost everything.

Daniel stares at the table. "It's going to take some time." He nods and grips my fingers. "For all of us."

I breathe out and squeeze back. "God, who am I to complain?" I mutter. "You're the one who got the worst of it..." I look up at him. "You never did say what happened—how you ended up on 3."

Daniel pulls away, tucking his hands between his legs. "It doesn't matter," he says, then instantly starts coughing.

I sit back and sigh as he wipes his mouth. "Daniel, I know about the coughing... and the lying. You can tell me." I tuck my hair behind my ears, frustrated.

Daniel catches his breath and squints out at the ocean. "I thought he might have told you—or that you'd figure it out on your own," he scoffs, rolling up a paper napkin.

I shake my head. "I feel like there is so much you're keeping from me. Whatever is going on, you can talk about it," I insist. "I know it wasn't Alden—"

He holds up his hands. "I know that, but there are some things I just want to be..." His brow crinkles. "... some things that *need* to be private. You have *your* secrets." He peers over at me. "And I don't have that same right as everyone else; I know I lost it a long time ago, and I deserved that." He sighs. "But maybe you could give it to me, every once in a while—just let me keep a little mystery."

I smile. "Mystery Date," I say with a nod. "Okay, you got it."

He sighs and takes my hand again. "Thank you. Now, we still haven't addressed what happens next." He reaches up and scratches his head.

I look at him. "Like, in the next five minutes, or next... in the Universe?" I reply coyly.

He takes a deep breath. "Like what happens tonight when you go home." He blinks. "Or, more specifically, *where* you're going to go, period."

I take my hands away and nod. "I see." I chew a nail. "That *is* an interesting quandary."

Daniel stacks our trays together. "So... I know you might not be wild about this next idea, but I really think it's worth exploring..." I watch him shift in his seat. He sighs.

"Since your mom is going to be gone for the next couple months, I was thinking that you might want to take on a roommate. And by that, I mean move out of your current scary apartment and find somewhere, slash someone else to live with." His eyes dart to the side.

My heart skips a beat. I try to hold back my excitement. "Daniel, are you asking me to move in with you at the Factory?" I giggle, tilting my head. I grin, picturing us cuddled up together listening to old records late into the night. "I don't know... Where would I plug in my phone?" I laugh, tugging at his sleeve.

Daniel coughs and picks at his leftovers. I frown. "What?" I ask cautiously.

"That's not exactly what I was thinking…" Daniel murmurs, looking away.

My face grows hot. "What *were* you thinking?" I demand.

His eyes widen, and he shrugs. "Well… Mary Carmen has a very nice two-bedroom house, and I know she would love to have you stay with her." He smiles, biting his tongue.

I glare. "Mary Carmen's? Seriously? The same Mary Carmen with the old-lady living room and the serious sense of self-righteousness? You've got to be kidding me!" I shout. I leave out the part about her wanting me dead if things go south. I'm still a little raw about that.

Daniel sighs and rubs the back of his neck. "She's not that bad, once you get to know her," he mutters.

I shake my head. "But she doesn't… *like* me," I scowl, remembering how relieved she was when it was me Alden picked instead of Daniel. "Why would she even want me to come stay with her?"

Daniel stares at me. "You need protection. Now that you and everyone else knows you're the Catalyst, we have to be more careful—at least until the Fate of the Universe has been determined." He fidgets with the buttons on his jacket.

I sit up. "*You* can protect me! Why can't I come stay with you?" I bark.

He looks down at the sand. "That would probably be… inappropriate," he mumbles.

I flush. "Well, that's kind of the point, right? I thought, after everything that happened, that we were, you know… *together.*" I pick at my shirt sleeve.

"Christa," he sighs, "it's not that I don't want that too, I—I do." He looks away. "So bad that every time I'm with you, I have to remind myself that we could never… that I can't…" He shakes his head.

"What? What can't you do?" I ask quietly.

His face tightens. "Be... *with* you," he says with a blush. "I can make you breakfast, I can be your friend, I can save your life, but," he laughs dryly, "Mary Carmen reminded me when we were at her place that Guardians are not allowed to... um..." He searches for words.

"Fraternize with the inmates?" I growl.

He cringes. "That is not how I would have phrased it, but essentially, yes. She also made me check my priorities in a big way—"

"Of course she did," I snap.

Daniel rolls his eyes. "My number one being your safety!" he shouts. I cross my arms. "My second being your happiness." He stares at me. "And I would do anything to make you happy, Christa. You have to know that." He winces. "But to cross that line, it would be... blasphemy." He looks down at his lap.

I gaze out at the water. "Oh." I nod. "I guess it's all a little more dogmatic than I realized." I scrunch my nose.

He smiles weakly and crumples up the burrito wrapper. "Yeah."

I pull my knees up to my chest. "But I'm not a regular mortal. I'm the Catalyst," I say after a minute. "Surely that comes with some extra benefits, right?" I grin, arching a brow.

Daniel laughs. "You looking like a sexy Smurf is not a 'Get out of Jail Free' card! No, it goes for everyone, Mortals, Demons, other Guardians... They're all off limits." He draws a hard line with his hand.

I look up at him, my eyes soulful. "You think I'm a sexy Smurf?" I beam.

He rolls his eyes. "Blue, green, purple, peach... Yeah, you're sexy, Christa." His mouth twitches. I smile and settle back into the bench. He sighs. "But just cuz I think that doesn't mean I can do anything about it. All right?"

I nod. "Fine," I sigh. "And... if you want me to go stay with Mary

Carmen, I'll do it." I frown. "At least she has a bunch of books. Give me something to read when she makes me go to bed at 9 o'clock."

Daniel smiles and reaches over, chucking me on the arm. "That's the spirit! Cool... We'll go by there later today."

I rub the bridge of my nose. "I'm glad one of us is excited." I take a shaky breath, the music from the merry-go-round down the pier tinkling in the background. I look at Daniel as he watches the Ferris wheel go around above us. "Daniel?"

He turns to me. I frown. "Alden said something, during your fight back at the Warehouse... about a... a girl, I guess."

The corners of his eyes crinkle, and he nods. "Yeah, he did."

I bite my cheek. "He wasn't talking about me, was he?" I murmur.

Daniel shakes his head. "No." He stares out at the sky, a light breeze picking up.

I push my hair off my face. "All of the crap that's happened between the two of you—is it all because of her?"

Daniel smiles sadly. "Isn't it always because of a girl?"

I watch sadly as he stands up and motions toward the Ferris wheel, pulling his hat from his jacket. "What do you think? Probably a great view... You game for a ride?"

I shake my head and get up, smiling by the time I make it to the other side of the picnic bench. "I think you should know the answer to that by now." I sigh dramatically. "But I have to tell you, I'm not crazy about heights." I crane my neck back. "And that's pretty high."

Daniel grins, tugging on his hat. "Hold my hand; I've got you." He winds my fingers with his, and we walk into the California night, the city lights coming to life behind us.

END OF BOOK ONE

EPILOGUE

"THAT'S TIME."

I get off my stool and stop the small clock sitting on the shelf. The red bulb I'd switched in provides little light as I squint down into the shallow tray, my nose burning from the smell of chemicals.

"There's definitely something there." I use a pair of tongs to pull the photo from the tray, its sides slick with developer. "Guess that rat Sergio wasn't a total liar."

I bring the image closer, the strong vinegary smell enveloping me. If I cross my eyes, I can see the faint outline of a human, slashed in half by an angry shadow across the foreground.

"That damn refractor," I grumble, pulling a loop from the desk drawer. I lay the photo down, pressing the magnifier to the person's face. While it's highly overexposed, I can just make out a pair of shockingly light eyes.

Coal black hair, no horns.

I stroke the face with my finger, thinking that it's like looking at a long-lost relative. "Remarkable," I murmur. "The portrait of a dead man." I reach up and gently tug on the silver cross around my neck.

"Well, Jilly." I smile, staring down at the picture. "Not exactly up to your standards, but it's a start." I lift the cross to my lips and kiss it softly. There's a loud knock at the door.

"Wait—" I yell, but it's too late. The door swings open, light pouring into the room. I look down at the paper in my hands, the photo burning away like newspaper at a bonfire.

"Damn it, Frank!" I bark. "I said WAIT." I toss the lost photo on the desk, rubbing the bridge of my nose.

"Sorry, Mr. Alden. You wanted me to let you know when we were ready," he mumbles, his large, hulking form filling the doorway.

I sigh. "It's fine. Give me a second." I grab my jacket that's hanging off of the back of the stool and follow Frank out the door.

We walk briskly down the corridor, Frank struggling to keep up with my pace despite his long gait. We stop in front of a white door on our left. "Where did you find him?" I ask, my hand on the knob.

"7-Eleven parking lot down on Olympic. He was trying to bribe a homeless guy to buy him a pack of cigarettes," Frank replies, folding his hands in front of him like a fig leaf.

"Classy," I snicker, opening the door. Frank looks appropriately bemused as we step inside.

"Well hello, hello! Boyfriend! We meet again!" I call out, my voice echoing around the room. Aside from several bright, swinging halogen lights, the room is dark. Sitting center in a high-back chair flanked by Vince and Tony is the guest of honor. He stares up at me, his eyes wide, his mouth gagged, and a touch of blood at his temple.

"Riley, right?" I cross over and sit on the arm of his chair, checking the ropes securing him in place. He frantically tries to rip his hands away, but my boys have done a good job. I pull a handkerchief from my breast pocket.

"Looks like you've got a little something there." I dab at the side of his head. He screams into his gag, shaking his head from side to side. I sigh and tuck the napkin back into my coat.

"I don't think proper introductions were made the other night at Trinity." I stand in front of him and hold out my right hand. "I'm Alden, your host for the evening."

He splays his fingers out like stars, panicked. I chortle and pat him sweetly, then saunter back over to Frank and take off my jacket.

"I'm so glad you could make it; I hated how things ended at the club," I murmur, handing my coat to Frank, who hangs it on a hook behind him. "But you know how people get when emotions are running high, hormones flowing..." I spin back and look at Riley. "I bet you had big plans for you and Christa that night. I'm sorry I had to go and spoil them."

He arches his head back and groans. I nod, putting my hands on my hips.

"Ah, where are my manners. You're grieving." I let out a heavy sigh. "So terrible to hear about your friend... Tom, was it?" Riley goes still. I frown. "A true tragedy, to lose one so young with so much promise. But some injuries are just too great to overcome." I puff out my cheeks. "You must feel absolutely terrible, being the responsible party."

He whines. I roll my eyes at Frank. "Listen, kitten. How about we all just take a deep breath. If I take off that gag, do you promise to be a good boy and not blow out all of our eardrums with useless screaming?" I arch a brow.

Riley bobs his head desperately up and down, so I gesture to Vinny, who unties his rag from the back, the cloth falling into his lap.

Riley stretches out his mouth. "What the hell is this place?! Why am I here? Get your goddamn filthy hands offa me!" he screeches, trying to head butt Vinny.

I give a light tut. "Oh, take it easy on poor Vinny! They're not the ones you need to worry about; everyone around here knows I like to do my own wet work." I turn toward the door.

"Who the fuck are you?!" Riley shouts, his eyes wild.

I take a step back and shake my head at him, bewildered. "Do you really not remember me from the other night? Ah, that is very disappointing! I used to make such an impression." I remove my cufflinks and hand them to Frank, who places them on a small table by the door, and start unbuttoning my shirt. "Oh well, something to cry about in my diary later." I pull off my shirt and crisp the sleeves before giving it to Frank, shaking out my arms and jogging in place, dressed in a sleeveless undershirt and slacks.

Riley looks on, terrified. "What the fuck are you doing?" He cringes.

I throw a couple air punches. "Just getting warmed up, Big Boy! Don't want to catch a cramp." Frank hands me a water bottle. I take a quick swig and gargle before swallowing. "I wouldn't want you to have come all the way down here to watch me get a charley horse. Tape, Frank." I hold out my fists in front of me. Frank comes over and rolls white boxer tape around my hands.

"You are one seriously twisted freak," Riley says, trembling. "Why the hell am I here?!"

I sigh and crack my neck. "Because I'm bored." I motion to Frank, who hands me a long, wooden baseball bat. I slink over to Riley and sit down on his lap, choking the bat up under his chin. He swallows, his Adam's apple bobbing against the wood as he glares back at me, nostrils flaring.

"You see, Riles—can I call you that?" I begin. He lets out a grunt. "Right now, I'm trapped between a rock and hard place. I lost all my toys, and now I'm left with nothing to play with." I sigh, Riley's knees jittering underneath me. "Stuck in the long game with Christa and Danny… They're off making moony eyes over tacos and arguing about whose jeans are tighter. Disgusting."

I lean in close, placing my face inches away from Riley's. He tries to look away, but can't turn his head. I crush the bat into his windpipe. He gasps.

"But *we* can have a bit of fun, can't we?" I simper, brushing my lips against his.

I climb off, taking the bat with me. Riley coughs, gulping in big lungfuls of air. I skip over to Frank, swinging the bat in my hand.

"You're fuckin' crazy!" Riley rasps once he's caught his breath. "A crazy... screwed up Mick!"

I crane my neck back and grin. "'Til the bloody, gory end, baby," I purr. "Right? But really, flattery is totally unnecessary. You had me at 'What the hell is this place?'" I tap Frank on the arm. "Can you give me a beat?"

Frank pulls his iPhone out of his jacket. He looks at me expectantly.

I nod. "Dealer's choice. Whatever you've got... Wait, let me clarify." I hold up the bat. Frank's smile falters. "*No* Aerosmith. I get enough of that in the car."

I arch a brow. He nods oafishly and hits play. Katy Perry's *Dark Horse* blasts around the room.

I pucker my lips. "Really, Frank?" I shake my head.

"There's this really great PiYo class up in the Hills. Totally got me hooked on her." He shimmies along with the music.

I sigh and clear my throat, moving toward the center of the room. "So be it." I look over my shoulder at Frank. "Never say I never gave you anything."

The bass thumps under my feet. I strike a pose and set the bat out in front of me, like a cabaret dancer with a cane. I twist down low, splitting my knees and rolling up on the balls of my feet, like only the most gifted strippers can. Riley recoils in his chair, his face cemented in a horrified grimace. I glide over to him and grind into his lap, twisting my torso back to lick his cheek.

"Hey, man... I'm not like that," he bleats. He shifts in his chair.

I rise and grin at him wickedly. "HAHAHAHAHAHAHAHHAH!" I cackle, Vinny, and Tony joining me. I prop myself up on the bat, pivoting my hips. "Oho, Big Boy... By the time I'm through, you're going to be *begging* for me to have my way with you—make you my sweetheart!"

I twirl the bat in the air, bringing it down hard on Riley's left kneecap. He screams in agony, his eyes popping out of his head. Vinny and Tony glance at each other knowingly, before stepping back just as I bring the bat back down on his right.

Riley convulses in the chair, held in place by his wrists and ankles. I do a jaunty spin in time with the music and come again, this time swinging at both sets of fingers. The bat comes down with a *crack*, shattering every bone in his hands. He squeals like a pig, the telltale sign of wet pants creeping across his groin. I throw the bat to Tony and lean over Riley, my mouth next to his ear.

"Do you have something you want to ask me?" I coo.

His jaw shakes. "Please… please…" he whimpers.

"Please 'make me your sweetheart,'" I coach, nodding up at Vinny, who just shakes his head.

"P-p-please make me your sweetheart!" Riley's voice cracks.

I sigh. "Unfortunately for you, you're not my type." I shrug, stepping back. "I much prefer redheads."

I sink down on him and position my thumbs over his eyes— but just as I'm about to go for the gold, there's a knock at the door. I spin and look curiously at Frank.

"Hello? Alden?" a bright voice calls from the hall, the door opening. "Are you in here?" Mandisa smiles from the threshold.

I motion to Frank to cut the music. "Yes? What is it?" I answer, swinging off of Riley.

Mandisa sighs. "Vesper's asking after you, wondering when you're coming…"

I narrow my eyes as I approach her. "Coming for what?"

She checks her manicure. "Did you forget? It's 2 o'clock!" she exclaims. "You're late!"

I spin to Frank. "What day is it? Is it Thursday already? Ah!" I clap. "You're right. My, how time flies…" I nod at Frank, who hands me my shirt. "Thanks." I point back to Riley. "Keep that one warm for me."

Riley shakes from head to toe and starts screaming. I roll my eyes. "Gag him if that gets annoying." Frank nods as I step out with Mandisa.

"How much have I missed?" I ask as we take the stairs up to Level 2.

"Not much. They just wheeled her out."

We step through the main auditorium doors and make our way down to the stage. The theater is full; I take my regular place standing off to the side.

Vesper is center stage behind the podium, a spotlight reflecting off of his black suit. He turns and sees me, giving a short nod. "Ah, Mr. Murphy, so glad you could join us," he drawls into the microphone.

I grimace. "Apologies, sir. I was wrapping up a few loose ends."

He waves me off. "No matter. We got the weekly business out of the way, and now we can get to the gravy." He turns his attention back to the audience.

"Thanks to Mr. Murphy, we have learned that, over the last twenty years, Heaven has doubled the amount of souls it admits into the Guardian program. Reaching beyond just addicts and whores, they've widened their net to also include repentant lower-level criminals. And if they could overturn the ban on mortal sinners, they would do it in a heartbeat."

A low murmur goes up in the audience. Vesper arches a brow. "In an effort to combat our numbers on the ground, they've also started allowing select members of the Seraphim to come down from Heaven to fight alongside the Guardians, which was unheard of in the past. I'm sure some of you have had the pleasure." He nods. "Along with more bodies on the ground, Guardians are also being forced to remain on the mortal plain longer, some of them staying and serving for fifty years or more, whereas it used to be that they only remained on average for about twenty-five years. They're getting to be worse than roaches." He snorts, looking over at me. "That about cover it?"

I nod. "Yes, sir," I reply.

He grins. "How *did* you find all this good stuff out?" he asks, crinkling his nose.

I shrug. "Keep your friends close…" I murmur.

He winks at me, then faces the crowd again. "So, as if it isn't enough that there's more of them and they're staying longer, we come to the final brick wall: that there is no way to *kill* a Guardian." He smiles. The crowd lets out a low laugh. I keep my eyes focused on the stage.

"We've all watched them burn, drown, suffocate, bleed out…" Vesper ticks off his fingers. "… and then bounce right back like a kid jumping out of bed on Christmas morning. They're unstoppable." He leans over the podium. "Until now."

A low tittering comes up from the audience as they excitedly whisper amongst themselves. Vesper, microphone in hand, steps over to the side of the stage.

"I wanna direct your attention to my friend back here." He steps between his two men over to an office chair, a topless black woman splayed across it, her large wing tattoo visible to the audience. Vesper spins the chair around so that we can all see her: it's the Guardian from the club last week. Vesper grabs a chunk of her hair, pulling her face to the light. She's been badly beaten, her lip fat and bloody and her left eye swollen shut. The crowd laughs as her head droops from side to side.

"All right, settle down, settle down." Vesper motions for quiet. "This is my friend, Emily. I had the joy of knowing Emily during her human life, when she was just a miserable crack addict, like so many that roam the streets of our shining city." He smiles down at her. "We were recently reunited when she was working a case dealing with another one of my junkies, although this time, she was on the other side." He cranes his neck back and laughs.

"Oho! You can imagine my surprise to discover that she had died and become a Guardian, turning away from her old life and working for all that was good and just." He lets go of her hair. "Well, I just had to know more—what was she up to now? How much further did she have to go before Ascension?"

He steps across the stage. "I spent the next several weeks following her every move like a bloodhound, tracking and seeking her through every back alley and bus station." He shrugs. "Finally, our paths crossed one final time, and I found just what needed." Vesper flashes his teeth. He has the audience in the palm of his hand. I rest against the wall.

"Along with Mr. Murphy's intel," he nods briefly in my direction, "Emily has been a very valuable asset to the research team up on 3. Without her, I wouldn't be able to share our amazing findings!"

He turns as Emily lets out a low moan, her eyes fluttering open. "Where... where am I?" she mumbles, barely audible.

"You're front and center at our weekly meeting," Vesper answers, his mouth to the mic. Mandisa stifles a giggle from the second row. Emily looks down and sees that she's topless. She hugs the back of the chair, trying to cover herself.

"Oh, no need to be modest now, Emily; we're all friends here." Vesper leers, cocking his head.

Emily looks at him blearily. "What am I—what is this?" she stutters.

Vesper nods and twists her chair around, her back once again facing the audience. "You are about to become the epicenter of a very important demonstration." Vesper clears his throat. "Now, I would like to direct your attention to the large tattoo on Emily's back." He lightly grazes his hand down her side, her dark skin flinching under his touch.

"After many hours of research, our team discovered that a Guardian's power lies in his or her tattoo. Upon accepting their mission from an Archangel, all Guardians are given the same mark:

the geometrical, folded-wing tattoo." He traces the lines with his index finger and steps away.

"Also during tireless interrogation, we learned that, along with their mark, Guardians are given another gift by the Archangel: a small, golden knife. Ah." He reaches into his breast pocket and pulls out a pocket knife, glinting in the lights. "Just like the one I have right here."

Emily glances up and sees him holding the knife. She falls off the chair and frantically tries to crawl away across the wooden floor. Vesper gestures to the goons, each grabbing one of Emily's arms and forcing her back onto the seat.

"No—NO!" She screams, struggling. Vesper nods to one of the men, and he cracks her across the jaw. She slouches back down, going still and silent. The crowd exhales.

"Just hold her there, boys," Vesper grumbles before continuing. "This knife is of great significance to a Guardian. They cannot hold it in their personal possession for more than 24 hours at a time, or Heaven will revoke their Guardian status. Upon receiving their knife, they must present it to one of their charges, someone they've saved out in the field. The knife can move from charge to charge, but this system ensures that the Guardian is constantly serving… It cannot be in their possession."

Vesper holds the knife up to the light. "Now, we were all under the impression that it is impossible to kill a Guardian. We've all seen them die in a hundred different ways, haven't we?" Vesper smiles out at the crowd. They chuckle in response. "Well, today, I am happy to report, that is no longer the case."

He turns on his heels and crosses over to Emily, who is sitting in profile. "Just keep her still, guys; we want to make this look good." Vesper sets down the mic and holds up the knife like he's about to conduct an orchestra.

"Your first step, of course, is to procure the Guardian's knife. This is no easy feat," he calls out, looking down at Emily. "We only just found hers about a week ago." He adjusts his shoulders. "Once you've got the knife, you need to exhaust your Guardian to prevent them from Altering. It could be after an attack event, when the Guardian is at his weakest—still regenerating—or through your own desired means. Whatever you do, it needs to be constant and brutal." He smooths her forehead with his palm. "We've been working on poor Emily here for the last 72 hours or so." He lifts her limp chin with his hand, only to let it droop back into place. "But that's what you've got to do, they regenerate so quick—like mayflies mating on a hot August night."

He pauses to wipe the knife on his jacket before he grinds his teeth and plunges it into her back with a grunt. Emily's eyes pop open, and she lets out a deafening scream.

"Get offa me, you sonofabitch! NOOO!!!!" she wails.

Vesper's hair gets mussed as he tears into her flesh. "You're going to want to trace the knife along the lines of the tattoo!" he instructs, yelling over her screams. Demons are standing on their seats to get a better look.

"While the technique may seem arduous, after doing a few, you will find that the pattern is the same every time!" He carves into her back, blood spurting all over his shirt. Emily bucks and stamps her feet like a wild horse, unable to shake him off.

"You can see now why it's important to prevent them from Altering: you're putting yourself at major risk, being so close..." Vesper nods to one of the men, who reaches up and mops his sweaty brow with a cloth. Emily's screams turn to moans, and her limbs stop flailing as he keeps cutting. The audience grows more and more excited.

"One more here, and there—" Vesper mutters, his eyes narrowed as he completes a final swipe and turns her back toward the audience, showing off his gruesome portrait. The outline of the tattoo is now clearly visible, deeply etched in blood. Emily is quiet, the only movement coming from her shallow breath.

"Once the trace is complete, there is usually about a minute before they go to ash," Vesper pants, taking the cloth and cleaning himself up. The goons step away from her, and one of them hands Vesper the mic. He walks back behind the chair and kneels down in front of Emily.

"Anything you'd like to share with the group?" he asks smugly.

She drags her head up and mumbles something.

"I'm sorry, I didn't catch that," Vesper snickers. The audience jeers along with him.

"Thank you," she slurs into the mic. "Thank you for... the chance... I tried. I hope it was enough..." Her neck goes slack.

Vesper chuckles. "I don't think that was for us." The crowd laughs with him. "Shhh, shh!" He waves his hand, watching Emily. "Here we go!"

I lean forward.

Emily's breath rattles in her lungs, and she throws her head back and howls—before bursting into a shower of gray ash. The audience lets out a collective roar and bolts up in a standing ovation, pieces of Emily raining over their heads. Vesper rises and holds out his arms, dipping into a low bow. The crowd is in full frenzy, horns and empty eyes bucking through the theater, performing every act of jubilation possible—from high fives to hugging and jumping on the seats.

I arch a brow and reach into my pocket, running my index finger over cold metal, letting the sharp point of the knife prick my fingertip. I put my finger to my lips, suckling the blood, and I can't help but smile.

END

SPECIAL THANKS

THIS BOOK WOULD have never been possible without the support from my wonderful friends and family. Thank you to my parents and Michael and Jared for their love and encouragement. Thank you to the entire Jaros clan for being such amazing in-laws, and to my three girls, Lorelei, Sophia, and Elizabeth, for being patient (most of the time) when Mama was in the middle of a page and couldn't play with/speak to/feed you at that exact moment. I love you all more than you'll ever know.

Thank you to Michael and Danica over at Edit 24-7 for helping make this book the best it can be. As well as to Alyssa Martoccio for her fantastic Spanish translation skills, and Grady over at Damon Za for his gorgeous cover art.

HUGE thanks to my fantastic readers: Megan Mackinnon, Kinzie Ferguson, Elizabeth Abbott, and Corrine Banach. I would not have the story I have now without your notes and insight. Hope you're ready for Round 2!

And finally, to Dunkin Donuts for making the best coffee— ever. I can only find your wares at Target and Safeway now, as I think, by law, you are not allowed to build stores anywhere west of the Cascades... but I think of you often and miss your delicious, delicious donuts. You keep the trains running around here.

Author's Note

The lullaby that Alden sings to Christa is called the *Ballyeamon Cradle Song*. It is a traditional Irish lullaby.

Coming Soon…

HELLBOUND

BOOK 2 OF THE LOST SOULS TRILOGY

New York City—September, 1975

HELL IS A waiting room.

All waiting rooms have several things in common: bad light-ing, out-of-date reading material, and loads of impatient peo-ple who are usually about to go through something unpleasant, like a driver's education test or a medical examination. This place embodied all of that and worse.

"Number 26!" a gorgeous girl in a tight gold macramé dress calls from behind the counter, her cocoa-colored skin glowing under the fluorescent lights. A woman in a headscarf sitting across the way with her five children crowding round looks anxiously at her ticket, hope shinning in her eyes, before sitting back and shak-ing her head forlornly. I sigh and scuff my loafers against the hard linoleum; looking down, I realize that I didn't return them with the rest of my uniform. I shrug to myself. They owed me that and more.

"Number 26!" the girl yells again, tapping her pen irritably against the partition window. A long wall painted vomit green separates us from them, the dream-makers and truth-sayers. Everyone's future on this side of the wall lies in their hands.

"Sir, are you number 26?" the girl asks a man standing at the bank of payphones opposite the desk. He shakes his head, pulls a cigarette from his bellbottom jeans pocket, and goes back to shouting into the phone in a language that no one else in the room understands. I slouch down in my chair, my arms crossed across my chest.

"Long day," a screechy voice murmurs next to me.

I turn and see an old woman hunched over a sandwich, her silver hair pulled into a tight bun at the nape of her neck. She wears a faded red cardigan, buttoned up to her chin. She nods at me and takes a bite of her food.

"Yeah. At least you had the good sense to bring lunch. I should've grabbed something before I walked in," I chuckle, fondly remembering the rows of hotdog carts waiting on the other side of the double doors.

She tuts. "Where I come from, you learn to always be prepared—especially when it comes to food." She pulls the uneaten half of her sandwich away from the foil in her lap. "Sometimes the only thing between you and death is a sandwich." Her tongue twists in a Slavic manner over her Ls and Rs. "We also learn that it's useful to make friends. You hungry?"

She gives me a gummy smile, offering up a handful of turkey and mayonnaise. I shake my hand kindly. "Thank you, but I'll be all right. They should be calling me soon." I look down at my ticket and back at the girl behind the window, now reorganizing a stack of files.

The old woman lets out a grunt. "You think just because they call your number, you're in and out, hello, goodbye?" She smirks. "No, no, boy. Once you get back there, that's when the real adventure begins." She chews thoughtfully for a moment, watching me out of the corner of her eye.

"Where you from? English?" She taps my knee.

I clear my throat and sit up. "Ireland, actually." I smile, my best attempt at being rakish. "First time in the States." I nod excitedly.

She shakes her head. "It shows." She purses her lips. "Let me give you a bit of advice…"

"Number 27!" the girl calls from the door on the wall, staring down at a clipboard.

I get to my feet, turning back to the woman. "That's me," I say with a grin, grabbing my beige canvas jacket from the back of my chair. "Best not to keep them waiting." I scramble into the arms and zip midway up the a clean, light-blue button down that I'm wearing underneath. "How do I look?"

The woman sighs. "Like a lamb walking into a lion's den." She shakes her head and shoves the rest of the sandwich into her mouth. "Get your head out of the clouds, boy. Before it gets chopped off by an airplane propeller." She shifts heavily in her chair.

"Is that an old Russian proverb?" I joke, bending down to pick up the brown, crinkled shopping bag that holds all of my worldly possessions.

She glares at me, her mouth drawn into a grim line. "I'm Czech," she mutters. "Good luck."

"Thanks." I smile widely. I rush over to the girl, who is still waiting by the door, my ticket in hand.

"That's me, I'm number 27. Here, I have it…" I breathe, pressing the ticket into her palm.

She raises a stylishly shaped eyebrow and seems to bite the inside of her cheek, holding back a laugh. "Okay, Number 27," she giggles, holding open the door. "Let's go." The door clicks closed behind us.

"Mr. Burman is just finishing up with another case, so he should be in shortly." Her hips sway from side to side as she guides me into a small office, tall stacks of files surrounding the desk. She gestures to a chair that's wedged between a storage cabinet and a pile of cardboard boxes, 'Altair 8800' printed in thick black ink on the side. Atop a cluttered desk sit the contents of that box: a new computer with a whole mess of wires coming off of the back like it's on life support.

The girl smiles and scratches her ear. "Sorry about the mess. Mr. Burman is very busy, and housekeeping is at the bottom of his list." She clears her throat. "Can I get you a cigarette or something to drink? Water? Coffee?" She leans coyly against the doorframe, her dark eyes scanning me.

I sit down, placing my bag under the chair. "Water would be great, thanks." I fidget with my jacket zipper, my knees jittery.

The girl nods and grins. "Sure. Don't be nervous. Mr. Burman is the best agent we have here. Whatever your situation, Mr. Burman has seen it all." She drums the door with her nails. "I'll be right back with that water." She disappears down the hall.

I take a breath and glance at the contents of the desk. Beyond the sea of papers and computer parts, there's a gold nameplate labeled *Jay Burman: Employee of the Year, 1962*. There are a couple of small, framed black and white photos of a large black man shaking hands with several severe-looking white men in suits— American politicians, by my guess. Next to the photos, half hidden under a greasy fast food wrapper, is an old baseball, its skin browning. I lean over and pick it up, seeing that it's signed by Don Newcombe... whoever that is. I hear heavy footsteps coming down the hall.

"Sorry to keep you waiting. Just had a rough case with a Dominican family that took nearly all morning." The large black man from the pictures comes through the door, several files in hand. He's older now than he was in the photographs, a touch of gray at his temples and a pair of large glasses perched on the end of his nose. He grins when he looks up and sees me holding the baseball. I quickly put it back on the desk.

"That's all right, you can look at it. You like baseball, Mr....?"

He scrunches his mouth and flips through the envelopes in his arms.

I stand and shake my head. "Murphy, Alden Murphy. And I don't think you'll have a file for me yet. This is my first time here," I ramble.

He nods and moves behind his desk, maneuvering carefully so as not to knock over the papers on the floor. He sits down heavily in his chair, smoothing out his rumpled suit jacket as he does so. He spins and faces the computer.

"Okay, Mr. Murphy. Mr. Murphy who likes baseball..." He punches a couple of keys with his index fingers and furrows his brow, letting out a long sigh. "What is your original country of origin?" he asks, not looking up from the screen.

"Um, Ireland, s-sir," I stutter.

He nods and clucks his tongue. "Should have guessed from the accent. Hang on, we're still getting used to the new system..." He taps one button repeatedly, getting more forceful with every hit. "God dammit... Excuse me." He glances at me, shaking his head. "We just started switching over all the files. I swear—this thing is gonna put me in an early grave. REGINA!" he yells out into the hall. A moment later, the girl in the gold dress returns and saunters over to the desk, a glass of water in her hand.

"Here you go," she purrs, handing me the water. She then sits on the edge of the desk, her long legs pressing into mine. She's so close that I can smell her perfume: lilac. I cross my legs to hide my erection.

"What's up, Mr. Burman?" She leans back over the desk, peering at the screen.

He sighs and rubs tiredly at the bridge of his nose. "I need to access the U.K. files, but it's stuck on Central America. I keep pressing the E.S.C. key," he grits out, baring his teeth.

Regina smiles and picks up the keyboard. "You can say 'Escape,' Mr. Burman. But that's not the command you need anyway." She deftly hits a few buttons, and the box makes an uplifting robotic sound.

Mr. Burman leans forward, nodding. "All right, all right. Thank you, Regina!" He looks over at me and grins sheepishly. "This is how I know I'm getting too old for this." He pushes his glasses up his nose and takes the keyboard back. Regina hops off the desk and gives me a wink.

"I'm taking Computer Science at City College. Expecting a promotion over here any day now," she says with a laugh.

Mr. Burman shakes his head. "You and me both…" He squints at the computer. I cautiously sip my water.

"Is there anything else you need, Mr. Burman?" Regina asks.

He nods, not looking away from the screen. "Yeah… the Mankowitz files on the floor there need to get put away. They're coming back on Monday to finish up their paperwork. Can you file those now, so we'll at least have a chance of finding them next week?" He purses his lips, lost in thought.

"Sure, Mr. Burman." She picks up a few files off the rug and opens up one of the storage cabinets, occasionally glancing over at me as she does her work. I give her a tight smile and turn back to the computer, staring at Mr. Burman apprehensively.

After a moment, he looks up at me. "Are you sure you went through processing in Ireland?"

I furrow my brow. "Processing?" I repeat.

Mr. Burman nods. "Yeah— when you filed for your visa to come here. You would have needed to go through processing in either the Dublin or Cork offices before you left. Unless you maybe did it in London… Did you go through London?" He taps at the keyboard, shaking his head.

"I would expect this from maybe South America or Russia, but the U.K. usually has their act together and mails their applicants to us as soon as they're filed." He scratches his head. "Takes a couple of weeks. Maybe your paperwork is still on its way. When did you say you filed?"

I shake my head, dumbfounded.

"Lemme see your passport and visa." He motions with his hand.

I lick my lips hesitantly. "Well, here is my passport..." I reply, reaching into my jacket. I place the little green notebook with the Irish flag stamped across the front on top of the desk. "But... I... um... I didn't know I needed a visa. They just told me I needed to come here."

Regina looks over as Mr. Burman stops typing.

"Who's 'they'?" he asks suspiciously.

"K-Kenny... and Mark from... dining services," I stammer. I gulp, spit catching in my throat.

He stares at me over his glasses. "So... you didn't go through Processing," he states wearily.

I shake my head. "No, I... I guess not. The guys on the boat said I only needed a passport to work." I can feel my palms starting to sweat. I wipe them on my slacks.

"What boat?" Mr. Burman demands. Regina quietly closes the file drawer.

I clear my throat. "The—the boat I worked on. The QE2?" My knees bob uncontrollably. "I um, work... I *worked* in the Engine Room. But I don't... anymore." I look down at my lap.

Mr. Burman sighs and sits back in his chair. "I see. Were you recently... let go... from this position?" he asks carefully.

I shake my head. "No—nothing like that! This was our first time... well, *my* first time docking in New York. We were given a couple of hours leave to see the city, and I just, um, decided to... stay." My eyes darting nervously around the room.

Mr. Burman closes his eyes and blows out his cheeks.

"I'm sorry." I sit forward in my seat. "Am... am I in trouble?"

Mr. Burman cocks his head to the side. "That all depends on

your definition of 'trouble'…" He pops his tongue into his cheek and keeps his eyes trained on the screen.

I shake my head and chuckle uncomfortably. "I don't understand. Everyone I talked to said I just needed to go through immigration in New York, and I would be fine." I pause and cough. "I'm fine, right?"

Mr. Burman holds up his hands. "Let's get the facts established before we get hysterical," he sighs. "You arrived in New York…?" He looks at me tiredly.

"Last night," I fill in.

"Yeah, last night." His voice is low and gravely. "Got a good look at Lady Liberty beckoning majestically in the harbor, bright lights, big city… maybe took in a show?" He raises his eyebrows.

I shake my head. "A couple of the engineers and I went out for Chinese in Greenwich Village…" I mutter, looking down at the floor.

He laughs. "They *do* make good Chinese down there. I get it. Anyway…" He shifts in his chair. "After taking in some of the tourist attractions and a couple of A-MAZING egg rolls, instead of heading back to port with your fellow travelers, you decided to stay on land and pursue U.S. citizenship… Am I getting this straight?" He looks at me.

I nod. He cranes his head back. "No premeditation, no paperwork, just pure passion?" he asks with a squint.

I smile. "Um, yeah. I guess so…"

He groans. "You know that's illegal, right? You just entered this country *illegally*." He crosses his arms in front of his chest and sits back like a frustrated bear, pondering a particularly nasty patch of honeycomb.

I put my head in my hands, my whole body starting to shake. "That's why I came here," I mumble. "The guys on the ship said that immigrants went through Ellis Island, and then they could stay here. I... I went there this morning... but it was all boarded up..."

"That's because it closed in 1954! Holy mackerel!" Mr. Burman crows.

Regina busies herself with papers, keeping her eyes down.

"Okay, so, you took the ferry over to Ellis and realized that there were nothing there but a bunch of bums and junkies, and then what? You came all the way up here to Harlem from Port Authority?" Mr. Burman continues with a laugh.

I nod. "Walked, yes," I grumble.

Mr. Burman whoops. "Unbelievable! Wow, son, you are either incredibly stupid or incredibly honest." He grins with a shake of his head.

I grimace. "Guess which one it is remains to be seen," I say, slumping down in my chair. My hands tremble, and I close my eyes.

Mr. Burman sits back and nods. "Guess so. You know, most people in your situation would have just walked away, disappeared into the city, started new lives, new families—probably never encountering any trouble until they needed heart surgery or a bail out from jail. But you came here to talk to me. That's admirable." He smiles, bright white teeth glinting.

I look frantically back and forth between him and Regina, who suddenly seems to have forgotten that I'm in the room. She looks everywhere but in my direction.

I grip the arms of my chair. "Please," I whisper. "Please don't send me back."

Mr. Burman sits in silence, rubbing his forehead. "So when does your ship leave?" he asks after a while, straightening some papers in front of him.

I feel my stomach sink into my shoes. "I think it already left, sir," I mumble.

He nods. "Of course it did." He clears his throat and taps the stack of papers neatly against his desktop. "Well, I'm not going to let my hard-earned tax dollars go to sending you back, so I guess we'll have to figure this out." He looks at me. "Unless you *want* to go home?" he asks, his brows raised.

I shake my head. "No, sir, Mr. Burman. No… I don't." I sigh. "I don't ever want to go back there." I stare at him earnestly.

Mr. Burman lets out a small chuckle. "A young, good-looking kid like you—must be girl trouble." He snickers over his papers.

I scoff. "No, I've never been with a…" I glance over at Regina, whose fingers have stopped flicking through the files. I clear my throat and blush profusely. "I've never had a girlfriend before," I mutter.

Regina turns to me, her eyes wide. "Seriously? How is that possible?" She gawks at me. Red creeps up over my collar, my face burning like a matchhead. She purses her lips coquettishly.

"Thank you, Regina. I think I've got it covered from here," Mr. Burman interjects with a sigh. Regina shuts the file drawer and slips out of the office, closing the door behind her. Mr. Burman turns to me and rolls his eyes.

"You gotta watch out for the women here, Mr. Murphy. They're a new breed… liberated, you dig?"

I sit up straight. "Yes, sir." I nod, looking down at my lap again.

He sighs and looks at his computer screen. "Okay, we're just going to let this machine hang out and do its thing…" He slides the keyboard under the monitor and opens a file drawer next to his knee, taking out a long piece of carbon print paper.

"It's more reliable the old-fashioned way, anyway." He grabs a sharpened pencil from a coffee mug next to a very heavy-looking black telephone and wets the lead with the tip of his tongue. "Plus, a little extra red tape will buy us some time." He unbuttons his shirt sleeve and rolls his cuff, revealing a shiny gold watch face, the brown leather band starting to crack.

I smile. "That's a nice watch, sir," I comment, thinking a little flattery couldn't hurt the situation.

Mr. Burman looks down at his wrist casually. "Thanks. Gift from everyone here at my retirement party six years ago." He snickers and looks up at me through his foggy lenses. "All right, full name: Alden Murphy, yeah?"

I nod. "Yes, sir."

He writes my name on the top line. "Al-den. Interesting name, kind of like Aladdin… from *Arabian Nights*?" He chuckles to himself. "Guess that makes me your magic genie," he adds with a grin. "Okay, birthdate?"

"15 March, 1955," I answer.

He juts out his chin as he writes. "Dangerous birthday. Explains a lot." He pushes his glasses up his nose. "Reason for leaving Country of Origin?" He stares at me placidly.

I bite my tongue. I'm guessing 'escaping a dismal existence' isn't going to look too good on paper. "Um, work," I say with a cough.

He nods. "Popular answer. Okay, Mr. Murphy, here's how this is going to work. I think this goes without saying, but given my role in your current predicament, I feel the need to express it."

He settles into his chair and glares at me over his glasses. "This is not a vacation. You are not here to drink, do drugs, gamble, or chase fast American tail." He takes a breath. "You are here for a fresh start to your young life, a second chance. The American Dream *is* possible, if you are willing to work for it."

I put my shoulders back. "I am giving you one week to find work and a place to live," he continues. "So that puts us at…" He brushes away the debris in front of him and looks at his desktop calendar. "I'm taking off that Friday, so let's call it next Monday, October 4th. On the fourth, you will return here and regale me with your new job and living situation… at…" He glances up at the wall clock. "2 p.m." He furrows his brow. "No, let's make that noon. Show up on time, and I'll buy you lunch." He clears his throat and stares at me sharply. "So, what do you say, Mr. Murphy? Do we have a deal?" He holds out his right hand.

I grin, jumping out of my chair. "Yes, of course, Mr. Burman!" I grab his hand and shake it wildly, my heart beating madly out of my chest. "Thank you! Thank you so much!" I bend down and pick up my bag. "Can... can I go now?" I want to get out of here before he comes to his senses and throws me into a detention center.

Mr. Burman nods. "It's a free country. But hang on a second." He sits back, scratching his temple. "Is that all you have on you?" He points at my grocery bag.

I nod and sit back down on the edge of the chair. "Just a couple of things from the ship." I rifle through it, pulling out the contents to show him. "Toothbrush, razor, pair of socks..." I reach down to the bottom of the bag and pull out a white envelope, then count its contents. "Fifty... no, forty... forty dollars cash in furlough." I fumble with the bills. "Sorry, still getting used to American money." I wipe nervously at my brow.

Mr. Burman lets out a heavy sigh and reaches into his back pocket. "That's all they paid you on that ship? That's not going to get you very far around here." He snorts.

I shake my head. "Well, they also covered room and board, and you know—gave me the priceless chance to see the world." I look down at the money, my jaw tightening.

Mr. Burman nods. "Yeah, yeah, I got it. I was a Navy man myself." He pulls out his wallet and counts out his cash.

"I've got $60 on me right now, and I want you to take it." He pushes the money across the desk.

I shake my head. "Thank you for everything, Mr. Burman, really—but I can't take your money." I purse my lips, painfully pushing it back with the tips of my fingers.

Mr. Burman sighs and pushes it back toward me again. "Yes, you can. Believe me, you're going to need it. And I'm going to do you one better." He grabs a notepad and scribbles down a name and address.

"I have an old friend I knew back in Korea that now runs a kitchen in Midtown. Pretty fancy place." He rips off the note and hands it to me along with the cash. "He always needs more guys to wash dishes, bus tables, whatever. Go see him, and I bet he can set you up with a job. You said you worked in dining services, right?"

I shake my head. "No, that was Kenny and Mark—"

He clears his throat and glares, holding out the paper. I shut my mouth and take it. He nods.

"It won't pay much," he continues, "But it's honest work. Tell him Jay sent you."

I stare down at the note in my hand, my eyes wide. "Wow, thank you, Mr. Burman. I don't know what to say." I grin. I read the name: Eddie Robbins. "I didn't know 'Robbins' was a Korean last name," I chuckle.

He looks at me, his expression pained. "The Korean *War*, son! You're going to need to brush up on your American history if you're planning on staying!"

I nod vigorously, my eyes wide. He shakes his head. "And stop looking so surprised every time a black man does something nice for you. This is New York... we are everywhere. There's a lot of *everybody* everywhere, here." He checks the clock again. "All right, Mr. Murphy, get outta here. Go get your dream." He smiles and picks up the baseball from his desk.

"Yes, sir, Mr. Burman!" I reply, getting back to my feet. I reach for the knob and turn back. "Thank you again, sir," I murmur. "I won't let you down."

"Mm-mm." He nods. "Noon on Monday. Do not make me come looking for you, Mr. Murphy." He glares at me over his glasses, tossing the ball back and forth.

I smile tightly. "Of course. Noon on Monday." I step out into the hall and run into Regina. She winks again as she walks into the office.

"Good luck, 27," she hums.

I grin and head down the corridor. "What do you think, Mr. Burman?" I hear Regina ask as I leave.

"I think one of two things," he replies. "Either this city eats him alive, or he eats all of us. Only time will tell."

www.ingramcontent.com/pod-product-compliance
Lightning Source LLC
Chambersburg PA
CBHW051516250626
47156CB00001B/108